DIAMOND EXPRESS

For years the cartel controlling the global supply and demand of diamonds feared that the Russians would release their reserves and render the gemstones worthless. Now it seems that their worst fears are about to be realised. But the Israelis, also economically dependent on the diamond trade, decide to send a crack commando squad into Serbia to thwart the Russians' actions... Pitted against each other are Viktor Ruchkin and Israeli army officer Mikhail Sapir. The two men have an old score to settle and now is their chance.

DIAMOND EXPRESS

DIAMOND EXPRESS

by

Derek Lambert

Magna Large Print Books
Long Preston, North Yorkshire,
England.

British Library Cataloguing in Publication Data.

Lambert, Derek
Diamond Express.

A catalogue record for this book is
available from the British Library

ISBN 0-7505-0903-1

First published in Great Britain by Judy Piatkus (Publishers)
Ltd., 1994

Published in Large Print January, 1996 by arrangement with
Judy Piatkus (Publishers) Ltd., and the copyright holder.

Magna Large Print is an imprint of
Library Magna Books Ltd.
Printed and bound in Great Britain by
T.J. Press (Padstow) Ltd., Cornwall, PL28 8RW.

For Barbara, wife of Frank Blair

It remains in the power of the Soviets to preserve or destroy the diamond invention—
Edward Jay Epstein

When the trains stop that will be the end—
Lenin

Acknowledgements

Diamonds
Diamonds, by Eric Bruton; *The Diamond*, by George C Blakey; *Gems, The Gemmologists' Compendium* and *Practical Gemmology*, all by Robert Webster; *Gem Testing*, by B.W Anderson; and, in particular, *The Rise and Fall of Diamonds*, by Edward Jay Epstein, a brilliant exposé of the vulnerability of the diamond market. My gratitude, too, to the National Geographic Society.

Railways
To the Great Ocean, by Harmon Tupper; *A History of Russian Railways*, by J.N Westwood; *Guide to the Great Siberian Railway*, a David and Charles reprint; *Trains and Railways*, edited by Alan Williams; *How to Drive a Steam Locomotive*, by Brian Hollingsworth; *Engine Drivers of the Great Steam Trains*, by Melville Wallace; *Trans-Siberian Rail Guide*, by Robert Strauss; *Trans-Siberian Handbook*, by Bryn Thomas; and *The Armoured Train*, by G. Balfour.

General

Spetsnaz, by Viktor Suvorov; *Soviet Union*, by Martin Walker; *USSR, A Travel Survival Kit*, by John Noble and John King; *Afghanistan, Travels with the Mujahideen*, by Sandy Gall; *Modern Elite Forces*, by Max Walmer; *Weapons of the Modern Soviet Ground Forces*, edited by Ray Bonds.

I should also like to thank Karen Marriott for the diamantine precision of her word processing, Beryl Croydon, Margaret Collins and Annette Mattock for visiting the Spaniards Inn on my behalf—they displayed no reluctance, Irene Malcolm for her cuttings service, Tony Knight for his financial acumen and, finally, Andrew Waylett for his expertise in the glittering showcase of jewellery.

Prologue

In April, 1993, the G7 countries, the wealthiest industrial nations in the West, agreed in Tokyo to inject 43.4 billion dollars into the floundering economy of Russia.

The staggering generosity of this package surprised many Western pundits and astounded most Russians. Especially when the following July the seven countries—America, Britain, Germany, Japan, France, Italy and Canada—set the seal on their good intent by allocating the first 3 billion dollars.

Why was the West which, since the end of World War II, had spent billions in girding its loins against the menace of the Kremlin, suddenly so eager to sustain the Russian republics which had survived the break-up of the Soviet Union?

The reason cited was reluctance to allow Russia to fall into the hands of the old communists who would once again create a regime which would be hostile to the West.

But surely such beneficence to a fallen foe was unparalleled. Or was there perhaps an ulterior motive?

Part I

Package

Chapter One

The intoxicating idea came to Viktor Ruchkin in a sobering-up station.

He held the rough diamond between thumb and forefinger and said to the thief: 'Where did you get this?'

The thief, a skinny junkie and police informer, who was strapped naked to an iron bedstead, said: 'I can't remember.'

Viktor Ruchkin sighed. 'Don't give me shit.' He beckoned the attendant, a former butcher, more beefy than anyone in Moscow had a right to be these lean times. 'Hose him down.'

The attendant wheeled the bed into a white-tiled cubicle fitted with a drain, a tap and hose with a brass spout. The cubicle had once been a chapel in the wooden church built in honour of St Nicholas the Miracle Worker, but the church had been abandoned when Lenin deposed God.

As the attendant adjusted the nozzle of the hose a few flakes of snow, the first that autumn, found their way under the great oak door of the church, fluttered down the aisle and came to rest at the foot of the ruined altar. There were frescoes of angels on the wall behind and, observing them, some drunks brought in to be sobered up, believed they were in heaven. But not for long.

The attendant said: 'Before we hose them we usually unstrap them. You know, in case they choke.'

'Unstrap him then.'

'The water's very cold and he's in a bad way—it could kill him.'

'One of my men who broke into the American Express on the Garden Ring Road was shot dead outside the Planetarium because of him.' Ruchkin fingered the rough diamond—it looked more like a nugget of bottle glass washed up on the sea shore than a precious stone—and whispered: 'But don't overdo it, I need him.'

The attendant unstrapped the thief and told him to stand up.

Had the militia who had picked him up at midnight in Hermitage Gardens, once a lovers' rendezvous but more favoured these days by whores, realised that he was an informer? Probably not. They would have known the sobering-up station was on my territory, Ruchkin told himself, would have realised they were handing him over to his executioner.

The thief stood on buckling legs. His hair was as long as Rasputin's, draped from a bald patch that looked like a skull cap. Appropriate, Ruchkin thought.

'So, who did you lift this from?' raising the diamond to the naked light bulb.

'I didn't steal it: I traded it.'

'For what?'

'The best currency in town, vodka. Golden Ring.'

'Who did you trade with?'

'I can't tell you.' The thief sought the bald patch with the tips of his fingers and Ruchkin noticed the punctures on the insides of his forearms.

'Another *zhid?*'

'I don't know if he was Jewish,' the thief said. He shivered, a single spasm that reminded Ruchkin of a gust of wind plucking waves from the sea.

'But you knew him?'

'I'd only just met him.'

'Where?'

'Outside the Dostoyevsky Baths,' the thief said.

'He'd been inside them?'

'He smelled of eucalyptus.'

'And you traded with a man you'd never met before?'

'You know how it is these days... He saw the bottle of Mother Russia's milk. Who wants roubles?'

'He knew what he was getting. You didn't.'

21

'A diamond is nothing?'

'Supposing it's a fake?'

'Then you wouldn't be so interested, would you?'

'Have you just had a fix?'

'What if I have?'

'I merely wondered. You're acting out of character, acting smart. Who did you trade with?'

'A stranger, I just told you.'

'And he didn't ask if you could get him any more Golden Ring and you didn't ask if he,' knuckling the diamond into the thief's chest, 'had any more like this?'

'Just a one-off deal,' the thief said.

'His name?'

'Josef Stalin.'

Ruchkin said to the attendant: 'See to him.'

The jet of water hit the thief in the chest, pushed him against the tiled wall and held him there.

The attendant, aiming the nozzle with cleaver-scarred hands—one finger missing —said: 'Do you mind if I ask you a question, Comrade Ruchkin?'

'I'm not your comrade,' Ruchkin said. 'There aren't any comrades anymore. Not even today, the anniversary of the Revolution. There are only survivors.'

'Where do you come from Com—Citizen Ruchkin? You're not a Chechen or a

Georgian or a Tartar like...'

'The rest of the crooks? You've got a dangerous tongue: it will choke you one day.'

The attendant adjusted the nozzle of the hose; the jet of water lost its momentum and dropped into an arc; the thief slumped on to the floor, the attendant sloshed across the tiles in his rubber boots and turned off the tap.

Ruchkin pointed to the thief. 'Strap him back on the bed. Put a blanket over him and leave him to refresh his memory.' He shivered. 'Have you got any vodka?'

'Of course, for you.'

The attendant led the way into the vestry, ferreted beneath a pile of rotting vestments and produced an unlabelled bottle of moonshine and a bottle of Narzan mineral water. He cut fingers of black bread from a loaf and opened a jar of pickled gherkins.

Ruchkin tossed back a measure of vodka—some of the stuff they distilled these days could burn a hole in your stomach but this was smooth enough —gulped mineral water and chewed the gritty bread.

Watching him respectfully, the attendant waited until he was on his second shot of vodka, then said: 'I asked because you've got fair hair, blue eyes...'

'A butcher with a poet's soul. Shit!'

'Siberia?'

Ruchkin almost smiled. If you had been interrogated by professionals you treated any other variety of inquisition indulgently.

He slipped one hand into the inside pocket of his thermal jacket and felt the plastic containing what had once been his credo, his soul. Disclose any details of your calling and you were punished under article 64 of the then Soviet criminal code—by death.

The butcher felt for his missing finger. 'It aches sometimes,' he said, 'even though it isn't there. Do you know how I lost it? On the chopping block, thinking about a girl in a striped apron who worked in the central market. You see, you were right, a butcher can be a poet.'

'So why did you stop being a butcher?'

'Because there isn't any meat,' the butcher said, nipping vodka and snapping at a gherkin with piano-key teeth.

'I have a cold store full of meat,' Ruchkin said. 'You can have a job there—if you stop asking questions.'

'In Siberia?'

'There you go again.'

'I'm sorry. I have an inquisitive nature.'

'Do you want the job or not?'

'What sort of meat?' the attendant asked. 'Moose?'

'You just lost yourself a job,' Ruchkin said.

He went back into the nave of the church just as the lights went out. Power cuts, like queues and crime, were part of the daily scenario now and everyone had a reserve supply. The attendant lit altar candles stored in the crypt before the Revolution. Ruchkin glanced at his watch in the flickering light. It was 12.45, the anniversary was over. Not that there had been anything to celebrate anyway.

Angels and cherubs peered at him roguishly from the penumbra of the candlelight. A trapped bird beat the darkness with its wings and settled, breast pulsing, on the altar. Superstition had it that a bird inside a building was a precursor of death. Ruchkin wasn't superstitious but this bird, a starling, knew what it was about.

The candlelight found the thief's eyeballs. Ruchkin angled the candle so that the flame lit his own face ghoulishly.

He held up the diamond. 'What were you going to do with it?'

'Take it to a cutter,' the thief said. 'A lot of them working in the Moscow Jewellery and Clock Factory are moonlighting.' The light went out from his eyes as he closed them. 'Get this strap off me, I can't breathe.'

Ruchkin told the attendant to undo the straps. 'And then what?'

'Sell it in a hotel—the Kosmos or the Mezh—to a tourist. For dollars,' he added. 'Or Deutsche marks or yen.'

'You've done it before?'

'Twice.' The thief was shaken by another bout of shivering as though he were coming out of a fix. 'Christ, I'm cold.'

'You give the impression,' Ruchkin said slowly, 'that rough diamonds are easy to come by...'

'So is crack,' the thief said. 'If you know where to go.'

'But rough diamonds...'

'Are available. Until the Syndicate gets hold of them.'

'The Syndicate?'

'Look, I don't know much about any of this. All I know is that the Syndicate controls the world's supply of diamonds and they've set up an office in Moscow.'

The intoxicating idea began to take shape.

'You make diamonds sound like pebbles on the beach.'

The thief sat up, shrugged his coat-hanger shoulders beneath the grey blanket, Patriotic War issue. 'All I know is Muscovites prefer potatoes: diamonds are strictly for foreigners. Can I go now?'

'So if...' But he was thinking aloud. 'The

name of the man outside the Dostoyevsky Baths, I want it.'

'I told you, I don't know it. Dima maybe...'

'Or Boris or Ivan?' Ruchkin turned to the attendant. 'Turn on the tap.'

The thief said: 'No, please.'

Ruchkin heard the beat of the starling's wings behind him and the flame of the candle wavered.

The attendant said: 'He's sober now. If he was ever drunk, that is.'

Ruchkin said: 'The tap, turn it on.' And to the thief: 'The name?'

'I'm not a grass.'

'But that's exactly what you are,' Ruchkin said. Water flowed thickly from the hose and splashed on the floor, a few drops sputtering in the flame of the candle. 'Does Dima, Boris, Ivan, have many diamonds?'

'He had three when I met him yesterday.'

'And he would have been willing to trade each of them for a bottle of Golden Ring?'

'That's just part of the deal,' the thief said watching the lazy curve of the water. 'We also split the profits from the sale.'

'So what's your contribution?'

'I know the cutters,' the thief said.

'I understand, *zhids*...'

'Best cutters and polishers in the world,'

the attendant said. 'Most of them went to Israel.'

Ruchkin said: 'For the last time, the name?'

'On my mother's grave, I don't know.'

'Then you will shortly join your mother,' Ruchkin said.

'He does have a nickname—the Miner.'

'That wasn't the first time you met him, outside the baths, was it? You were already on a business footing. Inside the baths?'

'You think they'd let me in?' He raised his arm and the puncture marks danced in the candlelight.

'Where then?'

'At the Kirov-Turgenev metro station. I used to do a bit of thieving there.'

'He approached you?'

'He knew about my contacts at the factory.'

'The Miner, that's all?'

'That's all I've ever known him by, I swear it. Now can I go?'

Ruchkin said to the attendant: 'Spray a little water on him. Not too much.'

'I don't understand.'

'This is a church. Holy water...a last benediction.' Ruchkin pulled the blankets off the thief's shoulders.

The attendant said: 'I don't think—'

'Pretend you're a priest,' Ruchkin said. 'Think to yourself, "This is the way God would have wanted it." Judas was an informer, wasn't he?'

He pushed the thief down on the bedstead and watched water from the hose descend thinly on to him, drops like the gentle rain from heaven. Then he buckled the straps, handed the attendant the candle and began to pull the bedstead towards the main door. The lights came on when they were halfway down the aisle and the attendant snuffed out the candle.

When Ruchkin slid the bolts the cold rushed in. He wheeled the bedstead into the courtyard outside and hesitant snowflakes fell on to the thief's body and melted. Finally they began to settle, covering the puncture marks on his arm, blinding his eyes, whitening his hair so that soon the skull cap of skin was indistinguishable from the snow.

As Ruchkin re-entered the church the starling flew out through the doorway. And the intoxicating idea took wing.

In the morning a November mist had replaced the snow, squeezing the city, settling like a grey wig on Tsarist mansions; severing spires of Stalinist Gothic and the roofs of penitentiary apartment blocks. From the windows of his apartment Ruchkin could see the golden husks of the Kremlin floating in a cloud.

The apartment, formerly the home of a privileged *apparatchik*, was luxurious by Moscow standards. Five carpeted rooms, decadent chandeliers, wide-eyed TV and VCR recorder, telephone and answering machine and fax. Beefeater gin and Chivas Regal whisky behind the bar, refrigerator stuffed with food imported from Helsinki, furniture as heavy as tombstones. An apartment befitting a godfather in the Russian mafia.

Being close to McDonald's in Pushkin Square, fulcrum of all real estate estimates, it was valued at 200,000 blackmarket dollars: it had cost Ruchkin nothing.

Still preoccupied with the possibilities that had occurred to him in the sobering-up station, Ruchkin showered, dressed, put on a heavy black topcoat and sealskin *shapka*, and took the antique caged elevator to the ground floor. His driver was waiting outside with the black Zil.

Ruchkin told him to drive to the Dostoyevsky Baths. They were in his territory—he had renamed them because Dostoyevsky had been imprisoned in a penal camp near his home in Siberia—so the staff would be co-operative.

The Zil circumvented Red Square and picked up the Boulevard Ring, passing the headquarters of Tass and the Church of the Ascension where Pushkin, now host to McDonalds, had been married. Mist drifted along Alexei Tolstoy Street, once the home of Mikhail Gorbachev, covering a drunk discarded by the night with a grey sheet.

The baths were in Trubnaya Ploshchad, formerly the heartland of prostitution. Under Ruchkin's patronage the trade was being rehabilitated—but not street-lamp harlots, only *putana,* classy whores.

He opened the double doors of the baths and entered the rest room where clients, prawn-pink from steam and the impact of birch twigs, were drinking Zhigulovsky beer, chewing dried fish and playing chess beside stacks of Marlboro and Winston cigarettes, packets of antibiotics and condoms and cans of corned beef. Some wore off-white towels; others were naked; most of them regarded Ruchkin respectfully, a few warily.

He took off his fur hat. Silence.

He said: 'Where can I find the Miner?'

An Uzbek, genitals hanging like tassels beneath the drum of his belly said: 'He's upstairs.'

'Who with?'

'Natalya,' the Uzbek said.

Ruchkin remembered her. A girl with smudged eyes and a flour-white skin who carried a parasol in the brief summer. A native of Leningrad, now St Petersburg once again.

'How long?'

'Ten minutes maybe. Time enough.'

Ruchkin climbed the marble stairs, trailing his fingers along the brass rail that had grown fragile with the years. It was indelibly Romanov this place: a palace of indulgence sacked by peasants.

The girl was in the shower. The bed was rumpled. On the bedside table a book of pornographic pictures—Russian because the man was wearing socks—and a rough diamond. On the wall a photograph of Vladimir Vysotsky, the singer who had made a libretto of anarchy before drinking himself to death during the Moscow Olympics. That was nearly 15 years ago but to the young he was still the personification of protest. What to protest about these days? that was the problem—there was just too much choice.

'Who's that?'

'Me, Ruchkin.'

The shower spent itself. Through plastic curtain, cornflowers and poppies, he could see her silhouette. Small breasts and cramped hips—a grandchild of starvation during the Siege of Leningrad.

'Do you want—'

'No,' Ruchkin said, 'I want information.'

'That comes cheaper.'

'How much?'

'A kind word,' she said, emerging from the shower, dark hair seal-slick at the nape of her neck. She put on a black robe with rearing dragons on the back, sat on the edge of the used bed, lit a Marlboro and said: 'So what do you want to know?' Pearls of water clung to her crossed legs.

Ruchkin pointed at the diamond. 'Where did you get that?'

'From the Miner. I'm sure you know that.' Her smudged eyes regarded him with the gentle cynicism of one who had heard many lies.

'What will you do with it? A piece of compressed carbon...'

'Trade it with someone who will get it cut.'

'Who?'

'A friend,' she said.

The thief, he thought. 'Does the Miner always pay with diamonds?'

'Just recently.' She inhaled Marlboro fumes and spoke in syllables of smoke. 'You mean it *is* a diamond? The last time...this friend... He said it was a fake and traded it for a bottle of perfume from Paris because he felt sorry for me. It smelled like cat's piss,' she said.

'It probably was.' He watched the drop of water zig-zag down her leg. 'This Miner, he seems to dispense diamonds like duck eggs in the market.'

'Not many of those around these days.' She pulled the skirts of the robe over her legs. There was no one quite so prim as an unpaid whore, Ruchkin thought. 'Are you sure it's a diamond?' She touched the undistinguished pebble on the bedside table. 'He had some more, in a pouch tied with string.'

'Where is he now?'

'Where's the payment?'

'A kind word? Vysotsky would have been proud of you.'

'He's in the steam room,' she said.

Wearing a towel high on his lean body so that it hid the scar below his heart—the scar beneath his left eye was enough for public display—Ruchkin felt his way blindly through the steam, catching his breath as the heat reached his lungs.

A voice with a Ukranian accent issued from the steam. 'Last one in throws water on the bricks.'

Ruchkin took a couple of steps forward. The steam cleared. He saw naked men sweating on tiers of benches encircling the floor and they saw him.

The owner of the Ukranian accent said: 'I'm sorry, I didn't realise...'

Ruchkin picked up a galvanised bucket and tossed water slugged with eucalyptus on to the hot bricks. Steam billowed. 'My duty. In a *banya* we're all equal.'

No one spoke. Two men who had been beating each other with birch twigs stood motionless. The *banya*, Ruchkin reflected, was the Russians' ultimate catharsis, the haven where they could joyously indulge their need to suffer.

As the steam rose to the highest tiers Ruchkin, ringmaster in the small arena of cracked tiles, said: 'Where is the Miner?'

No one answered but their glances were signposts. And there, unmistakably, was the Miner sitting on the lowest bench, shoulders bowed by the confines of subterranean tunnels, towel lying across bandy legs.

Ruchkin said: 'I want everyone out of here except him,' pointing at the Miner, 'and myself.'

When they had gone he sat beside the Miner. 'So what brings you to Moscow?'

'I have relatives here.'

'Where?'

'To the east. Between the Mikoyan canning factory and the bird market. Near the cemetery,' he added.

'You have a *propiska?*'

'I don't need a permit to visit.'

'But you work here, don't you?'

'I'm a miner, you know that. Look.' He stabbed his thumb at a dark glitter beneath the skin on the other hand. 'Coal dust, trapped there forever. And in my lungs.' He coughed.

'The Kuzbass basin?'

'How do you know that?'

'I guessed because you have an accent. Western Siberia.'

And the independent spirit of a Siberian! Ruchkin imagined him in the pit-head showers, jostling against the slippery bodies of the other miners, bellowing rousing songs about unity, freedom and defiance—when they had been in fashion. But a long time ago, Ruchkin decided, because he wasn't fit enough now to hew coal.

'So when did you move to diamond mines?'

The skin tightened on the miner's flat features. 'Who says I did?'

'Those weren't lumps of coal you've been trading in Moscow.'

'I don't know what you're talking about.'

'Your payment for services to Natalya...a bit extravagant, wasn't it? Or are there so many diamonds around?'

'I found it,' the Miner said. He coughed again. 'I've got to get out of here. I only spend a few minutes on the bottom bench.'

Ruchkin hauled him up two tiers. The Miner was muscular enough but the muscles were wasted. 'You can do better than that,' Ruchkin said, sitting behind him.

'All right, I got a job in a diamond mine near Mirny. A casual job, nothing too strenuous. I have relatives there...'

'You seem to have relatives everywhere.'

'And I found this rough diamond buried under the snow.'

'Just one?'

'How many do you want?' the Miner asked. 'I'm going now. The heat... You can't keep me here.'

'You're on my territory,' Ruchkin said. 'The girl says you had a pouch full of them. Where's the pouch?'

'Up my arse,' the Miner said.

Ruchkin pulled him up another couple of tiers. 'You've also been handing over diamonds to a police informer.'

'The skinny bastard told you?'

'How many diamonds have you got?'

'They're paste,' the Miner said. He coughed extravagantly. 'Now let me go. I can't tell you anything more.'

'Imitation *rough* diamonds?' Ruchkin placed his hands under the Miner's arms. 'Now that's a novelty.'

The Miner said: 'I've got five genuine stones left.'

'Value?'

'It depends on their quality. Flaws, colour, clarity.'

'Many more where they came from?'

The Miner shook his head. Ruchkin could see sweat beading his greying hair like dew. He heaved him up two more tiers. They were almost at the top now and the heat came from hell and the Miner's lungs played reedy music in it.

The Miner said: 'You want a cut?'

'*I* want a cut? You do know who I am?'

'I know you've got a lot of interests in Moscow but you haven't got the Jewellery and Clock Factory.'

'I don't want it: I want the source of the diamonds. Shall I throw more water on the bricks?'

'I can't talk here. Can't breathe...'

Ruchkin led him down the steps and across the floor to the rest room.

He ordered a jug of beer and sat at a battle-worn chess table. A few pieces, mostly pawns, still stood on the squares but the black king lay on its side as though it had been swiped into submission.

Ruchkin waited until the Miner had cooled his throat with Zhigulovsky, then said: 'Are you ready?'

'You play?' The miner picked up the king.

'If it doesn't distract you.'

The Miner fisted his hands, white pawn in one, black in the other. Ruchkin got white. He moved his king's pawn two squares. 'Now tell me about the mines,' he said.

Like the rest of Russia they were in chaos. Ethnic minorities which had trekked east to pick up fat wage packets were at each other's throats, management was in shock.

Jet engines for blasting permfrost had run out of power, X-ray machines for sorting diamonds had run out of electricity, steam shovels for loading kimberlite on to trucks had run out of steam.

Did Ruchkin know where the mines—Mir, Aichal and Udachnaya—were? He nodded. In Yakutia, the size of India, in Siberia which was itself the size of the United States.

Westerners had never really comprehended the size of the old Soviet Union—one-sixth of the world's land surface, 150 languages spoken... Nor, for that matter, could they visualise the infinite dimensions of the Russian Republic which embraced Siberia.

Sure, he knew Yakutia where the cold—minus 60°C sometimes—splintered steel, froze oil and murdered exposed flesh. Where body mist wreathed the capital, Yakutsk, and human breath fell rustling to the ground—'the whisper of stars', as they called it. Where, in summer, permfrost melted into mud thigh-deep and mosquitoes as big as MiGs sought blood.

The storehouse of Russia, the Miner said, moving a knight. The world maybe. Gold, coal, oil, uranium, almost every known mineral.

Diamonds, Ruchkin reminded him, that's what they were discussing. He swept a bishop across the table, pinning the black knight.

The Miner gulped beer. There were still a few diamonds to be scavenged, he said. At the extremities of the open-cast mines, in the sorting chambers and beside the 180-mile motorway linking the diamond town of Mirny to the Lena river, tossed there by optimistic pilferers intending to return.

But there weren't any *sizes* anymore. The Miner winked, communicating esoteric knowledge. Only *smalls*—'less than one carat'—and industrials.

He castled on the queen's side relieving the pin on the knight.

The double doors of the rest room opened and two militiamen in blue-grey coats, boots and fur hats, came in bringing a gasp of cold air with them. They noticed Ruchkin, nodded respectfully, and went to the changing room.

Ruchkin drank beer and began to mount an attack on the now vulnerable black king. What had happened to production? he asked. Where were the rest of the diamonds that had been mined?

The Miner brooded over his stretched defences but was diverted by a fit of coughing. When he had recovered he moved a pawn one square.

Ruchkin repeated the questions.

Production was still going ahead fitfully, the Miner said. But because transport was so unreliable a hoard of roughs had accumulated. They were being guarded by the army. Spetsnaz, the best.

Spetsnaz? Ruchkin's breathing quickened. 'They can't leave a hoard like that in the mines for ever.' He moved his queen diagonally. 'Check.'

'They're moving them to Moscow. The Syndicate... You've heard of the Syndicate?'

Ruchkin said he had.

'Well, they're waiting for them in Moscow so they can absorb them. Stop the market from being swamped.'

'Moving them by air?'

'Too risky. Hijacks, blizzards, airfields snowed in...'

'Snow? Not now.'

'They're not moving them now. In three weeks' time. On December 1st. In an armoured train.'

Ruchkin swooped with a bishop. 'Mate,' he said. 'Estimated value of the diamonds?'

'Fifty billion dollars,' the Miner said.

41

Chapter Two

From the baths Ruchkin went underground. To a subterranean city six miles south-west of the Kremlin beneath the suburb of Ramenki.

It had been built in the Brezhnev era to accommodate communist leaders and staff in the event of a nuclear attack. Its 500 acres, contained bunkers, recreation centres, a swimming pool even, and had many exits—beneath the homes of the then elite, the Defence Ministry in Taganka Square and the former KGB headquarters in Dzerzhinsky Square.

But the easiest way to gain access was through a secret underground railroad, Metro 2, which snaked through the bowels of Moscow below the public metro. Ruchkin told the driver of the Zil to take him to the concealed station near the banks of the Moskva river.

The mist had lifted but Muscovites in damp fur hats were already leaning into winter. The Zil passed Petrovka, the police HQ, and the offices of *Izvestia* and *Moscow News*, the theatres on Tverskoy, Gogol's house and the Defence Ministry, seat of

Ruchkin's betrayal.

Sitting in the back of the limousine, Ruchkin drew the curtains, took his out-of-date ID from his pocket and pondered the fate that had led him from a regiment of brutal honesty to that betrayal.

A young man with a scar on one cheek, wearing a beret the same colour as his eyes, ice-blue, stared at him from behind yellowing plastic. To all intents and purposes a conventional paratrooper, but to the initiated, who noticed that he wasn't wearing a Guards unit badge, a member of Spetsnaz, the elite.

What else? It had been written ever since his father had emerged from the 900-day Siege of Leningrad in the Great Patriotic War with Germany and sworn that any son of his would belong to a peerless breed who would transcend the ineptitude of Stalin and his generals who had dispatched more than a million citizens of Leningrad to their deaths.

A breed not unlike Hitler's dream of an Aryan race, vowed Nikolay Ruchkin, who was as anti-Semitic as any Nazi stormtrooper.

And when, as a pioneer, he had moved east to Siberia and married a girl with flaxen hair and blue eyes who had given birth to Viktor, dying in the process, he had put the boy down for Spetsnaz, a derivation of *spetsialnoye nazhacheniye*, meaning 'special purpose'.

In his late-teens Viktor had plunged with grim intent into the evolution of a *Spetsnaz* officer, first as a *salagi*, a raw recruit, then into the ranks of the *stariki*, the old sweats, all of 20 years old, who made it their business to humiliate recruits.

A snow white towel inside the door of a tent. One after the other the *salagi*, wearing boots weighted with mud, jumped the towel because presumably that was what they were expected to do. Not Ruchkin. He pulled up short and wiped his boots with the towel.

He was given a top bunk with the *stariki*. That night the newcomers were beaten up, heads shoved down lavatories, and Viktor Ruchkin was in there with the tormentors. Why not? He was adapting to the toughest initiation ceremonies in the Soviet Union.

From there he progressed to the training camp near Kirovograd in the Ukraine where he was introduced to the Devil's Ditch.

You weren't forced to jump the ditch, seeded with metal spikes, but if you didn't your moral fibre was questioned. The narrowest width was two metres; on seeing the ditch for the first time Ruchkin jumped it at its widest extremity wearing full combat uniform and carrying an AKS-74 assault rifle.

Thereafter, first as a junior sergeant, then as an officer, having passed tests that included fighting with a rabid dog in a hut, Ruchkin invoked the ditch. Particularly if there was a Jew to be intimidated. Jew, Ruchkin had learned from his father, was a synonym for traitor.

'We were all born in the Soviet Union. Georgian, Moldavian, Tajik, Russian... Why should a Jew be so different? Why should he want escape to Israel? Shit, we all fought for the Soviet Union, didn't we?'

His father died soon after that particular outburst but its venom stayed with Viktor as though it had been imparted with the fangs of a cobra. And when a muscular but clumsy Jew presented himself for training at a camp near Sverdlovsk in the Urals, Ruchkin suggested that they should compete with each other across the ditch.

The Jew, named Rozen, remained singularly unintimidated. 'Why not?'

'Starting at the narrow end wearing track suits and trainers.'

'If you say so.'

'If you say so what?'

'If you say so, *lieutenant*.'

They progressed from the narrow end of the ditch to the widest reaches and,

45

although he was ungainly, Rozen always landed comfortably, staring amiably at Ruchkin.

'How about full combat gear?'

'If that's the way you want it, lieutenant.'

Rozen carried his pack and his AKS-74 easily enough but on the last jump but one he stumbled on the far side of the ditch.

'Had enough?'

'If you think so, lieutenant.'

'It's up to you.'

'No, lieutenant, it's up to you. If you don't think you can make it, I will understand.'

Ruchkin jumped, feeling the black earth crumble beneath the heels of his boots. He called across the ditch: 'You don't have to.'

'Stand back, lieutenant, I can see Jerusalem over there.' He paused. 'Do you know about Masada?'

'Everyone killed themselves rather than surrender to the Romans.'

'And recruits in the Israeli Army have to go to the hill and swear an oath.'

'Tell me one thing, Rozen, what the fuck are you doing in Russia?'

'Jewish mother, Russian father, how the hell do I know, lieutenant?'

He ran lead-footed at the ditch, stumbled on the other side and fell back. A spike took him in the back. As he died in hospital three days later he said: 'Masada shall not fall again.'

After Rozen's death—private conflict was accepted, its outcome tolerated—Ruchkin prospered, abiding by the creed of the wolf, unofficial symbol of Spetsnaz. Wolves disposed of their weaker brethren but only in the interests of the pack. The wolf, Ruchkin believed, was a noble animal.

He fought in Afghanistan, winning medals and a reputation for indifference to the plight of both friend and comrade, if the latter jeopardised the safety of the pack. 'Never fear, never trust,' the manual said. 'Compassion is a fiction of Mankind.'

Honour, well...a soldier in Spetsnaz had the licence to make his own definition. And questions of honour were settled with the fighting spade, a weapon with a handle 32 centimetres long and a razor-sharp, green-painted blade. Thrown, the spade could take a man's head off at 50 metres. It was just such a spade that had left the scar on Ruchkin's chest while a matter of honour was being settled. A knife had left its signature on his cheek.

Ruchkin became the youngest major in Spetsnaz and would doubtless have become the youngest general if Gorbachev hadn't surrendered the empire, divided the Soviet Union and grovelled to the United States, thereby drawing the teeth of the army and its *raison d'être.*

For defying this craven spirit—by putting down a demonstration of Jews wanting to emigrate—Ruchkin had been disciplined and posted to the Middle East to train Arab freedom fighters. On his return he found not only the republics at each other's throats but regions within them. The way things were going village would be marching on village, neighbour upon neighbour.

So Ruchkin followed his own interpretation of honour, quit Spetsnaz and took up arms in the battlefield of organised crime, taking his fighting spade with him.

The Zil stopped outside the entrance to Metro 2 beside a curve of the river beneath the Lenin Hills and the wedding cake battlements of the university.

Two guards toting Stechkin machine pistols and wearing Afghanistan campaign pins on their Michelin-Man jackets waved aside Ruchkin's ID and watched him, almost reverently, into the elevator.

The stainless steel doors sighed and closed and Ruchkin began his descent into the vaults intended for Kremlin gangsters but occupied these days by their heirs, the mafia.

According to the constructors some of the tunnels dated back to the reign of

Ivan the Terrible in the sixteenth century, built so that his *oprichniki*, forebears of the KGB, could visit his palace secretly. And it sometimes seemed to Ruchkin that his presence still brooded in the catacoombs. Lost pigeons and bats ranged the corridors; cats already mutating into an underground species fought with rats that had grown fat on the stores of black market food.

At the foot of the elevator Ruchkin boarded a two-coach train on a track that terminated at Vnukovo airport 30 kilometres from the centre of Moscow—in case the US 82nd Airborne or the SAS dropped on the Kremlin!

He was the only passenger in the train and he alighted at Ramenki on the same level as the chamber where a politburo in subterranean exile would have met. Today the centrally heated chamber was occupied by three godfathers.

At the head of a long table sat a Chechen, on either side of him a Georgian and an Armenian. Sink a shaft anywhere in the Caucasus and you would unearth a conspiracy.

The Chechen, hirsuite, soft-eyed and inwardly coiled, said: 'You're late, Viktor Nikolaevich. We had almost given up hope.'

'I was taking a bath.'

49

'We're honoured.'

Ruchkin took off his coat and fur hat and sat at the other end of the table.

'So,' the Chechen said, 'let's get down to business.' He took off his tie and watchspring hair sprouted from the V of his shirt.

The Georgian handed him a map. He was old—possibly more than 100 if you believed those stories about Georgian longevity—with mottled skin and a white bandit's moustache. He spoke with a Georgian croak and wore a bandolier slotted with bullets.

Ruchkin stared at the blank, yellow-painted wall, looking instinctively for a window. The complex was supposed to have been built to accommodate 30,000 occupants for up to 30 years. But how could they have lived without sunlight?

The Chechen unrolled the map, securing two of its errant corners with flasks of drinking water. Moscow had been divided into areas with incisive strokes of coloured felt pens.

The Chechen said: 'We have been re-adjusting our boundaries.'

'We?' Ruchkin addressed a square on the wall where a portrait of a fallen hero had once hung—Lenin, Stalin, Brezhnev, Gorbachev?—and composed a window out of it.

'Those of us who bother to attend meetings.'

'You mean, those who know about them.'

The Armenian, dark and angular with a slithery quiff of blue-black hair, said: 'You have become too greedy. You had the market, the prime site, but you weren't content.'

'I should be content with a market?'

But the Armenian was right, of course. The big, glass-fronted market on Tavetnoi Boulevard was the most lucrative scam. Private enterprise stallholders paid handsomely for protection—the whole market police force had been arrested once for collusion—and for produce from Ruchkin's warehouses. What hurt the Caucasians was that they couldn't sell their southern comforts, fruit and flowers, without paying Ruchkin for the privilege.

'You took over the currency operations in the Savoy and Metropol Hotels,' the Armenian went on. 'The whores *and* the male prostitutes outside the Bolshoi. TSUM department store. The baths, the circus, the Blue Bird jazz club. You even moved north to the river beaches at Serebryany Bor. I'm surprised you didn't take over Lenin's tomb.'

'I left you all the drugs. Do they still

51

shoot up behind the Hard Rock Cafe in Gorky Park?'

'Don't talk to me about dope,' the Armenian said. 'It was the army who brought it here from Afghanistan.'

'Not Spetsnaz.' Ruchkin balled his fist and his knuckles shone.

'Maybe not Spetsnaz.' The Armenian toppled his quiff with his fingers.

The Chechen said: 'No more personalities. *We* have a proposition to discuss.'

'Where are the Tartars, the Assyrians, the Lyubertsy weight lifters?

'We have reached agreement with them.'

'You shot some of them?'

The old Georgian lit a *papirosa* and said: 'A few Siberians wouldn't be missed.' His voice was like parchment.

The Chechen raised one hand, fingers splayed. 'Listen,' he said to Ruchkin. 'And stop trying to be fucking smart. We are going to be very reasonable.'

Ruchkin stood up and, knuckles on the table, examined the map of Moscow. 'I see you've *re-adjusted* the central market. Have you moved your carnations in yet? Your pineapples?'

The Armenian said: 'You can always have Gastronom No. 1.' A joke. Its manager had been executed for corruption and today the ornate halls were as bare as those in any other store. The Armenian grinned, showing Ruchkin his gold teeth.

The Chechen thumped the side of his fist on the table. 'Stop sniping. The truth is we're offering you much more than you had before. But not in Moscow.'

'Leningrad?' Ruchkin didn't subscribe to the restoration of the name St Petersburg: it was retrograde, back to tsars and serfs. 'I never liked the place. Too much water, I always feel as if I'm standing on a raft.'

'Bigger than Leningrad—we're offering you Russia's treasure chest.'

'The Kremlin?' Ruchkin sat down again.

The Armenian said: 'Siberia.'

The silence expanded and small noises grew in it: the old Georgian's breathing, a hiss in a ventilator shaft, the scutter of rodent feet.

'You're right,' Ruchkin said, 'it is bigger than Leningrad.'

The Chechen said: 'If you don't agree...'

'I won't get farther than the metro station?' Ruchkin had noticed two more Chechens with pistol bulges in their leather jackets on the platform.

The Chechen shrugged. 'When American pioneers went west, Russians went east. Why not follow them?'

'So did the convicts,' the Armenian said. 'Go and pack your bags, Ruchkin. Take all your Siberian hooligans with you and thank God you're not going in chains.'

The Georgian stubbed out his *papirosa* and ran the tips of his clawed fingers down the bullets in his bandolier.

Ruchkin heard a train pull up.

He said: 'I think you're being very generous and I'm honoured.'

The new silence was a concentrate. The Georgian's claw rested on his bullets, the Armenian's lips opened over his cave of gold— It was broken by a watch beeping on the Chechen's wrist.

The Chechen said: 'You agree?'

'Of course. The *taiga*, the snow, every patch of sky with its own eagle. You know what they say out there: "A hundred roubles isn't money, a hundred versts isn't distance, a hundred grams of vodka isn't even a drink".'

The Armenian said: 'It's a trick.'

'No trick, you have my word.' Ruchkin extended his hand but no one took it.

He stood up and made for the door. Turning, he said: 'If you ever want to come fishing...'

The Chechen said: 'You must have reasons?'

Fifty billion of them, Ruchkin thought. But he didn't elaborate.

The Chechens were lying on the platform of Metro 2. Their pistols were in their hands but they had not had time to fire them.

The fighting spade of one of the two ex-Spetsnaz who had arrived on the second train had almost severed one of their heads; the other spade was buried deep in the second Chechen's chest.

One of the former Spetsnaz spread his hands. 'Where to now?'

'Siberia,' Ruchkin said.

From Moscow he took a six-hour Aeroflot flight to Yakutsk, capital of cold, in northeast Siberia. There he chartered an A -2 bush plane from Polar Aviation and flew to Mirny, city of diamonds, to await the others who were travelling on the Trans-Siberian.

Snow hadn't yet settled on this expanse of Siberia, Sleeping Land, and beneath him he saw the pencil-point pines and matchstick birch of the *taiga,* marsh tissued with ice, a herd of reindeer running ahead of the AN-2's shadow, river upon river—the arteries of Russia clogged with the cholesterol of disuse.

Then he picked up the spider footprints of the new railroad which, when finished in a couple of weeks, would link the diamond fields with Yakutsk and the Trans-Siberian to the south.

He imagined an armoured train nosing

through the wilderness towards Moscow and a terrible exultancy settled upon him. The biggest heist in the history of crime... He could imagine only one man impeding him: Mikhail Sapir, a Jew.

Chapter Three

The Dead Sea, lowest point on earth. Scarcely more than a lake, 45 miles long, nine miles wide, filled with thick brine—Yam Hamelach, Sea of Salt, in Hebrew—which kept the semi-conscious man drifting across its southern tip afloat, provided he stayed on his back.

The salt and other minerals stung his lips and eyes. Blood from the wound on the side of his head hung clotted in the water. The sun reached inside his skull.

From time to time he made unco-ordinated movements, propelling himself towards the Jordanian border and into Israeli waters.

To the north-west lay the Judaean Hills where Abraham had once journeyed and the West Bank which had been under Israeli military control since the Six Day War in 1967. To the east the salt pans and bleak baked hills of Moab in Jordan from which he had just escaped.

Six hours earlier Mikhail Sapir, 30 years old and a major in the 269 Counterterrorist Unit in the IDF, the Israeli Defence Forces, the elite within the elite, had led a punitive raid into Jordan as a reprisal for a terrorist attack at Eilat on the Gulf of Aqaba to the south in which Israelis on vacation had been gunned down.

But their armoured personnel carriers had met a detachment of the Jordanian Special Forces, its members all Bedouins with tribal links to King Hussein.

Sapir had always believed they were one of the best fighting units in the Middle East and so they had proved themselves. The battle in a wadi had lasted 20 minutes and Israelis and Jordanians had savaged each other to a draw.

Sapir's APC had been knocked out and he had been hit by a fragmentation grenade. Only a superficial wound but he had lost a lot of blood as he ran through the drainage ditches in the salt flats to the lifeless shores of the Dead Sea.

Ahead lay the shallow waters where the Biblical cities of Sodom and Gomorrah, destroyed by God for their decadence, were said by some to have drowned; on the Israeli shore to the south-west Lot's Pillar.

He had taken off his combat boots and

57

lowered himself into the brine and begun to swim, weightless as though he were in space, towards the rust-coloured shores of the Promised Land. Overhead clattered a gun-ship of the Royal Jordanian Air Force. He had floated motionless like a thatch of reeds, hoping that the blood trail in his wake couldn't be distinguished from the air.

When he had started to swim again he found he had lost power. Was he over Sodom or Gomorrah? He smiled weakly and his mouth filled with saline water.

By the time he reached the point where he estimated the frontier to be he could barely move his arms or legs and the flow of blood behind him was dwindling.

He turned and, unable to right himself, buried his head in the water.

When he came to there was an oxygen mask on his face and a drip feed in his arm.

A brawny young medic winked at him and said: 'Don't say "Where am I?" You were picked up by an army dinghy and you're in an ambulance on your way to Jerusalem, compliments of King Hussein, i.e you're on the road he built on the West Bank before we took it away from him.' He checked Sapir's pulse. 'You lost a lot of blood but we're refuelling you.'

In hospital in Jerusalem Sapir lies in a private ward and listens to the gunfire in his skull. He closes his eyes and the gunfire recedes and he smiles as a familiar smell reaches his nostrils.

The smell is the compound of borscht forever bubbling on an antique gas stove, the smoke from spluttering candles and suds strenuously lathered by his mother in their cramped apartment with a shared bathroom in Kazan 800 kilometres east of Moscow.

Kazan, capital of the Tartars, where Chaliapin was born, where Gorky worked, where Lenin and Tolstoy studied, is still Sapir's vision of quiet and considered normality. He sees himself sitting in the botanical gardens on Taktasha Street, sharing them with a breeze from the Volga.

Kazan is also the cradle of his reluctant militancy. Because he is a Jew, a *zhid*, a *pyaty punkty*, a fifth pointer—so called because Point No 5 in a domestic passport revealed Jewish nationality. And so at school he fought the Jew-baiters whose parents had taught them bigotry along with table manners and road sense.

When it became known that his father, a teller with the state bank on Bauman Street, had applied to OVIR, the Office of Visas and Registration, seeking exit visas for himself and his family to emigrate to Israel, the persecution became more inventive.

From his bedroom, scarcely more than a partition, he heard his father recounting his experiences to his mother. How he had been beaten, spat upon and interrogated. On three occasions he didn't return from OVIR—he had been imprisoned, Mikhail learned later—and the only sound in the apartment was the weeping of his mother.

Where had his father accumulated enough money even to think about journeying to Israel? When a rumour circulated in school that his father had stashed bearer bank books from numbered accounts, used by profiteers, under the floorboards of the apartment, Mikhail sought out the author of the rumour, loosened his teeth and broke his nose.

By the age of 16 he was, much against his will, a renowned street fighter. His black hair was cut ferociously short, his face scarred by conflict. And when, one June morning, Zionists staged a demonstration on 1st May Square beneath the walls of Kazan's own kremlin he was there, fists balled, beechwood club under his jacket.

But neither fists nor club were any match for Spetsnaz fighting spades.

The Spetsnaz looked magnificent—everyone agreed on that—as they marched on to the square in their blue berets and combat fatigues, sunshine splintering on the razored blades of the spades. Fine young men, Siberians by the look of them, disciplined and fit, the personification of Soviet manhood.

Old men with chests armoured with medals bought *kvas* from the vendors and raised their glasses. Babushkas turned the heads of dumpling babies in the direction of the young lions. Girls blew kisses. A smattering of applause was heard.

At the head of the Spetsnaz stood a captain, as lean as an Olympic sprinter, as fair as a Viking, spade in one hand, hailer in the other.

He gave one command: 'Jews, disperse. This is an unlawful assembly.'

Instead the Zionists carrying Stars of David on blue banners dimpled by the warm breeze, and placards asserting their right to go to the Promised Land, closed their jumbled ranks and began to converge on the blue berets.

The Viking raised the hand grasping the hailer.

The Jews, beards angled with Biblical conviction, continued to advance at a leisurely pace as God looked down upon them from behind the blessed sunlight. The same God who had many houses waiting for them in Israel.

The spades, hurled with the accuracy of medieval spear throwers, decimated the front line of the Zionists, severing limbs and tilting heads to unlikely angles. Black hats ran like cartwheels, banners fell and became funeral shrouds on faces still bearing, even in death, fatalistic optimism.

Those who fell were either very old or very young.

One spade sliced the shoulder of Mikhail Sapir, causing him to drop the beechwood club that he had been about to throw. Then he, too, dropped bleeding on to the sun-warmed ground.

The rest of the demonstrators dispersed.

So did the old men and the babushkas and the kissing girls.

Ambulances that had been waiting behind the town hall trundled into the square.

The hammer and sickle continued to snap over the Spassky Tower of the kremlin.

And the incident might have been forgotten by Soviet chroniclers in the pre-glasnost days when anything as unseemly as a massacre was not allowed to pollute the barren columns of *Pravda* or *Izvestia* if a deputation of Tolstoy buffs from Baltimore had not been visiting the city at the time.

One of them, a Russian-speaking blue-rinse named Mary Heinzel, who claimed to be distantly related to Tolstoy, filmed the Spetsnaz preventative operation and recorded a brief interview in English with Mikhail Sapir on cassette.

Mary Heinzel: God, what happened? Why, why...

Screams, running footsteps and wailing sirens.

Sapir: I didn't know I was hit so badly. The blood...it's warm...mine.

Mary Heinzel: Here, I'll try and stem the bleeding... But I don't know where... Shit, so much blood... Now, I think it's stopping. What...

Sapir: Are you Jewish?

Mary Heinzel: No, but everyone has the right...

Sapir: No rights here. All we want to do is go home. Home, do you understand?

Mary Heinzel: Israel?

Brakes squealing. A crisp military command. Boots marching.

Sapir: Not China, ma'am.

Mary Heinzel: I know... I'm sorry. Why spades?

Sapir: The weapon of Spetsnaz.

Mary Heinzel: Spetsnaz?

Sapir: The cream...

A cry of pain, presumably from Sapir.

Mary Heinzel: I'm sorry.

Sapir: What are you doing with this tape?

Mary Heinzel: I don't know...

Sapir: The officer in charge of the Spetsnaz was Ruchkin. I heard someone shout his name. Keep that on tape...

A man's guttural voice: What the fuck's going on here? Give me that...

Mary Heinzel: Get your hands off me, buster.

A shout, a thud. (Sapir remembered later that he had hooked one foot round a militiaman's legs.)

Sapir: Ruchkin gave the order to kill these Jews, I *saw* it. Now run...

Slurred sounds and an ever-increasing thump that may have been the beat of Mary Heinzel's heart.

Back in Baltimore she handed the film and the tape to a TV network. They went round the world.

The Kremlin, hungry for grain, investment, tourists and recognition as a misunderstood power, ordered an inquiry.

At the inquiry held in Moscow in the Ministry of Defence building, which had once been the Officer Cadet Academy, Sapir was called to give evidence and advised before he mounted the stand that if he implicated Ruchkin he would join the martyrs of lst October Square.

State investigator: You say you *saw* Major Ruchkin give the order?
Sapir: He raised his hand.
Investigator: Scarcely an order.
Sapir: Then why did his men throw their spades at that moment?
Investigator: I ask the questions, Comrade Sapir.
Sapir: Anyway, he *was* in charge.
Investigator: Could it not have been a misunderstanding?
Sapir: Twelve dead, three of them teenagers, a misunderstanding?

Ruchkin stopped Sapir on Gogol Boulevard near the Ministry complex. 'Just you and me now, *zhid.*' His voice was ice cold on the sweating air. 'Don't worry, I never forget a face.'

Ruchkin was reprimanded, demoted and posted out of sight and mind to the Middle East. And for a long while he, in Syria, and Sapir, in Israel, were neighbours.

Sapir opens his eyes as a nurse who looks like Sigourney Weaver enters the room, checks his temperature, pulse and drip, gives him an injection in his buttock and says: 'You've got a visitor.'

Rachel Wolf, as fiercely beautiful as

ever. Hair thick as harvested wheat, a fine questing nose...a warrior risen from mythology.

She wears combat fatigues and smells of expensive perfume and battle. She says: 'So where are the grapes?'

'You can speak Russian if you want.'

They had spoken Russian instead of Hebrew when making love.

'So what happened?' She is still speaking Hebrew.

'A punitive mission... Only it was I who was punished.' He watches a bubble rise in his drip feed. 'Why have you come here?'

'For old times' sake.'

'Good times,' he said.

'Good times.' She moves her chair fractionally closer to the bed. 'This mission...your last?'

He touches the dressing on the side of his head, conscious that it does not cast him in the heroic mould. 'I guess so. I've only got three more weeks to serve.'

'You could sign on again.'

'You know I don't want to do that. You of all people.' He shakes his head and pain darts from ear to ear. 'I'm going to the Negev desert to grow oranges.'

'You were meant to defend Israel not breast feed it.'

'I wasn't born a fighter, I was manufactured. First in Kazan and then here.

66

'Officer material, Sapir, your country needs you.' Well, I've served it and now I'm going to feed it.'

She regards him speculatively. 'Odd, isn't it, you and me? The roles should be reversed. But everything is circumstance...'

The Wolfs had arrived in Israel from Russia at about the same time as the Sapirs, ten years ago. Her father had been a diamond cutter in Novosibirsk, Chicago of Siberia, and as soon as she was 18 she joined the Israeli Army as though she wanted to distance herself from life behind the loupe, from the eternal search for flaws in compressed carbon.

Her father decided to invest his expertise in Israel's diamond industry which, since cutters from Antwerp—rescued by the British from under the noses of the marauding Germans in World War II—had settled in what was then Palestine, had become the country's most lucrative export.

He had opened a factory in Ramat Gan, the diamond district of Tel Aviv, but hadn't prospered because the Syndicate that controls the supply and demand of diamonds all over the world had decided that the Israelis, buying rough diamonds from unauthorised suppliers and smugglers, had to be cut down to size. It scared off the banks financing the cutters and polishers, reduced suppliers, and put hundreds of small firms out of business, Josef Wolf's among them.

After this humiliation, not dissimilar from those he had endured in his campaign to reach the Promised Land, Joseph Wolf withered. The end came on a bus near the Sea of Galilee, his daughter sitting beside him.

They were on their way to a kibbutz to spend a couple of days with a family of Polish Jews from Siedlice and the single-deck bus was labouring up a sun-baked hill.

Outside a young shepherd sat among his sheep and yet somehow appeared to be isolated from them; inside adults drugged by a day's sun dozed while children bit deep into watermelons, spitting out seeds that glistened like black pearls.

Suddenly the shepherd raised his hand—when Rachel relived the moment Sapir remembered Viktor Ruchkin raising his hand in the sunlit square in Kazan—and half a dozen young Arabs materialised from behind a hillock covered with scrub and boulders.

Instinctively Rachel, trained soldier, knew what was happening. She shouted, 'Get down,' but the elders were too anaesthetised to comprehend, the children too deep into their watermelons. 'In any case,' she said later, 'why should they take any notice of a madwoman in civilian clothes screaming at them?'

As the bus slowed to take a curve the Arabs opened up with Kalashnikovs. The bullets took out the windows of the bus and buried themselves in young and old alike and only then did the Israelis get down, some of them never to rise again.

Rachel snatched the automatic pistol she always carried from her purse and fired through the shards of a window at the Arabs still standing among the panicking sheep. The shepherd fell; the rest fled, firing their Kalashnikovs into the air.

Her father died in hospital two days later; her mother, who had been waiting for them at the kibbutz, followed soon after.

Rachel continued to serve in the army and such was her vengeful application that she was transferred to the elite 269, the unit which supplied the crack troops who in 1976 rescued hostages held by Palestinian terrorists in Entebbe.

Her commanding officer was Mikhail Sapir and six months after she joined they became lovers.

Sitting upright in his hospital bed, Sapir remembers a hotel room in Haifa, a sliver of Mediterranean visible through the window. He is inside her and she is crying out exultantly; after their abandonment the peace is like a shared dawn.

It all ended the following day.

The ambush was set up in the Golan Heights, captured from Syria by the Israelis in the Yom Kippur War in 1973, on information laid by a Druze.

A unit of Arab guerrillas trained by Russians in a camp outside Damascus was poised to cross the Syrian border and attack the En Gev kibbutz on the north shore of the Sea of Galilee.

Sapir, with Rachel Wolf at his side, deployed his men in a ghost village—devastated in the 1967 conflict with Syria and then again in '73—overlooking a modest valley in the bleak tableland.

Through his field glasses Sapir could see hang gliders sailing over the waters of Galilee and, in the distance, the hotels and palm trees of Tiberias.

Rachel was leaning against the wall of what had once been a school, a warm breeze teasing strands of her hair that had escaped from her combat helmet. A muscle twitched in her jaw and her finger massaged the trigger of her Galil assault rifle. Sapir knew that she was thinking about her father.

Sapir said: 'Hatred never solved anything.'

She frowned disbelief at him. ' "Eye for eye, tooth for tooth"...We read the same Bible, don't we?'

' "Blessed are the merciful: for they shall obtain mercy." '

'Not our Testament, Mikhail. We are still waiting for the Messiah.'

'And when he comes he will preach that.'

Inside his camouflage jacket his handset beeped. He spoke into it, then said to Rachel: 'They're coming.'

The first figure he saw through his field glasses was unmistakable—blue beret, hand raised to the invisible men behind him, just as it had been raised on 1st May Square in Kazan many years ago.

Pistol in hand, he waited. Five minutes. Too long. And then he thought: This is the obvious place to spring an ambush and he knows it—I'm not dealing with kids, I'm dealing with a professional.

Spetsnaz versus 269.

So Ruchkin would be reconnoitring *behind* the deserted village.

Sapir concentrated his squad behind a tooth-stump wall on the far side of the ruins and waited for another sighting of a blue beret. Like a cornflower blossoming, he thought.

Then he reasoned: If I were Ruchkin I would anticipate this too. And I would withdraw and wait until we break cover. Stalemate?

If Israelis had ever philosophised as

defeatistly as that they would have been driven into the sea years ago. *Mount an attack from the rear.*

He led them in a crouching run back the way they had come. Then a wide flanking movement through rocks and scrubs and the shell craters of long ago conflict.

In front of them a cornflower...

'Down!'

They hit the parched ground as the Arabs opened up with automatic fire. Ambushers ambushed?

Not quite so dumb, Comrade Ruchkin! Two Israelis who had continued the flanking movement opened up with their Galils from behind a rust-red tumili of rocks.

Sapir shouted: 'Throw down your guns, you're surrounded.'

An exaggeration.

Two smoke grenades exploded in the no-man's-land between Arabs and Israelis.

Sapir ran into the smoke.

Halfway through a gap like a window. Ruchkin peering through it...

'You,' he said.

'Your weapon,' Sapir said.

Ruchkin tightened his grip on his fighting spade. 'To a *zhid?* Fuck you.'

Sapir aimed his pistol—just as a grenade hit the ground between them and danced for a fraction of a second before exploding.

When Sapir got to his feet Rachel was beside him and Ruchkin had disappeared.

As they emerged from the smoke three young Arabs carrying AK-47's came at them.

Rachel aimed her Galil. 'They're the ones who killed my father!' Her finger tightened on the trigger.

'They aren't shooting. They're out of ammunition.'

'Murderers!' she screamed.

'They're only kids.' Just like the kids who were murdered in Kazan, he thought, as he knocked the barrel of Rachel's Galil aside and wrestled her to the ground.

When he let her go the Arabs had gone. Rachel was weeping; he could see her tears on the thin soil.

Outside the hospital, as Rachel Wolf leaves, the first stars of the Sabbath glimmer in the darkening sky. Faintly he hears the strains of *Lekha Dodi*, Come My Beloved, issuing from a synagogue. And smells the candles spluttering in his parents' home in Haifa, where they had lived for five God-given years before dying peacefully. Three more weeks before he leaves the army on December 1st. He watches another bubble rise in the drip and burst prettily. Where, he wonders, is Viktor Ruchkin now?

Chapter Four

Ruchkin went first to Diamond Factory No 3 where, according to the Miner, the hoard of rough diamonds had been stored.

To get there he hired a black Volga and drove through the city of Mirny built on foundations of permafrost. Past apartment blocks painted in pastel shades and supported on stilts sunk deep into the concrete ground—glue on the surface in summer—past a hospital, library, cinemas, theatres and a vodka distillery.

The factory stood near a pit 1½ kilometres wide, testament to the greed of the diamond pioneers who desecrated the countryside.

The extraction of roughs from kimberlite, the sorting and grading, was carried out in a windowless obelisk, 14 stories high and covered in an aluminium skin.

On the plane bringing him to Yakutsk Ruchkin had done his homework. Firestones had first been mentioned by Cossacks pushing east in the seventeenth century. But it wasn't until 300 years later that Vladimir Sobolev, a young graduate of St Petersburg Mining Institute, went to

Siberia and prepared a report for Gosplan, the state planning agency. He told them that the geological platform of the region was similar to the diamond-bearing region of South Africa: in particular in the valley of the Vilyui river.

Then the Germans invaded the Soviet Union and all prospecting was abandoned. The West supplied the Russians with all the industrial diamonds they wanted—until the end of the war when the West, fearing the Russian bear, restricted supplies to their erstwhile ally. So prospectors once more began to poke around Siberia, but it wasn't until 1953 that a geologist, a girl named Larissa Popugayeva, followed a trail of tell-tale garnets—found in kimberlite in South Africa—which led to a volcanic pipe near the Vilyui basin, just as Sobolev had predicted. They called the pipe Thunder Flash, but it was short on diamonds.

Now everyone was looking for blood-red garnets. And in 1955 another young geologist, Yuri Khabardin, found kimberlite in a fox's lair. This time it was studded with diamonds.

He sent a coded message to Moscow: *I am smoking the pipe of peace.* It meant that he had positively tested the kimberlite—the host matter of diamonds—and it was a message that horrified the Syndicate which, since the turn of the century, had controlled the world diamond trade. What if the Russians dug up so many diamonds that they were able to flood the market? Why, gemstones would become as worthless as glass baubles and the Syndicate would have to start trading in soapflakes.

The pipe was called *Mir*, Peace, but it was, according to the Syndicate's spies, a small one. And conditions in the region of Yakutia were so dire that further prospecting was restricted. But by 1960 the Russians, using steam power, had found more pipes and built diamond cities, Mirny and Aikhal, on steel stilts that reached deep into the permafrost to prevent them buckling in the summer.

Time for the Syndicate bosses in Johannesburg and London to do the decent thing. They pointed out that only they had the know-how to market uncut gemstones. Furthermore, it wasn't in the best interests of the Soviet Union to debase this hardest of hard currencies. So a deal was struck in which the Soviets agreed to market all their uncut gemstones through the Syndicate—two million carats in a good year—and the threat to the world's most enduring monopoly had passed.

Until now.

Ruchkin stopped outside the aluminium-sheathed factory, flashed his old plastic ID through the window of the Volga and asked to see the Spetsnaz officer in charge of security.

The officer, a young lieutenant, sat in a glass partitioned cubicle on the first floor of the factory. His eyes were as dark as ink, his skin as pale as a submariner's. His booted feet were perched on a desk and Ruchkin wanted to kick them off.

The lieutenant said: 'I've heard of you. To what do I owe the honour?'

He reminded Ruchkin of a recruit cautiously cheeking a *stariki*.

'A proposition,' Ruchkin said.

'You're a deserter, aren't you?'

'I quit, that's all. I was betrayed. We were all betrayed.'

'What had you in mind?' the lieutenant asked, a tremor in his voice. Ruchkin understood: once he would have been standing to attention in front of Major Ruchkin, now he was in charge. Or was he?

Outside Yakuts and Evenki with Eskimo eyes listlessly swept the floor around Sortex machines, all idle.

Ruchkin said: 'You're not entirely stupid. You must have an idea.'

'If I do?'

'It depends to whom you owe your allegiance, Spetsnaz or Mother Russia.'

'I thought they were one and the same.'

'Not any longer. Spetsnaz is the fighting

arm of GRU, military intelligence. And GRU is the brain of those who betrayed us. We should talk...'

'But not here.'

'Where had you in mind?' Ruchkin admired his initiative but not his anticipation —if the office was bugged then the eavesdroppers would pick up the suggestion of duplicity.

'In the *taiga*,' the lieutenant said.

A true Siberian, Ruchkin thought.

They drove in a GAZ-69 jeep into the forest beyond the ground desecrated by bulldozers in the early days, and stopped in a clearing. There was a black scar in the centre of the grass where a fire had burned.

The lieutenant said: 'I come here to get away.'

'From what?' Ruchkin climbed down from the GAZ.

'The inefficiency. It sickens me.'

'I thought the Syndicate had moved in?'

'Into Moscow. But they're working with Russians, and what do they care about diamonds? They want food, clothes.' He walked to the edge of the clearing. 'Help me get some wood.'

'We're building a fire?'

'We're going to eat,' the lieutenant said.

He read the temperature on a thermometer hanging from a birch tree. Minus 10. He pulled the flaps of his *shapka* over his ears.

When the fire was blazing the lieutenant handed Ruchkin a flask. *Spirt*, 95 per cent alcohol, Siberia's answer to vodka. It didn't freeze until—170°F so you kept it close to your body in case you forgot and took a swig that would freeze your stomach.

Ruchkin dashed some on to the fire and it flared. 'A Yakut custom,' he said. 'First drink to Bayonai, god of hunters. It means good luck—and we're going to need it.'

The lieutenant fetched smoked reindeer meat and Siberian salmon, *omul*, from the GAZ, cut it with a clasp knife, brewed tea and served it in dented tin mugs.

'It's not often I eat with a hero,' he said, sitting beside the fire.

'Ex-hero.'

'Do you ever feel bad about it?'

'They gave me no choice. They destroyed everything they had taught me to believe in. Unity... Where is it? Loyalty... What happened to that?' Ruchkin drank scalding tea. 'America...I was taught to fight Americans and now we're begging from them.'

Kazan, he remembered. Demoted, put out to grass in Syria. Recalled after the failure of the raid in the Golan Heights and put behind a desk... Mikhail Sapir, he remembered.

'That wasn't what I asked.'

'Yes,' Ruchkin said. 'Sometimes I feel bad about it.'

The lieutenant fetched a pan, cut the ice on a stream skirting the clearing, filled it with water and placed it on the fire. Into the water he dropped potatoes, *amul*, onions, and salt.

'Fish soup,' he said. 'What do you mean, good luck *we're* going to need it?'

'You said Russians weren't interested in diamonds.'

'Why should they be? What can they do with diamonds?'

'Use them,' Ruchkin said.

'I don't understand.'

He explained over the fish soup with the fire hot in front of them and the cold laying its fingers on their backs, and when he had finished the lieutenant sat very still staring into the embers of pine.

Then he said: 'We?'

'You agree?'

'We could be court martialled. Shot. We're supposed to be guarding that armoured train all the way to Moscow.'

Ruchkin poured another shot of *spirt* on to the fire and they watched it flame in the glowing ash. 'But that's the point,' he said. 'You won't be.'

The following day Ruchkin drove from his hotel to the skeleton railhead where the armoured train was parked. It was called *Little Eagle* after the train in which the Czech Legion terrorised the Trans-Siberian railway when the Bolshevik's quit World War I, leaving their former allies stranded.

It comprised an electric Skoda engine and two coaches reinforced with 120mm armour taken from T-72 tanks, each with its own mobile turret.

Ruchkin trailed his fingers along the flanks of the bullet-nosed locomotive. It had been camouflaged with paint, the green of the *taiga* and the black of the steppe, but that wouldn't hide it when the snow settled. Always the third fall—so far there had been one.

He stopped beside the two steps leading up to the footplate on which the driver, Ivan Chukovsky, a 65-year-old veteran, blunt-faced and shiny-palmed, was checking the controls with his assistant.

At the diamond factory the Spetsnaz lieutenant had shown Ruchkin the dossier on Chukovsky, chosen to make the journey to Moscow because of his knowledge of the terrain and the Trans-Siberian railway.

For 45 years he had stood on the footplate of nearly every type of engine in service on the Trans-Siberian. And here the author of the dossier had sneaked in some of his own knowledge.

'Old 2-4-4-0 Mallets; S.O. classes from Ulan-Ude and Krasnoyarsk; massive P-36 steam locos, American lend-lease 2-8-0's built by Baldwin and ALCO for the US army which became the Soviet Sh (111), eight axle N-8 electrics...'

He had added: *'Chukovsky likes to talk about his days on the footplate of a steam loco, red scarf at his neck, peering down the track through his goggles...'*

Ivan Chukovsky obviously bored the arse off the author.

Ruchkin shouted 'Can I have a word?'

'Who the hell are you?' Chukovsky wiped his hands on a rag.

Ruchkin flashed his out-of-date ID. 'I'm going with you to Moscow.'

'I thought—'

'A change of plan. The lieutenant will tell you all about it. Can you spare half an hour?'

Chukovsky climbed down and Ruchkin led him to a timber hut, a legacy of Mirny's frontier days. It was called the White Nights and it served pepper-flavoured Pertsovka vodka. All it lacked, Ruchkin thought as they walked in, was sawdust on the floor.

A waiter in grease-stiff black trousers served them a 500-gram flask of Pertsovka,

Barzhomi mineral water, black bread and pickled cabbage.

Ruchkin spread a map of the Russian republic on the table and gave Chukovsky a pencil. 'Show me the route.'

Chukovsky drew a line east to Yakutsk, then a long haul south to the BAM railroad.

'And where do we join the Trans-Siberian?'

'At Tayshet, the junction,' Chukovsky said.

'Time?'

'To Moscow? Nine days from here.'

'And what are the most vulnerable points on the journey?'

'From here to the BAM line. In winter the cold could snap the line.'

'I wasn't thinking about the weather—I was thinking about an ambush.'

'I could tell you about the most dangerous stretches in the old days.'

'Please don't,' Ruchkin said.

'A lot of the Trans-Siberian was built by convicts. The *varnaki*—escaped convicts—used to attack them for food. Catch a *varnaki* and you ground powdered glass in his eyes so he couldn't find you again.'

Ruchkin sighed. 'We don't have convicts anymore. Or hadn't you heard? What are the most dangerous points *now?*'

'Lake Baikal, I suppose, the deepest lake

in the world. You have to slow down for the curves there. The track went across the ice once when Russia was attacked by Japan. The first engine went straight to the bottom.'

'Lake Baikal,' Ruchkin said, 'is to the east. We're going west. And why do I get a history lesson every time I ask a simple question?'

'Because history repeats itself. Do you know where the Czech Legion was taken by surprise by the White Russians? There.' Chukovsky pressed a broad and oily thumb at a point 50 kilometres west of Novosibirsk. 'Near a saw mill called Naked Boy Halt.'

Standing beside a discarded grease-sorting machine outside the factory, the manager of the first floor, who sported a small pointed beard, watched the stranger walk to the battered black Volga. He had observed him earlier in the day in the glass-walled office with the Spetsnaz lieutenant and had made enquiries from a Spetsnaz soldier guarding the diamonds.

Apparently he was a former Spetsnaz officer, a hero of the war in Afghanistan, who had been feared for his ruthlessness even within a special force which prided itself on its pitiless applications.

But according to the soldier, he had been

made the scapegoat of a massacre in Kazan and put out to grass in the Middle East. There he had led an aborted raid into Israel and, although the failure wasn't his fault, had been recalled to Russia to do a desk job. The final humiliation!

So he had quit Spetsnaz, taken other disenchanted officers and men with him and created his own fighting unit in the no man's land of organised crime.

He was also violently anti-Semitic, said the soldier, gazing speculatively at the manager who was a Jew from the Ukraine.

The manager watched Ruchkin climb into the Volga and drive off. Should he immediately call the Syndicate who paid him in dollars for information? He shook his head. Wait and find out what Ruchkin was planning, then the reward would be more generous. 'Big bucks' as the Americans put it.

When his men had arrived and dispersed in the town Ruchkin flew back to Moscow to invoke *blat,* influence, the common denominator of all Russians' aspirations. You had to have *blat* to get your son or daughter into university, to get an exit visa, to acquire *Playboy* or *Penthouse,* to pull off a 50-billion-dollar heist... What better custodian of *blat* than the Minister of Defence?

From his apartment Ruchkin called a former colonel in GRU, Gregori Bykov, who had been sacked in a purge of hard-line communists but had been given a job at the Ministry of Defence because he possessed dossiers on corrupt officials, the highest quality *blat* in the land. He also sold arms to Viktor Ruchkin.

The met in Sokolinki Park, once the haunt of tsarist falconers, *sokolniki*, and struck out from the shabby pavilions left over from international exhibitions across the broad pastures where cross-country skiers would soon be training. Snow was peeling hesitantly from an aching sky—the second fall, the last before winter settled.

Bykov, face beneath his fur hat creased by cold and intrigue, said: 'So what do you want this time, a tank?' He clasped and unclasped one gloved hand as though he were holding an invisible pistol.

'Protection,' Ruchkin said.

'Who from? The Chechens, the Tartars?'

'The enemy at large.'

'I didn't come here to listen to riddles.'

'I want to see the minister,' Ruchkin said.

Bykov put away his phantom gun in the pocket of his topcoat. 'You want to buy direct?' He creased a smile to show he was joking.

'Can you arrange it?'

'Impossible. In any case he's away most of the time, back in the 40s fighting the Great Patriotic War all over again.'

'Tell him to take some leave.'

'At the gates of Berlin?' Bykov arranged another smile. 'Are you serious?'

'Tell him I have some information—'

'Of mutual advantage? Have you taken leave of your senses, Ruchkin?'

'About the Great Patriotic War.' Ruchkin considered the lie. 'A question of patriotism.' Better!

'I'm sorry,' Bykov said. 'It can't be done.'

'I understand you sold fold-butt AKS-74 assault rifles to the Chechens...'

'I'll see what I can do,' Bykov said.

He turned on his heel, drew his invisible pistol and headed towards the frayed pavilions.

The minister's dacha was near Zhukovka, some 30 kilometres from Moscow, where Stalin, Khruschev, and Brezhnev had lived idyllically within the deprived territories over which they ruled.

It was made from pale wood and it smelled warm. Beyond the green fences, past frozen-faced militiamen on patrol, lay a tidy curve of the Moskva river, birch trees with peeling bark and ruts in the turf where in World War II, the Great

Patriotic War, the last-ditch defences of Moscow had been dug.

When Ruchkin was admitted the minister was patrolling these scars of historic heroism just as he had patrolled them in 1941 before the Germans pulled back.

He was stumpily built and wore medals on the chest of his heavy topcoat as though he had just returned from the funeral of another ancient campaigner.

He kicked a stone and said: 'Even now we find cartridge cases here. Did you know that in Stalingrad or Volgograd, whatever they call it these days, they rebuilt parts of the city on shell cases, shrapnel, bullets...'

'Were you there, Comrade General?' Ruchkin admired the chronicle of the old warrior's life.

The Minister shook his head regretfully. 'Moscow, Voronezh. Finland, Berlin... The Fritzes were wonderful fighters, very brave.'

'It's a pity we don't have anyone to fight these days. Anything to defend,' Ruchkin added.

'Of course we have something to defend. Mother Russia.' He swung towards Ruchkin, medals jingling, belligerently.

'I meant values, Comrade General. We fought a revolution and a war against fascism and we had stability for 70 years.

Then the crusaders took over. But instead of handing over the country to God, they gave it to the devil.'

Through the birch trees Ruchkin could see a boy with a rod pulling in a catch from the river. Perch, carp, roach? As a boy he had fished at night through a hole in the ice on a lake at his home in Siberia near Omsk and even now he could smell the naptha from the flare.

'We lost 20 million lives,' the Minister said. 'Are you telling me they died in vain?'

'Not necessarily,' Ruchkin said. 'Russia could rise again, the Soviet Union even. All we need is one strong man. By which I mean a military man,' he added.

'Me? Are you crazy? I'm 70 years old. They only keep me in the Kremlin because they know I command loyalty in the army.'

'Exactly,' Ruchkin said.

On the bank of the river the boy hauled his catch out of the water. A stick dripping with weeds. He began to disentangle the line.

The minister said: 'If you are so patriotic, Comrade Ruchkin, why did you leave Spetsnaz?'

He stumped along the rut of a filled-in trench, Ruchkin beside him.

'Because Spetsnaz was betrayed. Along

with the Red Army.'

'So what's changed?'

'It's what could change...'

Ruchkin told him about the diamonds.

'You want me to be an accomplice to a robbery?'

'A robbery, Comrade General? Who said anything about a robbery?'

The world's diamond markets, Ruchkin said, were monopolised by a cartel known as the Syndicate. Swamp those markets with 50 billion dollars worth of really big rough stones and the Syndicate would be ruined.

So, too, would the economies of South Africa where diamonds were mined and Israel where they were cut and polished.

Other countries where they were processed and marketed would also be affected—Holland and Belgium in particular, the US, Japan, Australia, Brazil, Britain, Germany, France, Italy, Spain. Nor would Canada escape unscathed because diamonds had recently been discovered there.

The domino effect, Ruchkin said, would be incalculable.

Supposing left-wing Africans took over a devastated South Africa and started exporting uranium and other resources to China? Supposing Arabs occupied a crippled Israel and America lost its influence in the Middle East?

World-wide, Jewry would be in disarray. Not merely because of the fate of the Promised Land but because Jews were the pillars of the diamond industry—had been since the Middle Ages when they took up the new trade which was exempt from the influence of anti-Semitic guilds.

Robbery, no. Ruchkin shook his head. Extortion, yes! A nice round figure. Fifty billion dollars or we flood the markets.

The Syndicate itself could get together 15 billion from its investments, the Jews maybe ten billion, South Africa five...all the other countries affected would contribute.

The package, boosted by injections from the World Bank and, say, the European Bank for Reconstruction and Development—'They're on record as saying they've got more money than projects'— would be delivered under the guise of aid from the G7. countries.

'Who in any case are proposing to give Russia aid in hard currency.'

'But not 50 billion dollars' worth,' the Minister said.

'No, Comrade General, not 50 billion dollars.'

'Why me?'

'Because you have the authority to make the demand. Because you *are* the Military. This,' Ruchkin said softly, 'could be your greatest victory. You could make Russia into a super power once more.'

On the river bank the boy began to haul in his line again.

The minister stared through the birch trees as though gunsmoke were drifting through them. 'You would need protection to bring off such an exploit.'

'Just a little co-operation as the armoured train makes its way to Moscow. And a promise that no action would be taken against the Spetsnaz supposedly guarding it.'

'Where would you keep the diamonds?'

'In the Ministry of Defence, Comrade General. Will you do it?'

The minister made a last inspection of the ruts in the ground, the scars of collective heroism. 'Why not? Marx said: "The workers have nothing to lose but their chains." I have nothing to lose but my medals.' He stopped, faded eyes considering Ruchkin. 'What do you hope to get out of it?'

'A billion dollars,' Ruchkin said. 'You see, for me there's no going back.'

The boy landed a muscular fish which whipped the ground despairingly with its tail. He removed the hook from its mouth and threw it back into the water.

Natalya lay beneath Ruchkin.

'You fuck me as though it were a duty,' she said.

He rolled clear. 'I've always found pleasure in duty.' He sat on the edge of the bed in the room above the bath house.

She touched the scar on his chest. 'Were you ever married?'

'To the army,' he said, reaching for his shirt.

'A good marriage?'

'While it lasted.'

He finished dressing and handed her the rough diamond he had taken from the thief in the sobering-up station.

'Another diamond? Has someone pinched the Diamond Throne from the Kremlin?'

'Get it cut and polished and sell it in the Mezh as soon as you can in case it loses its value.'

In case *all* diamonds become worthless, he thought, letting himself out of the room into the eucalyptus-smelling corridor.

Chapter Five

'Mazel und Brucha.' In the London headquarters of the Syndicate the chairman responded guardedly to the Yiddish salutation with which diamond deals are

93

traditionally clinched because he suspected that good luck and blessings were the last commodities his visitor had in mind.

Suspected, in fact, that the visitor, a Russian, was the bearer of a threat to the diamond monopoly that the Syndicate had preserved for more than 100 years.

There were too many coincidences. First the report from their new office in Moscow that rough diamonds smuggled out of the chaotic mines in Siberia were circulating in the capital. Then the decision jointly taken by the Syndicate and Rosalmazzoloto, the Russian diamond trading company, to transport diamonds valued at 50 billion dollars from the mines into safekeeping in Moscow.

Finally a tip from an informant in Mirny that a godfather of the Moscow mafia, a former officer in the Russian elite force, Spetsnaz, had been seen at the No 3 factory on the outskirts of Mirny.

Was the threat, feared by the Syndicate since 1955 when a geologist had found diamond-bearing kimberlite in Siberia, about to be implemented? A profusion of diamonds on the world markets that would decimate their value...

Until now the Russians had cooperated with the Syndicate for two reasons. One, they took advantage of the Syndicate's

94

expertise in mining, processing and marketing. Two, there is no point in devaluing your own assets.

But now the old Soviet Union was no more. And what was left of it, the Commonwealth of Independent States—the major partner the Russian republic which contained Siberia—was a floundering hulk of ineptitude and corruption. Anyone would do anything for a quick buck—or 50 billion of them.

The chairman settled himself behind his leather-topped desk and studied the messenger, a first secretary at the Russian Embassy.

He was in his thirties with high Slavonic cheekbones and wary eyes which were focused on the oil painting hanging behind the desk and the chairman knew he was making the inevitable comparison between the old diamond baron who had licked the company into shape in South Africa all those years ago and his son.

Same deceptively soft eyes; broad forehead; expression radiating a sort of amused pugnacity.

Son? A misnomer because it implied youth. I'm an old man, levered out of retirement to combat the new wave of prospectors and smugglers, heirs and upstarts, inside and outside the family, snapping at my arthritic heels. Is this stripling here to tell me, before I finally quit, that my life has been a sham?

The Russian pointed at a photograph of Cecil Rhodes on the walnut-panelled wall and said: 'The greatest imperialist of them all; I'm honoured to be in his presence.'

'He had some equals. Josef Stalin for one.'

'Ah, the Rise and Fall of the Soviet Empire... You know the real tragedy? The man who gave us freedom, Gorbachev, was destroyed by it.'

'I'm sure you haven't come here to talk politics.'

'Hard to resist sitting here at the fount of capitalism.'

'You and your countrymen should have realised earlier that communism is the equal distribution of poverty.'

'But we did. The trouble is we're masochists at heart. Didn't someone say that the true masochist is the one who asks the sadist to stop whipping him?'

The chairman took his gold hunter from his waistcoat pocket. 'I really don't have much time...'

'I understand, all those diamonds to count. It doesn't matter—I only came to deliver a message.' He opened his briefcase, took out an envelope and handed it to the chairman.

Inside was a sheet of embossed writing

paper from the Russian Embassy. A hand-written note. The Defence Minister of the nine republics comprising the CIS would consider it a great honour if he would call at the embassy at 16.30 hours that afternoon 'on a matter of extreme urgency'.

The chairman, who remembered reading that the minister was in London on a private visit, said: 'Have you any idea what this is about?'

'I'm only a first secretary.'

'There was a time when first secretaries knew more than ambassadors.'

'But that,' the first secretary said, 'was in our decadent, colonial past. These days spies are on the dole.'

The offices of the subsidiary through which the Syndicate controls most of the world's supply of diamonds occupies a block in the City of London near Hatton Garden, the ancient centre of Britain's gemstone trade.

But the power exercised by the Syndicate lies not in the discreetly appointed offices and sorting rooms but in the four levels of vaults below the street. Here lies a hoard of diamonds so abundant that if it were released in its entirety the diamond trade would exist no more.

As it is the hoard is carefully rationed

according to the fluctuations of the market. In the 30s the market was so depressed that the Syndicate closed its mines in South Africa. And only recently, hard hit by recession and smuggling from Angola, dealing had been so bearish that quotas had been imposed on mines.

After the Russian had gone the chairman made a tour of his fortress. It was the day of the sights, the sales to 150 or so selected clients which take place ten times a year in London, Lucerne and Kimberley, and the reception room on the second floor was occupied by dealers and cutters from London, New York, Tel Aviv, Bombay, Amsterdam, Antwerp, Tokyo, Hong Kong...

The chairman hovered on the fringes and watched as clients were escorted to private viewing rooms—all facing north for the purest light—to examine their allocation contained in envelopes inside a box.

Certain rules were inviolable: clients couldn't question the Syndicate's authority to apportion the diamonds, they weren't allowed to haggle, they had to take all or nothing, they couldn't re-sell the diamonds still uncut.

An absolute cartel.

The chairman nodded approvingly. Just as it should be. The market was controlled. Diamonds retained their value. The industry from mine to jewellery store was protected. The third world countries were saved from penury. The stability of the West was maintained. Trust endured.

One man who did not agree with this philosophy approached. Harry Sampson. Born in the 20s on New York's Lower East Side, he had clawed his way up Manhattan—largely by buying diamonds from estates and recutting them for mass-market outlets—to the rarified reaches of Fifth Avenue.

Harry, dapper and nimble-brained with grey hair slicked back from fragile temples, was angry; the chairman didn't blame him.

He prodded a manicured finger at the chairman. 'There's been a fuck-up. My sight's been cut to 2 million dollars, all shitty quality. Macles, flats, more spots on them than a kid with measles, nothing whiter than pale yellow.'

The chairman said: 'The Tiffany is yellow.'

'You know what I'm talking about: I'm talking about crap.'

'Keep your voice down, Harry,' as heads swivelled. 'In any case, you know we never discuss sights.'

'Just who do you think you are, mister?'

'Better come into my office, Harry.'

The chairman sat in front of the painting

99

of his father, felt his magisterial strength. 'Don't ever talk to me like that again.'

'I'll talk to you any way I want.' Harry Sampson, holding his box, paced up and down the grey carpet. 'Why was my sight reduced?'

'You know perfectly well—you've been a bad boy.'

'Don't talk to me like a schoolmaster.'

'You tried to outbid us for diamonds in Angola, right? Promised the Portuguese a steady market in the United States. Promised them dollars which they badly wanted...'

'That was centuries ago, for Christ's sake!'

'And we promised you that if you stopped meddling we would guarantee you the best sights.'

'Big deal.'

'Which we did.'

'Not today you didn't.'

'Because you haven't stopped meddling. Sierre Leone, Harry?'

'What about Sierre Leone? I wanted my own mine, was all. That's what I've always wanted. But you bought me out. A quarter of all the alluvial diamonds found in South West Africa. The biggest source of gemstones in the world. How could I refuse?'

'Indeed you couldn't. That's what made

you the richest jeweller in the US.'

'A kept man.'

'A greedy man.'

'So what's wrong with wanting to be independent?'

'IDM, illicit diamond mining? Stones smuggled from Angola via Lisbon to Antwerp where you bought them illegally.'

'Who says I bought them illegally? The Syndicate? Who says I have to abide by your laws?'

'No one, Harry. But you know the penalties.'

'Maybe I don't want to buy any more of your diamonds. Certainly not garbage like this,' holding aloft the box containing inferior stones, but 2 million dollars worth just the same.

'It's your privilege.'

'Yeah, right.'

Harry Sampson took the lid off the box and began to open the envelopes one by one, dropping their contents into the box.

'What are you doing, Harry?'

'Going private is what.'

He opened a window and turned the box upside down.

By the time the chairman reached the window pedestrians were already scrabbling on the pavement, in the gutter, searching for the fragments of compressed carbon that had suddenly descended like manna from heaven.

The chairman said: 'Have you booked your fare from New York for the next sights?'

'What's it to you?'

'Save the fare, Harry, there won't be any for you.'

Harry Sampson tossed the box out of the window and together they watched it sail across the street and fall spinning to the pavement.

He said: 'I wasn't planning to make the trip anyway. Haven't you heard? The Russians are coming.'

Reclining in the sighing cushions of the black Rolls-Royce, the chairman agonised. If Harry Sampson knew about the diamonds in Siberia, who else did? The Israelis? Probably only key merchants in Ramat-Gan who had hacked into the intelligence networks of Rossalmazzoloto and the Syndicate.

Of the top jewellers in the world—companies such as Cartier, Tiffany, Van Cleef, Garrard's—maybe only Harry Sampson was privy to the secret, the chairman consoled himself.

The Rolls crawled through the West End. On either side of him the chairman saw jewellers, diamonds sparkling in lights specially angled to pick up maximum brilliance, some even resting on hidden springs to make their facets dance.

Quality gemstones, graded on the criteria of the four Cs: colour, clarity, cut and carat; flawed stones containing carbon spots or bubbles or cleavage cracks; tiny crystals that had narrowly missed being classified as industrials; out-and-out fakes.

Even the chairman had been taken in by stimulants such as Yttrium aluminium garnet, also known as diamonair, and YAG, which was really only distinguishable from diamond by its lower refractive index.

The old hunger for diamonds stirred inside the chairman like an old man's sexual desire that can no longer be fulfilled.

From his childhood in South Africa his father had fed him diamonds in the family home in Kimberley not far from the Big Hole, the gaping mine, now defunct and partially filled with water, which had once been worked by armies of diggers beneath a chaotic canopy of ropes and pulleys.

He had regaled him with stories about the nineteenth-century pioneers who had made glittering fortunes dug from kimberlite, named after the town; had sat him in the red leather chair in which Cecil Rhodes, crusader of the Holy British Empire and founder of the diamond cartel, had once

103

had his hair cut; had shown him the brass arrow outside the Kimberley Club placed there to remind Rhodes which direction was north. Rhodes, the first entrepreneur to realise that, if diamonds were to retain their value, their output had to be controlled...

The chairman's father had worn Rhodes' mantle of artful resolution with bravura. And so have I because the intrinsic beauty of diamonds must be preserved. It's regrettable that beauty is related to rarity but there it is; that's why an orchid is exquisite, a nasturtium vulgar.

I would kill for diamonds, the chairman thought.

Betray them, so it was said, and you risked a curse. The Hope Diamond was said to be cursed...

The chairman wasn't convinced about curses. But if there were any around today he hoped they would be directed towards the Russians.

The Rolls turned into Kensington Palace Gardens and stopped outside number 13, the Russian Embassy, one of the dreariest of the nineteenth-century mansions strung along a private road which is as quiet as the Sabbath even on weekdays. It's only concession to its homeland a silver birch in the front garden.

Dig up that tree, the chairman thought,

and you would uncork a mausoleum of mildewed secrets.

The first secretary led him into an office on the second floor with a dismal view through the flaking branches of the birch. On the desk stood the white, blue and red tricolour in miniature, a silver cigarette box and a photograph of a woman with beefy arms akimbo.

As the first secretary excused himself the Defence Minister entered through another door. His dark suit looked like a uniform and his square old face was pitted with battle.

He sat opposite the chairman and pushed the cigarette box across the desk. They were in Marlboro country, the chairman noted, no Belomor. He shook his head.

'Wise man,' the minister said, taking a *papirosa* with a long cardboard filter from a packet, lighting it and blowing a smokescreen across the desk. 'The ceremony, that's part of the addiction. Gives you time to settle, assess.'

'To assess what, Comrade Minister? The enemy?'

'I prefer Comrade General,' the minister said. 'It has...purpose. Purpose... Is that good?'

'Spoken like a true soldier,' the chairman said. 'I don't think we're all that different, you and I. Both still fighting when we should be enjoying retirement.'

I should be with my wife in South Africa, in the vineyards of Cape Province where the vines, descendants of seedlings brought from France by Huguenot refugees in the seventeenth century, stand sturdily in parade ground order.

In small towns steeped in South Africa's ferocious history; in Cape Dutch houses as white as chalk in the sunlight; in the bone-bare Atlantic coast of Namaqualand; on the soft beaches of the south...

To roam the Kalahari to the north; spend nights there when the hot sand is cooled by the freezing air and dark-maned Kalahari lions roar desolately and shepherd trees are as grey as phantoms in the moonlight...

'You may be right,' the minister said. 'A pity we are enemies.'

'Adversaries would be better.'

'You don't know what I'm going to propose.'

'I think I do,' the chairman said.

'Then you are very wise.'

'Street wise. That's what you become when you defend a legacy.'

'Diamonds?'

'Are trust.'

'Diamonds are also bullshit,' the minister said, discharging another smokescreen and peering through it cannily. 'Bullshit... Is that good?'

'Very eloquent.'

The chairman stood up, walked to the window and stared at the naked fingers of the birch. Rain had begun to fall and in the dusk they were jewelled with water.

The minister said: 'At Stalingrad General Friedrich von Paulus was much admired by us Russians.'

'You're comparing me with von Paulus? Well, the Russian commander, General Vasili Ivanovich Chuikov, was much admired by the Germans.'

'You know your generals,' the minister said.

'I'm older than you,' the chairman said. 'Did you know that a lot of South Africans wanted the Germans to win that war? Why not? They hated the British. Makes you wonder about values, doesn't it?'

'*You* hated the British?'

'I *am* British,' the chairman said. 'And South African. And Jewish. That's why I believe in diamonds. They're the testament of the birth of the world because that's when they were born. And thrust to the surface of the world to remind us.'

'I don't go back that far,' the minister said. He stared into the corner of the room and the chairman noticed an oil painting of Lenin on the floor. 'But I had values. Serfs of the tsars, that's all we were. Until the Revolution. Then we became men. And we had a man to lead us, Stalin. So why did the do-gooders—is that right, do-gooders?—throw our pride away? Give us begging bowls instead of guns?'

'Perhaps,' the chairman said carefully, 'they believed that the most important value of all was liberty?'

'More bullshit. I like that word.' He said it again. 'Do you realise that Siberia itself could become a super power in its own right? Every known mineral. Gold, titanium, nuclear materials—caesium-137 and strontium-90.'

'What you're a little short on,' the chairman said, watching rain drops weep on the window, 'is organisation.'

'What we are a little short on is cash. Hard currency.'

'Which is why we're here?'

'Street wise...I like that. We need dollars, pounds, yen, Deutsche marks.'

'In exchange for diamonds?'

'Fifty billion dollars, Comrade Chairman. As you know, the diamonds being taken to Moscow are being guarded by the army. Well, I am Minister of Defence...'

'But this isn't you talking, is it?'

'I'm sorry, I don't understand.'

'You have been asked to make this

demand because they, whoever *they* are, know you will be taken seriously.'

'Street wise.'

'Mafia?'

'The money will go towards the re-establishment of old values. True values like diamonds.'

'You really think we, the West, could get together 50 billion dollars?'

'Of course. I read only yesterday that a bank, the BCCI, owed 12 billion. If one bank... Maybe you, the Syndicate could raise 15 billion.'

'Supposing we let you dump all those diamonds on the market? That would be the end of your diamond industry.'

'But you wouldn't, would you? Because if you did that would be the end of the Syndicate. The end of faith,' he added slyly.

'We would need time to consider your proposal.'

Time to bluff.

'You wouldn't need long, not with your resources. The G7 countries, the IMF, the World Bank, Israel, South Africa... After all, you *are* South Africa.'

Time enough to intercept the diamonds en route from northern Siberia to Moscow. The chairman was calculating as quickly as he had when he was a young man. Well, almost.

He said: 'How long?'

'From now, obviously.'

'Until?'

'The diamonds arrive in Moscow.'

Time enough to hijack them?

'But,' said the minister, 'we will require a gesture of good will. Five billion by midday on December 2nd.'

'If we can't get it together by then?'

'Then the deal is null and void and the diamonds will be sold on the open market.'

The chairman took his gold hunter from his waistcoat pocket. The gesture he had used down the years to conclude fraught meetings. 'We'll be in touch,' he said.

The minister picked up a photocopy of a newspaper cutting. 'You once said, "Carats are units of trust".'

'Originally the seeds of the locust or carob tree.'

How could we get a hit team into Siberia of all places?

'I hope you won't betray their trust.'

'Trust? We're discussing blackmail aren't we, Comrade General? Incidentally, did you know that it was probably locust beans that John the Baptist ate in the Wilderness, not locusts themselves?' He stood up.

And how could we get it out?

'I admire your...your cool. Is that right?'

'A good word. A *cool* 50 billion.' The

chairman stood up and made his way to the door past the recumbent Lenin. 'By the way, what about all those diamonds in the Kremlin? You wouldn't want those to become worthless, would you?'

'Would your Queen want the Crown Jewels to be devalued?' The minister stood up and joined the chairman at the door.

The chairman said: 'Your last battle, Comrade General?'

'Your last conspiracy, Comrade Chairman?'

The minister offered his hand and, after a moment's hesitation, the chairman took it. What he had learned to distrust over the years was the too-firm handshake, the steadfast gaze. The minister's grip was a vice, his eyes unwavering.

Outside a wind sprang up and blew the raindrops off the branches of the birch.

The Rolls was waiting for the chairman in the rain-streaked glow of a gas-lit street lamp, an anachronism of Kensington Palace Gardens retained from the days of Jack the Ripper.

The Rolls glided past Kensington Palace, emerging in Kensington High Street. The chairman noticed a young couple, oblivious to the rain, gazing into the lighted window of a jeweller's. Choosing a diamond engagement ring.

The chairman knew of only one man who could save diamonds, symbols of love, from the grasp of the extortionists. He picked up one of the two telephones and called security at the Syndicate's headquarters. 'Get Loder,' he said.

Chapter Six

In Namibia on the south-west coast of Africa it was high summer and at the time the chairman was calling security Loder was making love to a German girl beneath the scything blades of a ceiling fan in a hotel in Luderitz.

The room facing the Atlantic Ocean was tacky, the girl beautiful, bronzed and bleached with a slender body and fine breasts. But her blue eyes were often squeezed by perplexity as though she were sighting secrets, particularly those she tried to keep from herself.

But there was no perplexity there now as she held him deep inside her, arms tight round his back, shivered and called out. Then she held him at arm's length and, head to one side, studied him. Like a doctor unable to make a diagnosis, he thought.

He kissed her mouth and her puzzled eyes. Then he lay back on the pillows and listened to the frayed whirr of the fan.

'Next time,' he said, 'Cape Town, the Mount Nelson.'

'I don't care where it is.'

Or when or if?

He went to the bathroom and ran a shower. Rust-coloured water fell lazily from the clogged sprinkler. The hotel depressed him but this was where the miners and smugglers and informers stayed so it was where Loder, aged twenty-eight, lean and dark and alone even in company, stayed.

He picked up a wafer of soap curled by the heat and attempted to lather himself. And, as the tepid water danced on his shoulders, tried to work out how long ago it was that Cronin had recruited him, paving the way to flophouses like this. And some of the finest hotels in the world.

Ten years?

It had been the oldest robbery in the book. Wealthy dude walks into a jeweller's on 47th Street, hub of New York's Diamond District, and asks to see some stones.

Certainly, sir, three bags full. Out come the rocks but none of them are quite good enough for this dude with the 10 x loupe. One's been scratched by another diamond, another's flawed by a cleavage crack known as a feather, a third burned during polishing.

The owner of the store reluctantly admires this would-be purchaser with the expert knowledge although he can't understand why he rejects a stone of VS quality, only three grades below flawless. His admiration alters course when it is discovered that two of the 12 stones exhibited are missing.

The dude agrees to a body search, at the same time threatening to sue for damages. Not a single carat is found on his person. With magnificent aplomb the dude leaves, mingling with the dealers and brokers, cops and con artists who throng the street between Fifth and Sixth Avenues.

The following day a darkly handsome young man wearing a decent suit and a shy smile asks to see a modest engagement ring.

He is busted as his fingers search for the two stones the dude had stuck beneath the counter with chewing gum the previous day. Rightly busted—this scam was first pulled in Tiffany's in 1893.

But busted by whom? He is taken to an austere office in the same block as the Diamond Dealers' Club at number 30 West 47th where he is introduced to a bleak-faced Englishman who buys

114

his clothes from thrift shops and regards compassion as the eighth deadly sin. This is Cronin.

'Crummy,' Cronin says, feet on the desk, while Loder stands loose-armed in front of him.

'Sir?'

'A hoary old scam like that. You should be ashamed of yourself.'

'I don't know what you mean, sir.'

'Don't weary me, son. It went out with the ark.'

'I don't understand—'

'We're on to you, laddie.' He spoke like a sergeant in the British military police which he once was—although, of course, Loder does not appreciate this. 'Have been for a long time. Want to know about yourself?'

Cronin leads him into an adjoining office equipped with a computer and punches out digits on the keyboard. Loder's short life quivers on the screen.

Born April 18, 1965, in Queens. Mother, Mary Helen Loder, aged 33, of Irish ancestry, died in childbirth. Father unknown.

'You got it,' Loder said. 'I'm a bastard.'

Believed to be of Italian extraction.

'Believed to be?' Cronin said.

'My mother got around. I'll say it for you so I don't have to slug you.'

'And you would, wouldn't you?'

'Try me,' Loder said.

'Italian... That accounts for your looks.'

Brought up by the State.

'With Orphan Annie,' Loder said. 'What the hell is this all about?'

Trained as an electrical engineer.

'That must have come in useful,' Cronin said.

'As what?'

'As a thief. Knocking out alarm systems, that sort of thing.'

'Who says I'm a thief?'

'I do.'

Absconded.

'Lovely word,' Cronin remarked.

'Better than busted.'

Taken under wing of jewel thief named Marchetti living on the Lower East Side.

Cronin said: 'The dude, right?'

'A gentleman,' Loder said.

'A gentleman thief? A long-dead breed, laddie.'

'I don't give a shit,' Loder said. 'He is a gentleman. Maybe you wouldn't recognise one.'

'I admire your loyalty. In fact, that's one of the qualities that attracted our attention.'

'*Our* attention?'

No known Mob connections.

'Not for the want of trying,' Loder said.

116

'Untrue.'

'You know more about me than I do?'

'Maybe—the privileges of the observer.'

'I asked you what this is all about.'

Loder glanced round the room for ways of escape but few offices on Diamond Row had rear exits, one of the unwritten laws of self-preservation. Security was tight in this district—40 alarm buttons in the Diamond Dealers' Club.

Cronin said: 'Don't even think about it.'

Never been known to inform.

'A good honest thief,' Cronin said. 'An honourable crook. Just what we're looking for. Born in April, too.'

'What's that got to do with anything?'

'Birthstone diamond. Maybe that's why your mentor picked you.'

'Mentor?'

'The dude,' Cronin said.

'I've had enough of this,' Loder said, backing towards the door.

'But you've stood up to it well. Another plus.'

Loder reached behind him for the door handle.

Cronin said: 'You want a future?'

'I've got a future.'

'Okay, you won't go to prison. Not this time. But with his record your mentor, the dude, will be looking at eight to twelve.'

Loder's tensed muscles slackened. 'So what's the deal?'

Cronin switched off the computer. 'Simple.'

First he explained about the Syndicate, about its monopoly over most of the world's rough diamonds and its indirect control over cut stones.

But, Cronin told Loder, there were many threats to this distribution which kept the market stable. Not the least diamonds smuggled via Antwerp into New York, from illicit diamond mining operations.

'We need an informant,' he said.

'A grass? Forget it.'

'You won't be betraying criminals to the police. What you will be doing is saving the livelihoods of millions of honest people. People like your mother who believed in diamonds.'

'What makes you think she believed in them?'

'She left you a diamond ring.'

'Jesus, you've been thorough.'

'You were set up, laddie. The stupidity and vulnerability of the owner of the store you tried to rob was leaked to the dude and we knew he wouldn't be able to resist the temptation. But, one, the owner's not so stupid, two, he will be quite happy not to press charges if—'

'I co-operate?'

'If you don't your *gentleman* gets eight to twelve.'

Instead of jail Loder's mentor moved to a condominium, near St Augustine in Florida where he settled down with a woman with a blue rinse and skin the colour of teak who owned a boutique specialising in costume jewellery.

Loder settled into 47th Street congenially enough but such was his commitment—more like the burgeoning crusade of a man who has just been handed a belief—that Cronin decided he was destined for more ambitious duties and dispatched him on a crash course on diamonds.

He went to South Africa and learned how diamonds, crystals of carbon, were formed by heat and pressure millions of years ago and pushed to the surface of the globe by explosions of gas.

He learned about the host rock, kimberlite, which someone had christened geological plum pudding—a dessert studded with minerals, coal, fossilised ostrich eggs, human bones.

He watched kimberlite being mined in chambers sunk 1,600 feet deep; observed rough diamonds putting on their first display of magic—sticking to beds of grease while mundane detritus was washed away by water.

From mining he progressed to sorting. From flawless stones to heavy spotted. From finest white to Dark Cape. Such colours! Lilac pink, yellow, blue—the chocolate brown of the 248-carat Earth Star, the impenetrable black of the Amsterdam.

Then he went to Amsterdam to study cleaving. Get the grain wrong and with one blow of mallet on blade you presented the owner with a hatful of splinters and took to the hills.

In Antwerp he witnessed the bruting of the facets–58 for a fashionable brilliant cut—and the polishing with diamond powder mixed with olive oil, egg white, spit even.

Antwerp was also the sorting house of smuggling.

Wherever they originated, most contraband roughs found their way to the docks beside the Scheldt or Deurne airport—he had once seen stones changed hands in Rubens' house—and thence to some dodgy merchant on Pelikaanstraat or Schupstraat.

In the early days IDB, illicit diamond buying, had flourished in stones spirited out of South Africa and South West Africa, in the digestive system, in wounds, in orifices. Once, in furniture owned by a retiring mine manager—he had subsequently been burgled in Durban but all that had been stolen was a leg of his dining table.

Piracy of one kind or another, it seemed, had been the common denominator of the diamond industry ever since Cecil Rhodes and the other barons had first plundered the diamond fields of South Africa. Barney Barnato, the Cockney Jew, pugilist and conjurer, who had finally leaped to his death from the deck of a ship... Or was he pushed? His nephew, Woolf Joel, shot by an adventurer calling himself Baron von Veltheim... Rhodes himself pursued almost to his death at the age of 48 by Princess Catherine Maria Radziwill...

Loder was initiated into all the modern scams. Switching stones, and salting them —introducing them into a worthless site and then selling the land to a mug. Simulants and synthetics, fakes and frauds — the application, for instance, of violet dye to the rear facets of a yellowish Cape stone to whiten it.

Finally he was initiated into the highest echelon of the Syndicate's operations, CONTROL. The purchase of new sources of diamonds, manipulation of prices, threats to cut off outlets to rebellious traders, cultivation of contacts in high places, stockpiling.

Loder was such an adept pupil that he became the Syndicate's chief trouble shooter. But even Cronin, head of security, was sometimes worried by the ruthless diligence of his protégé, the son of a whore from Queens.

Loder finally lost the sliver of soap, switched off the shower, began to dry himself with an off-white towel and looked back on the perilous path he had trodden from New York city to Luderitz.

He had severed smuggling routes through Liberia, Lisbon and Antwerp, snuffed out IDM sources in India and Zaire, *negotiated* with the Australians when they discovered diamonds in Argyle, bought out mines before the owners were tempted to market their stones outside the Syndicate's channels.

His toughest adversaries had been the Israelis. In pursuit of survival, they had threatened to take over the cutting of mêlée, small stones, from the Syndicate's other trusted clients. And at the same time to stockpile a hoard bigger even than the Syndicate's by purchasing unseen from other Syndicate buyers.

Loder had advised the Syndicate to move against the banks financing the purchase of the diamonds. To scare them by slapping a capricious surcharge on the price of diamonds. You bought a sight for 50,000 dollars on Monday, by Tuesday it was only worth 30,000. What bank was going to finance a deal like that?

Loder had also suggested that the Syndicate should cancel sights to those dealers who had been re-selling to the Israelis. Finding supplies cut off, the Israelis began to sell their own hoard; prices fell, banks began to call in their money and hundreds of dealers in Tel Aviv were ruined.

Towel round his waist, Loder returned to the scruffy bedroom. The girl lay naked on the bed, eyes closed.

Loder began to dress to confront the latest threat to the cartel, a disreputable prospector named Vogel.

Vogel had once worked in the *Sperrengbeit,* the Forbidden Territory of Namibia, so named by the Germans when in 1908 diamonds were discovered on the wild coast of what was then South West Africa.

After World War I possession of the desert territory had been transferred from Germany to South Africa and the Syndicate had acquired the Forbidden Territory, scooping the highest quality gemstones in the world from a ledge where oysters once bred, sometimes from the beach itself.

Smuggling from the *Sperrengbeit* was strictly controlled and Vogel had been caught with three gemstones in his stomach. When he had passed them he was fined and sacked. So he became a prospector convinced, like all his nomadic kind, that one day he would find a diamond as big as the Ritz.

And he had. One day when he had left the matronly Germanic town of Luderitz, where you could still buy a stein of beer and eat frankfurters, and had taken up residence in a ghost town abandoned in 1938 when its mine had run out of diamonds.

That evening he had dodged a herd of wild horses, descendants of Teutonic cavalry chargers, climbed a towering red sand dune and gazed down on what looked like an old river bed exposed by the movement of sand.

He had scrambled down the precipitous flank of the dune, scratched around for a couple of hours, found the diamond—and sent the Syndicate into shock.

The alluvial diamonds found in Namibia had been washed there by the Orange River. Everyone knew that. What no one knew was the location of the source—the kimberlite pipe over which the river, long since diverted, or tributary had passed.

Was this the extinct water-course? The signpost to a source that could devalue diamonds overnight?

Loder finished buttoning his shirt and walked to the door. When he turned the girl's eyes were open, full of questions.

There was a cable waiting for him at reception.

He said to the fat receptionist in the damp-patched shirt: 'Why didn't you call me?'

The receptionist shifted a toothpick to one side of his mouth and said: 'I thought you were otherwise engaged.'

Loder read the cable. AUTHORISE PAYMENT AND COVER SOURCE STOP THEN DROP EVERYTHING AND RETURN LONDON SOONEST STOP EMERGENCY STOP CRONIN.

Loder walked to a diggers' bar near the Magistrate's House where Vogel was waiting for him. He wore a greasy nautical cap and thickets of stubble grew deep in the creases of his cheeks.

Loder slipped him an envelope. 'Stick that in your pocket and when you leave here, run like hell.'

Vogel peered inside the envelope. 'How much?'

'More than you've ever owned in your life. Ten thousand rand. Now sign this.'

Loder handed him a statement to the effect that the stone he had found was zircon. 'A mistake anyone can make.'

'But it was a diamond.'

'Okay, give me back the money and keep the crystal.'

'Ten thousand rand, that's a lot of beers.'

'Then sign.'

Loder then went into the Bay View Hotel and made a call to the Syndicate's headquarters at Oranjemund on the border with South Africa and authorised the biggest sand-moving operation in the history of diamond exploration. But not to recover gemstones, to cover their traces.

Watched by the German girl, he packed his bag in the bedroom in the flophouse, kissed her and hurried away from the questions in her eyes.

He took the company Lear jet to Windhoek. From there he flew South African Airways to Frankfurt and from Frankfurt by British Airways to London.

DROP EVERYTHING. Cronin wasn't noted for melodrama so what had prompted the note of near hysteria? As the aircraft lowered itself over London's spangled lights Loder was visited by the spirit of the old robber barons, Rhodes, Barney Barnato, Woolf Joel...

The meeting was held in the chairman's penthouse in the Barbican in the City. In attendance were Cronin, Loder, and the director of the Syndicate's trading subsidiary.

The chairman poured himself a Scotch

and soda, planted himself in front of the grate where an imitation coal fire burned and said: 'Gentlemen, we are facing the greatest crisis in our history.'

Loder frowned. Greater than a prospector uncovering the source of Namibia's alluvial diamonds?

'Greater,' the chairman said, reading his thoughts. 'There we can cover our tracks. Russians with snow on their boots are harder to obliterate.' He told them about the extortion demand.

The director of the subsidiary, a plump executive with polished cheeks who smelled of hotel soap and cigars, said: 'I still think we should call their bluff.' He buried his face in a gin and tonic; ice clicked against teeth which looked younger than the rest of him.

Cronin, bleakly ageless, drank Vichy water, stared into the anaemic flames of the fire and said: 'What makes you think it's a bluff?'

'Why would they jeopardise their most lucrative export? Kill the golden goose, if you'll excuse the change in elements.'

The chairman waved his glass at Loder. 'What do you think?' He paced the elegantly uncomfortable room.

'I don't think the Russians give a damn about long-term prospects. They want hard cash now.'

'Hard cash has to have hard backing,' the director said. 'What makes you so sure they've got enough diamonds to swamp the market?'

'They've got them. Didn't you read my report?'

'I read it,' Cronin said. 'I wasn't totally convinced.'

At least he doesn't call me laddie anymore, Loder thought.

'Why not?' The director of the subsidiary had trained himself to find cracks in Loder's reasoning.

'Because we're relying on one informant in Mirny,' Cronin told him.

'A good one,' Loder said.

'How do you know?'

'He's never been wrong yet. And he's Jewish and he's Ukrainian.'

'So?'

'No love lost between Ukrainians and Russians.'

'They were all Soviets not so long ago.'

'The Bosnians and the Croats and the Serbs were all Yugoslavs not so long ago.'

The chairman said: 'What we have to appreciate is that the threat has been posed by, arguably, the strongest man in Russia. Backed, I suspect, by organised crime. And we have two alternatives—pay up or fight. Which is it to be?'

'Fifty billion dollars?' The director

peered into his glass for enlightenment. 'Where do we get that sort of money from?'

'The usual aid sources. The G7 countries ...'

'I suggest we call their bluff,' the director said, reaching for the bottle of Beefeaters.

'Whatever, don't pay them,' Cronin said, fingering the lapel of his disgraceful suit like a tailor searching for pins.

The chairman said: 'What do you think, Mr Loder?'

'I figure we should *pretend* we're getting the money together.'

The chairman stared thoughtfully at him. 'And meanwhile?'

'Get our hot little hands on those diamonds, sir.'

'And who will put them in our hot little hands?'

'I think you know, sir. The Israelis. Who else?'

Chapter Seven

The oranges were beginning to blush, heavy clusters of them dropping from the trees as far as the eye could see.

Mikhail Sapir cupped one in his hand,

felt the weight of the juice inside the peel and was suffused by a deep contentment. Not merely to make the desert blossom but to make it ripen, gestate. Belligerence had been thrust upon him; now at last he was at peace.

A truck drew up spitting sand from beneath its tyres, and an orange picker—a Falasha from Ethiopia by the look of him—began to unload plastic crates.

When he had piled them into a stack the driver and his mate climbed down. Viktor Ruchkin and Rachel Wolf, looking flustered as though surfacing from a long embrace.

Arm in arm, they made their way into the grove. To make love, no doubt about it. Sapir gave them a couple of minutes then threw the grenade cupped in his hand. It exploded pithily and blood dripped from the oranges draining the colour from them.

Sapir cried out. Whimpered on his lounger on the terrace of the convalescent home on the coast between Caesarea and Netanya.

The man standing beside the lounger shook his shoulder. 'You were having a bad dream,' he said. 'Welcome back to reality—it's even worse.'

Brooklyn-born Theo Reisfeld was a brigadier

130

in the Israeli Army, *Zahal* and Sapir's commanding officer in the 269 elite force. As a young lieutenant he had taken part in the Entebbe raid in 1976 when the Israelis had flown 2,000 miles to Uganda to rescue hostages hijacked in an Air France airliner.

He was aggressively built, neck sunk deep in his shoulders, with sparse hair the colour of the desert. He wore combat fatigues, red paratroop beret in one paw, and Sapir did not think he had come bearing grapes.

He sat on a wicker chair which creaked under his weight and regarded Sapir speculatively. Like a hangman sizing up a doomed prisoner, Sapir thought. Finally he said in Hebrew: 'So how are you feeling?'

Sapir said the wound on the side of his head was much better because he knew that was what Reisfeld wanted to hear. Sometimes he heard palm fronds in the breeze. Sometimes gunfire. He stared through the mauve bracts of a bougainvillaea at the tranquil Mediterranean.

'Good, because we have a mission for you.'

'But I'm on convalescent leave. In any case I've only got one week left to serve.' He tightened the belt on his blue dressing gown.

'Time enough.'

A beaky-faced doctor approached, stethoscope hanging from his neck like a pendant.

He said to Reisfeld: 'I told you, Major Sapir suffered concussion and compression. He's not fit for active service.'

'When is he going to be discharged?'

'Tomorrow, but that doesn't mean he can return to duty.'

Reisfeld, paratrooper's wings bright silver on his camouflage jacket, turned to Sapir. 'How do you feel?'

'I told you, better.'

'Well enough to fly one last mission?'

Gunfire rumbled distantly inside Sapir's skull. 'May I ask what sort of mission?'

Reisfeld addressed the doctor. 'Did I hear another patient calling you?'

'You didn't,' the doctor said, sighing theatrically. 'But I'll go just the same.'

Through the bougainvillaea Sapir noticed a white sail on the sea. The PLO had once mounted a commando assault somewhere near here, he recalled. They had all been killed, but not before they had killed. Would it always be like this, the Promised Land?

Reisfeld said: 'Israel is facing its worst crisis since the Yom Kippur War.'

'Worse than the Iraqui Scuds?'

'Potentially... You see, our economy

depends on diamonds.'

The white sail edged into the centre of Sapir's vision. 'Diamonds?'

'Maybe half our total exports apart from agriculture. Diamonds, Mikhail, are as Jewish as *knaidels.*'

Another ship appeared in the limit of Sapir's vision. A gunboat? Rachel's father had cut and polished diamonds, he remembered. Before he had been murdered. 'So?'

'What I'm about to tell you is classified.' Reisfeld traced a Star of David in the dust on his boot. 'The Russians are threatening to swamp the market.'

'Why would they want to do that? They export them too.'

'They're more interested in hard currency than diamonds. They're holding the Syndicate to ransom. The Syndicate—'

'I know about the Syndicate,' Sapir interrupted him. 'Rachel Wolf told me. How it nearly brought the diamond industry here to its knees. Hundreds of small firms went under, Rachel's father among them. And you want to help them?'

'If the Russians flood the market, the Syndicate will go under and Israel with it.'

'Then the Syndicate must find the ransom money.'

'Fifty billion dollars?'

The gunboat was approaching the sail

resting like a butterfly on the blue sea.

'That's a lot of dollars.'

'Not even the Syndicate could get that much together. So they propose a ploy. Pretend to get the money together—'

'While we steal the diamonds?'

'They're being taken from northern Siberia to Moscow on an armoured train.'

'A hijack? In Siberia?' Sapir stared at Reisfeld in disbelief.

'After Entebbe anything's possible. Our intelligence has been in touch with guerrillas in northern Afghanistan who fought the Russians. They captured a Russian transport plane, an Antonov-12, and they've got an armoury of Russian weapons.'

Reisfeld picked up a dusty briefcase and took out a map. 'Look. Not so far from Novosibirsk.'

Sapir examined the map. 'That's on the Trans-Siberian Railway.'

'And the armoured train will be on it: it's the only route to Moscow. The Russians will think twice about shooting down one of their own planes, in any case their radar isn't so hot over the Pamirs, Uzbekistan, Kazakhstan... Maybe not so hot anywhere if a German pilot can land a Cessna in Red Square.'

'Why me?' Sapir asked.

The wicker chair creaked. 'Because you're the best.'

'After what happened in Jordan?'

'Could happen to anyone.' Another creak. 'And you speak Russian.'

'My main objection,' Sapir said, 'is that I would be risking Israeli skins to save the wallets of the diamond cartel.'

'You would be doing it to save Israel.' Reisfeld leaned forward. 'Do you know who's leading the Russians?'

'How could I?'

'Viktor Ruchkin,' Reisfeld said.

The patrol boat churned a circle round the white sail and departed leaving it fluttering in its wake.

'I'll do it,' Sapir said, gunfire loud inside his skull.

Although it has been tarted up, Moscow's National Hotel where Lenin once stayed—in Suite 107—still carries itself with an air of aristocratic decadence. Waitresses bringing *champagne* to the rooms act like bit players in scenes of seduction; as the elevator doors open conspiracies escape into the high-ceilinged lobby.

Because of its furtive graces the National, Viktor Ruchkin reasoned, was the obvious hotel in which to accommodate his distinguished visitor while the Minister of Defence was discharging his threats in London.

His room had a view of yellow-walled

Kremlin buildings and, if you dislocated your neck, the ice-cream cornet spires of St Basil's Cathedral in Red Square. The furnishings were sombre—a table covered with a vermillion cloth with a fringe that trembled in an imperceptible breeze, heavyweight chairs, funeral parlour drapes.

On the table stood a bottle of Novi Svyet, champagne in all but name, in a silver bucket beaded with moisture, a jar of Beluga caviar, black bread, slices of cucumber, and sour cream.

All the trappings of capitalism, Ruchkin thought. He had once fought for communism, for equality. But all along the line ideals had been debased by the preachers. How many cars had preacher Brezhnev possessed? A Rolls-Royce, Maserati, Cadillac, Lincoln, Mercedes... You lost count.

A knock at the door. A porter carrying the capacious hand baggage of a seasoned traveller came in first followed by the guest who tipped him with a five-dollar bill, passport to a week's decent food.

Ruchkin shook his hand, pointed to a chair. 'Please sit down.' He poured *champagne* and offered the jar of caviar.

'The old Russian schmaltz?' Harry Sampson accepted the sparkling wine, waved aside the caviar. 'I suggest we get down to essentials. You paid my fare, first class, from New York. You're picking up the tab here... Why?'

'I have a proposition.' Ruchkin spoke slowly, picking at his sparse English.

'Who gave you my name?'

'Contacts.'

'Mafia?'

'Contacts,' Ruchkin said, smearing black pearls of caviar on a finger of bread. 'But you are probably the most famous jeweller in the world.'

'Flattery,' Sampson said, 'will get you everywhere. What's the deal?'

'I believe you have fought many battles with the Syndicate.'

'And lost them all.'

'Then it's about time to win the final victory.'

'Saturate the market? That's been on the cards for 40 years. Why should Russia cut its own throat?'

'Because,' Ruchkin said, choosing his words with care, 'Russians don't care about diamonds anymore. All they want is hard currency.'

'Blackmail?'

Ruchkin nodded.

'I'm interested,' Sampson said, combing grey hair from his temples with the tips of his fingers.

Ruchkin dipped a slice of cucumber into sour cream, and told him about the ransom demand which he had designated Operation Orloff after the 200-carat diamond, now in the Kremlin, given to Catherine the Great by Count Gregory Orloff in the hope that she would reinstate him in her court. She had taken the diamond and left him out in the cold.

Ruchkin chewed the cucumber.

'So you see,' he said, licking cream from his lips, 'whatever you do, you win and the Syndicate loses.'

Sampson unbuttoned the jacket of his pin-stripe suit, crossed his legs. His black shoes were made of leather as soft as skin. 'How come?' he asked.

'If the Syndicate accepts the terms they will have to provide a fortune in ransom money. And you will make it clear that you were responsible.'

'And if they don't play ball?'

'Then diamonds will become worthless. But you, Mr Sampson, will have taken the precaution of selling your diamond stocks and moving into emeralds, sapphires... We have plenty of those in the Russian republic. Emeralds on the Asian side of the Urals, sapphires nearby.'

'So what do I have to do?'

Ruchkin handed him three rough diamonds, each of more than 30 carats, and told him.

Nearby, *beneath* the city of Moscow, three mafia godfathers and six of their lieutenants were also discussing diamonds.

Seated at the table in the underground complex flanked by the Armenian and the ancient Georgian, the Chechen said: 'We put a trace on Ruchkin. He wouldn't have allowed us to throw him out of Moscow unless he was on to something very special.'

The Georgian lit a *papirosa* and coughed gently; the Armenian felt for his quiff and patted it with the tips of his fingers.

The Chechen went on: 'No easy task in Siberia but we got lucky. Here in Moscow. As you know we took over Ruchkin's territory. And what did we find?'

'Tell us,' the old Georgian said.

'Diamonds.' The Chechen rasped his hand against the thick stubble on his dangerous face. 'In the bath-house that Ruchkin calls Dostoyevsky. A whore with four roughs in her purse. Payment for services rendered, she said. Now who pays a whore with diamonds? A miner for one, she told us. For another Viktor Ruchkin. So what does that tell us?' He pointed at the Armenian.

'Ruchkin's made a strike?'

'Close. We checked out the diamond fields in Siberia and found that Ruchkin had booked into a hotel in Mirny. From there it was easy. And guess what—a hoard of diamonds is being shifted to Moscow. Estimated value?'

'Maybe a few million dollars?' one of the lieutenants ventured.

The Chechen held his audience for a moment, then said: 'Fifty billion dollars. Billion,' he repeated.

Another lieutenant said: 'Shit, I didn't know anything was worth that much, not even life.'

'Maybe not yours,' the Armenian said. 'Fifty billion, are you—'

'Sure? We checked it out with a floor manager at the No 3 Diamond Factory who would slit his mother's throat for the price of a fix. The diamonds are coming on an armoured train and he's heard from a Spetsnaz guarding them that Ruchkin's going to be on the footplate.'

'Not for long,' the Georgian said in between phlegmy coughs.

'So where do we hit it?' the Armenian asked.

'According to the floor manager the train will change engines at Novosibirsk. There will be some unexpected passengers waiting for it. You,' to the lieutenants, 'organise the advance party and fly there. Fold-butt AKS-74s, grenades and armour-piercing cannon. I'll make the final arrangements and follow by rail.'

'Fifty *billion* dollars?' the Armenian said. 'What would we do with that much money?'

'Count it,' the old Georgian said.

The Minister of Defence, inspecting once more the scar tissue of Moscow's last ditch defences, said: 'The chairman, I liked him.'

Ruchkin kicked a hump of earth and a brass cartridge case coated with verdigris sprang out. 'Two old warriors?'

'Maybe. One thing worried me: he seemed to know what this was all about.'

So did Harry Sampson, Ruchkin thought. Which meant that there was a spy somewhere in Mirny. A spy who would have to be eliminated if Operation Orloff was going to succeed.

First Ruchkin handed the Spetsnaz lieutenant in charge of security a letter from the Minister of Defence ordering him to hand over control of the armoured train to a major in GRU, military intelligence. 'Me,' Ruchkin told him.

Then he went looking for the spy. The first-floor manager if his deputy, jealous of his *blat,* was to be believed. The manager had been acting furtively, frequently visiting the White Nights where there was a telephone, one of the few in

141

Mirny. More pertinently he had *zeliotes*, greenbacks, to spend.

Ruchkin held a meeting with the lieutenant and the manager, with the pointed beard, and told them that the armoured train was now scheduled to leave Mirny a day later, December 2nd.

Then he staked out the White Nights.

The manager arrived during the lunch-break. Ruchkin signalled to two of his men and, carrying his fighting spade, went into the log cabin. The phone was behind a door leading to the lavatory.

Ruchkin pushed his way past the waiter with the greasy trousers and kicked open the door. Just as the manager slammed the lavatory door itself behind him, leaving the phone dangling from the wall.

Ruchkin kicked it but it was tougher than the dividing door. He heard the sound of breaking glass inside the lavatory and ran on to the street.

What he hadn't anticipated was that a factory manager would pack an old TTR4 target pistol with a barrel like a cannon.

He fired two shots, winging one of Ruchkin's lieutenants. Then he dived into the indoor market where women in scarves were queuing for food—salted fish, dried fruit, reindeer meat sparkling with ice—and clothes.

Ruchkin shouted. 'Get down!' but the

shoppers who, with glasnost, had learned disobedience, stayed where they were.

Ruchkin's other lieutenant, a pale-eyed marksman named Gusev, materialised at another entrance on the far side of the white-tiled stalls. He fired his pistol at the manager briefly isolated among the shoppers; the bullet chipped a stall and ricocheted into a side of reindeer meat.

'Get down,' Ruchkin shouted again.

The women stared at him. A rare commodity had been sighted—a tottering pile of Chinese-made women's shoes in cardboard boxes. Most of the women hit the ground, others made it to the shoes.

The manager fired at Gusev. The bullet smashed a naked light bulb and glass fell on to a counter of salted fish.

The manager dodged between the women lying on the floor and those who had made it to the queue for shoes. A mistake. The recumbent women, identifying him as the obstacle between them and the shoes, rose as one. And that most frightening phenomenon, a pack of bargain-hunting Russian women, trampled over him.

When the sturdy feet had passed the manager stared into the barrel of the pistol held by Gusev. And from the stall beyond him came the lament: 'The shoes are all left feet.'

Ruchkin strapped the manager to the broad trunk of a pine where he and the Spetsnaz officer had drunk *spirt* and fish soup. Legs apart, arms stretched high, as though he were the target in a knife thrower's act.

'So,' Ruchkin said, standing eight metres away, spade loosely held in one hand, 'what did you tell them?'

'Them?'

'The Syndicate,' Ruchkin said. 'In Moscow. The *zhids*...'

'I was calling my mother.'

'Why is it that informers have so many relatives?' Ruchkin asked, remembering the thief in the sobering-up station.

'Everyone has relatives.'

'What did you tell them?'

'My mother? That I was in the best of health.'

'But you're a junkie, aren't you?'

Ruchkin threw the spade. It hit the bark of the pine just below one of the manager's crucified arms.

He shouted: 'For pity's sake...'

Ruchkin retrieved the spade. 'I can take your ears off with this,' he said. 'One by one. Without even touching your head.'

'I told them nothing.'

'Them?'

'All right, the Syndicate. Nothing, I promise.'

'So why did you call them?'

'To keep in touch.'

This time the razored blade of the spade pinned the edge of his padded jacket to the pine.

Ruchkin took up his position again. 'What did you tell them?'

'What could I tell them?'

'For a *zhid* you're a brave man.'

The spade clipped a segment off his ear.

'All right, what does it matter? I told them you were leaving a day late.'

'Good,' Ruchkin said, 'because we're leaving a day early.' He stepped to one side and threw the spade with unerring aim at the side of the manager's neck.

Chapter Eight

The briefing was held in the mildew-smelling classroom of a recently abandoned school to the east of Tel Aviv near Ben Gurion airport.

Paintings of orange trees beneath strips of sky and sunflower suns were still pinned to the wall. The Negev, Sapir thought.

He sat in front of the class—nine specialists, one of them a pilot. In front of them on a platform sat the Israeli chief of

145

staff, a general, the director of Intelligence, Mossad, and Theo Reisfeld.

The general, whose fringe of hair made a battlefield of his scalp, said: 'Good news, gentlemen—the Cabinet has given us the go-ahead. You,' to Sapir, 'will be in charge. Brigadier Reisfeld...'

Reisfeld looking, Sapir thought, as though he had been scooped from the desert, leaned his elbows on a magisterial desk complete with an old-fashioned inkwell, and said: 'All members of your team are Russian Jews. Everyone will therefore be able to speak Russian—and know their way around. You will be wearing Russian uniforms and you will be flying in a Russian aircraft. From Afghanistan,' he added.

Sapir asked: 'May we know how we're going to get to Afghanistan, sir?'

The director of Mossad, brown eyes and sunspots at his temple—everything about him was brown, even his shirt—took over from Reisfeld.

'You can forget about Entebbe,' he said. 'I know that pains Brigadier Reisfeld but we can't fly four C-130 Hercules transport planes and two Boeing 707s across Turkey and 2,000 miles of what was the Soviet Union without getting them shot out of the sky.'

The director opened a dossier. He

146

reminded Sapir of a friendly-looking dog he had once owned which had to be destroyed after it savaged a pedestrian. He put on a pair of rimless glasses and summarised the contents of the dossier.

Those taking part in Operation Joshua—'We don't want to give the game away by calling it Flawless or anything like that'—would fly to Kabul, capital of Afghanistan, on scheduled airlines as private passengers in three parties, two or seven operatives, one of six.

Each party would depart from Tel Aviv to a city served by Ariana, the Afghanistan airline. 'Your party,' pointing at Sapir, 'will catch an Ariana flight from Rome at 17.10 arriving at Kabul via Delhi at 8.30 the following morning. There is a conference taking place in Kabul to try to defuse the military situation there. You will fly as delegates from three foreign countries. Your passports are being manufactured now.'

The pilot, a 25-year-old from Netanya whose stern features belied a sometimes misplaced sense of humour, held up his hand. 'With respect, sir, if I am an Italian, shouldn't I be able to speak Italian?'

'Each party has a spokesman who speaks his appointed language.' The director consulted the dossier. 'You're American. You do speak English, don't you?'

He sat down and the chief of staff took his place. 'We now move to the second phase. Kabul to the far north of Afghanistan. Theo...'

Reisfeld, combat boots clumping on the worn platform boards, planted his hands on the desk. 'You will rendezvous at Kabul's Khwaja Rawash airport. Not a problem because the flights land there within a couple of hours of each other.'

'Provided they're on schedule,' the pilot whispered to Sapir.

'There you will be met by a member of the Mujahideen—holy warriors fighting for Islam—who has infiltrated Kabul.'

Silence. Sapir broke it. 'Moslems are going to co-operate with Israelis?'

Reisfeld said: 'What you've got to understand is that after the atrocities they've suffered, they hate Russians more than Israelis.'

'In fact,' the Mossad director broke in, 'they don't really hate Israelis at all. They're not Arabs: our war is remote from them.'

'And we're paying them well,' the general observed. 'With diamonds. They can cross the border into Pakistan and sell them in Islamabad. Am I right?' looking at the Mossad director.

'Correct. And from Islamabad they will be smuggled to Antwerp. Good business all round. With the money they get in Islamabad the Mujahideen will buy arms from the French, Belgians, British...maybe even the Israelis.' He smiled.

Reisfeld pulled open a map hanging from the top of the blackboard and prodded it with a ruler. 'From Kabul you will be driven through the Hindu Kush mountains to a valley near the border with what was the Soviet Union where the Russian An-12 transport plane crash landed and was captured by the Mujahideen.'

The pilot's hand shot up. 'How bad a crash landing, sir? Does it still have wheels?'

'And wings,' the Mossad director said. 'Our information is that the aircraft is in good order. And, yes, there is fuel.' The smile was beginning to fade from his brown simian eyes. 'There you will be given Russian combat uniforms, weapons and equipment.'

Reisfeld pulled down another map of central Asia, mostly Kazakhstan, the newly independent republic five times the size of France stretching from the Volga to China.

The general said: 'The land of the Silk Roads. Deserts, steppe, mountains.' He explored his rugged scalp with his fingertips. 'Not to mention Baykonur, launching pad for space shots and Semipalatinsk, a nuclear test site.'

'Avoid them like the plague,' Reisfeld said. 'This is your route.' He pointed the ruler at a line inked in red. 'You cross the Pamirs here,' tapping the map with the ruler, 'then fly roughly parallel with the Chinese border but well west of it. You then cross Lake Balkhash and fly north-east to the border with the Russian republic, giving Semipalatinsk a wide berth.'

'Let's hope the Migs give us a wide berth,' the pilot said.

'Don't forget you will be flying a Russian plane so they will think twice about shooting you down. Mossad has drawn up a precise flight plan, and given you a call sign. You will be far enough away from China to avoid their border patrols and, according to the met office, the weather will be bad.'

'Great,' the pilot said.

'Blizzards—good cover. From the Russian border you will strike north east to Novosibirsk.'

The Mossad director said: 'We have also created a convincing reason why you've suddenly appeared on the Kazakh and Russian radar screens.' He patted the dossier. 'A secret mission authorised by GRU, Russian military intelligence, which still holds sway in Kazakhstan.'

Reisfeld said: 'If you lose your way look for the railroad linking Novosibirsk with

Alma-Ata, the capital of Kazakhstan.'

'Father of Apples,' the pilot said. 'That's what it means,' he said quickly, catching the Mossad director's gaze.

Sapir intervened, nudging the pilot with his elbow. 'And at Novosibirsk we take out the armoured train carrying the diamonds on the Trans-Siberian railroad?'

Reisfeld said: 'Ten of you drop from the An-12 at a point 50 kilometres west of Novosibirsk. It's called Naked Boy Halt; it used to be a saw mill and it's on a disused loop of the Trans-Siberian. The An-12 flies on to an airstrip 25 kilometres closer to Novosibirsk.' He turned to the Mossad director. 'Your turn, Yosef.'

The director moved to a screen beside the blackboard and nodded at a pro-jectionist at the back of the classroom. A satellite photograph appeared on the screen.

'The airstrip, gentlemen. Virtually disused. At one end of the strip a helicopter, an unidentified aircraft, possibly an Illyushin 76—we're doing a closer check on it—and an ambulance. There, you can see the red cross. You,' to the pilot, 'will land there and the rest of the squad will overpower any staff there may be there and make their way to Novosibirsk in the ambulance—they're always mobile. There you will take over the railroad control centre and switch the points as the armoured train approaches the feeder line to Naked Boy Halt.'

He nodded at the projectionist and another satellite picture appeared on the screen. Naked Boy Halt. A loopline leaving the main Trans-Siberian, nosing through 15 kilometres of *taiga* and hills until it reached a tiny station in front of the saw mill. Then a bridge across a ravine. At the other end of the bridge a small building. To the right of that what looked like a pit filled with monsters. Then the single-track continued on its way back to link up with the Trans-Siberian again further down the line.

The director said: 'The building at the end of the bridge was an overnight rest house for locomotive drivers and stokers. The cavity across the track to the right is a cemetery for old steam engines. But we expect your team,' nodding at Sapir, 'to hit the armoured train before it reaches the halt and the bridge. The track is electrified. We have Pavel Shapiro to thank for a lot of this information. Stand up and take a bow, sergeant.'

A bulky red-haired sergeant stood up bashfully, then sat down again.

'Sergeant Shapiro,' the director told them, 'is the son of a former railroad controller in Siberia—in Irkutsk. He was training to follow in his father's footsteps before the family got permission to emigrate to Israel.'

Sapir said: 'So what if the loopline *is* electrified, sir?'

'The team in Novosibirsk will activate it. When the armoured train has progressed far enough—only an idiot would stop, guessing he was about to be ambushed—you blow an electric pylon. The train stops: it's yours.'

'An armoured train?' Sapir frowned.

'Among the weapons you're collecting in Afghanistan is a Russian RPG-75 shoulder-fired rocket launcher. Does that answer your question?'

The general looked at his watch. 'We'll take a break now. Any more questions so far?'

'One,' Sapir said. 'Who is going to lead the team to the control room in Novosibirsk?'

'A good question,' Reisfeld said. 'There are only nineteen of you here and the missing member is the leader of the Novosibirsk squad.'

'Who is he, Brigadier?'

'*She,*' Reisfeld said. 'Lieutenant Rachel Wolf.'

Snacks were brought in—pita bread stuffed with deep-fried chick-pea dumplings and salad—and sodas.

Sapir approached Reisfeld who was

standing beneath a crayoned drawing of a citrus grove hung with ambitious oranges watching a couple of bearded Orthodox Jews wearing black hats and long coats walking down the street.

Reisfeld said: 'I know what you're going to say.' He took a hungry bite out of his pita.

'You know how it was with Rachel and me, Theo.'

'She's a good soldier,' Reisfeld said, chewing.

'Not good enough.' Insubordinate, he thought, remembering how she had tried to shoot the young Arabs. No place for private feuds on a mission like Operation Joshua. 'She hasn't got the experience.'

'The general's mind is made up.'

'Why, for God's sake?'

'Because she knows the terrain. She was born in Novosibirsk near the railroad control. She also speaks a couple of Siberian languages, Yakut and Buryat apparently. You, Mikhail, were born in Kazan and only speak Russian.'

'I think she will be a disruptive influence.'

'Because you were once lovers? Don't talk crap, Mikhail. You're both professional soldiers. Anyway, perhaps you'd better tell her your views yourself,' as the door opened and Rachel entered the classroom.

She was dressed in uniform, silver parachutist's badge on her breast, but Sapir saw her naked standing in the doorway leading from the bathroom to the bedroom in the hotel in Haifa.

He said to Reisfeld: 'She can't even get to a briefing on time.'

'Special dispensation,' Reisfeld said. 'The anniversary of her father's death.'

'Who's going to brief her then?'

'You are,' Reisfeld said.

The general called them to order once again and took up his position behind the desk. He welcomed Rachel and said: 'Since the original tip came from the Syndicate we have received more detailed information.'

The Mossad director took over. 'The Russian operation is being mounted by a man named Viktor Ruchkin, Moscow mafia and former Spetsnaz. An old adversary I believe,' he said, nodding at Sapir.

'A highly competent operator.'

'And a murderer?'

'Ruthless, yes.' Not answering the question directly because in a way they were all murderers.

'As Spetsnaz are guarding the diamonds it's reasonable to assume that Ruchkin will be on the armoured train. Which, incidentally, is leaving a day late. The informant,' he explained.

Sapir closed his eyes and became Viktor Ruchkin. Then he opened them and raised his hand. 'Can I ask a question, sir?'

'Of course,' but the director sounded irritated.

'Has the Syndicate heard from the informant since?'

'As a matter of fact, no. Why?'

'Because I reckon he's dead, sir. That information was fed to him. When he had passed it on, he was killed.'

'An interesting theory, major. Unproven but...a possibility. Why,' striving to be fair, 'do you think Ruchkin would have let him send that message?'

'Because he intends to set out a day *early*.'

'You anticipate each other, you and Ruchkin?'

'As you said, sir, he's an old adversary. And if you receive any more intelligence from Mirny, via the Syndicate, I should treat it with the utmost suspicion.'

'Really, major? You should have been in intelligence.' He favoured Sapir with a warm and dangerous smile. 'So if you're reasoning is correct we have a day less to mount Operation Joshua and we didn't have much time in the first place.'

The pilot asked: 'Exactly how long do we have?'

Reisfeld made his way to the desk,

dwarfing it. 'The armoured train *was* due to leave Mirny in three days, on December lst. If Major Sapir's reasoning is correct it will leave in two days, on November 30th. From Mirny it will take three days on the new track and the BAM railroad to link up with the Trans-Siberian at Tayshet. Tayshet is 1,179 kilometres from Novosibirsk—that's 1,229 to the feeder line to Naked Boy Halt. If the armoured train travels at the same speed as the Trans-Siberian that will be another 17 hours and 51 minutes.'

The pilot said: 'But it won't, will it, because the Trans-Siberian stops at stations.'

'Very good. In fact I have deducted 50 minutes for those stops—the longest are at Krasnoyarsk and Novosibirsk itself, 15 minutes each. So that's 17 hours. The armoured train will also have to change engines, probably at the half-way mark, Novosibirsk. So let's say 17½ hours.'

Sapir said: 'Today's November 28th. We have five days to get to Naked Boy Halt. That's cutting it very fine. When do we leave?'

'Tonight,' the general said.

The pilot said: 'One last question, Brigadier. 'You've told us how we get into Russia. How do we get out?'

'We're working on that,' Reisfeld said.

157

They sat in a McDavid's eating hamburgers and French fries and drinking orange juice. Outside Sapir could see Israel passing by. Ashkenazi Jews from Europe, Sephardic Jews from Africa and the Middle East; American Jews and Russian Jews; old German Jews carrying memories of concentration camps on crooked shoulders and young black Falasha from Ethiopia escaping from famine. Arabs from the West Bank and the Gaza strip working in Tel Aviv. What should have been a market of peaceful co-existence and yet we've been at war for 45 years. Who was the culprit, religion? Two separate gods? Why couldn't gods get together....

Rachel said: 'What are you thinking about?'

Her wheat-coloured hair had been cut short for battle. Did she still use lemon-scented soap?

'Checking on what I'm fighting for,' he said.

'You shouldn't have to check.'

'Reminding myself that the diamond cartel is incidental.' He bit into his hamburger. 'Shouldn't you be thinking about that?'

'My father? What would you care about him? You saved his murderers.'

'Kids,' Sapir said. 'Kids with no bullets.'

'Because they had fired them all at Israelis.'

'Because they were told to. Because that's the way they've been brought up from the crib. Killing, a way of life...'

'And dying,' Rachel said. She forked French fries. 'Strange, isn't it,' she said. 'You look more like a fighter than a pacifist.'

He touched the scars on his face, legacies of fists and stones—one from a knife behind a mosque in Kazan. He felt the wound healing on the side of his close-cropped black hair like an angry parting. Heard distant gunfire.

'Are you all right?' She chewed slowly, searching his face.

'I'm fine.'

'Fit enough to lead the mission?'

'Orders are orders. In any case, who else could do it?' He put down his knife and fork and wagged one finger. 'No, not you.'

'Because I'm a woman?'

'Because you haven't got the experience.'

'Jewish women have always been tougher than men. Golda Meyer, now there was a woman.'

'All women are tougher than men: that's why they live longer. But you don't have to be tough to be strong.'

'So if some Russian soldiers come to

you and say, "Shalom, zhid, don't shoot us because we haven't got any bullets left", you'll slap their wrists and let them go?'

'I don't think we should be on this mission as first and second in command.'

An old woman sitting at the next table smiled at them fondly.

'We don't have any choice,' Rachel said.

Sapir drank orange juice. The gunfire in his skull faded. Wrong, he thought, I do.

In London it was raining, drizzle that blew through the streets looking for the Thames. Loder caught a taxi from Brown's Hotel to the Syndicate's headquarters in the City where he surprised the chief accountant by asking for 50,000 dollars in cash.

The accountant, who spoke in figures and possessed an admiral's eyebrows, said he would have to get the chairman's authority. When he had done so he said he couldn't get the money together for sixty minutes—not one hour, Loder noted.

From there Loder went to a travel agent in Hatton Garden, squeezed between shop windows sparkling with jewellery, and booked the daily 10.30 a.m flight from Heathrow airport to Warsaw and an ongoing Ariana flight to Kabul.

Back at the Syndicate's offices the

accountant told him the money was waiting for him in the chairman's office. In 100-dollar bills.

Why, the chairman asked, did Loder want so much cash? Insurance, Loder told him.

'And I'm flying to Afghanistan in the morning.'

'Why, for God's sake?'

'In case the Israelis get the wrong idea. You know, sir, finders being keepers.'

Eight thousand five hundred miles away Viktor Ruchkin watched the huge safe containing the diamonds being welded to the floor of the first carriage of *Little Eagle*.

Beside him, wearing a cheap nylon and rabbit fur hat, stood a gemmologist named Suvorov from the Crimea, chief executive of the Mirny Diamond Administration, a bespectacled and miserly pedant with a small, damp moustache who had once worked in the Special Collection of Jewellery in the Hermitage in St Petersburg.

Through the open door in the 120mm-armoured plating Ruchkin could see a plume of soft sparks falling from an acetylene torch held by a welder wearing goggles. Spetsnaz wearing blue berets aimed Stechkin machine pistols at the coach.

Suvorov touched his moustache—to see if it had frozen, Ruchkin thought—and said: 'Not much work for military intelligence these days, major?'

'Different sort of work,' Ruchkin said. 'GRU has to keep a fatherly eye on the breakaway republics. Make sure the Ukraine hasn't kept too many missiles for its own good.'

'Guarding precious stones must be a departure for you.'

And stealing them!

'We get involved in all sorts of projects involving security. As you know, Spetsnaz is our fighting extension.'

'Will you be travelling on the armoured train?'

'Part of the way,' Ruchkin said. 'To make sure security is water tight. Radio communication with the helicopter, that sort of thing.'

A few flakes of snow peeled away from a bruised sky. The third fall. This one would settle. Ivan Chukovsky, leaning against the Skoda, gazed skywards, greeting an old friend.

The sparks spent themselves; the welder climbed down from the coach and said to Suvorov: 'It would take a missile to shift that.'

'Not much chance of that, major?' Suvorov said to Ruchkin.

Ruchkin took his elbow. 'A word in your ear.'

'Where are we going?' Suvorov asked as Ruchkin led him away from the improvised railhead.

'Out of earshot.' Ruchkin stopped behind a prefabricated office separated from the track by a pile of sleepers, predictably over-ordered.

Ruchkin said: 'I want the combination of the safe.'

Suvorov stared at him. 'Why? All you have to do is deliver the safe to Moscow.'

'I am in charge of this operation: give me the combination.'

Fear dawned on Suvorov's cramped features. 'I haven't got it. Only the Syndicate in Moscow knows it.'

Ruchkin drew a pistol fitted with a silencer. 'You're lying.'

'I'm not, I swear it.' Then, momentarily, a lifetime of self-importance wiped away the spiderwebs of fear. 'In any case, you're not GRU—I phoned Moscow.'

Ruchkin shot him through the heart.

Suvorov's body was buried in the obdurate soil of the *taiga*—Ruchkin said he had accused him of stealing diamonds and he had pulled a gun but he had been quicker. After the burial Ruchkin went to his hotel and revised the timetable he had drawn up

163

before making the departure a day earlier.

They would leave in two days, reach Novosibirsk, where they would change engines, in five. Provided nothing went wrong. But it couldn't, could it?

Part II

Passage

Chapter Nine

November 30th. 14.05 hours.

As always the Trans-Siberian, the *Rossiya*, left Moscow's Yaroslav station on time. It would traverse 9,297 kilometres, pass through eight time zones, and reach Vladivostok on the Pacific coast in 7 days 16½ hours. On time.

It would pass the Monument of Tears, the boundary between Europe and Asia where families had once bidden farewell to convicts exiled to Siberia; circumvent Baikal, the deepest lake in the world holding 20 per cent of the world's fresh water; skirt the Sino-Soviet border where gin-seng grew, where sabre-tooth tigers still roamed, where the Chinese had once shown their bare arses to the Soviets over the River Amur.

Among those on board was Frank Blair, 45, redundant British spy and disgraced journalist hopelessly seeking an exclusive on the last leg of his career.

Blair, modestly drunk, herring-bone jacket and charcoal-grey trousers rumpled, sat in the restaurant car, laptop in front of him, and watched his home for the past six years retreat. Komsomol Square with its three railroad stations where junkies and hookers had first challenged the pristine visions of the new Russia; Gorky Park, its iced pathways singing with skates; jugglers and gypsies and Baskin-Robbins ice cream on the Arbat; ice dust sparkling in the air in Red Square and the mossy smell of river beaches and the music of winter melting.

He nipped from a silver flask of vodka—the Trans-Siberian was dry these days—closed his eyes and opened the door of the cavernous apartment he had shared with Barbara on Kutuzovsky Prospect. Two flats, in fact, knocked together in a ghetto block reserved for foreigners opposite the Stalinist wedding cake hotel, the Ukraina.

Purple borscht in the kitchen, stirred and conducted by their 18-stone maid Nina with a wooden spoon; champagne on ice; cassette of a melancholy women's choir singing about a birch tree on the imported tape deck; playing darts in the spare bedroom and making love on two single beds roped together.

But the love-making had been a long time ago when they were breathing the same air as each other, the first fresh draughts of revolution. The biggest story out of Moscow for 70 years, the collapse of the Soviet Union, the passing of communism.

Blair, dark hair tracked with silver, leanness of cheek still palpable beneath punished flesh—Barbara had told him he looked like an American Indian corrupted by white man's baubles and booze—stared out of the window. A line of women carrying their ubiquitous string bags out of a store. Snow was settling on their headscarves.

It had been threatening to snow when he had been recruited in the chillingly diffident style of the British in the days before spies had become an endangered species.

A phone call to his apartment in South Kensington. An anonymous informant, a political exclusive for his paper. Could they meet beside the Joy of Life fountain in Hyde Park opposite Mount Street? He, the caller, would be wearing a yellow rose in his lapel.

His name was Lomax and he carried a furled umbrella which, as they walked through the dormant park, he pointed in front of him like a mine detector. A crumpled man in a black overcoat with clipped tufts of hair in his ears and the hesitant authority of an officer on the retired list.

There was, he confessed, no story but he had heard that Blair had been posted to Washington. There, with contacts beyond the reach of British diplomats—'Russians spring to mind'—he would be in a privileged position to help his country wage the good fight. Did Blair get his drift?

Blair got it all right. Understood, too, that his whole life had been processed by computers. *Young and patriotic but flawed by a well-concealed sense of inferiority that could be assuaged by clandestine activity.* Something like that. *And studied Russian at Cambridge.*

'So what do you think?' Lomax speared a crisp leaf with the tip of his umbrella.

Why not? He could discern nothing disreputable in serving his country covertly and, at the time, did not acknowledge that it was the prospect of a second, secret life that gave him a buzz. And it was only much later that he realised that, in the jargon of that period, he had been enlisted as a sleeper. Finally posted, presumably at the behest of Lomax, to Moscow.

'But you must never confide in your wife,' Lomax had warned him before swivelling on his umbrella and heading for Park Lane at a brisk, parade ground clip. And he hadn't until it was too late.

He was joined at the table in the restaurant car by his companion in the two-berth sleeper, Tom Noland, a bird watcher. In the few minutes they had been together Noland, pale hair damply combed, small features intent, had confided that he lived in Muswell Hill in North London, that he worked as a clerk at the offices of the Comptroller and City Solicitor, and that he was in Russia because of a bet. An unlikely proposition, Blair had thought, seeing an unremarkable but thoroughly contented man, and escaping down the corridor.

Noland ordered a fizzy cherry drink from a waitress wearing a white tiara. 'You look a bit down in the mouth,' he said brightly. 'Want to tell me about it? It always helps.'

That I am a passed pawn in the game of espionage? That my wife has left me because our marriage was a lie? That I'm a failed journalist recalled to London to write obituaries?

Wondering how he could distance himself from the bird watcher, Blair tipped vodka down his throat, stared out of the window at a playground full of children welcoming the snow and began to compose an obituary. His own.

After Cambridge he worked as a reporter on a provincial daily before joining the staff of a leading national newspaper where, after three years as a general reporter, he became

171

deputy political correspondent. It was at this stage of his career that, covering a visit to Canada by the then prime minister, Edward Heath, he met his future wife, Barbara Brunet, a researcher for an American news magazine.

From Montreal he had taken Barbara, delicately boned with a neat blonde head, warm hollows at her throat, back to London where he had proposed. They were married in New York, spent the first couple of days of their honeymoon in Vermont, and then caught the Montrealer train at Bellows Falls, home to 60 acres of old steam locos and rolling stock beside the Connecticut River. It was the season of the foliage and even in the moonlight the trees seemed to find colour.

Barbara's parents picked them up at Montreal's central station and drove them to the clapboard house they owned on the banks of the St Laurence near Quebec City. Snow geese excavating the mud, a lost wind raising ruffs on the water, exhilarating plans hatched in the deep, lavender-smelling bed. The bed was the future and in its depths they found each other many times.

By day they walked among Douglas firs and watched the big ships shouldering their way to Lake Ontario or the ocean and drove into Montreal to eat steaks and drink French wine in the old town and stood on the throne that is Quebec City where Samuel de Champlain once stood. And he learned some French because if you marry a Quebecoise it is criminal folly not to do so.

They stayed one night in her parents' smart apartment in the Montreal suburb Ahuntsic. It contained a lot of flowerless plants with polished leaves and photographs, and Blair was an intruder. There on top of the TV was Barbara graduating in cap and gown from college; there she was with a group at Sir George Williams; there she was ski-ing, sun-bathing, dining, but always in control.

The rationale for her parents' existence and here I am, a British Philistine who can scarcely speak French, abducting her.

His own parents who lived in Lavenham in Suffolk, and hadn't seriously recognised any hostilities since the end of World War II, accepted her on sight.

From Washington Blair was dispatched to the paper's Moscow bureau where, for several years, he prospered, providing his paper with a string of exclusive stories that were the envy of his competitors. Then, inexplicably, his star waned.

In fact it had all but evaporated in the heat of a July day. They had escaped that

Sunday, their wedding anniversary, from the reproving icons in their apartment on Kutuzovsky and driven to a beach on the River Moskva packed with Russians embracing summer before it escaped once again.

They swam in mud-coloured waters and sank bottles of Narzan in the shallows to keep them cool. Played ping-pong on sagging tables and picnicked off cold chicken and cucumber salad, black bread and blue cheese.

'Not quite the St Laurence,' said Blair watching a woman, aggressive bosom contained by a khaki brassiere, fit a cardboard protector to her nose and raise her face to the sun.

'St Laurent, French spelling.' Barbara wore a black one-piece, looking as sleek as a seal, blonde hair still wet at the nape of her neck.

'Independence for Quebec? You're going to be as sore as hell if it happens while you're away from the action.'

'It won't,' she said. 'One day perhaps but not now. But everyone's fighting for something, aren't they?' She looked at him quizzically and he wondered, as he had wondered before, if she suspected. 'What are you fighting for, Frank?'

He took evasive action, extended one arm to embrace the beach. 'You know there's a lot to be said for old-style communism on a day like this. Everyone collectively enjoying themselves. The Pentagon wouldn't like that: they prefer their Russians bowed into a Kremlin-inspired blizzard.'

'And the Kremlin prefers its Americans puffing on torpedo-sized stoogies evicting black slaves from their hovels.'

'What we need,' Blair said, 'is a summit on public relations.' He leaned forward and squeezed water from her hair, kissed the back of her neck.

'This evening,' she said. 'When we get home. Immediately.'

'I love you,' he said.

A white pleasure boat pushed its way along the river, decks crowded with waving passengers, just as the big ships had once passed them on their way to Lake Ontario.

They stopped on their way home to pick wood anemones in a forest, tiger-striped with sunlight, and they made love, immediately, on their bed, out of sight of the holy vigilantes on the walls of the living-room.

Then they went to dine in the Aragvi, carton of Winston the key to closed doors, to eat Georgian food.

Which was where Denikin, formerly KGB, his contact at the Ministry of the Interior, found them.

For a few moments he hovered beside their table next to the marble wall near the musicians' gallery, until Blair, in wonderment and fear, asked him to join them to share their 200 grams of vodka.

Denikin's face, creased with suppressed subterfuge, was grey and his fingers shook as he lit a yellow cigarette.

Blair introduced him. Vladimir Denikin from the Foreign Ministry. Good contact. Good friend, he almost said, to which she would have replied: 'Then why haven't I met him before?'

What the hell was Denikin doing here? They always met in parks, like all good agents, at twilight times of loneliness. So what had brought him to the Aragvi, haunt of former Party *apparatchiki* and deadbeat spooks from home and abroad?

'I was just passing.' Denikin answered the unspoken question.

Pathetic. Denikin seemed to have acquired another incipient crease below one cheekbone and he kept touching his stone-coloured hair.

'Aren't you eating?' Barbara asked, and when Denikin shook his head: 'I'm surprised they let you in if you're not. Are you a privileged guest?' She ordered beans in walnut sauce followed by *shashlik*.

'A bribe,' Denikin said. 'Cigarettes.'

'The doorman should be able to open a tobacco store. I thought you were just passing?'

Denikin tossed vodka down his throat and didn't bother with the chaser. Blair ordered another 200 grams.

Denikin said: 'It isn't so difficult if you're a Georgian. Anyway this place isn't what it was. I recommend the Mukuzani red.'

A waiter served the food and the band struck up a bouncy tune.

Barbara spooned beans. 'I'd love to visit Georgia. Frank's been there. There are a lot of places Frank doesn't take me to.'

Blair said: 'Does a plumber take his wife to every bathroom he fixes?' He picked at his food, appetite dispatched by anxiety.

'You *must* visit Tblisi. It's full of gangsters and students. And the streets are laid out for intrigue. The Russians are very jealous of us,' Denikin said. His eyes pleaded with Blair.

Barbara scooped up the last of the walnut sauce. 'I'm going to powder my nose,' she said. 'Go to the little girls' room... Why is it that only men are allowed to say, "I'm going to take a leak"?'

When she had gone Denikin leaned

across the table and whispered: 'We're blown.'

Not *us* exactly, Denikin told Blair later as they walked along Tverskaya Street, formerly Gorky Street, beneath a sky smeared with summer stars. *Me!*

Had Blair passed on the information about the new compound near Archangel where nerve gases GA (Tabun), GB (sanin) and GD (soman) were stored? Of course Blair had. The disclosure of such cynical disregard for human suffering had made the front page.

'Well, it doesn't exist,' Denikin said.

'What the hell are you talking about? The photographs...'

'The new young Turks are busily trapping all the old guard. Well, I was well and truly snared. All those death's heads and warnings on yellow flags and zombies wearing masks with elephant trunks. A little obvious, wasn't it, in retrospect?'

Denikin spoke almost perfect English learned when he worked at the Soviet Embassy in London in the good old days when spies outnumbered diplomats.

Blair said: 'So what's going to happen?'

They reached Arts Theatre Street. Blair had taken Barbara to the theatre to see *The Seagull* and there had been a seagull painted on the curtain.

178

'I will be reprimanded, held up as an example of an outdated spook trying to make mischief with our new allies, The West, then sent to a camp to make chessmen, castrated, executed...'

'You told them I worked for British intelligence?'

'I had no choice. And now I suspect you will be fed stories.'

'And if I don't file them I will be exposed as a former spy and expelled?'

'If I were given the job of handling such an exposure, I would leak it to your main rival newspaper.'

He told Barbara in Gorky Park the following day. Always parks; perhaps he had been born in one.

The ferris wheel carted lovers and children up to a prairie sky and down again. Soldiers and sailors paraded the tree-lined walks where in winter promenaders buckled on skates. Old men played chess and young men guitars. Balloons strained to join the clouds, vendors dispensed *kvas*, the juice of fermented bread. The River Moskva idled past and, in the distance, you could see Stalin's wedding cake palaces perched on the skyline.

'Who was that man?' she asked. She was wearing a yellow blouse with an extravagant collar that fluttered in a breeze that had found its way up the river; he would always remember that collar.

He had drunk a lot of wine at lunch and suddenly he wanted more than anything to tell her, to abandon his *alter ego* in this sunlit confessional.

'Last night?'

'Sure last night. The man who was so important that you abandoned me on our wedding anniversary.'

'Only for half an hour. I told you, he's a contact.' He had found in the past that half truths brought a little solace; not today.

He led her to an arbour near the boating lake and they sat on a sun-warmed bench. And then, with relief and astonishment, he listened to himself.

The approach by Lomax in Hyde Park...the sleeping years in Washington...the awakening in Moscow.

He paused as a flushed girl being chased by a soldier allowed herself to be caught in front of the arbour; the soldier squeezed her hips and she squealed happily. Barbara twisted the wedding ring on her finger.

He believed, he said, that he had done the right thing. Wouldn't every patriotic young Englishman have given his right arm—'His soul?' Barbara queried—to stop the communists taking over the world?

Guilt dripped from him like grease from

180

a lighted candle. Then she began to ask nibbling questions, often repetitious but sharp-toothed just the same.

Their posting to Washington. Whose doing was that? The newspaper or MI6?

'Both probably. Does it matter?'

It mattered, she said. 'And Moscow?'

'Likewise.'

He hunched his shoulders, spread his hands.

'So who was I married to, spook or scribe?'

'You married me, Frank Blair.'

'Or had you already been approached?'

'No, you've got to believe me.'

'Why should I? Our whole marriage has been a lie.'

There was an edge to the breeze now and the soldier's jackboots rang on the path.

'It's all over now.'

'Why should I believe that? Why should I believe anything? When we made love, who was I fucking?'

There was a salty timbre to her voice, words like unshed tears.

'Me,' he said.

'Who are you, Frank?'

'Me,' he said again.

'But who's me? Who was I married to?' She frowned. 'One of you could have told me.'

181

Lightning fizzed between storm clouds that had slyly gathered, thunder rumbled and fat drops of rain fell releasing the scent of dust. Families gathered themselves together and made for shelter. A lone guitarist continued to play.

Blair sat with his wife for a while until the collar of her yellow blouse lay down in the rain. Then they went home.

She screamed once that night.

After his wife left him and returned to Canada his coverage of the Russian scene deteriorated. He filed stories which were patently fabrications; he missed significant events covered by other correspondents. He began to drink heavily and was finally recalled to London. He returned to England via Japan and the United States with the intention of breaking his journey in Montreal to seek a reconciliation with his wife.

Just one more exclusive, Blair thought, so sensational that it will be picked up by the press, TV and radio from Boston to Bangkok. He would get hold of a copy and show her the front page. 'There, that's the Frank Blair you married. The spook is dead, dead, dead.' He took her in his arms and felt her warmth and his breathing quickened.

'Are you all right?' Tom Noland asked.

'I'm okay thanks.'

Then maybe a job as a roving correspondent, a house in the Cotswolds...

The train stopped at Zagorsk, seat of the Russian Orthodox Church, 73 kilometres out of Moscow. Blair could see the blue and gold domes of its cathedrals. He had driven here with Barbara in 1987 when Margaret Thatcher had lit a candle in the Cathedral of the Holy Trinity.

The train inched out of the station, picked up speed. Just one exclusive... Don't bullshit yourself, Frank, it's the vodka talking. An exclusive on a train passing through the infinite wilderness of the Sleeping Land? Fat chance.

When he turned his head away from the window he noticed another passenger sitting at a table across the aisle. His face was familiar. Blair tried to discipline his rioting thoughts.

Then he had it. A Chechen, a mafia godfather whom he had interviewed in Moscow. Now what was he doing on a train taking him far away from the battlefield of organised crime?

He saw recognition in the Chechen's eyes and a reflex reaction of wariness. His journalistic instincts stirred. He took the silver flask from his hip pocket, considered it for a moment, then replaced it without unscrewing the top.

Chapter Ten

November 30th. 19.10 hours.

Little Eagle pulled out of the railhead at Mirny five minutes after the Trans-Siberian left Yaroslav station. But in darkness because Mirny was five hours ahead of Moscow.

It had stopped snowing and stars sparkled through rents in the cloud but the snow that had already fallen lay thinly on the ground, there to stay.

On the footplate of the Skoda the driver, Ivan Chukovsky, stared malevolently at its console, wishing he was at the controls of a roaring-lunged 0-6-6-0 Mallet from the Putilov Works, one hand on the regulator, one eye on the water gauges and steam pressure indicators, accompanied by a stoker feeding the incandescent firebox, frying breakfast on a shovel on the coals...

Such camaraderie, such high adventure, the story of the Soviet Union written in steam—even the gauge, 5ft instead of 4ft 8½ in, introduced it was said to deter foreigners from nosing into its vast secret hinterland.

184

And here he was at the controls of a computer on wheels.

His co-driver, a thin young man with sleek hair who regarded old age as a terminal disease, rested his hand on the air brake. The lieutenant charged with shepherding the train to Moscow rested his hand on the holster of his pistol as though expecting trouble already.

Behind the Skoda the two armoured coaches, the first containing the diamonds, three Spetsnaz to each of them.

Cautiously *Little Eagle*, lit by a spotlight from a Mi-8 helicopter overhead, picked up speed on the virgin track which led first to Yakutsk, capital of the region, to the east, before striking south to the BAM railroad.

Chukovsky said: 'I remember the days—'

'Please don't,' the co-driver said. 'And keep your eye on the automatic warning system.'

'We didn't have those in the old days.'

'I know,' the co-driver said. 'You crashed instead.'

The lieutenant snapped: 'Shut up, both of you,' and peered anxiously through the bullet-proof windshield.

Scattered pines stuttered past on either side of the track like a reel of black and white film in the light from the Mi-8.

The lieutenant showed both drivers a

letter signed by the Minister of Defence. 'You must carry out Major Viktor Ruchkin's orders without question.'

'Who the hell's Major Ruchkin?' the co-driver asked.

'Military intelligence,' Chukovsky said importantly. 'I met him the other day.'

'I was told to answer only to the lieutenant.'

'I don't think you will argue with Major Ruchkin when you meet him, will he, lieutenant?'

'Only if you want to argue with the devil.'

A reindeer ran towards the track. Chukovsky took over the brake from the co-driver, clipping *Little Eagle's* wings, and the reindeer escaped into the *taiga*.

The train was beginning to pick up speed again when a red light appeared beyond the penumbra of the spotlight glittering like a shooting star that has fallen and is about to explode.

Chukovsky applied the brake again.

The train stopped and stood throbbing. The lieutenant opened the door and Ruchkin climbed on to the footplate. 'Gentlemen,' the lieutenant said, 'I want you to meet the devil.'

The lieutenant ordered the Spetsnaz out of the armoured coaches and Ruchkin's men, wearing combat uniforms and blue berets, moved in five to each coach.

When the lieutenant had gone the co-driver said: 'What's this all about?' He caught Ruchkin's gaze and began to wipe the spotless console with a rag.

Ruchkin said: 'It's none of your business but I suppose you're entitled to an explanation. GRU heard rumours that some of the soldiers guarding the diamonds were planning to steal them.'

'Spetsnaz? I can hardly believe it.'

Ruchkin warmed to him. 'These are hard times: they're only human.'

The unexpected glimpse of compassion encouraged the co-driver. 'And your men are incorruptible?'

'Absolutely. Hand picked.'

Chukovsky pointed at the Mi-8 hovering above the pines. 'What about that?'

'Already carrying my men,' Ruchkin told him. 'Also hand picked. Now let's get moving.'

Chukovsky engaged the power control on the console and *Litte Eagle* once again began to burrow through the night, animal eyes watching from the *taiga*, guardian angel clattering above.

The Israeli hit team left Tel Aviv's Ben Gurion airport at different times that day, three parties each with a destination served by Afghanistan's Ariana airline.

Mikhail Sapir flew to Rome with the pilot, a demolition expert, a medic, a marksman and the Russian railroad expert Pavel Shapiro. Not, thank God, with Rachel Wolf.

They were all Americans, passports to prove it, and if some of their accents were peculiar then, boy, you should hear some of the New York cab drivers—Sapir's explanation if they were challenged. They carried expensive bags and wore blazers and slacks and lightweight suits, and if they looked ill at ease in them then it was the fault of a tailor in Damascus where they had also been talking peace.

At the airport in Rome they split to avoid drawing attention to themselves among the stylish Italians and wealthy tourists.

They boarded the blue and white Ariana jet at 16.55 and took off on time at 17.10. They flew non-stop to Delhi, then north-west to Kabul arriving at 09.45 the following morning, three-quarters of an hour late. They waited in the arrival lounge for the other two parties to join them, one from Prague, one from Teheran.

From time to time Afghan officials wearing conference identity buttons approached, offering to take them to their hotel, but Sapir told them that they were awaiting colleagues. 'Men of peace, like us.' From the city of Kabul came the rattle of small arms fire as the feuding factions within Afghanistan fought it out.

Turkomen from the north wearing little beaded hats and carrying carpets wandered by. Veiled women walking with slumbrous grace; a Pathan with bright blue eyes; young bloods assessing the talent; two Pakistani businessmen wearing identical silk suits, grey flecked with black; a leper with a clubbed stump instead of a hand.

A young Afghan wearing a turban, a scar reaching from his downy beard to one eye, approached Sapir. 'I am your driver, Haji,' he said. 'Your guide and your protector. You have the diamonds?'

'You'll get them when the others arrive,' Sapir said.

'I'll be waiting outside,' the Afghan said. 'I have a message for you from Tel Aviv via Islamabad. I don't understand it.'

Sapir sat down and decoded it. He smiled. Thank God the Afghan hadn't understood it.

The second party arrived from Teheran. There were now thirteen of them including a radio operator. Rachel Wolf's squad from Prague was due in half an hour.

An hour later it hadn't arrived. DE-LAYED, according to the casually enigmatic parlance of all flight information. Whether an aircraft hadn't taken off, whether its bones were scattered over the desert, it was DELAYED.

Sapir began to worry.

Another half hour.

He went to the information desk. It was DELAYED. A weary official punched buttons and a message on a screen confirmed his prognosis.

The clerk said: 'There's a flight just landed from Warsaw,' as though that might appease the irritating interrogator.

Sapir waited in front of the exit from customs in case Rachel's flight plans had been changed. There was always one passenger who swept out well ahead of the others and this time it was a man in his thirties, an Italian by the look of him, with razored features and a cleft in his chin.

To Sapir's surprise he made straight for him. 'Mikhail Sapir? I recognised you from your description. My name's Loder.'

They sat at a small table and drank black tea, interrupted from time to time by flight announcements. The quality was bad, like a mountain echo, and Sapir listened for one word. Prague.

He said: 'I've heard of you,' touching the angry scar on the side of his head as though Loder had inflicted it. 'I know a girl, Rachel Wolf. Her father was ruined by the Syndicate.'

'I'm sorry,' Loder said. 'But they got greedy in Ramat Gan.'

'He was an old man, a Russian. He had campaigned all his life to come to the Holy Land, the Promised Land.'

'Then he should have blamed the guys who should have known better.'

'What are you doing here?' Sapir asked, sipping the sweet, inky tea.

'Going with you,' Loder said.

'Like hell you are!'

'I know diamonds: you need me.'

'Forget it,' Sapir said.

'Aren't *you* forgetting something? Those diamonds belong to us.'

'I don't give a shit who they belong to.'

'Then you should. You really should.'

Another reverberating flight announcement. Prague. Sapir strode across the lounge to the information desk. 'What did it say?' he asked the fatigued clerk.

'It said the flight from Prague was delayed.'

'Is it airborne?'

'Delayed is all I can tell you.'

When he got back to the table Loder, wearing a blue mohair suit, pale blue shirt and black knitted tie, seemed to have consolidated his case, like an attorney after an adjournment.

He said: 'You're going to take me on

that plane. Or else—'

'This is an Israeli operation. No place for a gangster.'

'You're all fucking gangsters,' Loder said.

'But not thieves.'

'Ah, Mossad's been busy, busy. Turning up juvenile crime records?'

'You're not coming with us,' Sapir said.

'Know something? That's really funny, because it was me who put you up for the job. Now you listen to me. You're in this because Israel needs diamonds, right? Well, have I got news for you: if I don't fly to Russia it won't get anymore because the Syndicate will cut off its supplies.'

Sapir must have missed an announcement because suddenly there was Rachel Wolf emerging from customs.

'Let's see what that lady thinks,' Sapir said. 'Because she thinks you're an even bigger asshole than I do.'

Although the diamonds were being transported across Siberia, the first warning shot in Operation Orloff was fired in Belgium, in Antwerp, diamond capital of the world. By Harry Sampson.

He arrived at Deurne airport at 0740 on British Airways flight BA8012 and, such was his renown in Rubens' home town, was untroubled by formalities. Which was

192

convenient because one of the three rough diamonds given to him by Viktor Ruchkin in Moscow nestled in a pouch in his ostrich-skin shoulder bag.

A black Mercedes with smoked windows took him to the Eden Hotel in the centre of the diamond district. The driver, young with hair too long for his peaked cap, pointed out Gothic churches and fourteenth-century merchants' houses and, after a while, Sampson told him to keep quiet: when a life's crusade is drawing to a climax Rubens and Breughel can be a pain.

All his working life Sampson had fought the Syndicate.

By the late-50s he was the biggest wholesaler and retailer in the US and was reluctantly allotted the largest package of roughs at the sights in London. What he really wanted was his own mine, a source from which to circumvent the Syndicate's monopoly, and when a strike was confirmed in Tanzania, within British Commonwealth, he tried to buy the concession from the prospector. But at the behest of the Syndicate, the British Government threatened to nationalise the mine and the prospector capitulated and sold out to the Syndicate.

When another mine came up for grabs in Angola, the then Portuguese possession in West Africa, he outbid the Syndicate with dollars instead of pounds sterling. But his contact in Lisbon died suddenly, the Portuguese expelled Harry and the Syndicate warned that if he continued to flout them they would cut of all his sights.

Why had he been thrown out of Portugal? The answer, he discovered later, was port wine. The British Government which had a cosy relationship with the Syndicate had threatened to stop importing port if the Portuguese allowed Sampson to buy a mine.

When he personally went mine-hunting in West Africa the Syndicate offered him 20 per cent of all alluvial diamonds harvested from the coastal strip, the *Sperrengbeit,* the forbidden zone of what was then South West Africa, now Namibia. Sampson decided to take their diamonds and secretly continue the vendetta.

What he did was make overtures to the Russians. Now those overtures had suddenly come good and he was in a position to devastate the Syndicate. Cutting his own throat? Not if the market heard about the Russian threat—which was why he was in Antwerp—and prices slumped, because he would be in a position to buy at knock-down prices and sell high if the Syndicate bowed to blackmail. Meanwhile he would buy emeralds, sapphires and rubies in case the Russians did flood the market.

Whatever, he had a third option. As the Mercedes pulled up outside the Eden a smile crossed his face and he drummed his small, ringless fingers on the leather upholstery.

After freshening up in the hotel room he walked along the nondescript Pelikaanstraat to number 62, the aloof block housing the Diamond Club, and took an elevator to the offices of a broker who specialised in hot stones from Ghana, Sierra Leone, Tanzania, Angola—and Russia.

The broker, plump and sandy with a bank cashier's downward gaze, acting like a peasant visited by royalty, ushered Sampson to a chair on the other side of a desk scattered with the tools of his trade—two loupes, one with a magnification of ten, the other eight, tweezers, Diamondite light box.

Sampson waited for him to say: 'To what do I owe this honour?' but instead he said: 'Can I get you anything?' Sampson asked for a glass of iced water, took the pouch out of his pocket, held the diamond between thumb and forefinger, and said: 'I want you to sell this.'

The broker made a one-act play of examining the stone through one of the loupes but didn't over-react. Good boy, Sampson thought. A pro. 'Russian?'

'As Beluga caviar,' Sampson said.

The broker weighed it in his hand. 'Thirty carats?'

'Close.'

'What sort of price were you thinking of, Mr Sampson?'

'Fifty thousand dollars.'

For the first time the broker showed emotion, holding his second chin as though it belonged to someone else. 'But it's worth—'

'I'm asking chicken-shit, I know that. But 50 grand, no more, is the price. And you can take your brokerage from whatever you think it should have fetched. Within reason,' he added.

'I don't understand, Mr Sampson.'

'You don't have to. Just do it, okay?'

'If you say so.' The broker peered at the diamond again through the loupe in case it was a fake. 'Now? It won't be difficult.'

'Sooner,' Sampson said. 'With one stipulation.'

'Ah.' The broker leaned forward, after-shave smelling like scented sweat.

'You've got to say it's Harry Sampson selling. You've got to remind buyers that Harry Sampson works closely with the Russians, that he knows a thing or two.

You've got to say he couldn't get rid of the stone quick enough because there are more, lots more, where that's coming from. Shout it from the rooftops. "The Russians are coming." '

The broker felt for the freckles on the sandy shallows of his hairline. 'Is it true? Or are you manipulating the market?'

'What should *you* do? Is what you mean? Well, you can't go wrong with emeralds, symbol of immortality. Unless they change colour which means you've been unfaithful and your old lady hits you with a baseball bat. Are you married?'

The broker said he was.

'Then stay with diamonds,' Sampson said.

They walked along a white and silver corridor and took the elevator to the bourse on the ground floor.

The dealers sat opposite each other at long tables placed at right angles to tall windows facing north to catch the best light. They looked as if they were playing checkers, but the pieces were gemstones and they were examining them for the four Cs, clarity, colour, cut and carat weight, on folded sheets of paper, some lined with pale blue for brilliant cuts, others black for rose cuts.

The dealers agreed on a price and the

day of payment, sealed the diamonds and took them to the bourse office where they were weighed and placed in a sealed envelope with the date and weight written on it. If a purchaser defaulted then the case was considered by the Board of Arbitrators. Ignore their finding and you were thrown out of the world federation and your name was displayed in every bourse and diamond club in the world—London, New York, South Africa, Amsterdam, Tel Aviv, Milan, Vienna, Paris.

Dealers stared speculatively at Sampson. Why was the king mixing with his subjects? Sampson saw them talking among themselves and approved.

The broker sold the Russian rough immediately, first come first served. Fifty thousand dollars. Observing the stone's brilliance—life and fire—shining from a window bruted on the surface, Sampson felt momentarily grieved.

Other dealers gathered round the lucky buyer. Sampson heard his name mentioned, fielded puzzled glances. Dealers headed for phone, fax and teleprinter.

One of them with a bald patch like a skull cap approached him. 'Mr Sampson,' he said, 'to what do we owe this honour?'

'You know what—I just sold a diamond.'

'For peanuts, if I may say so, Mr Sampson. Is there any ulterior motive?'

'Fifty thousand bucks *was* the ulterior motive.'

'You could have got more. Much, much more.'

'Mr—'

'Kochan.'

'When a deluge is threatened, what do you do, Mr Kochan?'

'Find a roof?'

'What you do, Mr Kochan, is sell umbrellas. Quickly and cheaply.'

The chairman of the Syndicate heard about the sale 30 minutes later, just before he was due to leave his office for Heathrow to catch a South African Airways flight to Johannesburg.

His brisk, grey-haired secretary who, according to his wife, had been in love with him for 40 years, placed a message from his personal fax machine on his desk. It was from the chief executive of their Antwerp operation.

A Russian diamond, a pure regular octahedra, 32.8 carats, second colour, has just been sold in the bourse for a mere 50,000 dollars. Vendor: Harry Sampson who has intimated that there may be many more where that came from. The market is currently holding firm but in a state of shock. I will keep you informed as reactions become clearer.

So it has begun, the chairman thought.

He summoned Cronin on the house phone. The head of security, face as bleak as moorland, sat facing him—and his father's patrician in oils.

The chairman said: 'The latest, Mr Cronin?'

'The Israelis have arrived at Kabul.'

'Loder?'

'No word, sir.'

The chairman felt a jab of pain in his chest. He took a tablet from a small gold box he kept in his waistcoat pocket and swallowed it with a glass of water.

'How much time do we have before this...this act of piracy on the steppe?'

'About 85 hours, give or take.'

'Tell me one thing, Mr Cronin. Have you any idea how the Israelis plan to get the diamonds *out* of Russia?'

'The Israelis will think of something, sir.'

'Hardly a satisfactory answer, Mr Cronin. Keep me in touch.'

The chairman summoned the director of the trading subsidiary. He looked as always as though he had just emerged, too closely shaved, from the shower.

The chairman said: 'Are we winning?'

'Up to a point, sir. The Americans are willing to go along with the bluff—the president apparently favours a little clandestine derring-do.'

'Perhaps that's why he's always smiling.'

'The British, Dutch and the Belgians too. And South Africa...'

'We *are* South Africa,' the chairman said.

'The World Bank, dodgy... Well, they would be, wouldn't they? But other banks are prepared to confirm that we are trying to get the money together. Banks dealing with jewellers, cutters, bullion dealers, all associated interests...'

'Swiss Banks?'

'Two of them,' the director said. 'Or so they led me to believe. You know how they are.'

'The Bank of England?'

'All that gold in their vaults? If diamonds become worthless then the public will ask "What about gold?" No, they will persuade themselves that it's the decent, sterling thing to do.' The director rubbed one polished cheek. 'Our greatest hazard is the Russians' new deadline for the first instalment. Five billion dollars in two days, midday on December 2nd as proof of good faith.'

'Show willingness, ask for an extension. Until we know whether we've won or lost. Have you been in touch with the Minister of Defence?'

'With an aide who has been sworn to secrecy. The Minister is getting...edgy.'

'Old soldiers often do, shaky trigger fingers.'

Another jab of pain but less vivid this time.

'I've been thinking, sir. Maybe we should do a deal, make them an offer.'

'Call their bluff was what you said.'

'If Loder and the Israelis don't pull this off, if they realise we've been deceiving them, they'll go right ahead and dump 50 billion dollars worth of diamonds on the market and we'll be finished.'

The chairman regarded him shrewdly, felt his father behind him doing the same. 'Someone been getting at you? A call from Johannesburg?' He shook his head. 'You must never give in to blackmail: it's a recurring disease.'

When the director had gone the chairman waited for another message from his heart but it was quiet now.

His secretary knocked at the door and when she entered he knew from her expression that he was about to be censured.

'I've got your tickets,' she said. 'But I don't think you should go.'

'I have to, you know that. I've got to talk to the other directors, my son...I'll be back soon.'

'Too much flying,' she said. 'At your age. You know what the doctor said.'

He stood up, walked round the desk, put his arm round her thin shoulders. 'Put it this way. My life has been the company. If the company goes under then my life has meant nothing.'

'It's your life I'm worried about.'

'But it has to have meaning.'

He kissed her on both cheeks. Awkwardly because he had never done it before. She turned and strode out of the office and he knew that she was crying.

Married to two wives for 40 years! He looked at his father and could have sworn that he winked. It must be the pill. He picked up the phone, called the car pool and told his driver to take him to Heathrow.

While the chairman was on his way to the airport *Little Eagle* was pulling out of Yakutsk, striking south towards the BAM railroad which joined the Trans-Siberian at Tayshet, 1,180 kilometres east of Novosibirsk, overall a two-day haul.

Sapir and the Israelis were leaving Kabul in a Zil 131 truck to take them to the far north of Afghanistan where, hopefully, an airworthy Antonov 12 was waiting for them, two days overall to the Novosibirsk region.

The Trans-Siberian was approaching Danilov, 357 kilometres east of Moscow—

two days to Novosibirsk. Unless anything unforeseen occurred. With a Chechen godfather on board, Frank Blair thought, anything was possible.

Chapter Eleven

The names of birds reached Blair like the distant beat of wings. Rubythroat, lammergeier—'Bearded vulture, that is'— Baikal teal...

'A stupid wager,' Tom Noland said. 'But Helen would have approved.'

'Wager?'

'You haven't been listening.'

They were sitting on snap-down seats in the broad corridor of the soft-class coach of the Trans-Siberian where, when they weren't eating, drinking or sleeping, passengers socialised. Through the parted curtains Blair saw a girl wearing a yellow scarf standing beside a duck pond tissued with ice. She waved and Blair waved back.

'Sorry,' he said. 'Miles away. You have to spot three birds, right?'

'I made the bet over a pint of bitter in the Spaniards. That's a pub on Hampstead Heath. With Harry Cardoza and Sydney

Collet who reckoned he had spotted a Tennessee Warbler in the Lake District. The bet grew from that.'

'You came all the way to Siberia to see three birds?'

'Harry Cardoza had been everywhere and he asked where I was going for my holiday. Out of perversity I said Siberia because, you know, I haven't been anywhere really, although Helen and I promised ourselves...'

'Helen?'

Blair was thinking about the Chechen godfather and Tom Noland at the same time. Perhaps he was a schizophrenic as well as a drunk.

'My wife. We always said we'd travel when I retired from the office of the Comptroller and City Solicitor. We used to talk about the various places we'd go to, Siberia was one of them...'

'I remember an evening in The Chine in Muswell Hill, little gardens, you know. On either side men were watering borders that seemed to have been picked from colour magazines. The TV was going, a newscaster addressing an empty room, and I could smell the scents from Helen's herb garden—rosemary, marjoram, curry plant, Sweet Cicely...

'She was reading a book. *Gorky Park* by Martin Cruz Smith, I think it was. She said, "You can feel Russia. Taste it".

' "Then we'll go there, one day," I said. "To Siberia. Would you like that duchess"—I always called her that—"I could take early retirement. The world will be our oyster."

'And she said, "I'll hold you to it," but she was pretending because she knew she had only a year at the most to go. Eight months, as it turned out.

'But I always remember her saying, "I want to see the real Russia. Not spies and stone-faced bureaucrats and May Day Parades. Siberia," she said, "yes, that's where we'll go." So when the wager was struck I leaped at it. One hundred pounds to the Royal Society for the Protection of Birds. Paid by Harry and Syd if I spotted the three birds. Paid by me if I didn't. I got a suitcase from the loft and there were still brochures in it from Intourist that Helen and I had picked up.'

'Let's hope Harry—Cardoza, was it?—and Sydney Collet have to pay up.'

Tom Noland, fringe of pale hair dropping over his forehead, said: 'Would you like a glass of tea?'

'I would like nothing better,' Blair said, feeling the vodka-filled flask in his pocket.

He watched Noland walk down the corridor to the *provodnik* serving lemon tea from a coal-fired samovar. Her green eyes were moist and, as she poured tea, she stared through the windows into the *taiga*, searching for lost love.

When Noland returned Blair said: 'What did your wife look like?'

'She was a Viking,' Noland said.

'I thought as much: she would have been proud of you.'

'You really think so?'

'Let's keep a weather eye open for a rubythroat,' Blair said. And a Chechen godfather, he thought.

In the sleeper, while Noland talked to the green-eyed *provodnik*, Blair, lying on the lower of the two berths, made notes about the Trans-Siberian to accompany any story he might write.

...easy staring out of the window to imagine mounted cossacks observing the train from the steppe...while American pioneers thrust west, Russians pushed east...all began in the sixteenth century when Yermak, a cossack, began to colonise in exchange for a pardon for his crimes...successors occupied Alaska, tunnel under Bering Strait considered, Soviet Union linked with United States, no Cold War?...exiles and chain gangs...penal camps...the taiga *where in the east tigers are still said to roam...*

Noland came in and lay on the upper bunk. 'Charming girl,' he said. 'But very sad. I wonder why?'

'Ask her,' Blair said. 'God gave you an inquiring mind: exercise it. That's what my first editor used to say.'

'What paper was that?'

'The *Dartmouth Chronicle*,' Blair told him and began to write again.

...the new Siberia...heated towns built to excavate the riches of the Sleeping Land, gold, silver, coal, uranium, oil, diamonds...10 million square metres traversed by the Trans-Siberian...

The Trans-Siberian first proposed by an American, Perry McDonough Collins... British -built ferry assembled from 7,000 parts to cross Lake Baikal...permafrost, scurvy, floods—wall of water swept away track in Yablonovy mountains...one strip 67 kms. dynamited, 50 wooden bridges on it... Chinese coolies eaten by Manchurian tigers...

'Dartmouth,' Noland was saying. 'I once spotted an Eskimow curlew there, *Numenius borealis*, but no one believed me.'

'I believe you,' Blair said.

'I don't think the Baikal teal will be too difficult, not when we get to the lake. It's the lammergeier that worries me. You see, its habitat is really a little to the south. Although they are found in the Altai Mountains... Did you know they drop bones on to rocks to break them and get at the marrow?'

Blair didn't. Why didn't Noland go into the corridor in case one was poised to drop a bone beside the track? he asked.

'I read once that there are 750 species of birds that never nest outside the Soviet Union.'

'I wonder if they know it doesn't exist anymore?' Blair said.

He swung his legs off the bunk and peered through the double-glazed windows. Sunlight splintered on patterns of frost, ferns and palms. Through them he could make out a parade ground of plastic-covered green-houses, a cluster of pink and blue *izbas*, wooden cottages with fretted eaves as delicate as lace.

He glanced at his watch. Midday local time, confusing because the Trans-Siberian kept Moscow time for the whole journey. In 36 minutes they would stop for 12 minutes at Perm where the Great Siberian Post Road, a rutted track, had once started.

He and Barbara had once stayed overnight there. He remembered joking about the British cyclist, R.L Jefferson, who in the 1890s cycled from London to Perm and onwards on an Imperial Rover wearing Jaeger cellular underclothes and carrying infinite supplies of Bovril. He found that he was smiling. Sharing was everything. The smile spent itself.

A knock on the door. He opened it. The

provodnik. A message from the Chechen. Could they meet in the first of the hard-class coaches in ten minutes? Blair's journalistic reflexes quivered. Why not here? he wondered. But to a Caucasian— Armenian, Georgian, Chechen—intrigue is normality.

As he made his way down the corridor he heard Noland ask: 'Is there anything troubling you?' and heard the girl launch enthusiastically into an explanation.

He passed through the dining car, tables and red seats between transparent plastic screens colonised by Australians and Japanese, danced with a waiter carrying a tray of beef Strogonov, and entered the video coach where *The Sound of Music* was playing.

He was stopped at the swaying connection to hard class by a woman with arms as thick as legs wearing a pink blouse and a blue skirt tight across sandbag buttocks.

'Only hard-class passengers.' She wrestled her arms together.

Blair gave her 10 US dollars. She untangled her arms and spirited him past her defences. Into a commune. Bunks stacked on both sides, laundry hanging between them, babies crawling among husks of sunflower seeds unshaven troubadors, assassins every one, playing guitars and singing wistfully. Families eating black bread, onions, dried fish and pickled mushrooms on sheets of newspaper...stout women cuddling autumn-leaf babushkas...men becalmed over the black and white battlefields of chess.

No sign of the Chechen.

Blair made his way to the end of the carriage where he was stopped by a giant with Eskimo eyes. 'Who are you looking for, comrade?'

When Blair told him he took his arm and piloted him through the door. His fingers bit into Blair's bicep. No going back, the fingers said.

The train whooshed through a tunnel.

The giant knocked three times on the door of the toilet with a fist like a mallet. The door opened and he pushed Blair into the presence of the Chechen. The giant stood behind them.

The Chechen said: 'We meet again, Mr Blair. With a difference. This time I'm asking the questions.' His voice was surprisingly soft. 'What are you doing on this train, Comrade Blair?'

'Going home,' he said.

'To England? Via Siberia?'

'Stopping off in Canada. To see my wife,' he added.

'You could have flown.'

'I like trains. Memories...'

'I think you're lying.' The Chechen took

a knife from his belt. 'Have you had a tip, a big news story ahead?'

'You mean, there is one?'

'I think you know, Comrade Blair.'

'Not until now I didn't.'

The Chechen lunged. The point of his knife pricked Blair's throat. Blair put a finger to his throat. It came away wet and red.

'The truth, comrade...'

'A last story? Nothing would give me greater pleasure.'

The blood cooled on his finger. He was scared but it wasn't the ultimate fear of death: he had already encountered that.

The Chechen said: 'Why do you think I'm on the train?'

'Like all of us, going somewhere.'

The Chechen nodded at the giant.

He hit Blair in the kidney with the blades of both hands. Blair felt fluid spurt inside him. It burned like acid.

The Chechen said: 'Why are *you* on this train?'

'I told you.'

A knee in his back, hands on his shoulders, pulling back. He waited for his spine to snap.

The Chechen nodded again.

The giant released Blair.

He caught sight of himself in the mottled mirror behind the Chechen. There was dirty sweat on his forehead as though the silver tracks in his hair had been bled of pigment; the shadows beneath his eyes slipped over his cheekbones.

The Chechen said: 'For the last time.'

'I'm on my way home,' Blair said.

The Chechen tested the blade of the knife with his finger. 'I almost believe you. In any case, who wants a corpse?' He looked over Blair's shoulder. 'No stories, no communication with your office, nothing. Do you understand?'

Blair said he understood.

'Just in case you don't...' The giant's hands hit Blair in the back simultaneously just below the ribs. Another spurt of acid. He could taste it.

The Chechen nodded at the giant. Two kicks into Blair's calves that made him bend as though he had been tripped.

As the door burst open.

Blair saw it in the speckled mirror. Saw the giant lurch. Saw Tom Noland peering into the toilet, saw the green-eyed *provodnik* behind him.

Noland was babbling: 'I've seen it.'

'Seen what?'

'A rubythroat,' Noland said. 'In a thicket beside the track. Just asking to be spotted.'

They drank Narzan mineral water in the restaurant car.

'Did you really see a rubythroat?' Blair asked.

'Bird spotters don't lie,' Noland protested. 'Although I was never too sure about Syd Collet's Tennessee Warbler in the Lake District...'

'So why come bursting into a toilet to tell me?'

'Lidiya—that's the girl at the samovar—said she thought the Chechen was carrying a knife. A flash of metal in his belt.'

'So how did you get past the female at the door to hard class?'

'Lidiya knows her.' Noland sipped his fizzy water. 'What did they want, those two men?'

'They want to stop me sending a story to my newspaper. The trouble is, I don't know what the story is.'

The train slowed at the approaches to Perm, 1906 kilometres from Novosibirsk.

Chapter Twelve

Little Eagle took the thin bridge carefully. Below a modest river poised to freeze oozed south. Above the helicopter banked playfully in the sunshine, its pilot a restless young Tartar.

Ruchkin, standing on the footplate, felt the bridge sway—there hadn't been time to check the line—and told Chukovsky to accelerate. The driver made a marginal adjustment. Something would have to be done about Chukovsky, Ruchkin decided.

A length of metal detached itself from the overhead span and fell lazily into the water.

When the train reached the far bank Ruchkin relaxed. Bonnets of snow sparkled on pine, birch, larch and spruce. Eagles searching for prey floated in the blue sky.

As the train nosed south history tapped Ruchkin on the shoulder. He heard the snap of the *plet,* the three-tailed lash, threatening convicts labouring on the Trans-Siberian; the chatter of machine guns as the Czech Legion on board *Little Eagle* chopped down Bolsheviks who believed the Czechs were being used as a pretext for an Allied invasion of Siberia after World War I.

The train rounded a bend, needle-bright track leading to a village of wooden, gingerbread cottages silhouetted on a rise in the taiga. The village had been discovered by the new railroaders and bared like a colony of insects hiding beneath weed. It was said to have been five years before the inhabitants, Yakuts, had realised that the Great Patriotic War had ended: Ruchkin doubted whether they had ever known it had started.

The Yakuts gathered round the train and the children touched the flanks of the Skoda, snatching away their hands when they felt its body heat. The helicopter settled beside the track, a weary insect, its blades dispatching miniature blizzards of snow into the forest.

Ruchkin approached the headman. He wore felt boots, a grimy sheepskin coat and a moth-eaten sable *shapka*.

Ruchkin asked in Yakut if they could have tea. He offered dollars or roubles. The headman said they would prefer bullets and took Ruchkin on a tour of the village built round a pump. Regulation geese slapped their feet on a frozen pond; wild horses stood in a paddock daring the Yakuts, famous riders, to break them in; faces peered from behind lace curtains like nosey neighbours.

The headman led them into a hall carpeted with skins. They ate buckwheat porridge and hunks of bread, washed down with scalding tea served from a samovar by a shyly flirtatious girl.

Accompanied by the pilot, the restless Tartar who should have been born a bird, Ruchkin walked to the Mi-8 and radioed the Minister of Defence's aide in Moscow.

When he removed the earphones the pilot looked at him quizzically. 'What's the matter?'

'Why do you ask?'

'Your eyes...they're glittering.'

Ruchkin said: 'Unconfirmed reports from the GRU that members of a crack Israeli paratroop unit have left Tel Aviv.'

'I'm sure they do it all the time.'

'GRU asked their informant in Mossad to find out why those particular men had been chosen.'

'And?'

'They're all Russian,' Ruchkin said.

The train crossed another river. Fifty-three thousand rivers in Siberia, he had learned at school. A million lakes. Who counted?

Israelis! Could they possibly be planning a raid into Russian territory?

Who, South Africa apart, stood to lose most if diamonds became worthless? Certainly the Israelis were up there among the front runners. Who would be asked to make one of the biggest contributions to the ransom demand? Well, the Jews *were* diamonds.

Incredible. Israelis versus Spetsnaz. If it were true, and Ruchkin couldn't quite believe it was.

Circumspectly he approached the question that had been flitting behind his deliberation.

If it were true, who would lead the Israelis?

Silently he mouthed the name.

The final encounter...

Get smart, Viktor Ruchkin. You've already left a day early. He thought with Mikhail Sapir's brain. Shook his head, watched curiously by Chukovsky. No, Sapir wouldn't have been deceived by the false information transmitted by the floor manager at No 3 Diamond Factory. A day *early*, that's how he would have interpreted it.

Little Eagle flew across a bridge spanning a gorge.

So what I have to do is throw my timetable so that the Israelis cannot anticipate accurately my ETA at any given point.

The factor that dictated the progress of the train into western Siberia and beyond to Moscow was the engine change at Novosibirsk.

He said to Chukovsky: 'Change of plan, old timer. We're not going to stop at Novosibirsk.'

'We have to,' Chukovsky said, peering down the track as though an iron horse breathing steam might materialise.

'Adapt, Chukovsky. That's the secret of staying young.'

'*Little Eagle* won't stay young if we don't

change engines: she'll die.'

'Bullshit, Chukovsky. It's habit that kills people. Drive through Novosibirsk like a bat out of hell.'

'Sorry, major, it can't be done. With a head of steam maybe...'

'Chukovsky...'

'Major?'

'I'm relieving you of your command. As from now your co-driver is in charge.'

Ruchkin went to the first of the two armoured coaches where the co-driver was sleeping. He woke him. 'Any problem going through Novosibirsk without stopping?'

The co-driver blinked his way out of a dream. 'Not as long as we radio ahead.'

'Okay, you're in charge as from now.'

Where was it that Chukovsky had anticipated an attack, based on historical repetition?

Naked Boy Halt.

Ruchkin returned to the footplate and stared down the track disappearing beneath the wheels of *Little Eagle*.

Six thousand kilometres to the south-west the truck carrying the Israeli hit team began to crawl up the shell-pocked side of a mountain in the Hindu Kush in Afghanistan.

Rachel Wolf had agreed with Sapir that Loder could accompany them—'The bastard gives us no choice'—and he sat in the cabin beside the Mujahideen guerrilla, Haji. The rest of them huddled in the back.

Before departing Haji had warned them: 'We have to be very diplomatic... We are Moslems, you are Jews. But after what the Russians did to us we hate them so much that anything is possible. In my village the Mujahideen operated from underground tunnels. Spetsnaz found the tunnels, pumped gas into them and exploded it. All that was left of my brother was a ring on his finger.' He turned to Sapir. 'How do I know your diamonds are genuine?'

'You don't. But we're coming back this way and we would be stupid if we deceived you.'

A lie!

At first the truck took the road that had been used by the Russians entering and leaving Afghanistan. According to Haji, they could come under fire at any time—from Mujahideen or government troops. 'The situation is very confused.'

Thirty miles north of Kabul the truck swung on to a dirt track and began to bounce higher into the mountains, their fangs snagging motionless clouds.

In the back of the truck Sapir briefed the Israelis, still incongruously wearing city slicker clothes although they had ripped off their ties as if they were throttling them. Rachel Wolf wore a green lightweight suit with brass buttons.

'From the Afghan border we fly north-east to Novosibirsk, 2,200 kilometres away. Visibility is bad, we're in a Russian plane, the pilot speaks Russian and we've got a call sign.'

'What is it?' the pilot asked. 'Diamond?'

'Falcon,' Sapir told him. 'Those of us who are parachuting will drop at Naked Boy Halt, 50 Kilometres west of Novosibirsk. The An-12 with the rest of you on board will put down at the strip half way between the halt and the city.'

'Supposing it's snowbound?' Rachel Wolf said. 'That's the reason why they're transporting the diamonds by rail—in case the airports get socked down with snow.'

'An Antonov-12 can land on a snow cap. Right?' he asked the pilot.

'Right. The problem is getting it off again.'

'We've got more information about the strip. It's only used in emergencies but, for that reason, it will have adequate back-up—fuel and transport. You,' to Rachel Wolf, 'will make your way to the railroad control centre in Novosibirsk in the ambulance. Who challenges an ambulance?'

221

Rachel said: 'Luckily the control room is to the west of the city centre by the main station, at the junction of Cheluskintsev and Vokzalnaya.'

'There shouldn't be any problem there,' Sapir said. 'You'll be wearing Russian combat uniforms and there are plenty of soldiers in Novosibirsk—it's the GHQ of the Siberia military district.'

'And I was born there,' Rachel said. 'And I speak two Siberian languages.'

'Russian would have been enough,' Sapir said.

'If you want to be accepted, go native. Once inside the control centre we hold it at gunpoint and throw the points so that the armoured train diverts on to the feeder line leading to Naked Boy Halt.'

'You will also activate the current,' Sapir said. 'Overpower the staff and get out quickly. We will blow a pylon, stop the armoured train—and take it out.'

'And then?' The voice of Shapiro, the red-haired son of the former controller at Irkutsk.

'Get back to the airstrip in the ambulance.'

The pilot said: 'So now we have to get 50 billion dollars worth of diamonds *out* of Russia. Has Tel Aviv come up with anything?'

'I received a message in Kabul.'

'What do we do, bury them?'

'According to the satellite pictures the chopper is still parked at the end of the runway, presumably serviceable. You fly to Naked Boy Halt, pick us up and fly back to the strip.'

'And then we all climb into the old An-12 and fly back to sunny Afghanistan? Of course the Russians won't have been alerted by the capture of a rail control centre, a missing armoured train... Stupid, aren't they?'

Sapir said: 'Forget Afghanistan.'

He heard their breathing quicken. Lowered his voice. 'Mossad has identified the aircraft at the end of the strip beside the chopper. It's an Ilyushin-76.'

'So?'

'Even when the Soviet Union and China were at each other's throats Ilyushins were built in China under a licence granted before 1960.'

'Il-28s,' the pilot said.

'And later Il-76s,' Sapir said.

'This has got Chinese markings?'

'According to Mossad. And the Chinese border is only 700 kilometres from Novosibirsk. So that's where we're going,' Sapir said. 'To sunny China.'

From Johannesburg the chairman and the director of the subsidiary flew to Kimberley in a company jet. The chairman's son picked them up in a Range Rover at B.J Vorster airport seven miles outside the town.

The sun was high in the summer sky and in its heat the weary chairman fancied he saw mirages of history.

Rhodes directing Kimberley's defences when the Boers laid siege to it in 1899...diggers' camps mushrooming after the first diamond strike in 1870—3,600 claims in the area by 1872...Rhodes and Barnato, battling it out for control of the mines...

More and more that was what Kimberley was—a museum. The mines were becoming exhausted and its only claim to recognition in the 1990s was the company's tall tinted-glass sorting office in the centre of town.

Here all the diamonds from South Africa and Namibia were roughly classified by machines before being X-rayed for colour and checked by sorters.

Cronin had always considered the offices to be the weak link in the company's security operation. All that crystalline wealth concentrated in one building— 5,400,000 carats dispatched in a single consignment to London.

Accordingly he had installed computers which reacted to any weight loss at any time during the whole sorting process and triggered alarms. And you couldn't leave the building until the loss was made up: the computer wouldn't let you.

Ironic that the weak link was now somewhere in the wastes of Siberia.

His son, built like a tennis player but balding a little now—the chairman could never think of him as middle-aged—negotiated the streets of the town which still followed the outlines of the old mining claims and turned into the drive of his fine old mansion.

A *brasi*, a barbecue, was being prepared in the garden and all the top executives of the company and its associate companies were drinking cold beers at a table beneath a false pepper tree.

His son, groomed to take over the reins of the parent company, offered his father a beer but the chairman asked for water and sipped it beside a fountain flanked by red and orange canna lilies.

What did these men really think of him? A dictator who had grown too old to exercise power? Had they practised the manipulative arts for so long that they could not recognise the need for a gamble when it arose?

Rhodes would have recognised it. And Barnato and Solly Joel, another of his nephews—hadn't he once bought all the Tsar's diamonds *unseen* when the Bolsheviks threatened to flood the market with them?—and all the rest. And, of course, my father...

A couple of the executives were telling Van der Merwe jokes but the laughter was uneasy. Fat spluttered on glowing charcoal: black servants served spare ribs, chops and sausages. The chairman took his place at the long table and waited.

Finally his son said: 'So, how are the negotiations with the Russians coming along?' He gnawed a spare rib.

'As planned: we're buying time.'

A husky Afrikaner who had once played rugby for the Springboks and had obviously been appointed troubleshooter, said: 'There is a feeling among some of us that the Russians' demands should be met.'

His voice was loud with hesitant authority.

'Some of us?'

'Most of us.' The Afrikaner gulped beer.

The chairman pushed aside his plate. 'Is that true, gentlemen?'

Murmurs of assent.

His son said: 'They feel they should have been consulted.'

'Do you?'

'I believe the company has always been family and you are—'

'Its patriarch?'

'If you like.'

'That has an antediluvian ring to it.' He paused. 'I will have a beer.' He watched while his son poured a bottle of Castle, frothing, into a glass.

It was true, of course. The group had always been family and he had been at pains to keep it that way. Takeover bids, for instance, had been financed with non-voting shares to pre-empt hostile action by the victims.

The chairman sipped his beer and noted the cousins, nephews and in-laws at the table. Obviously some of them had faltered in their family loyalty.

He turned to the Afrikaner. 'Well, get on with it, man.'

'The truth is, sir, that recent results have been disappointing.' Understatement of the year, the chairman thought. 'A dividend cut for only the second time in recent history. Quotas imposed on producers, shares down by 25 per cent in three months...'

'Recession is bad news,' the chairman said. 'Or hadn't you heard?'

A South African of English stock, Harrow and Balliol, said: 'But *we* don't want it to get worse. Are you aware that 1 million dollars worth of diamonds are being smuggled out of Angola every day by a 50,000-strong army of diggers?'

'I am aware of it,' the chairman said.

'As you know we market 80 per cent of all rough diamonds mined in South Africa, Namibia, Australia—the biggest but not the best source—Tanzania, Botswana, Zaire...*and* Angola. We are negotiating with the Angolan Government and they are co-operating.'

'And the Russian Government? The Minister of Defence, that is.' The Old Harrovian inclined his distinguished head towards the other executives and favoured them with a gentle smile.

The Afrikaner said: 'Gemstones have even been discovered in the North West Territories of Canada. A mini diamond rush. Maybe there are more diamonds in the far north than in the south.'

The chairman sighed. 'You must be aware that the world's richest diamond mine, Jwaneng, is in Botswana? That another mine has just started production in the Transvaal?'

The Old Harrovian, who clearly believed that the Balliol experience invested the prosaic with the prophetic, said: 'Sales in America and Japan have dropped. They account for two-thirds of our total sales.'

'I'm afraid,' the chairman said, watching the bubbles spiral in his beer, 'that you don't understand recession. It is merely a predictable fluctuation of the market. Between 1981-86 the retail price of a good quality one-carat gemstone dropped from $60,000 to $10,000. In 1987 sales increased by 20 per cent.'

'If the Russians release all their diamonds, sales will never increase again.'

'Which is precisely why we've taken a certain course of action.'

'An act of piracy!' The Old Harrovian shook his head in disbelief. 'If it were ever made public it would finish us. Which is why I—we, that is—feel we should make the Russians an offer.'

'You sound like a second-hand car salesman,' the chairman said. 'What sort of offer, 25 billion dollars?'

The Afrikaner said: 'Why not—if all interested countries contributed? 'And we put up, say, five billion.'

'In a situation where, as it has just been pointed out, we have had to cut our dividends?'

But it was possible, he privately conceded. With the value of the stockpile of diamonds in London as yet intact and the cash reserves deposited in bank accounts all over Europe.

'Don't you understand,' he said, 'that this demand would just be the beginning? That the Russians, having smelled weakness, would strike again and again?'

'And if we fail we will stand exposed as gangsters and still have to pay blackmail money,' said the Old Harrovian.

'And what do members of my family think?' The chairman looked from one to the other but they averted their eyes. All except a nondescript and normally reticent cousin. 'Most of us agree,' he said into his beer.

Most? Here perhaps, but not elsewhere. But patently a serious bid to oust him from the leadership of the group was being mounted.

The Afrikaner folded his formidable arms on the table, lowered his head as though he was butting into a scrum, and said: 'Some of us think that we would be doing you a favour by allowing you to retire at a difficult time like this.'

His voice cracked as he cleared his throat.

'Retire? Do me the favour of saying what you mean. What you're doing is calling for my resignation.'

Silence except for the clatter of plates and the splashing of the fountain.

The chairman turned to his son. 'What do you think?'

'I think you should stay on until you want to quit.'

'Thank you.' But it was time for him to retire—not resign—the vineyards of the Cape. To vacations in the Kalahari. He heard the dark-maned lion roaring...

His son said: 'We seem to have lost you.'

'No such luck,' the chairman told the others. 'But you're right, I should retire.'

Heads jerked.

He smiled. 'But not now. You're not in a position to pull off a palace coup and you know it. But I promise you that I will quit—when all this is over.'

'Which may be too late,' said the Old Harrovian.

'You are entitled to your opinion.' The chairman addressed his son. 'I wonder if there is any place in this organisation for such a defeatist executive?'

He stood up and wandered into the cool living room of the old house, built on the profits from crystals plundered from blue ground.

So now he had issued his own ultimatum. To retire with honour, or quit admitting that his life had been a sham.

From the back of the Rolls taking him from his Johannesburg office to Jan Smuts airport, the chairman made two calls.

First to his wife at their home among the vines. He told her about his decision and her voice followed him down the years and was still young.

'But don't leave it too late,' she said. 'We've been waiting a long time.'

Then he called one of the advertising agencies that had helped perpetuate the mystique of diamonds. Spread the word that they were a symbol of enduring love...given them to movie stars to wear... encouraged the Japanese to become the biggest importers after the Americans... He should have contacted them before.

The voice of the managing director of the agency was brisk although in London he was probably in bed.

The chairman told him he wanted an instant campaign to counter rumours emanating from Antwerp that the Russians were on the rampage.

'First resurrect that old chestnut that Russian gemstones are manufactured. Mêlée of inferior quality—silver bears as we call them—and dreary regular shapes, mostly one-fifth of a carat. Greenish, too.'

'Is it true?'

'You immediately establish quality doubt. Who wants diamonds like that even if they are readily available?'

'You should be in PR,' the dry voice on the other end of the telephone said.

'How about: "Diamonds are forever provided they're not Russian"?'

'I thought you had an agreement about that with the Russians.'

'*Had.*' The chairman gazed out of the window at the vibrant city his ancestors had helped to found. 'Then you have to trample on the rumours.'

'These days people interpret denials as confirmations.'

'You're probably right. Deny them just the same. In other words, confirmation that the Russians are going to put a lot of inferior diamonds on the market. Pre-empt the bastards.'

'Until the world discovers that the gemstones aren't that bad after all?'

'Always ahead of the game?'

'With you I have to be.'

The chairman smiled at the receiver. 'All we're doing is buying time.'

A commodity, he reflected, that, at the moment, was even more valuable than diamonds.

Chapter Thirteen

Like many of the world's diamond centres Hatton Garden in London is a lacklustre clasp for its merchandise. A street of unpretentious offices just outside the boundaries of the actual City, its showcase shop windows of jewellery an aberration in such an unfashionable setting.

Even more unassuming than most was

an office rented by a haggard merchant not far from the sites of the infamous police court where Mr Laing, model for Mr Fang in *Oliver Twist*, had dispensed his own interpretation of justice, and the premises where Sir Hiram Maxim had perfected his machine gun.

On this the first day of December, a Tuesday, he stood at the grimy window of the office, examining a diamond which, being a rough, didn't brighten the gloom but brought joy to his soul. A beautiful stone, probably VS clarity when cut, colour champagne.

It was a long time since he had handled such a diamond. Back, that was, in the days when dealers had ill-advisedly believed that his air of uncompromising honesty must surely be the outward manifestation of even more steadfast inner probity. Then he reneged on a deal clinched in the bourse in Amsterdam and his name had been circulated to affiliated bourses and clubs.

Since then he had made a sort of a living dealing in smuggled diamonds, resorting even to simulants, YAG mostly and variations of Strontium titanate, but when the call came that morning he had been desperate, unable even to pay his rent.

Could he present himself at the entrance

to Burlington Arcade in Piccadilly at 9.30 a.m?

'Where I will learn something to my advantage?' It wasn't the first time he had received such calls.

'Very much to your advantage.' Strong American accent.

The caller was silver-haired and dapper wearing a camel coat and a soft grey scarf. He looked vaguely familiar.

He offered his hand. 'My name's Harry Sampson, you may have heard of me.'

'*The* Harry Sampson?'

'Only one as far as I know.' He took the merchant's arm. 'Let's take a walk along the arcade. I love it. Did you know it's got a resident poltergeist?'

The merchant, awed by the identity of his companion, said he didn't.

'Americans know more about London than the British.' He nodded at one of the uniformed beadles. 'They're here to stop you carrying large parcels or open umbrellas, running or singing. I hope you don't feel like singing. Or running.' He squeezed the merchant's arm.

'What can I do for you, Mr Sampson?' Had some shady deal from his past suddenly surfaced?

'I want you to sell a diamond for me.'

The merchant frowned. 'Why me?' Because it was stolen, smuggled... No,

Harry Sampson didn't deal in hot stones. Why should he?

'Why not?' Sampson took a small brown pouch from his pocket. 'The stone in there is worth 750 thousand bucks, probably more. I want you to sell it for 50 thousand, commission to be calculated on its real worth.'

The merchant took the pouch, felt the hard pebble inside between thumb and forefinger.

'Don't take it out here,' Harry Sampson said. 'Is it a deal?'

'Yes, but—'

'And don't get smart. Nobody crosses Harry Sampson.'

'When do you want me to sell it?'

'Now. And I want everyone in the London Diamond Club to know that you're selling it on behalf of Harry Sampson. And I want them to know there are lots more where that came from.'

'Are there?' The merchant was beginning to understand: word had swept Hatton Garden about the sale the previous day in Antwerp of a big Russian stone for peanuts.

'I said, don't get smart.' Sampson stopped. 'Do you know why this arcade was built?'

The merchant didn't.

'To stop pedestrians throwing garbage into Lord George Cavendish's garden. Do you really want to know why I chose you?'

'I can't imagine.'

'To really rub the Syndicate's nose in shit is why.'

He turned on his heel and walked towards Piccadilly as though he owned the arcade. Even if he opened his umbrella, the merchant didn't think the beadles would object.

By mid-afternoon reverberations of the second warning shot had spread round the globe. From the mines of Guyana to the jewellers in the Rue La Fayette and La Place Vendôme in Paris. From the Meisters of Zurich to the Bulgaris of Rome.

To Tokyo, Berlin, Madrid, Stockholm, Copenhagen, Rio de Janeiro, Caracas... In Hong Kong merchants touched the paws of the sculptured lions outside the Hong Kong and Shanghai Bank because they were reputed to bring good fortune.

Some dealers tried to unload but, by and large, markets that hadn't already closed for the day froze.

In London the *Evening Standard* carried the story by its financial editor as second lead on the front page.

RUSSIAN CARATS AND CHAMPERS MAKE RUMOURS FIZZ

A 32-carat rough diamond from Russia, champagne in colour, was sold in London today for a song. The sale, accompanied by hints that there were many more in the kitty, followed a similar one in Antwerp yesterday.

It also revived speculation that the Russians might be planning to renege on an agreement that effectively controls their stocks of diamonds.

Such a move would depress the value of diamonds. In the past the trade has become resilient to such rumours emanating from Moscow but on these two occasions speculation has been heightened by the identity of the vendor, Harry Sampson from New York, one of the world's most illustrious jewellers.

If Sampson is selling, goes the smart thinking, then get out because he has dealings with the Russians—he recently flew to Moscow—and knows a thing or two.

If the market was really flooded with quality stones then diamonds could become virtually worthless.

A dealer in London told me: 'You would

be able to buy the Crown Jewels on Saturday morning in Portobello Road.'

But he cautioned: 'My advice is not to panic. This would not be the first time that an attempt has been made to manipulate the market.

'In any case, why would the Russians want to devalue their most profitable export? They may be paranoic but not suicidal.'

The chairman was given the news in the first-class cabin of a SAA Boeing-747 London bound from Johannesburg. A told-you-so radio message from Kimberley.

He asked the blonde stewardess for a Scotch and soda and, sipping it, wondered how many more stones Harry Sampson intended to sell.

Could he damage the market irre-deemably? No, not Harry. He wouldn't want to lay waste his own business: he would carefully gauge reaction to the two sales before making another move.

But supposing Operation Joshua failed? The Russians, realising they had been tricked, would dump the trainload of roughs on the market and diversify into some of the other treasures buried in Siberia.

The chairman visualised an old woman

in Brooklyn forced to sell an item of antique jewellery to Empire Diamonds on the 66th floor of the Empire State. A diamond stomacher, perhaps, that she had worn across her bodice when she was young and beautiful.

She would be turned away, along with an army of similar old women in straitened circumstances.

What the public didn't realise was that diamonds had never been a profitable investment. A beautiful buffer against inflation maybe, but nothing more. What was always cited was the $1,100,000 diamond Richard Burton bought Elizabeth Taylor. It was sold 10 years later for $2 million but what with sales tax, insurance over the years *and* inflation that probably represented a loss.

He remembered, too, the young couple he had seen on his way back from the Russian Embassy, window-shopping for an engagement ring. What we shall lose, he thought, is trust.

The stewardess brought him another radio message. This time from Cronin in London: 'Loder has reached the border but there have been developments. No further details.'

What developments, for God's sake? The chairman closed his eyes and tried to transport himself to the vineyards of the Cape. The ripening grapes became rubies in a world where diamonds were no longer of any value. Seeing him shiver, the stewardess gently placed a blanket over his legs and tucked it in.

The 'developments' had occurred on a hillside in a valley of the Hindu Kush at daylight: a crackle of gunfire from the flanks of the mountains and the whine of wandering bullets.

The truck left the dirt track, lurched across an expanse of grit studded with boulders and came to rest behind prickly oak scrub on the brow of a hill.

Sapir ordered the Israelis out of the truck, a sitting target. Rachel Wolf rolled down the hillside and came to rest at the mouth of a cave. She crawled in. Two brass buttons from her green suit were missing: the fact that she had made this discovery annoyed her—she was a soldier first, a woman second.

A bullet thudded into the hillside and soft rock spilled outside the cave. An irritated bat hanging upside down from the roof flew into the alien dawn.

Crouching, Rachel gazed across the valley. Below a collection of flat-topped, khaki-coloured huts and an old fortress surrounded by cultivated fields. Beyond the fields the haunches of the mountains

241

climbing to crumpled white peaks that had been floating there forever.

She heard a slithering above her and Mikhail Sapir, wearing white shirt and dark trousers, pistol in his belt, materialised outside the cave in a shower of rubble. He came into the cave.

'Did you follow me?' she asked.

'I knew you'd find good cover. A professional.'

'Not what you told Reisfeld.'

'Ah, he ratted.'

'Ratted? It wasn't any secret that you didn't want me along. You told me yourself.'

'I don't think we're good for the mission together.'

'Then you should have stayed at home.'

He smiled, a revelation. The smile wiped away years of warfare. You should never have been a soldier, she thought. Which was probably true of most servicemen called to arms. But not me, I was born to fight. How dare he, a conscript of Israel's need, challenge me, a professional?

He was looking at her breasts, partially exposed when the buttons had been ripped from her jacket. She pulled the two borders of green cloth together.

He put one hand to the side of his ear and said: 'Did you hear more gunfire?'

'I don't think so. Are you all right?'

'I'm fine.' He forced another smile on to his face. 'I was pronounced fit.'

'That depends on what you told the medic.'

'Fitness tests aren't based on what the subject says.'

'They are,' Rachel said, 'if a general says: "We want him if he's fit. He is fit, isn't he, doctor?" '

'Did you hear that?'

'What?'

'Birdsong?'

She relented. 'I heard it.'

'At this time of the day the valley would be full of birdsong if it wasn't for the guns.'

'Guns are the reality,' she said.

'Birds were here before the guns.'

'Hunters killed the birds with arrows.'

'The birds were here before the hunters.'

She was about to leave the cave when the shooting started again. A bullet hit the pitted wall behind them. The birdsong stopped.

Sapir lay beside Rachel peering at the foothills across the valley through a pair of field-glasses. She had often wondered whether a face truly portrays its owner. Is the brute necessarily brutish? The angel necessarily angelic? Sapir's features defied analysis because they had been sculpted by vengeful circumstance. She remembered him asleep, features in repose, a visionary's face.

She picked up a small blue stone. 'Lapis lazuli. They mine it around here.'

'How would you know?'

'My father knew about such things.'

'His memory would always have been with us, wouldn't it?' He put down the field-glasses, leaned his head to one side. 'Gunfire?'

'Yes,' she said, 'gunfire.'

She saw puffs of smoke on the sides of the mountain like cotton tufts growing there.

'Why are they firing at us?' she asked.

'Because we've come from Kabul. Because they think we're agents of the other Muslim faction entrenched there. Because communications are bad here in the mountains. Did you know the Mujahideen fly a black flag over their camps?'

'Death?'

'When the Prophet's warriors went to a Holy War, a *jihad*, they always carried black flags because they believe war is bad.'

'But necessary,' Rachel said. 'Human nature being what it is. Look into any school playground.'

'You're right, of course,' he said. 'Only the really strong know how not to fight.'

She felt a sudden urge to place a finger

244

gently on the angry scar on the side of his dark head.

He said: 'I still don't understand why they chose you. Reisfeld knew how it had been between us.'

'Because he assumed we were two adult people who could put the past behind us. Because he knew I was the officer for the job.'

She was glad she hadn't touched him.

'It was stupid: Reisfeld isn't stupid. It was almost as if there was an ulterior motive,' Sapir said.

Which there was, of course. But she couldn't tell him.

She became aware that the shooting had stopped. Above the cave the noise of scraping. Dust and stones fell into the entrance of the cave. Sapir drew the pistol from his belt.

Haji said: 'Everything is okay. I got through on the radio. The Mujahideen send their apologies.'

As they climbed the hill to the truck birds began to sing again.

The Russian helicopter lay on its side at the end of the valley like the husk of an insect abandoned by summer, beneath the buckled rotor blades a row of rusting bullet holes. It had lain there, according to Haji, since 1985 when the Russians had been flying sorties from Bagram. Before, that was, their ignominious retreat from Afghanistan, their Vietnam.

The An-12 stood beyond it, a handsome aircraft, belly close to the ground, four single shaft turbo-prop engines snouting. But it didn't look in good health.

The Israeli pilot said: 'How do I know this thing will even take off?'

'You have my word,' Haji said.

'Has it ever taken off since it was captured?'

'Once,' Haji said. 'Last Thursday,' he added.

'How far did it fly?'

'Not far, there was no need. And it scraped a mountain.'

'Scraped?'

'Just a scratch.' Haji waved vaguely at a tear on one wing tip.

'Armament?'

'Tail turret with two 23mm cannon.'

'Do they work?'

'You are not mounting an invasion,' Haji said.

Watched by the other Israelis, the pilot walked under the rear ramp door touching the camouflaged metal as though he were establishing rapport.

'Fuel?'

'Enough,' Haji said.

'For what, take-off?'

246

Haji stared at the young, serious-faced pilot and said to Sapir: 'He is a comedian?'

'How much?' the pilot asked.

'Fuel?'

'Price.'

'I have reached agreement with Mikhail Sapir.' He spread his hands. 'But alas there is a problem.'

'We agreed payment,' Sapir said. 'In diamonds.'

'The Mujahideen will not accept diamonds.'

'But you said—'

'They are meaningless up here in the mountains.'

'They can be sold in Islamabad.'

'They prefer dollars. You do not believe me? I will prove it to you.'

He cupped his hands and called out in Persian. Two men in their thirties, both dark-skinned, one with a conspirator's beard, the other clean-shaven with the hollowed cheeks of a zealot, appeared from behind the helicopter. They were both smoking cigarettes and carried AK-47 Kalashnikov assault rifles.

Haji spoke to them, turned to Sapir and said: 'It is true, dollars only.'

'Can't they speak for themselves?'

'You speak Persian, Mr Sapir?'

Sapir spoke abruptly: *Skazhee'tye pazhalsta gdye zdyes ubor'naya?'*

The bearded Mujahideen laughed and pointed at the aircraft.

Loder said: 'I didn't know you spoke Persian.'

'I don't. That was Russian—these two men are Soviets. From what was Soviet Central Asia. Right, Haji?'

'It doesn't matter where they're from,' he said sulkily.

'But it does: that's why they don't want diamonds, because they're scared to travel cross-country out of Mujahideen territory. Not much love lost for Russians around these parts...'

Loder said: 'You mean they're deserters?'

'And probably gun-runners. A lot of Soviets deserted during the war in Afghanistan, bringing arms with them. Ethnically, soldiers like these two were closer to the Afghans than the Russians. For them it was like a civil war, a dirty war.'

The hollow-faced Mujahideen spoke in thickly accented Russian.

'They insist on dollars,' Sapir told Loder. 'If we don't pay them they keep the aircraft and the diamonds—and kill us.'

'So what are you going to do?' Loder asked.

'Take them out. What else can we do? There are 20 of us...'

'And Christ knows how many guerrillas in the hills with guns trained on us.'

248

'So what do you suggest, Mr Loder?'

'Pay them,' he said. He addressed the two deserters. 'How much?'

Sapir, surprised, repeated the question in Russian. 'Two hundred thousand dollars,' he told Loder.

'Tell the sons-of-bitches I admire their style. Tell them 50 grand, no more.'

'You've got 50 thousand dollars?'

'Someone has to take care of the petty cash.' Loder turned to the pilot. 'Check the plane out.'

They walked to the truck. Sapir repeated the offer to the two deserters. Both shook their heads.

The flaps and the rudder of the An-12 moved. One Ivchenko engine fired, died. Another fired, coughed, gained power. Then another.

The scar reaching from Haji's beard tried to leap across his eye.

The third propeller started, stopped, started.

The remaining engine turned again, then died.

The pilot climbed down from the cockpit. 'I can probably fix it,' he said. 'We might clear the mountains, then again we might not.'

Loder followed Haji who had walked away. 'The pilot says the aircraft is a heap of shit.'

'He's entitled to his opinion.'

'So what I'm offering is half now, half when we get back.'

'What makes you think you're going to get back?'

'Ask them if it's a deal.'

'It's a deal,' Haji said. 'I'm in charge. They're only Soviets.'

'You know what I think? You rightly figured we had diamonds *and* money. You wanted both. Greedy.' Loder went to the truck, returning with two canvas bags. 'Twenty-five thousand dollars in there.' He handed Haji one bag 'Count it if you want to.'

'And the other twenty-five is in the other bag?'

'With an incendiary device which I can trigger if you figure you can blast the aircraft on take-off. That way you lose the Antonov and the 25,000 bucks.'

'Suppose I signal to the Mujahideen to open fire now?'

'Then you're dead,' Sapir said, taking the pistol from his belt and pointing it at the scar on Haji's cheek. The scar quivered beneath his eye, then lay still.

Sapir told a couple of Israelis to take the deserters' guns and tie them up.

Haji looked disgusted. 'Hostages? They're only Soviets,' he said again, as though they were serfs in his court.

Loder said to Sapir: 'How did you guess who they were?'

'I didn't guess. One had a tattoo on his arm. Something about Rodina, Mother Russia.'

'What did you say to him?'

'I asked him where the toilet was.'

Haji had lied—the An-12 hadn't flown recently.

Sapir pointed at the scrub and boulders lying undisturbed on the floor of the valley. 'Obvious, but we didn't have a choice.'

'And the gash on the wing is an old war wound,' the pilot said. 'They must have towed it here from wherever it crash-landed in case the Russians decided to cross the border and take it back.'

Loder said: 'Do you think you can fly it?'

The pilot shrugged. 'Have you ever taken a car out of a garage after it's been standing a long time? In any case, we'll have to clear some sort of runway.'

By dusk the aircraft was still standing at the head of the valley. Hearing footsteps, Rachel, guarding plane and prisoners while the others cleared a strip, reached for her pistol.

'It's me, your paymaster,' Loder said.

'Checking on the money, Mr Loder?'

'I want to talk to you,' he said.

251

'It isn't mutual.'

'About your father.'

He walked to the truck and leaned against it.

Still holding the pistol, Rachel joined him. 'What about my father?'

'I'm sorry about what happened.'

'Sorry? You ruined him. When he died he had nothing.'

Mountains reached for the stars on either side of them. The valley whispered with nocturnal sounds. A wolf sang in the distance.

'I had nothing against individual diamond cutters. But collectively they were about to ruin the market. Buying direct from smugglers in Africa. Increasing their stock-pile by half a million carats a month. With the diamonds they hoarded they could have flooded the world's bourses.'

'And cut their own throats?'

'No,' Loder said. 'They would have made a killing—and then got out. Not so different from the threat today: thousands of innocent people ruined.'

'You're breaking my heart,' Rachel said.

'So what we did was talk to the bankers financing them. We told them we were going to impose a surcharge on the sale of diamonds to the dealers and cutters. A surcharge that could be wiped away in an instant. So a dealer who paid say

252

10,000 dollars for a diamond suddenly found it was only worth say 6,000. No bank wants to finance a lousy deal like that.'

'And you cut the sights.'

'Only to 40 clients. Your father wasn't one of them. He was—'

'Small fry... But you ruined him just the same. Without the banks' support the dealers had to sell their stocks...had to repay their loans...they sold for peanuts. Scores went bankrupt, my father among them.'

'I'm sorry,' Loder said. 'He was—'

'Expendable? You know what you remind me of? A gangster who loves his mother. Your mother is the Syndicate.'

Loder's voice hardened. 'You must know why I'm here. You of all people.'

'To protect the Syndicate's interests, of course.'

'You know more than that, lieutenant.'

She touched the trigger of the pistol with her forefinger. 'I do?'

'A big temptation, 50 billion dollars worth of diamonds. The Israelis aren't above temptation, are they, lieutenant?'

'I don't know what you're talking about: we're here to hijack the diamonds for the Syndicate.'

'Or for Israel?'

The wolf sang again, about loneliness.

'I don't think so. Don't mess with the Syndicate. You just told me what happens if you do.'

'What's the deal, lieutenant? A partnership between Israel and the Syndicate?'

'Why are you telling me this, Mr Loder?'

'Because you weren't picked for this job for your beauty or your brains. Or your knowledge of Siberia. Or its languages. You were picked because you have the motive to stab the Syndicate in the back. Because it ruined your father.'

'Killed him.' Sweat oiled the palm of her hand gripping the pistol. 'He was dead before the Arabs got to him. That was all he talked about in Russia, you know, setting up a little business in Israel...'

'I told you, I'm sorry. But whatever you're planning, forget it.'

'Why should I? *If* I'm planning anything, that is.'

'Because pressure would be brought on Israel. Diamonds aren't your only export. Citrus, chemicals, textiles, guns... I think you'd find no one wanted them. And as for imports: food, crude oil, machinery. I wonder where you'd buy those? The Arabs would be laughing from Beirut to Baghdad.'

'Bastard!' Rachel remembered the despair on her father's face when he had lost his business; remembered his black hat cartwheeling down the aisle of the bus as he bled to death. She raised the pistol and pointed it at Loder.

He straightened up in the starlight. 'Syndicate trouble shooter shot? You'd have a lot of explaining to do.'

'For killing scum, no explanations necessary.'

'The Syndicate might disagree.'

Mikhail Sapir said: 'I might, too. Drop the gun, Rachel.'

She glanced over her shoulder. Sapir had taken a Stechkin machine pistol from the equipment stashed in the An-12. He was pointing it at her.

'You heard what he said?'

'I don't care what he said.'

'About bringing Israel to its knees...'

'He would only have said that if the Syndicate was threatened. What was the threat, Rachel? Were you really going to steal all those diamonds?' He jerked the machine pistol. 'Now, drop the pistol.'

It fell heavily, striking a boulder.

Sapir picked it up. 'As of now,' he said, 'you are relieved of your duties as second in command.'

In the distance the wolf laughed.

The pilot pronounced the patient fit—or as fit as it ever would be—at 9.00 a.m. Loder and the Israelis, who had slept in

Soviet sleeping bags and breakfasted on Soviet iron rations, boarded and changed into captured paratroop uniforms—heavy-lined camouflage jackets and trousers, blue berets, webbing, boots. Sapir wore the insignia of a major, Rachel a lieutenant.

Sapir issued those flying to the airstrip with AKS-74 assault rifles—the others to be parachuted in a back-up bag—and the whole squad with P6 silenced pistols and combat knives. He gave the radio operator a transmitter and packed the rest of the weapons and ammunition—PK light machine gun, hand grenades, mortars and the rocket launcher with two missiles—into the back-up bag. Then he handed out parachutes.

'How long to Naked Boy Halt?' he asked the pilot.

'If we get off the ground, you mean?'

'I'm not sure whether you're neurotically logical or just a pain in the ass,' Sapir said.

'In peak condition the An-12 has a top speed of 777 kilometres an hour, cruising 670. We should reach the Novosibirsk area at around 1300 hours.'

'Then we should be in position, with the points switched, by 1400 hours. Before Ruchkin gets there.'

'Ruchkin?'

'An old acquaintance,' Sapir said.

256

Chapter Fourteen

Little Eagle filtered on to BAM, the Baikal Amur Magistral, the new eastern back-up to the over-worked Trans-Siberian, during the night. No ordinary branchline, Ruchkin remembered—it crossed 2,400 bridges and was frequently imperilled by mudspills, avalanches and earthquakes.

All he could see from the footplate was a blizzard, snow flakes flying at the windshield and veering away into the night. The snow had grounded the helicopter and the armoured train's only protection outside was the darkness which closed around the beam of the Skoda's spotlight like a tunnel.

Ruchkin said to the co-driver; 'What time do you estimate we should reach Novosibirsk?'

'About 1400 hours tomorrow,' the co-driver said.

'Have you radioed ahead that we're not stopping there?'

The co-driver hesitated. 'They said it was impossible. We'd throw the whole schedule for the day.'

'What did you say?'

257

'I said we were going through anyway. Orders from the Ministry of Defence—check if they doubted it—and I told them to move the replacement Skoda to Tatarskaya 460 kilometres further west.' Anxiety shredded his voice. 'I had to—the Skoda will break down otherwise.'

Ruchkin patted him on his angular shoulders. 'You did well.' He took a couple of steps to the door leading to the first coach. 'I'm going to get some sleep. As soon as the snow clears hand over to Chukovsky: I'll need you at Novosibirsk.'

He unzipped a sleeping bag and lay down beside the other men. On the other side of the coach, an ex-Spetsnaz named Simenov hoisted himself on to his elbow and gazed at Ruchkin with dark sombre eyes. Simenov, on the clumsy side but tough enough with the honed instincts of a hunter, faintly disturbed Ruchkin.

He turned on his side to avoid his gaze, closed his eyes and slept.

The Trans-Siberian had passed the stone obelisk in the Urals marking the border between Europe and Asia, stopped for 15 minutes at Sverdlovsk, formerly Ekaterinburg, where in 1918 Tsar Nicholas II and his family were murdered, and where in 1960 American U-2 pilot Gary Powers was shot down.

It had passed the site of the Monument of Tears near Tugulym and at 0558 on the morning of December 3rd had reached Omsk where, Tom Noland read aloud from a guide book, Dostoyevsky had twice been flogged—once for complaining about a lump of dirt in his soup, once for saving a drowning prisoner after a guard had ordered him to let him drown.

As the train stopped Noland, wearing a duffel coat, camera and binoculars thumping his chest, jumped on to the platform followed by Blair. Despite the hour, the station was quick with activity.

Men in ubiquitous blue track suits jogged while their elders marched briskly, striped pyjamas protruding from below their trousers. Some queued for beer sold in fluted brown bottles, others for magazines and yesterday's newspapers crammed with tales of corruption. Angry passengers harangued implacable women selling mushrooms and gingerbread and meat pies at extravagant mark-ups.

A woman passenger with tightly bunched cheeks held up a pie. 'So that's where all the stolen meat goes.' She took an ambitious bite out of it. 'What have you got to say to that, you thieving peasant?' The woman behind the stall folded her arms across her robust chest and nodded at a lurking militiaman.

'Pay up and watch your tongue,' the militiaman said to the passenger. 'In Omsk we cut tongues out.'

Blair and Noland, flaps on their fur hats over their ears to stop the cold taking them off, walked the length of the platform. Past robust women washing the carriages as far as the pea-green, serpent-faced locomotive.

Outside the station snow poured from the darkness and a plough spewed white jets to the side of the track.

'If only Helen were here with me,' Noland said. 'You know, after she died I never really thought I'd make it. Suspected I was just a lunchtime traveller escaping over my sandwiches. Then Harry and Syd made the bet. It was the anniversary of Helen's death and here I am.'

He peered into the sky.

Blair said: 'Surely even bearded vultures sleep.'

'Strange bird, the lammergeier. Won't join other vultures at a carcase. Why are people so disgusted by vultures feeding off carcases? We eat them, don't we?'

Blair said: 'Speaking of carcases...'

The giant with the Eskimo eyes approached, the Chechen, wearing a long sheepskin coat, beside him.

He said: 'I'm glad you haven't contacted your newspaper, Comrade Blair.'

'No need to: I haven't got anything to send.'

'You use a laptop, I believe?'

'A Tandy,' Blair said. 'Why?'

'You will need a phone link to send a report and there won't be anymore until we reach Novosibirsk. There, Comrade Blair, you might have a story.'

He and the giant retraced their footsteps down the platform.

Blair and Noland climbed into their carriage, dark green flanks streaming with water, and ordered glasses of lemon tea from the *provodnik*.

Her eyes, Blair noticed, had lost their misty reproach. And she was conscientiously made up, lipstick as shiny as cherries. She smiled at Noland and refilled his glass.

'Nice girl,' he said as they made their way to their sleeper. 'Knows about birds, too. Used to go spotting with her father at Lake Ladoga near St Petersburg when it was Leningrad. She'll come in useful looking for the Baikal teal.'

At eight they went to the dining car where Noland ordered buckwheat porridge, fried eggs, toast, plum jam and tea for the two of them. Outside the lights of a small town burned in the snow-flying darkness, then fled.

Noland ate hungrily. Never, Blair thought, had he known anyone adapt so readily to

261

alien circumstances.

He said: 'What time are we due in Novosibirsk?'

Noland consulted his timetable. 'At 1313 hours. Unless something unforeseen happens,' he added hopefully.

In the cramped bathroom Blair's razor swathes through the aerosol foam on his cheeks. He remembers shaving in a hotel in Vermont during their honeymoon, kissing the hollows at her throat, making love, with small drifts of soap still on his face, driving like a maniac to the station at Bellows Falls to catch the train to Montreal.

Remembers the embers of summer in the foliage and the snow geese exploring the silver-shining mud on the banks of the St Laurence and ruffled water seen through slats in Douglas firs and brave plans hatched in the lavender-smelling bed.

Who were you then, Frank, spook or hack?

He washes his face, dries it, presses the tired skin beneath his eyes. *American Indian corrupted by white man's baubles and booze.* Where is she now? In a lavender-smelling bed with a man with only one identity? He turns away from the face in the mirror, eyes peering from a mask of past deceit.

In the corridor he peers through the centre-parted curtains. The train is passing through the Baraba swamps. The snow has thinned and he can see a duck settling, trailing feet tearing the tissued ice.

The train stops at Tatarskaya. He notices the engine of an armoured train standing on a siding, a Skoda. Now what is that doing in the middle of a swamp in Western Siberia? His instincts stir once more and he hurries to the sleeper to make notes.

One engine fired.

The pilot raised his thumb. 'Only three to go.'

'Get on with it,' said Sapir, sitting beside him. He stared along the valley. Beyond the *strip* which they had cleared stood a cluster of adobe cottages. The villagers, who had been evacuated by the Mujahideen, stood around a fire to one side of it; smoke from the fire rose in an unwavering stem. Beyond the village white peaks rode the blue sky, small clouds loitering in their grasp.

Sapir wondered what he was doing here. Was he truly crusading for Israel—or was he merely saving the Syndicate's skin?

A second engine fired.

Maybe he could grow cotton as well as oranges in the Negev. These days they were even irrigating saltbush for animal fodder with water piped from the Mediterranean.

What had happened to the third engine?

The pilot jiggled with the controls. Somewhere he had found a leather flying jacket; he looked like a bush pilot flying by the seat of his pants. A breeze found its way through the mountains and took the smoke from the fire with it.

The third engine fired. The propeller faltered, then picked up power and joined the other two.

'One to go,' the pilot said.

'I can count,' Sapir said.

The fourth engine coughed, subsided.

'That's the bastard I've been working on all night,' the pilot said.

'And you still haven't fixed it?'

'It stopped a bullet.' He took a dented bullet from the pocket of his flying jacket and showed it to Sapir.

Sapir glanced at Haji and the other two prisoners, hands bound behind their backs, in the back of the truck. 'Serve the bastards right,' he said.

'What serves them right?' The pilot's hands were as quick as spiders on the controls.

'They're going to be 25,000 dollars short. We're not coming this way anymore—we're flying back to China. Or had you forgotten?'

'And have you worked out how we're going to get out of China?'

The engine fired, roared, faded, stopped. The pilot went to work again on the controls.

'That's where Loder pulls his weight,' Sapir said. 'I've talked to him. Diamonds have been found in the northern Hunan province, but the Chinese haven't got the experience to mine or process them. Loder will promise them Syndicate money and technology.'

'Provided they let us out of China.'

'And then the Syndicate will do what it does best—control the output, just as they did with Russia.'

'The Russians aren't going to like the Syndicate helping China.'

'Screw the Russians,' Sapir said.

'All a bit academic, in any case, if this engine doesn't catch.'

At that moment it fired, howled and went on howling.

'Here we go,' the pilot said. 'Although, technically speaking, we can't clear those mountains.'

'So why are you trying?'

'I saw God beckoning to me from the other side of the peaks.'

'Maybe he doesn't like you,' Sapir said.

The Antonov inched forward and Sapir felt the wheels spitting aside the stones, the metal groaning as it picked up speed. The village loomed. Sapir fisted his hands, knuckles polished bone white, as the plane lifted, then subsided once more, wheels bumping. Any moment now they would plough into the village; he felt the wheels scrape a roof.

Suddenly, as though they had jumped seconds in time, the valley was below them. The Antonov slanted upwards at an acute angle—another degree and it would break its back.

Gunfire echoed inside Sapir's skull. They were so close to the sides of the mountain that he could make out small details: a honeycomb of caves, a broken pine, a thin waterfall... Now there were drifts of snow in crevices, boulders glistening with ice.

'Can you still see God?' Sapir said.

'No. But if we're going to heaven we're going in the right direction.'

Faintly, Sapir heard Israelis singing their anthem, *Hatikvah,* the Hope.

The Antonov's belly scraped a fang of rock with a noise like ripping calico. The snow was thick and soft, deceptively beguiling. *If we crash here we will be covered in a quilt and no one will ever find us,* Sapir thought. He remembered Rachel in his arms and he prayed.

The Antonov shook itself like an old dog shedding fleas, cleared the final crest, reached for the sky and headed for Russia.

Part III

Approach

Chapter Fifteen

Three in the morning, six hours behind Novosibirsk. Fingers of mist from the Thames infiltrated the square mile of the City of London. Police guarding the nation's wealth patrolled the silent streets; lights burned here and there. One of these was in the chairman's study in the post-war complex, the Barbican, where 6,000 City residents live.

Gingerly the chairman, just returned from South Africa, punched the keys on his private IBM. He felt uneasy in the presence of computers, remembering days when his own brain had done the job, but recognised their boundless worth.

Every available fragment of information had been fed into the IBM. Probable departure time of the armoured train, taking into consideration that, according to the leader of the Israeli hit squad, it would probably leave a day earlier than scheduled. Estimated flight time from the border of Afghanistan to Novosibirsk. Weather forecast in the area. Probable time of drop over Naked Boy Halt; expected time of Antonov landing; capture of airstrip, capture of railway control centre...

What came up on the screen was that, hopefully, Loder and the Israelis would be in position to divert and rob the armoured train 30 minutes before it was due to arrive at the feeder loopline to Naked Boy Halt.

London time that would be about 10 a.m, four hours before the midday deadline for the first payment of five billion dollars expired.

Cronin had asked for an extension but so far there had been no response.

The chairman switched off the IBM because it couldn't answer one vital question. Could stampede selling in Tokyo and Hong Kong which opened hours before London be prevented before the hijack?

Not if the Russians fired another warning shot. But Harry Sampson wouldn't be so stupid. Would he?

The chairman, disorientated by two long flights, prowled the apartment. His head ached, his eyes were dry and tired. He felt a hundred years old.

There was only one way to steady the market and that was to encourage buying. But who would buy prior to a possible spate of diamonds on the market? Futile to instruct the Syndicate's own agents to buy: such a ruse would be detected immediately and interpreted as panic.

A dangerous thought occurred to the chairman. He poured himself a whisky and soda and telephoned Cronin who lived in one of the top-storey residential flats in Gray's Inn.

Could he come over to the Barbican? Of course he could. Cronin had never been affected by time; nor emotions or lust or any of Mankind's failings. He had only one motivation: the Syndicate.

He arrived 20 minutes later, wearing a clerical grey suit and a striped military tie as though he had been expecting the call.

The chairman poured him a malt whisky. He drank it slowly and appreciatively as though he was drinking ice-cold water from a stream. The chairman imagined him fishing for salmon—tossing a grenade into the water if the fish wouldn't bite.

Cronin said: 'With respect, sir, you should be in bed.'

'You sound like my secretary.' The chairman stiffened his own drink with a measure of Black Label. 'Have you heard anything more from Loder?'

'Nothing since the mysterious developments.'

'He was always cagey,' the chairman said. 'You taught him that.'

'He's his own man.'

The chairman sat in an easy chair beside

271

the IBM and crossed his legs; his shoes felt like lead weights.

He said: 'Are we going to win?'

'We always have, sir.'

'Maybe it has to end one day. Maybe today.'

'You're over-tired, sir. Everything will seem brighter in the morning.'

'It is the morning,' the chairman said. 'If the Israelis fail then we can't possibly raise 50 billion dollars.'

'They won't fail.'

'I admire your unbridled optimism. Why do you think Harry Sampson is helping them?'

'That's easy. A life's dream—to outsmart us.'

'To cut off his nose to spite his face?'

'Harry will have hedged his bets. In the unlikely event of the Russians getting away with their blackmail threat he will be in a position to buy cheaply before the market steadies. If the Russians do saturate the market then I'm quite sure he has been promised unlimited supplies of alternative gemstones. We know, for instance, that emeralds are mined 70 kilometres north-east of Sverdlovsk on the Takovaya river. Alexandrites and cat's eyes too. Sapphires in the Urals and quite probably rubies—after all, they're the same mineral, corundum.'

The chairman undid his shoelaces. 'What Sampson doesn't know is that the Israelis have intervened.'

The skin tightened on Cronin's forehead. 'And he mustn't—he'd tell the Russians.'

'If he thinks the Israelis are going to pull it off, then he could be persuaded to buy now at rock bottom prices. Word will spread like wildfire, "Harry Sampson is buying", and a crash will be averted.'

'If he tells the Russians the game is up.'

'Why should he tell them? He'll never be able to buy as cheaply as he can now.'

'I don't think he'd risk the money, sir.'

'He might, Mr Cronin, if I gave him a cheque for five million dollars.'

The chairman eased his feet out of his shoes and sighed.

The Antonov was flying in a peerless sky of metallic blue. Just beneath it oceans of cloud pierced here and there by shark fin mountains.

'Let's hope the map makers are right,' the pilot said to Sapir.

'What are you talking about?'

'According to my British map the highest peak in the Pamirs,' gesturing east, 'is 24,590 feet. That gives us less than 500 feet clearance. And this old heap is so out of condition I daren't fly any higher.'

273

Sapir said: 'You really are a pain, aren't you?'

'Navigation is going to be tricky,' the pilot said.

'I'm sure of it. With you at the controls.'

'I'm flying INS. Inertial navigation system,' the pilot explained. 'Speed and direction are measured and a computer works out our position. Only one snag.'

'Only one?'

'On take-off you feed in the aircraft's *exact* position.'

'Which you didn't have.'

'Not precisely.'

'So we could put down in Delhi.'

'Or Beijing.' The pilot pushed the control column forward. 'As a matter of fact there is another snag.'

'Of course.'

'I can't radio for a fix because we're not supposed to be here.' He touched a pedal with his foot. 'On the other hand we should be able to fly a good distance without interference because aircraft aren't expected this far away from the Chinese border and radar is pretty basic.'

'When the Russians do come on the radio,' Sapir said, 'you know how to string them along. They won't shoot down one of their own aircraft.'

'Maybe they won't have to.'

'What's that supposed to mean?'

274

'This heap is like an overweight jogger with a heart problem.'

'Lots of fun in your house in Netanya, huh?'

'My father was a comedian.'

'Like father like son,' Sapir said.

He ducked as the fang of a mountain crusted with snow loomed out of the cloud.

The pilot kicked the rudder control pedal and the peak raced past on the starboard.

The pilot said: 'One of two things. Either the map maker was wrong about the highest mountain...'

'Or?'

'The altimeter's kaput.'

One hour later he aimed his thumb downwards. 'With luck Alma-Ata, capital of Kazakhstan, is down there somewhere. A big airport with sophisticated radar. We can expect trouble any moment.'

'And then?'

'We duck into the cloud and fly low over Lake Balkhash.'

A voice cracked on the headset. 'This is ground-control at Alma-Ata. Please identify yourself. I repeat, please identify yourself. You are endangering airspace...'

The pilot spoke in Russian. 'This is Red Falcon Three. I repeat, Red Falcon Three. Part of Operation Cossack, a classified project. Please get off the air immediately.'

'Operation Cossack?'

'You heard me. You are endangering the future of the state. Check with General Belov at Ryazan. Over and out.'

'Ryazan?' Sapir frowned.

'Headquarters of the Higher Airborne Command School where they train Spetsnaz officers for special missions. Kazakhstan is independent now but they still jump when they hear Spetsnaz. General Belov is the boss.'

'How do you know all this?'

'Mossad told me. The controller at Alma-Ata will be shitting blue lights. Should he call or shouldn't he? What the hell is Operation Cossack?'

'What the hell is it?' Sapir asked.

'Mossad's brainchild—it doesn't exist. And now the controller will be consulting our other ally.'

'Which is?'

'Bureaucracy gone mad. Down there in Kazakhstan,' pointing again with his thumb, 'they don't even know where their loyalties lie anymore.'

'Maybe *they* do.' Sapir pointed at the old MiG-23's with red stars on their silver tailplanes that had suddenly broken cloud.

'Terrific. They will see we're Russian and report back to ground control.'

The headset cracked again. 'Mikoyan One to Red Falcon. Do you mind telling me what the fuck's going on?'

'Wish I could, Mikoyan One. A classified mission. Ground control is contacting Ryazan.'

'Your name?'

'Belov. Now move your asses out of this patch of sky.'

The MiGs made one pass round the An-12. The pilot of Mikoyan One waved. Then they banked and disappeared beneath the cloud.

Sapir tapped the pilot on the shoulder. 'Belov?'

'The general's son.'

'Maybe he hasn't got one.'

'Maybe he always wanted one.'

Two minutes later the pilot eased the control column forward and the Antonov began to lower itself into the cloud. Gently like an old man easing himself on to his pillows.

Little Eagle stopped briefly at the market town of Bogotol on the banks of the Chulim river 510 kilometres east of Novosibirsk.

While the men wolfed bread and cheese and eggs in a spartan cafe that had been warned of their approach, Ruchkin radioed Moscow from the helicopter.

Was there any more positive news about the departure from Tel Aviv of members of the elite Israeli force?

None, said a reedy voice, scarcely audible in the static. In any case it was hardly likely that they intended to cross the Russian border...

'Do you know the identity of their leader?'

A pause. Then: 'Something like Shapir.'

'Sapir?'

'Sapir, that's right.'

Ruchkin breathed deeply, shut his eyes, smiled fiercely.

Static buzzed in the earphone like a trapped insect. He cut the connection and strode to the cafe.

His second in command, a deceptively languid Cossack, said: 'What's happened? You look as though you've dropped a kopek and picked up a rouble.'

'I've just had a fix,' Ruchkin said. He smiled to show he was joking and the men applied themselves uneasily to their food because Viktor Ruchkin never made jokes.

The Trans-Siberian made one more brief stop before the long run-up to Novosibirsk. At Barabinsk, in the centre of the swamps.

And, Blair noted, there was a telephone booth there despite what the Chechen had said. But in any case the Chechen was using it, talking urgently.

A few Kirghiz with high cheekbones, descendents of the Mongol hordes that joined up with Genghis Khan, strolled along the platform, waiting for a local train.

They were joined by Tom Noland searching the grey, water-colour sky for an errant lammergeier or Baikal teal. Binoculars in one hand, camera at his chest, he lingered near the phone booth.

Blair, sitting in the corridor, wondered why the Chechen was making a call at a station where the train stayed only a few minutes. Was the call connected with the armour-plated Skoda engine he had seen at Tatarskaya? The warning administered with the giant's bladed hands in the hard-class toilet?

The pulse of the train increased.

The Chechen hung up the receiver and exploded out of the booth, colliding with Noland. The Chechen's hands talked wildly. Then they were both sprinting for the train.

Noland, panting, sat beside Blair.

Blair said: 'Did you see either of your feathered friends?'

Noland shook his head. 'But I'm an incurable optimist. In any case it wasn't a waste of time... I caught a little of what

279

the Chechen was saying.'

'You speak Russian?'

'Not much. Only what I learned at night school. But the words he was using, you couldn't mistake them.'

Blair swivelled round. 'What sort of words?'

'Something about a train leaving a day early...Novosibirsk...guns...diamonds.'

Blair shivered.

Then Noland was on his feet. 'Look,' pointing out of the window at the drooping sky. 'A lammergeier.'

Blair saw a large bird with black wings, a pale belly and a *beard* floating over a cluster of atrophied birch trees.

Noland aimed his camera through the window. *'Gypaetus barbatus* as ever was. Oh, you beauty,' he said, clicking away.

'Congratulations,' Blair said. 'One to go.' If we ever get past Novosibirsk, he thought.

Chapter Sixteen

Novosibirsk is the third largest city in Russia and is labelled the 'Chicago of Siberia' by all modern tellers of tales about these parts.

Indeed it is a hustler. It first asserted itself when the Trans-Siberian was being constructed and needed granite footholds on either side of the Ob and since then it has capitalised on its river, its railroad, and everything viable that can be extracted from the surrounding terrain.

One train passes through its station every four minutes and its wide streets are busy with tramcars and trolley-buses. In fact it is not unlike Moscow, 3.343 kilometres to the west, although it is even farther from the Soviet capital than London.

It is also the coldest city that far south in the world. A possible 40°C in the summer, sometimes—50° in winter when its citizens use window ledges as deep freezes and the Ob is frozen six feet deep.

It is ambitiously planned—its main street, Krasny Prospect, is 10 kilometres long, its silver-domed opera and ballet theatre is one of the most renowned in the country, and its railroad station is built in the shape of a locomotive. Inside the station peasants camp, vendors sell pies and beer, watchmakers mend clocks, cobblers mend shoes, and gypsies beg.

The control centre for this stretch of the Trans-Siberian and the Turksib railroad which links the city with Turkestan in the south stands close by, a chamber of soft, phlegmy noise in which blips representing mighty or modest trains, freight or passenger, pursue each other on panels spread in a half circle around the walls.

On this day, December 3rd, the senior controller, pouter plump with soft, unused hands, regarded the blips apprehensively.

His life was ruled by these small flashes of light. Even when he was making love to his wife, which was not often, they winked at him.

In one week he was due to retire. He looked forward to mushroom picking and cross-country ski-ing in the *taiga* and hoped that the blips would usher him from one orderly timetable of life to another.

Then he had been told about a belligerent intruder into his territory. An armoured train. Well, it could be assimilated easily enough, especially as it was scheduled to stop at Novosibirsk for an engine change.

Total shock came later. A radio message from the armoured train: it was going to storm Novosibirsk without stopping. Impossible, he told the voice, imagining the blips blundering around on the panel and exploding the way they did in computer games. But the voice had said: 'We are going through, orders from the Ministry of Defence—check if you doubt it—and move the replacement Skoda to Tatarskaya.'

Obedience, sown and rooted in the Young Pioneers and the Komsomol, the Young Communist League, took over. He telephoned the Moscow number the impudent voice had given him and was told: 'Do it.'

He had worked all night on the revised schedule. According to the computer the armoured train and the Trans-Siberian would now pass each other 100 kilometres or so east of Novosibirsk.

At the moment the two blips were approaching each other on a collision course. Not an unusual contingency because the blips were also programmed to avoid each other.

The controller closed his eyes for a moment and imagined the tracks of his skis crossing the virgin snow like a new railroad leading to the Arctic. When he opened them again the blip that was the Trans-Siberian was winking furiously.

The Antonov dipped into cloud like a spoon into soup. One minute sunlight was glinting on the wings, the next vapour was streaming thickly over them.

The pilot said: 'All we have to do is keep below the radar while they sort out Operation Cossack and follow the Turksib railroad from Ayaguz to Novosibirsk.'

Sapir stared into the soup. 'How far?'

'About 900 kilometres.'

'You figure you can find Naked Boy Halt?'

'I wonder why they called it that?'

'I don't know but it must have been in the summer,' Sapir said. 'Can you find it, that's what I asked?'

'No problem once I pick up the Trans-Siberian. If there's any visibility,' he said. 'Which I doubt,' he added.

'And the strip?'

'Twenty-five kilometres west of Novosibirsk. In a blizzard? Nothing to it.' He eased the control column forward. 'You know this is crazy, don't you?'

'Entebbe was crazy.'

'That was for people not diamonds.'

'I know,' Sapir said softly.

The pilot glanced at the clock on the control panel. 'Roughly 90 minutes flying time before we drop you.'

Suddenly there was no cloud beneath them. Only water.

The belly of the Antonov hit it lightly but the whole aircraft shuddered.

The pilot heaved back the control column.

Another shudder.

The nose of the Antonov lifted. Hillsides loomed, disappeared. One wing reached out for a forest of pines.

The pilot juggled the rudder pedal.

Then they were in cloud again.

The pilot slumped. 'So who needs an altimeter?'

General Vladimir Belov had two daughters, both of them trouble, and all he needed was an imbecile on the phone suggesting that he might have a son.

The general, bulky and pouch-eyed, growled into the receiver, 'What the devil are you talking about, man? Have you been drinking?'

'Operation Cossack...' The voice of the ground controller from Alma-Ata faltered.

'Never heard of it. Stop babbling and explain.'

When the ground controller had explained the general replaced the receiver thoughtfully, then called the head of GRU, military intelligence, of which Spetsnaz was the fighting wing, in Moscow.

The reaction was more vehement than he had anticipated and this gave him considerable satisfaction because he had no time for spooks. 'An unidentified plane? What the hell are you talking about, Belov? I've got every frontier covered.'

For what? Belov wondered. 'Perhaps,' he said equably, 'you weren't looking for a Russian aircraft.' He hung up, the smile on his face an unexpected visitor.

The ground controller at Alma-Ata, a

285

young man with a lofty opinion of himself who aspired to high rank in his profession, took his second top priority call within a few minutes and stared at the receiver in his hand. The head of Russian military intelligence? Officially neither the GRU nor the KGB was recognised in Kazakhstan anymore but they still chilled the spine as icily as a 1 a.m knock on the door.

The voice said: 'For the last time, where is the An-12 now?'

The controller cleared his throat but his voice still quavered. 'We've lost it,' he said.

The laminated glass and plastic windshield of the An-12 pierced the blizzard at such velocity that the flakes of snow were scarcely visible. But they were there all right and the perspective was a white wall.

Occasionally the Turksib railroad became visible below. Occasionally a long freight train nosed south towards Alma-Ata or north to Novosibirsk.

Then Sapir glimpsed a town.

'Barnaul,' the pilot said. 'We just picked up a radio beacon on the HSI.' The aircraft banked in the white-out. 'We're flying north north-west. Not long now. Better get back there with your boys. And girl,' he added.

Sapir went back into the cabin. Rachel and the other Israelis were sitting in their Russian combat uniforms on either side of the fusilage, backs humped with parachutes.

He approached a lieutenant named Katz, a husky martial arts expert with high Slavic cheekbones from Jerusalem.

'When I've dropped,' he said, 'you'll be in charge.'

'I don't like it,' Katz said. 'It's in direct contravention of Brigadier Reisfeld's orders.'

'Brigadier Reisfeld appointed me as commander, didn't he?'

'Yes, but—'

'Then I'm perfectly entitled to alter the chain of command beneath me.'

'He's not going to like it,' Katz said.

'He isn't here,' Sapir said.

He made an announcement over the roar of the turbo-props. No explanations, a joint decision between himself, Katz and Rachel. He hoped Rachel would nod acquiescence. Her head remained rigid.

He had asked her in the valley in Afghanistan whether she would have shot Loder and she had replied: 'I don't know. He killed my father. Eye for eye, tooth for tooth...'

'He didn't kill your father.'

'Prepared him for death.'

287

'You realise I can't keep you as second in command? You're acting irresponsibly.'

'Unstable?'

'If you wish.'

'I'll make a full report when we get back to Tel Aviv.'

'Your privilege,' Sapir said, remembering how their words had once spilled into each other's as if the two of them were a single unit.

He looked at her now, pushed forward by the parachute, elbows on her knees. She caught his glance and swapped him contempt for regret.

He told those parachuting to make their way to the rear ramp door, take off their berets and put on their helmets. Even without a helmet Rachel looked the most implacable warrior of them all.

Ruchkin's handset bleeped. The pilot of the helicopter clattering above *Little Eagle*, the restless, questioning Tartar, said: 'You're not going to believe this.'

'But you're going to make me?'

'An unidentified aircraft has crossed the Afghan border into Kazakhstan. Thought to be heading towards Russia.'

'So? Shoot the bastard down.' The information took a moment to register in his brain. 'Israelis?'

'Moscow can't confirm. But apparently

they told you members of an elite Israeli force—'

'The 269. Has to be.'

'Had left Tel Aviv. They said it's beginning to look as if the Israelis might be on the unidentified aircraft. Israelis invading Russia? God in heaven!'

Ruchkin took off his blue beret, ran his hand through his blond stubble. Renegade Spetsnaz versus Jews? As if it was written.

Chapter Seventeen

The water was strong. It rose 50 kilometres north of the Trans-Siberian and, like a breaker crashing on to the shore, gained impetus and height on its journey south through the marshes.

It was spawned by a meteorite. Nothing on the scale of the Tungushka Marvel, an explosion 80 kilometres north of the Trans-Siberian which, in 1908 devastated 2,000 square kilometres of *taiga* and created an air wave that twice circled the globe—possibly a fragment of Encke's Comet—but a sizeable dent in the earth's crust nonetheless.

The wave took with it trees and reeds and frantic fish and broke, elongated brow clouded with snow, ice and sulphurous sediment, 10 kilometres north of the railroad.

There it spread itself but its dying impetus was still strong enough to put the track ahead of the Trans-Siberian out of alignment.

Just before it hit Tom Noland was saying to Frank Blair: 'Do you realise that we're going to travel the same distance as London to Chicago within one country?'

At that moment the driver braked. Sparks flew from the track. China and cutlery crashed from tables in the dining car. Tea from the samovars coursed down the corridors. Children cried. And in the control centre in Novosibirsk the Trans-Siberian's blip winked.

While Noland comforted the *provodnik*, Blair jumped from the carriage and walked down the line to inspect the damage. It didn't look serious. The vanguard of water had undermined a sleeper; the rearguard had thrust a short stretch of track to one side. But the delay would be considerable.

Returning to the carriage, he juggled the facts that had been tumbling in his brain before the locomotive braked.

What had he got? A mafia godfather on the train. A threat that he mustn't file a story. What story? Blair frowned as he

290

climbed the steps and sat in the corridor among agitated passengers.

What had Noland heard the Chechen say on the telephone at Barabinsk? Something about a train leaving a day early...Novosibirsk...guns...diamonds...

Blair squinted across the marshes which were subsiding after the departure of the rogue wave. Birds settled and adjusted their plumage.

He remembered reading about the chaos in the diamond mines in the north. How would they safeguard the gemstones? Ship them to Moscow on an armoured train! Blair leaped to his feet, pushed his way through the passengers to the sleeper and took his notebook from beneath his pillow.

Why was the Chechen so agitated? Because he was going to rob the armoured train before it changed engines at Tatarskaya. At Novosibirsk. And it had departed a day early.

Blair sat on the edge of the lower bunk and began to write. Another possibility occurred to him and he tore the page from the notebook, squeezed it into a ball and tossed it on the floor.

What good were diamonds in a country where women prayed for sausages and potatoes? How could the mafia sell them outside Russia when the Syndicate had a stranglehold on the market?

Simple—blackmail. His pencil snapped between his fingers. Pay up or else we saturate the bourses and make diamonds worthless.

Blair wrote swiftly, a linked scrawl he had developed when court reporting. But he couldn't write such a story on a speculative basis. Not even quoting 'usually well informed sources'. The foreign desk had grown weary of his sources.

What he could do was send an advisory memo before filing a story at Novosibirsk that would electrify the morning editorial conference. That way they could get to work on back-up material. A piece from the City anticipating the effect on stock markets, currencies, and the repercussions on national economies. Dispatch reporters to Hatton Garden and, later in the day, New York's 47th Street. Ask the woman in the street what her reactions would be if the diamond on her finger was worth no more than a piece of glass.

They might think he was drunk again but, by God, they would have to react positively in case he wasn't.

What he needed was a telephone.

He snapped down the lid of his laptop and returned to the corridor. Outside the flood water had made a paddy field of frozen grassland which stretched away to a belt of birch trees. Among them stood

292

a dacha and above it on the ashen sky a pencil line...telephone line! Blair made his way towards the end of the train, levering his way through passengers with his laptop.

The keep-calm music on the loudspeaker system stopped and a man's defensive voice said that, owing to circumstances beyond the control of the railroad, the Trans-Siberian would be delayed for an unspecified period. These things were sent to try us, the voice implied.

Blair saw a path raised on a dyke leading to the dacha. Two figures had already got as far as the birch trees. He jumped down from the last coach and began to walk along the top of the dyke.

Receding water gurgled; flakes of snow fluttered sparsely like winter butterflies. In the distance he heard a train approaching. A breakdown locomotive? He imagined the chaos along the length of the track. Scores of trains immobilised, some loaded with passengers, others with *defitsitny* merchandise. Black marketeers in Moscow and St Petersburg would be devastated.

He reached the dacha. It was made of wood seasoned silver-grey, probably the weekend home of an old *apparatchik* who, like anachronistic aristocrats in England, found escape from senility by shooting birds and sometimes each other.

Negotiating the claws of the birch trees, pausing to peel a strip of skin from one emaciated trunk, he negotiated the last stretch of woodland. The door of the dacha was open.

He hesitated. Strode in with an authority which was, of late, uncharacteristic. Into a long room which was incongruously baronial. You expected venison to be turning on a spit in the fireplace.

Instead the ash was cold and the only dead meat was the body of a corpulent, white-haired man lying on the floor. His throat had been slit from ear to ear and blood was still flowing on to the stone-flagged floor.

The Chechen put his hand over the receiver of the antique black telephone. 'Mr Blair, I warned you... Look what happened to him,' pointing at the body. 'He tried to stop me using his phone.'

Blair heard excited chatter on the other end of the line. Heard breathing behind. Turned. The giant was a wall behind him.

The Chechen said into the receiver: 'What time?'

More chatter.

The Chechen said: 'Do what you have to do even if I'm not there.'

'Not where?' Blair asked.

The Chechen replaced the receiver.

'Never mind, Mr Blair.' Bandit face above his long sheepskin coat, he looked a classic wolf in lamb's clothing. 'Why did you defy me?' He seemed genuinely puzzled.

'Because I'm a journalist.' A *self-respecting one once more.*

'Too bad because you'll never send your story.'

'You implied after Novosibirsk.'

'But this is before Novosibirsk.'

'Why can't I get my story out?'

'Because you'll be dead,' the Chechen said.

The blow on the back of his head wasn't unexpected. He was aware that he was being dragged out of the dacha. Dumped into flood water among the birch trees.

'Better this way—natural causes,' he heard the Chechen say as his face was turned into the water.

The parachutes were Russian D-1s operating from static lines but ripcords were also fitted in case of emergency.

Not, Sapir thought, that there would be much time to pull one—minimum height for a drop with a D-1 was 492 feet and the Antonov was going in at 500.

The eight Israelis and one American who were going to jump with him clipped their static lines to the anchor cable.

Loder was last.

Sapir stopped beside him. 'You did say you'd jumped before?'

'Would I be here if I hadn't?'

A red light glowed. Sapir opened the rear ramp door. Iced air sucked at him. He peered into a white well. They could land anywhere: in the *taiga*, in a pine forest, on the frozen Ob River.

Then he saw it, as though he were peering through gauze. A single track looping away from the iron road of the Trans-Siberian into hills. A toy station. A bridge spanning a ravine.

The light glowed green. 'Okay, go,' he shouted. He ran to the back of the line and clipped his static to the anchor cable.

Loder turned. 'I was lying,' he said. 'I've never jumped before.'

Then they were gone.

Rachel Wolf, sitting beside the pilot, imagined the hostile land leaping at Sapir and the others. Sapir who shouldn't have been jumping anyway, not with that wound on his head, only recently healed. Sapir, inside her in a hotel room in Haifa...Sapir, visionary turned brigand by circumstance. Sapir, cynical bigot!

The pilot, flying by dead reckoning, said: 'All I've got to find is an onion-domed church and a clump of birch. Shouldn't be difficult. Twenty thousand churches in

Siberia, birch trees growing like weeds...'

Rachel pointed. 'Hey, look.' It had stopped snowing and a cluster of baubles, gold on blue beneath caps of snow, stood beneath them like exotic fungi that had grown overnight.

'Onion domes,' the pilot shouted. 'And there are the birch trees. Okay, the strip is between the two, equidistant. I'm taking her in.'

Rachel watched him nurse the big turbo-prop into its glideslope, lower the undercarriage, extend the flaps. Ahead the runway was a broad white avenue only distinguishable from its surroundings because of its uniformity. No threshold markings, no touchdown zone, no ground control: a sparrow would have thought twice about landing here.

The pilot flared out—lifted the nose of the Antonov slightly. Throttled back. The Antonov hit, bounced.

Hit again, held. The pilot raised the spoiler, applied the brakes. The white avenue raced beneath them.

Then the undercarriage collapsed. The Antonov thumped on to the runway, skewered, sending up plumes of snow. The diminutive control tower loomed. The Antonov finished its long slide a few yards in front of it.

The pilot said: 'I want you to know that

wasn't the best landing I've ever made,' and slumped over the control column.

The Israelis in their Russian combat uniforms and blue helmets leaped out of the crippled aircraft as four armed and jack-booted soldiers in long greatcoats came running from the tower.

Katz held up one hand, flat-palmed in Rachel's direction. 'I'll take care of this.'

'You look as if you're warding off evil spirits,' she said.

'I didn't ask for this job.'

When the leading Russian, a sergeant, reached them, he said: 'What the hell's going on? This strip has been closed for two weeks.' He noticed the insignia of a lieutenant on Katz's combat jacket. 'I'm sorry, lieutenant, but we didn't expect—'

Katz said: 'I know you didn't. This was an emergency.'

His Russian was immaculate but a fancy Muscovite accent was no advantage in Siberia. He drew his pistol. Two Israelis stepped forward, assault rifles aimed at the Russians.

The sergeant spoke to the other three in Kirghiz.

Rachel said to Katz: 'They're going to try to take us, lieutenant.'

Katz fired his pistol over their heads. Snow fell from the tower. One of the Israelis stepped forward and took the weapons, AK-47s, from the Russians.

Katz said: 'Okay, lock them up in the control tower. You,' to the other Israeli at his side, 'guard them. Take any incoming calls. You,' to the pilot who had climbed down from the Antonov, 'breathe life into them,' pointing at the Mi-6 helicopter and the Ilyushin-76 with Chinese markings, red star set in a red strip, parked at the end of the runway. 'The rest of us will take a drive into Novosibirsk. In that.' He nodded at the ambulance.

Chapter Eighteen

In the control centre in Novosibirsk the controller stared in disbelief at the blips on the panel. All those moving eastward were stationary. It had never happened since the computers had been installed. And he had stopped them. One week before he was due to retire. His second chin quivered, his soft hands embraced.

First the rogue armoured train. Now this, the Trans-Siberian forced to stop for the first time since he had first reported for work as a junior signalman 40 years ago. His staff of five standing in front of the panel that stretched halfway round the wall were all looking at him, seeking advice.

He consulted the computers. Consulted other controllers—he was in charge of 300 kilometres of track—and eased a few blips on to sidings. Gave his staff instructions. Calmed them. He was in charge, gold clock and pension awaiting him.

He opened a drawer beneath the master console. A pistol, an old Nagant, lay there. It had been given to him when he was promoted to chief controller ten years ago. 'In case of trouble.' What possible trouble could there be short of another Civil War?

You learned survival on the streets where Loder had grown up in New York City: you didn't learn parachuting.

One moment he was tumbling towards the whiteness below wondering if he was going to die, a red stain in the snow. The next, as the parachute blossomed, he was swinging helplessly in space.

A gust of wind swept him to one side, probably taking him miles off course. The ground reached for him at an awesome speed and when he landed it was like jumping off an express train. As the parachute billowed and pulled he fell, twisting his left ankle.

Mouth and nostrils full of snow, he

chased the parachute, caught it, deflated it the way they did in the movies.

Then the pain made itself known. He sat in the snow and took off the combat boot and thick sock. The ankle bone on the outside of the foot was cushioned in swelling flesh. When he tried to move the foot from side to side pain leapt up his leg.

He hoped it was just a sprain. He put on the sock and boot and looked around. It had stopped snowing but there was no sign of the halt where they had been told to rendezvous. No sign of any Israelis either.

Behind him stood pines as quiet as a cathedral. In the distance a range of snow-covered hills.

He wondered, as he had wondered in the desert, bush and jungle, what he was doing in circumstances of such absolute desolation. Was it just because he and his mentor had been set up for a robbery? Was circumstance everything? Even life itself?

A train pierced the desolation. A freight a couple of miles away, travelling west, seemingly unending. The Trans-Siberian railroad. So he had landed south of it. Which meant that Naked Boy Halt was far away on the other side. To the east or west?

Loder limped west. The freight finally

301

spent itself, leaving him alone. His scalp felt tight with the cold. He took off his helmet and replaced it with the Red Army issue fur hat he had stuffed inside his combat jacket. It made him feel like a hunter and with one hand he sought the reassurance of the pistol in his webbing belt.

Another freight heading in the same direction briefly animated the stunned countryside. Five minutes later another. All heading in the same direction, west. Odd.

He came upon a wooden cottage, eggshell blue with a fringe of fretted wood. It had been locked and abandoned for winter, windows shuttered. There was a crack in one and through it he could make out the detritus of summer, husks of sunflower seeds, shrivelled fireweed in a vase, comics, two decoy ducks—mallards with green heads.

He walked on. Decoy ducks? Where there were ducks... Ice groaned and he plunged knee-deep into water. He waded back to the shore, boots breaking the ice. His legs ached with the cold. Some hunter! He changed the angle of his approach.

Another train. Passenger coaches this time, faces blurred at the windows. Also heading west.

He followed the train. Towards Naked Boy Halt or away from it?

Ten minutes later he rounded a gentle curve on the railroad. There was a lot of water about and ahead a stationary passenger train.

Loder approached stealthily. On the side of one green coach he saw a silver hammer and sickle, a relic of another era.

The Trans-Siberian, had to be.

Loder retreated into the pines, re-emerging like any conscientious Russian soldier on manoeuvres to see if he and his unit could be of any help.

Except that he didn't speak Russian.

He crossed the track and scanned the passengers who had alighted.

Two coaches away he saw a smallish man with soft brown hair wearing a very British duffel coat, peering through field glasses.

He approached hesitantly. 'You're British?'

'English.' He lowered the field glasses. 'Tell me, have you passed a sign pointing to a place called Naked Boy Halt?'

'I saw a sign. The name was in Cyrillics but a Russian said it meant that. Apparently it's an old saw mill and there's a feeder loopline to it about ten kilometres ahead. A warning to old time engine drivers...' He paused. 'You speak very good English.'

Loder ignored him. 'Have you seen any paratroopers?'

'Why, have you lost some?' He shook his head. 'No, none. You didn't say "Have a good day".'

'Should I have done?'

'You've got an American accent.'

'Some of us were taught English by Russians who had visited America.' Loder smiled. 'You take good care now.'

'As a matter of fact you might be able to help me. You see, I've lost a friend. You didn't see anyone? Tall, carrying a laptop...'

'Sorry. Where the hell would he be going?'

'I don't know—I'll have to go and look for him.'

So Naked Boy Halt lay in the opposite direction. Pulling down the flaps of his fur *shapka*, Loder began to limp eastwards.

The drive into Novosibirsk aroused more than memories for Rachel Wolf: it opened an album in which pressed flowers had been kept.

A wooden house with yellow curtains where a boy named David with a brace on his teeth had chased her round the garden and given her a steely kiss behind a patch of fireweed.

A lake with meadowsweet growing beside it in which she and two boys had half drowned the class *zvenovoi*, the official sneak, and laid him out to dry on the muddy beach.

A towering machine for washing gold-bearing gravel. Purple vetch threaded its rusty skeleton and she had searched beneath it for gold nuggets and found instead tin cans.

Thirty kilometres to the south lay the privileged scientists' city of Akademgorodok. City flowers, pansies and lobelia and salvias, in geometric gardens. Her father had taken her to the geological museum and had pointed at a diamond sparkling among the minerals and said: 'One day I'll be cutting stones like that—in Israel.'

A day in Central Park in Novosibirsk itself, flowers waiting for spring beneath the snow, a ride on the miniature railway. When she got on the train her parents waved; when she alighted two men in grey hats and funeral-black overcoats were leading her father away and she didn't seen him for another two days and when she did he was years older.

She remembered wild flowers, daisies and violets preserved inside two candles. They had taken them with them to Israel and on the day her father had died she had lit them and watched them burn; the petals of the flowers had fallen with the melted tallow like unanswered prayers.

The ambulance crossed the Ob with its hibernating beaches and headed for the railroad station which lay on the east bank which accommodated most of the city. On Prospect Dmitrova she stopped at a bakery and bought warm bread, then turned left at the new Hotel Sibir which hadn't been there when she was a girl, and sped along Ulitsa Lenina if that's what it was still called.

Katz, at the wheel, said to Rachel who was sitting beside him: 'I'm glad you're here—I wouldn't have been able to find my way around.'

'That's why I was chosen.'

'Look, I'm sorry...'

'Forget it,' she said.

Two GAI motorcycle cops drew level. 'Wind down your window,' one of them indicated, rotating one gloved hand.

Rachel said: 'Let me handle this.'

Katz wound down his window.

One of the traffic cops shouted: 'Is it an emergency? Do you want an escort?'

Rachel replied in Yakut: 'No thanks—it's an exercise.'

'How did you know I was a Yakut?'

'I married one,' she shouted.

'What's the matter with him,' pointing at Katz. 'No tongue?'

'He's from Moscow,' as though that explained everything.

The two policemen grinned, saluted and broke away.

Rachel told Katz to park outside the Novosibirsk Hotel at the apex of Ulitsa Cheluskintsev and Vokzalnaya Magistral. The railroad station loomed across the street. Snow ploughs were out; babushkas were scraping snow from the pavements with shovels; pedestrians approached the station with forlorn intent as though they were being evacuated.

Katz led the Israelis across the street to the control centre. A security guard challenged them. Rachel, recognising a Kirghiz, answered him in his own language. They were carrying out a peaceful army manoeuvre.

'Carrying rifles?'

'Where do you expect us to stick them?' The guard laughed and they mounted the stone steps.

Katz said: 'Is it necessary to keep speaking different languages?'

'For absolute authenticity? I think so, lieutenant.'

The control room was in shock.

The plump controller was shouting into a red telephone on the master console in the centre of the floor. His assistants were making urgent adjustments to the panels around the room.

307

The controller replaced the receiver with a soft, shaking hand. He turned. 'Who the hell are you?'

'Visitors,' Katz said. 'On an initiative test.'

'Not now.' He punched a button. 'We have a crisis.'

'No doubt about it,' Katz said, hand on the butt of his pistol.

Shapiro, the red-haired railway expert, stepped forward. 'I used to be in your business. What's wrong?'

'The Trans-Siberian was forced to stop. The Trans-Siberian! The track was buckled. We sent a breakdown loco there and now we've got to back it off.'

'Where?' Shapiro asked.

'Down a feeder line to a place called Naked Boy Halt.'

'I don't think so,' Katz said.

Shapiro held up one big hand. 'Where's the armoured train?' he asked, pointing at the wall panels.

The controller's head jerked up. 'What do you know about an armoured train?'

'We're Spetsnaz. Spetsnaz are guarding it.' He shrugged.

'There.' The controller pointed at one of the panels administered by a long-haired controller with a stud sparkling in one ear. Blips were heading steadily westward.

Shapiro crossed the floor. 'How are you coping?' he asked.

'We're coping all right. But we'd do better without him,' nodding towards the controller. 'All he does is press panic buttons.' He squeezed the stud in his ear as though it gave him strength.

'Naked Boy Halt. It was still operating when we went electronic, wasn't it?'

'We?'

'My father was controller at Irkutsk.'

'A good man, a legend. Not like this moron.' He felt the lobe of his naked ear; perhaps he was saving to buy a matching stud. 'Naked Boy Halt? Sure, it could be controlled from here.'

'Show me the armoured train,' Shapiro said.

The assistant pointed at a blip. 'Why do you want to know?'

'This *is* an initiative test,' Shapiro said.

He went back to the master console. 'How do you control the points at the feeder to Naked Boy Halt?' he asked the controller.

'There.' The controller indicated an insignificant green button. 'Now please, all of you, get out. Come back when the crisis is over.'

Shapiro nodded at Katz and he drew his pistol, pointed it at the controller and said: 'I'm afraid the crisis is only just beginning.'

Someone had pulled the plug. Blair felt the flood water receding rapidly as it found a natural conduit; the level on his face lowered so that he could just breathe.

He heard the Chechen talking to the giant. They had summoned a helicopter to fly them to Novosibirsk so that the Chechen would be there in time to supervise the diamond heist when the armoured train stopped there to change engines.

Change engines at Novosibirsk? So what was a spare Skoda doing at Tatarskaya? They couldn't have seen it, Blair decided.

His body was marble cold. His heartbeat had lodged in his ears and it was very slow.

He thought about making a run for it, but, one, he didn't think he could run and, two, they would see him on the dyke and pick him off with a couple of shots. If the helicopter arrived soon he might be able to make it back to the Trans-Siberian when it had gone.

Faintly he heard a locomotive engine. The sound died like a motorcycle on a summer evening. The breakdown engine departing.

Another engine noise replaced it. From above, a predatory clatter. He felt the breath of the helicopter's rotor blades on his face.

Footsteps approached, twigs snapped. He turned his face into the water.

The Chechen said: 'Is he dead?'

'He must be,' the giant said. 'But I can finish—'

A voice on a bullhorn above the slow swish of the blades: 'Hurry up, for God's sake—the train's almost at Novosibirsk.'

The giant's boot thudded into Blair's ribs. I am a dead fish, he told himself. I don't breathe, I don't move, I don't flap my tail.

'He's dead all right,' the giant said, and Blair heard his heavy tread as he followed the Chechen to the helicopter.

Blair turned his head and gulped air. Like a *dying* fish, he thought. The helicopter rose, banked and clattered away towards Novosibirsk.

Blair pulled himself to his feet, collected his laptop and leaned against a spindly birch. The Trans-Siberian sounded its horn. No way could he reach it before it took off again.

Noland said: 'All right, let's be having you.'

He took Blair's arm and pulled him towards the dyke. 'I saw the telephone line, I guessed...'

'I can't make it,' Blair said. His feet were weighted, his lungs lazy with cold.

'I told the *provodnik* to tell the driver to

311

wait. Five minutes. If we don't make it by then he'll go.'

Halfway along the dyke Blair stumbled, fell. Noland pulled him to his feet. The Trans-Siberian sounded its horn again. The halfway mark. Two and a half minutes left.

A hundred yards more. His vision was blurred but it seemed to him that the train was inching forward.

One door was open. The *provodnik* was leaning out. Calling to Noland.

The train gathered speed. Blair fell again. Stared at the wheels on the track. Noland grabbed his hand, pulled him to his feet and jumped on to the steps beneath the open door.

Blair ran with slow-motion strides. He found the bottom step with his left foot; his right dragged behind him.

Noland tugged but his grasp was slippery. The *provodnik* leaned forward and grabbed the laptop. A vision flashed before him—Barbara grabbing the laptop when he slipped on ice outside Novodevichy Monastery in Moscow.

He willed his right foot on to the steps, Noland heaved and he collapsed in the corridor. He could hear the wheels grinding on the rails, steel on steel, and it seemed to him that they were cutting through the crust of the world.

Chukovsky said: 'I must protest.'

'Protest as much as you like,' Ruchkin said. 'It's not going to stop the train.'

'An engine change is essential.'

'This isn't a clapped out old L class,' the co-driver said.

'I will make sure you're disciplined when we get to Moscow.'

'I'll make sure he isn't,' Ruchkin said.

The eastern suburbs of Novosibirsk began to thicken.

Ruchkin said to the co-driver: 'Increase the speed. Just in case there's a reception committee waiting for us.'

'No!' Chukovsky hurled himself at the co-driver. Ruchkin hooked an arm round his neck, pulled him away, wrestled him into the first coach and thrust him forward. His head hit the metal floor and he lay still.

Ruchkin returned to the footplate. Blocks of apartments were accelerating past the window. A red light glowed ahead.

The co-driver said: 'With respect, we're going too fast.'

'The control centre can deal with it,' Ruchkin said. 'Maintain the speed.'

The tracks were multiplying, melding, gleaming as bright as bayonets in the grey light.

A freight train whooshed past, workmen in blue overalls stared.

Platforms approached. The guardian helicopter slanted overhead.

Ruchkin saw the gunmen. They stepped from behind passengers waiting for the next train, straightening their fold-butt AK-47s. He spotted a rocket launcher. God willing they were travelling too fast for it to be effective.

He saw the Chechen and waved.

Passengers scattered, throwing themselves to the ground. Bullets splattered against the armour plating. The co-driver ducked, whimpering.

Ruchkin heard a thick explosion. Tensed himself. Glanced out of the window. Saw the missile hit an office block and explode in orange and blue flame.

Little Eagle swayed with its own momentum.

A last scattering of bullets as it flew past the end of the platform.

Ruchkin said to the co-driver: 'Okay, you can look now.'

The co-driver straightened up.

'No more problems until we reach Tatarskaya,' Ruchkin said.

Faintly they heard the rattle of small arms fire and an explosion.

The controller, gun pointing at his head, began to shake.

Katz said: 'What's the matter?'

'When I authorised the Trans-Siberian to start again, I forgot the armoured train. And it's accelerating.' He aimed one finger at the panel. 'They're on collision course.'

Shapiro said: 'Then stop them.'

The controller said: 'The armoured train's got priority. The computer can't cope with a counter command over priority.'

'You mean, you can't. Year after year trains have passed through here as scheduled. One rogue and you quit.'

'I retire at the end of this week.'

'You should have retired years ago. Here, let me take over.'

The assistant with the stud in his ear clapped.

As Shapiro approached the console the controller reached for the drawer beneath it.

Katz shouted: 'Look out,' and stepped between Shapiro and the controller as the controller, Nagant pistol now at his hip, pulled the trigger.

The bullet took Katz in the chest. Blood pumped rhythmically. As he fell he shot the controller in the shoulder.

Shouting: 'They're going to crash,' Shapiro navigated the bodies and squashed his thumb on the small green button and activated the electricity on the feeder line.

Rachel knelt beside the two bodies. The controller was alive, Katz was dead.

She stood up. 'I'm taking over because I know Novosibirsk and I know the way back to the airstrip. Does anyone object?'

No one did.

She pointed at a reel of electrical wire in the corner. 'Tie them up and gag them.'

She opened a first aid box on the wall, found a pair of scissors, took off the controller's jacket and cut away his shirt. A clean flesh wound just above the right nipple. She taped a dressing to it, propped him against the wall and tied his legs together.

The assistant with the stud in his ear said to the controller: 'I think you can forget the gold clock.' Shapiro gagged him with a strip of his shirt.

The co-driver of the armoured train pointed down the line, shouted in disbelief.

Ruchkin snapped: 'What is it?'

'The Trans-Siberian,' said Chukovsky, emerging from the first coach. There was a trickle of drying blood on his forehead below his sparse grey hair.

The co-driver's face was in wild angles of panic. 'What shall I do?'

'Brake, lunatic!' Ruchkin shouted.

Chukovsky pushed the co-driver aside and lunged for the air brake beneath the automatic warning system.

The train shuddered. Ruchkin held on to the console. The train plunged on, wheels screeching.

The Trans-Siberian closed on them.

The co-driver raised one arm to protect himself.

Chukovsky braced himself.

Ruchkin pressed his back against the side of the cabin.

Sparks sprayed...pine and birch flickered past...the helicopter hung impotently above the narrowing space between the two trains...

Chukovsky hung on to the handle of the air brake and stared ahead. Saw steam and smuts, felt a red scarf whipping around his neck.

Two hundred metres. Still on collision course.

'Oh, shit!' The co-driver flung himself to the floor. As *Little Eagle* swung right at a signpost pointing to Naked Boy Halt.

Part IV

Impasse

Chapter Nineteen

In Tokyo and Hong Kong it was easier to sell prime beef to vegetarians than it was to sell diamonds to a dealer. When the markets opened in London and the United States it would be the same.

Or worse, the chairman thought, as he shaved in his apartment in the Barbican: panic selling might begin.

It was now 6 a.m. After calling Harry Sampson at the Connaught and inviting him to an early breakfast in the directors' dining room at the company offices, he had catnapped for a couple of hours.

If anything he now felt worse. He stared into the shaving mirror and two pouched eyes stared back.

He dressed in a thick pin-stripe suit and black Crombie and took the lift to the ground floor. The black Rolls was waiting outside. Stifling a yawn, his driver tucked his peaked cap under one arm and opened the door for him.

The streets breathed quietly, the dormitories of the homeless sleeping in shop doorways covered with paper and cardboard blankets. Lights in shop windows wished them a Merry Christmas. Frost on the pavement sparkled in the lamplight. A burglar alarm severed the quiet. No one took any notice, no one ever did.

Sampson was waiting outside the Connaught in Carlos Place, as jaunty and fragile as an old actor.

Climbing into the Rolls, he gestured at the hotel. 'Used to be called the Coburg. They changed the name in World War I because of the anti-German feeling. Adaptable, weren't they?'

'And you, Harry, are you adaptable?'

'Depends on what I'm asked to adapt to.'

The streets were waking now. Vans delivering warm bread to coffee bars, milk vans rattling, women cleaners on the march, newsvendors unpacking the news, yesterday's yuppies hurrying to their computers to try and recoup their Porsches. The homeless slept on because there was nothing to wake for.

In the dining room the chef, summoned early by Cronin, had provided scrambled eggs, kidneys, beef sausages and tomatoes, tea and coffee.

Sampson and the chairman helped themselves and sat opposite each other.

The chairman said: 'You've probably guessed why I've asked you here.'

'The third diamond? Sure I guessed.'

He took a pouch from his jacket pocket. 'Look, a beauty.' The rough stone rolled on to the tablecloth. 'From the Udachnaya pipe 200 miles north of the Mir pipe in Yakutia, Siberia.'

'I know where the Udachnaya pipe is.' It was going to be more difficult than he had anticipated because he had never eaten humble pie before and it would stick in his gullet. 'You aren't going to sell it, are you?'

'Haven't made up my mind yet.' Sampson cut a fried egg and watched the yolk flow. 'Depends how the markets are reacting.'

'You know how they're reacting. You must have made calls before you came here.'

'Sure, but we may need a little more movement. You know, a whiff of panic to make you move ass. When's the deadline?'

'The first payment—midday today, London time. We've asked for an extension. Why are you doing this, Harry? Revenge?'

'That's about the size of it. Last time I was here you said, "You've been a bad boy," and gave me a lightweight pack of shitty stones.'

'If you sell that stone the market will collapse and you'll go under with it.'

'The market might collapse,' Sampson said. 'I won't.' He drank coffee. 'Hey, not bad—most coffee over here tastes like a third pressing.'

'All right, so you'll survive. Have you thought about all those others who will be ruined? Little stores, small investors, prospectors, miners, cutters...'

'And the Syndicate?'

'We kept the business stable, Harry.' The chairman, who had no stomach for food, drank iced water.

'Okay, let's cut the crap. Shall I tell you why you've really asked me? To persuade me not to sell the third diamond.' He picked it up, cradled it in the palm of his hand. 'Okay, but that's only part of it. Am I right?'

'You tell me,' the chairman said.

'You want me to buy, buy, buy. To give the world a lead. Rally the market. Compressed carbon must be okay because Harry Sampson, King of Diamonds, says so.'

'You'll do it?'

'Like fuck I will.' He speared a length of sausage and began to chew it.

The chairman considered the hazardous idea that had occurred to him earlier that morning: to tell Sampson about the Israelis. No, Cronin had been right: Sampson would tell the Russians.

He said, 'Supposing I told you I *know* diamonds are going to survive.'

'Why, are you going to hijack them?'

'That now *is* the time to buy them.'

'If you were so sure you wouldn't have invited me here.'

'You can help.'

'Not good enough.' Sampson put down his knife and fork, selected an apple from the fruit bowl and bit into it. 'Good for the caps,' he said.

'Supposing I were to arrange finance?'

'I haven't borrowed money for 30 years.'

'A gift.' The chairman slid his hand into the inside pocket of his pinstripe jacket, took out an envelope and handed it to Sampson.

He took the cheque out and studied it. After a while he said: 'Maybe I should get my loupe.'

'No flaws,' the chairman said.

'Five million bucks?'

'It's a buyer's market, Harry. You can buy a lot of gemstones with that.'

'Last time I was here,' Sampson said, getting up and walking to the window, 'I scattered diamonds in the street. Lousy diamonds but diamonds just the same. This time cash.'

He opened the window, tore the cheque into small pieces and threw them out. Together they watched the fragments disappear in the darkness.

8 a.m London time. 2 p.m Novosibirsk.

In the City it was the time the chairman liked best. The awakening. A distilled hush as the servants of Mammon arrived by road and rail, as computer screens blinked, as money began to move.

But this morning he didn't open the window to savour the rebirth. He was facing the worst crisis in the company's 100 years trading and pain was nudging his chest again.

He took a pill, washed it down with water and was caught in the act by his secretary.

'I hear you had an early breakfast,' she said. 'Very early. You know what the doctor said.' She patted a watch-spring curl of grey hair between thumb and forefinger.

'Get a good night's sleep. That's what every doctor says. Never mind, it will all be over today. One way or the other.'

Apart from Cronin, Loder, family and directors she was the only member of the company who knew what was happening and she nursed the trust placed in her jealously.

She said: 'Just supposing the Israelis fail.'

'Then we'll have to dock your pension,' he said, smiling.

When she had gone he scanned the

salmon-pink pages of the *Financial Times* and the digests of any financial stories in the morning papers collated from the early editions.

All of them carried speculative reports about the diamond crisis accompanied by quotes from spokesmen for the Syndicate and Rosalmazzoloto, the Russian diamond trading company that worked closely with the cartel.

All agreed that it was within the power of the Russians to devalue diamonds.

One correspondent had written about an existing diamond glut of 7 billion dollars. Not far from the truth. He also suggested that the Syndicate might sell to one of its own subsidiaries to promote the concept of healthy trading. Sell diamonds to itself? A spokesman for the subsidiary had vigorously denied such an absurdity.

The chairman turned briefly to gold. Healthy. Reserves of more than 30 million ounces with prospects for output bolstered ironically, by more chaos in the Russian mines.

But not healthy enough to sustain the group if diamonds crashed.

At the end of the digest a postscript. A picture of a pretty girl employed by Asprey in Bond Street wearing jewellery worth 3 million pounds on her birthday had been well projected in the newspapers.

So the advertising agency which 25 years earlier had sold the notion to the Japanese that diamond engagement rings were symbols of enduring love was still doing its stuff in the face of impending disaster.

He opened the wall safe and took out letters of resignation signed by directors when they took office—in case one day their services were no longer required.

Cronin came in while he was looking at them. He handed Cronin his. 'Do you want to get out while the going's good?'

'Do you want me to go?'

The chairman shook his head. 'We've been together too long.'

Cronin smiled, sunshine on a stony outcrop. 'Then I'll see it through.'

'Anything from Loder?'

'Nothing. It's as if he's got lost in Siberia.'

'The Israelis?'

'I wouldn't expect anything more from them,' Cronin said. 'Very resourceful people, the Israelis.'

'The first deadline runs out in less than four hours. Any response to our request for an extension.'

'Nothing, sir.'

'Let's pray it doesn't matter,' the chairman said. 'If my computer's right the robbery should be taking place about now.'

For the second time in two hours the Trans-Siberian ground to an unscheduled halt.

Blair, peering through the window of the sleeper, grabbed Noland's arm and pointed. 'Look.'

An armoured train was racing through marshy fields towards hills covered with pine.

Blair seized his laptop. 'Goodbye, Tom.' He hadn't fully recovered but news had always been a great stimulant.

'Goodbye? No, you don't—I'm coming too.'

'No place for you, Tom.'

'The dacha with the phone just now... Wasn't that a place for me?'

'I'm grateful. I'll write.'

'You can't, you haven't got my address.'

Blair pounded along the corridor.

Noland shouted: 'Wait for me.'

Blair turned. Saw Noland stop beside the *provodnik* and kiss her on the lips.

'If you're coming, hurry.'

They jumped on to the side of the track, ran past a sign proclaiming in Cyrillics 'To Naked Boy Halt,' and followed the armoured train. Just as I once chased ambulances, Blair thought.

Mikhail Sapir had reached the halt first. It was built from pine split in the forest ravaged long ago by lumberjacks feeding the saw mill. The walls were weathered, fancy eaves hung at forlorn angles, the bell was coated with verdigris. Inside the waiting room a wooden bench rested on its side beside a table; a timetable, four trains a day, was hung from the wall in a glass case.

On the wall a single slogan scrawled in Russian: ALL BYELORUSSIANS ARE PRICKS. So the commissar had been a Byelorussian. Sapir imagined the room thronged with *spirt*-nipping woodmen homeward bound. Heard the last train pull out leaving behind a wilderness of tree stumps and sawdust.

Why Naked Boy Halt? A boy, perhaps, observed bathing in a stream as the track was laid through the pines.

As the Israelis assembled one by one he stood on the rotting platform and surveyed the terrain.

He knew the single electrified track left the Trans-Siberian about 15 kilometres to the east. From there it lunged across the wet plain and wound its way through foothills on a gentle gradient until it arrived at the saw mill on a tree-stumped plateau.

330

To the south small hills screened the plateau from the plain below. To the north, beyond the saw mill which had collapsed leaving a rusty circular saw protruding like a rotted tooth from a gun, the wooded hillside rose steeply.

A ravine split the range from north to south and it was spanned just beyond the halt by an iron, single-span bridge with a curved girder above it. Leaving the bridge on the far bank, the track passed a low wooden building on the left and a windbreak of pines on the right before making a gentle descent to the Trans-Siberian some 10 kilometres to the west.

A lot of construction for such a minor project but the Russians had always lived by the rail and thus bridges. And there had always been slave labour in Siberia. First exiles and convicts, then prisoners in the Gulag penal camps. He possessed a chess set carved by Jewish *zecs*, prisoners, in Abakan 28.

Beyond the wooden building on the far side of the bridge—probably a rest house for drivers and firemen while their trains were loaded with timber—lay the broad hollow, backed by a steep rise in the hills, where retired steam engines had been laid to rest. Snow had been falling when he passed it and the old engines had looked like prehistoric animals emerging from the mists of time.

Statues of discredited communist leaders lay among them—Stalin, Khruschev, Brezhnev... Even Lenin lay there, eyebrows white with snow, staring into the tarnished future that had once seemed bright with visions of equality.

All the Israelis who had dropped by parachute had now reported to the little station. Missing: Loder. So God was with them!

They unloaded equipment, explosives, conventional weapons and the missile launcher from the back-up bag.

Then Sapir and a wiry demolition expert named Arie made their way along the track to one of the primitive pylons supporting the overhead cable.

Arie climbed halfway up, attached Semtex to a girder and inserted a detonator and a lithium battery.

He carried the transmitter, which would blow the Semtex, into the pine stumps beside the track. Sapir deployed the rest of the Israelis among the stumps. Then they settled down to wait for 50 billion dollars worth of diamonds to arrive, special delivery.

Chapter Twenty

When Rachel Wolf led the eight Israelis out of the control centre the guard had disappeared. Police cars and braying ambulances were converging on the railroad station. Firemen were aiming an extending ladder at a black-lipped mouth in an office block.

Rachel asked a woman with a string bag full of rotting potatoes what had happened. The woman shrugged her meaty shoulders. An armoured train had raced through the station without stopping. Armed men on the platform had tried to stop it. There had been some shooting and they had fired a rocket which had hit the office block.

So we aren't the only highwaymen abroad today, Rachel thought. The gunmen had expected the armoured train to stop. But Ruchkin, Sapir's old adversary who had led the Arabs responsible for her father's death, had outsmarted them.

Followed by the Israelis, she raced across the street to the ambulance outside the Hotel Novosibirsk. She took the wheel, Shapiro beside her. As the ambulance took off she heard more firing. Pistol shots and the throaty snarl of an automatic rifle.

Were they firing at the ambulance? She glanced round. Police were crouching behind their cars aiming their guns at a giant firing a Kalashnikov.

A black four-wheel drive Suzuki took off. The driver was dark-skinned, wearing a sheepskin coat. Across the street the giant staggered back, gun spewing bullets into the sky, and sprawled on the ground.

Rachel took a different route this time. Along Cheluskintsev, past the *beryozka* hard currency store, the circus and the Cathedral of the Ascension, turning right on Krasny Prospect and heading towards the main square and the theatre.

Ahead of her the brake lights on the Suzuki glowed red. It stopped and the man in the sheepskin jumped out and climbed into a Zil. The Zil took off along Ulitsa Frunze towards Central Park.

It had begun to snow heavily and the silver dome of the theatre floated. She had been there twice, ballet both times, *Giselle* and *Carmen Suite*.

She passed the cinema where her first serious boy friend, an architectural student, had taken her to see *The Red Snowball Tree*.

The ambulance charged a set of traffic lights as they changed to red and crossed the bridge over the Ob. The suburbs thinned. She came to a fork in the road. Was the airstrip to the left or right? She swung the wheel to the left.

Braking, Chukovsky juggled with the controls of the Skoda and wished he was applying air brakes in a steam locomotive, handle on the fifth emergency position—the 'big hole' that in a crisis allowed air to escape through a large aperture regardless of damage to the train.

Little Eagle still swayed dangerously but it was slowing.

Ruchkin, steadying himself, said, 'Where the hell are we?'

'On the way to Naked Boy Halt—I told you about it. A loopline feeding an old timber mill. They used to fell eastern white pines there but they got a disease, blister rust.'

'You know every kilometre of the railroad?'

'Every metre,' Chukovsky said. 'There's a bridge beside the halt, a beauty, single-span, lattice girder, over a ravine.'

'I underestimated you,' Ruchkin said.

What would I do now if I were Sapir? he wondered. An ambush obviously. Between here and the bridge.

But this is an armoured train. Only an anti-tank missile could knock it out. So of course they had one!

And if I were going to take out an armoured train, I would first make sure it was stationary. Cut the power...

So what *we* have to do is storm them. Get beyond their positions to the other side of the ravine and counter attack while they're still reeling.

He told Chukovsky: 'Stop braking, accelerate.'

'If we stop we can reverse on to the main line,' Chukovsky said. The co-driver was still crouching on the footplate and *Little Eagle* was his once more.

'We'd be sitting ducks. In any case, that would be retreat and we have to fight.'

'I'm not sure about the bridge,' Chukovsky said.

'What do you mean, you're not sure?'

'It's very old. I don't know if it will take our weight.'

'A risk we'll have to take,' Ruchkin said as *Little Eagle* picked up speed.

'It's not far now,' Chukovsky said.

The co-driver was getting to his feet. Ruchkin pushed him back on to the footplate. 'Where you belong.' He went to the door leading to the first coach and ordered three men into the two turrets, picked up his handset and called the pilot of the helicopter flying overhead. 'What do you see?'

'What I did see was an armoured train

going in the wrong direction,' the Tartar pilot said. 'What the hell's going on?'

'We've been diverted: the Israelis are going to try and jump us. *Did* see?'

'We've hit a blizzard.'

As he spoke snow hit *Little Eagle*, blinding it.

'What else *did* you see?'

'A tiny station, a bridge over a ravine...'

'Israelis?'

'Negative. But they wouldn't show themselves, would they?'

Ruchkin said: 'I'm going to cross the bridge. I want you to put the helicopter down on the other side of the ravine.'

'Using what for navigation?'

'You can handle it,' Ruchkin said.

'I would be risking the lives of the men on board.'

'Just do it.'

As Ruchkin spoke an explosion shook the track. Ahead flames blossomed in the thickly falling snow.

Instinctively Chukovsky braked. But they were losing power anyway. He released the brake and *Little Eagle*, carried by the momentum of the speed it had picked up, continued on its way down a slight incline. Past a crippled pylon, past a cable twitching beside the track.

Then the shooting started. Bullets hammered the 120mm-armour plating. Return fire poured from the turrets.

Acrid smoke drifted into the cabin of the Skoda. 'They're firing at phantoms,' Ruchkin said.

A whoosh, a flare of light and an explosion to the right of the train. 'A missile,' Ruchkin said. 'They can hardly see us either.'

The train proceeded inexorably towards the halt and the bridge.

A bullet punched out a panel of the windshield, ricocheted and buried itself in the co-driver's thigh. Screaming, he grabbed his thigh above the spouting blood.

Iced air rushed into the cabin. Ruchkin saw a blurred figure on the track. He aimed his pistol and fired. He didn't know whether he had hit; if he had the body was under the train...

Chukovsky, big hands clenched, urged on *Little Eagle*.

Blood pumped steadily from the co-driver's thigh.

The helicopter loomed. It fired from its outboard gun pods but it was more vulnerable than the train. A burst from an assault rifle and it veered away.

Little Eagle was trundling now.

Past a dark rectangle on the left. The station...

It couldn't be far to the bridge.

Ruchkin prayed to the God he had never acknowledged: 'Please don't let her stop, not now.'

A machine-gun snarled. Bullets took away the remainder of the windshield and flew around the cabin.

Ahead a void. The ravine. And *Little Eagle* was almost on the bridge spanning it.

Even if they made it, would it hold?

The shooting stopped. Ruchkin heard shouts. Had they mined the bridge? Urged *Little Eagle* to its destruction...

If they had then they were doomed because they would have to reach the bottom of the ravine to blow the safe and the team in the Mi-8 helicopter would trap them.

Unless they blew it with a rocket...

The bridge materialised like a gate.

The grip of the wheels changed: they were on it.

Ruchkin felt it sway.

Slowing...slowing...

Blood stopped pumping from the co-driver's thigh and he lay still.

Slowing...stopping.

Little Eagle finally folded its wings and came to rest on the middle of the bridge.

Ruchkin snapped: 'We can't stay here—Sapir will order saturation fire and hit us with a missile when there's a break in the snow.'

He ran into the coaches and summoned the marksmen from the turrets.

Chukovsky said: 'What about the diamonds?'

'We haven't got the combination of the safe and we can't carry it because it's welded to the floor. What we've got to do is eliminate the Jews, mend the electric cable and get it to Moscow.'

But first do battle. What we, the elite, were trained to do, attack not defend.

Ruchkin replaced his blue beret with a fur *shapka* bearing the unofficial badge of Spetsnaz, a wolf, and jumped from the footplate on to the track. The bridge moved a little in the wind whipping snow through the ravine. He grasped the rusty handrail. In the spaces between the sleepers he glimpsed space.

Ducking into the blizzard, he led Chukovsky and the others along the bridge towards the side of the ravine facing the invisible enemy.

Above them the Mi-8 scythed unseen through the snow. What if the pilot put down in the ravine?

Ruchkin strode on, fighting spade gripped tightly in one hand. Behind him he heard a cry. He swung round. One of the sleepers had snapped and the leg of one of the men bringing up the rear had plunged through the gap. He regained his footing and staggered on.

Suddenly there was no more bridge. On either side of the track nuances of substance and, to the left, the blurred outline of a log cabin.

Ruchkin kicked open the door.

Peering inside Chukovsky realised with joy that it was a rest house built by the old NKPS, the People's Commissariat of Ways and Communications, for drivers and firemen.

It contained four wooden bunks attached to one wall. A sink for washing oil and smuts from your body. A long table where crews had drunk cabbage soup bobbing with chunks of meat, and drunk vodka flavoured with pepper—provided they weren't returning to the footplate within six hours—and sweated in the heat from a red-hot stove and told tales of the great iron roads that clawed their way across a sixth of the world's land surface. Ah, such camaraderie.

Chukovsky wiped dust from a pair of goggles, picked up a cap and fingered its small, incisive peak. The clock on the wall had stopped at 9.13—ticked on after the last train loaded with timber had pulled out until it had finally run out of time.

Ruchkin said: 'We can stay here until the blizzard stops. Then get out fast, before the Israelis hit it with a rocket.'

One of the men said: 'Won't the Israelis go for the train? Blow the safe and get away with the diamonds?'

'Let's hope they try,' Ruchkin said. 'I've booby-trapped it.'

The helicopter came down tentatively opposite the rest house on the other side of the track. Standing outside the rest house Ruchkin saw its blurred shape settling. Heard the shocking noise as the rotor blades tore into the trunks of pine trees. Heard the ugly ineffectual rasp of the ruined engine.

Listened to the ensuing silence.

Chapter Twenty-One

Blair led the way along the track. He breathed heavily because his body had been punished and he was out of condition. But he was fired by a great exultancy.

Noland followed, hands plunged into the pockets of his duffel coat.

'What do you think's happening?' he asked Blair.

'I think the Moscow mafia are trying to steal enough diamonds to hold the West to ransom.'

'Maybe it's just an exercise?' Noland told him about the Russian soldier who had spoken to him. 'He sounded like an American,' Noland said.

'Maybe he was.'

'What would an American be doing in a Russian uniform in the middle of Siberia?'

'I don't know,' Blair said. 'What did he want?'

'Had I seen a sign pointing to Naked Boy Halt.'

Blair stopped. 'And now we're on a track leading to it.' Another heady possibility occurred to him. 'Supposing someone else is trying to get their hands on the diamonds? A foreign intervention...'

'Surely the Russians could handle it themselves?'

'Not if they don't know about it. What country would suffer most if diamonds became worthless?'

'South Africa?'

'And Israel?' Blair said, adrenalin surging. He began to walk again, lengthening his stride. 'Could the man who spoke to you have been an Israeli?'

'I suppose he could have been,' Noland said. He caught up with Blair. 'You mean something like Entebbe?'

'Either working for the Syndicate or themselves.' Blair pointed at Noland's camera. 'Are you any good with that thing?'

'I took photography at night school,' he said. 'I once had a photograph published in *Country Life*. Black and white, an Evening Grosbeak from North America which I spotted in Lancashire.'

'Good, because I'm not a photographer. So if you see anything significant, take a picture.'

They continued along the track. Somewhere in the muffled silence ahead they heard shooting and an explosion.

'Jesus Christ!' Gripping his laptop, Blair walked faster but he was no longer a match for Noland who overtook him.

Snow fell remorselessly, covering the rusty track exposed by the wheels of the armoured train, caking their clothes.

They had been walking for nearly two hours when Noland was taken from the side, arm round his throat, barrel of pistol to his neck.

Blair next.

Arms twisted behind their backs, they were frog-marched to Naked Boy Halt, paraded in front of a young officer in Russian combat uniform, with short black hair and features that were half saint, half assassin.

He said: 'So, what have we here?'

And when Blair told him: 'Your last story, huh?' and his smile was so sudden and unexpected that it seemed to Blair that he felt its warmth. 'Well, we can promise you a good one. My name is Sapir.'

'You're Israeli, aren't you?'

'You've been to our country?'

'Twice. But you were always fighting.'

'I wanted to grow oranges, Mr Blair.'

'I have the advantage over you: I always wanted to be a journalist.'

'And retire in a cloud of glory? Well, this story will be the biggest since...what?'

'The invention of the postcard? Think of all the work hours that saved.'

Sapir laughed. As though he hadn't laughed or years, Blair thought.

'You've got style, Mr Blair.'

'A sense of the ridiculous. We should teach it at school. Then perhaps we wouldn't fight.'

'Try telling the enemy that.'

'Enemy?'

'On the other side of the ravine.' Sapir wiped the laughter from his face but it stayed at the corners of his eyes. 'What the hell, what's the harm?'

'In what?'

'Telling you.'

Noland said: 'Telling him what?'

'Okay, the biggest scoop since the

invention of the postcard. The Russians are holding the West to ransom. Fifty billion dollars.'

'And the hostages are diamonds?'

Sapir looked surprised. 'How did you know that?'

'Intuition, a reporter's greatest ally.'

'Fifty billion dollars worth of diamonds, in fact. Stranded out there on the middle of a bridge. Israelis on one side, Moscow mafia on the other.'

Blair turned to Noland. 'It beats the hell out of the Baikal teal,' he said.

Rachel Wolf drove with verve but with waning confidence. Should she have taken the right fork?

It had stopped snowing and ice dust hung in the bright air. Pink and white apartment blocks had given way to open countryside. Snow-quilted pastures sprouted with silos and birch trees and the gathering sense of desolation made an oasis of the city she had left behind.

Once she skidded and managed to drive into the skid; twice the ambulance stopped, wheels spitting snow, but, being a 4 x 4—a UAZ-452 which she had seen in service in Lebanon—it managed to take off again.

If she failed to reach the airstrip Sapir would always blame her. Claim that his decision to relieve her of her command was justified. If she ever saw him again.

Finally the snow won. The ambulance ran into a drift which looked as though it stretched as far as the Arctic Circle and the Israelis piled out.

Even if the road led to the airstrip the snow was so deep that it was indistinguishable from the surrounding countryside.

She pointed with an authority she didn't feel, 'Follow me,' and struck forward into the wilderness as it began to snow again.

The small Kamov helicopter landed at the point where the track leading to Naked Boy Halt began to make its way through the foothills. One man alighted and, as the helicopter took to the sky again, began to walk along the track in the footsteps of Frank Blair and Tom Noland.

He carried a canvas bag, handling it with respect. He thought the contents were safe enough but with some volatile explosives you could never be quite sure.

In Moscow it had stopped snowing and the city lay stunned in brilliant sunlight. Muscovites emerged cautiously like cats testing the snow with their paws; street traders in the Arbat donned silver Grandfather Frost robes and wound up clockwork bears; bathers in the Moscva open-air

347

swimming pool splashed like frenzied wraiths in the rising steam; in Red Square a militiaman was seen to smile.

But there was no joy in a first-floor office in the hulking Ministry of Defence building on Ulitsa Frunze and Gogol Boulevard, Russia's Pentagon. Sitting at a swaggering desk littered with telephones of different colours, the minister agonised.

In front of him lay a confidential report from GRU. A concentrate of information that had reached it from diverse sources.

(1) Members of Israel's elite 269 force had left Tel Aviv. (2) They were all former citizens of the defunct Soviet Union. (3) Delegates to a peace conference in Kabul had mysteriously disappeared—in fact there was no record of their invitations. (4) An unidentified aircraft had violated Kazakhstan air space, presumed heading for the Russian republic. (5) An armoured train was transporting a fortune in rough diamonds from Siberia to Moscow. (6) Israel's economy depended largely on diamonds.

Conclusion: Israel had invaded Russia.

The minister rubbed his frosted eyebrows and owned up to another conclusion: he was responsible for that invasion. Wishing that he were once again at the gates of Berlin in 1945, he collected his disguise, low-brimmed hat, tooth-ache scarf and voluminous grey coat, and descended to the place where he deliberated best—the streets of Moscow.

He walked along Gogol Boulevard passing the Arbat which, as far as he was concerned, epitomised everything that was wrong with the rudderless country. Punks, poets, galleries of decadent art, handbag snatchers, seditious posters... He waved aside a tout offering cut-price 10,000 rouble share certificates in the new economy.

He attributed the decline to middle-aged *apparatchiki* who encouraged unbridled change in case they were branded as dreary old reactionaries. What had been so wrong with the days under communist rule when the streets had been free of crime and everyone had a home, a job, a vacation, and a saucepan of borscht bubbling on the stove?

He bought a copy of the hardline newspaper, *Dyen,* and turned into Prospect Kalinina, an avenue of heroic achievement fashioned in the old spirit of disciplined endeavour. Four ministries, soaring high-rise, grand shops that had once had something worthwhile to sell...

What GRU would now expect would be immediate action to take out the Israelis. With nightfall approaching in western Siberia, with a blizzard raging, he would be able to postpone such an attack until just after dawn.

He turned on his heel and strode back briskly to the Defence Ministry and authorised his confidential aide, a bespectacled young man who looked like Trotsky, to encode another message to Ruchkin. SEEK AND DESTROY ISRAELIS URGENTEST.

If they succeeded, the armoured train could proceed on its way to Moscow before the army intervened. He calculated that he had 16 hours in which to overcome the one obstacle to the final triumph of his life. If time ran out then he would have to do the honourable thing and blow his brains out.

Led by the Tartar pilot, the occupants of the crippled helicopter crossed the track and reported to Ruchkin in the rest house.

The pilot, dark with a thin, closed-in face, said: 'I knew it was crazy to try and land there.'

'Not so crazy,' Ruchkin said. 'We've consolidated. Once the snow stops we can take the Jews.'

'Is there something personal about this?'

'They're Jews who quit Russia, deserters. Now they've come back to rob us of our diamonds. Nothing personal in that, is there?'

'I don't know,' the pilot said. 'A strange phenomenon, anti-Semitism. Personally

I've always thought it was a question of jealousy.'

Ruchkin fingered the razored blade of his fighting spade. 'No one asked for your opinion.'

'Which doesn't stop me giving it. By the way, there's a coded message for you.'

Ruchkin took the message into the rest house and decoded it. SEEK AND DESTROY ISRAELIS URGENTEST.

Predictable. What he suspected the Defence Minister was saying was: *Take them out before I'm forced to send in the army.*

Ruchkin went to a grimy window and stared across the ravine towards the Israeli-held bank. How to attack? A flanking movement from the south of the ravine? From the north?

Maybe Sapir would try and blow the safe. In which case he would blow himself up. No, he would get someone else to do it. I would. After all these years we have to meet face to face.

Which is one reason why he won't try and hit the rest house through the snow. Another—he can't afford to waste ammunition. Only a guess but a stimulating one.

Ruchkin became aware of a presence behind him. Simenov, the awkwardly boned hunter who made him feel uneasy.

'What do you want, Simenov?'

'I want to ask you a question.' He hesitated, choosing his words. He reminded Ruchkin of an ox-like private soldier who would single-handedly fight a rearguard action until he had spent his last bullet. 'Did you let my brother die?'

Ruchkin stiffened. 'What the hell are you talking about?'

'A long time ago. His name was Rozen. You challenged him to a contest to see who could jump the widest distance across Devil's Ditch. You won. He got a spike through his back.'

'Rozen your brother? Why is your name Simenov?'

'His father died. Our mother married again. I am a son by her second marriage.'

'So you're half brothers?' Ruchkin said.

'We grew up like brothers. He was eight years older than me... Tell me, Comrade Ruchkin, did you let him die?'

'It was a fair contest.'

'Not really. You were an officer, he was a recruit. A clumsy one. Like me.'

'He was a good soldier. I told him he needn't jump any further but he insisted.'

'That's all I wanted to hear,' Simenov said.

Ruchkin said: 'Why have you asked me now?'

'Because of the ravine. A blown-up version of Devil's Ditch. Because there are Israelis on the other side of it.'

'They're Jews, they have to be eliminated. Executed. Wearing enemy uniform is a contravention of the Geneva convention punishable by death. But Judaism is a strong if misguided faith. Do you hear the call from across the ravine, Simenov? Are you Jewish or Russian?'

'Russian,' Simenov said. 'That's why I'm on this side of Devil's Ditch.'

A few hundred metres away Ivan Chukovsky contemplated the shadowy outlines of the venerable locomotives that had not been accorded any dignity in their retirement. Majestic P36s, possibly from the Moscow-Leningrad haul, antique R class 2-8-0s and, so it was rumoured, one of the engines that had hauled Stalin's Blue Express which, in the 30s, had transported communist leaders on their summer vacations—compartments sprayed with eau de cologne, rugs in the polished blue coaches costing 5,000 roubles each... That was equality for you!

As he peered through the snow the iron horses seemed to acquire substance and potency. And as they loomed Chukovsky was visited by an extraordinary idea.

Chapter Twenty-Two

Loder's foot felt as though it belonged to someone else, an aching package that he was dragging through the snow.

He had left the Trans-Siberian and was labouring along the exit from Naked Boy Halt past stumps of pines felled long ago.

He passed an old-fashioned signal drooping at a forlorn angle. A bird took off from a pine spared by the woodmen, dislodging fingers of snow.

To divert his mind from the pain and the cold he forced his thoughts into the past created by Cronin.

Where would he be now if it hadn't been for the head of security? In a white-walled villa in Jamaica listening to the rustle of palm trees? In a penthouse in New York overlooking Central Park? In jail?

Pain pierced his thoughts. He concentrated on the dunes of Namibia. Rearing waves of hot sand taller than houses. Had the prospector Vogel really discovered the source of Namibia's alluvial diamonds?

When this is over, he thought, I will have to go back. In case someone else discovers it.

Unless we fail here and the Russians release all their gemstones in which case my job is finished. What then? Emeralds, symbol of immortality, more valuable than diamonds?

He remembered the girl in the hotel room in Luderitz. Her beautiful young body and her eyes, searching for betrayal. Lying awake at night, Loder remembered lots of girls but she always returned and her eyes were always puzzled.

The track, only visible where the wind had blown away the snow, curved. He imagined wolves, sensing his infirmity, following him, tongues spilling hungrily from their mouths. But it was the silence that really got to him. Like fog drifting into his ears.

He stopped and sat on a tree stump, foot stuck out in front of him. He didn't think he could go on much longer. Was it true that, finally, you welcomed the cold as a friend and went to sleep with it?

Not yet, his foot said, dispatching another shaft of pain.

He got up and began to limp along the track once more. Further on, a mile perhaps, he got the feeling that he wasn't alone. Or was the fog of silence confusing his senses?

He stopped and listened. Nothing.

He walked on. Suddenly the wind blew

aside the falling snow like a hand opening a curtain and there in front of him were soldiers in Russian combat uniform. Israelis!

One of the soldiers came up to him.

'It's me, Loder.'

The soldier answered in Russian and it was only then that he realised the terrible truth.

Sapir sat at a table in the waiting room. The Chechen, who had reached the halt after alighting from the Kamov helicopter at the foot of the hills, stood in front of him. His long sheepskin coat was stiff with driven snow, his dangerous unshaven face brown against the whiteness.

He said: 'I have a lot to offer you.'

'What, apart from trouble?'

'I am a professional.' He spoke Russian with a sharp accent.

'So am I.'

'A professional criminal. Since we broke away from Russia our country, Chechenya, has become a Sicily of the Caucasus. Gun law rules. But it is crude. Just as many Sicilians moved from Palermo to New York, I moved from Grozny to Moscow. And pulled off the biggest fraud in Russian history, 60 billion roubles. Ask him.' He pointed at Blair who was leaning against the wall beside the old ticket window.

'True,' Blair said. 'He also tried to kill me.'

'Next time I'll succeed,' the Chechen said.

Sapir said: 'I still don't see how you can help us.'

'Even if you get your hands on the diamonds, how do you hope to get them out of Russia?'

'You don't expect me to tell you, do you?'

'There is only one way. To the east, to Japan. I have men working for me from here to the Pacific. This is the tradesmen's entrance to the black market. From America, Japan, Korea, Taiwan...this is the route to Moscow. You must take it in the opposite direction because no one wants diamonds in Moscow. Yokohama, now there's a city.'

'Except that in your hands they wouldn't get further than Novosibirsk.'

'Wrong.' The Chechen rasped a hand over needle-point stubble. 'Who wants 50 billion dollars worth of diamonds? They would devalue themselves. I would accept three billion as payment for my services.'

'I'll think about it,' Sapir said.

'Think about it? Is that all you can say? How else do you hope to get the diamonds out of Russia—on a magic carpet?' The Chechen lit a cigarette loosely filled with

357

tobacco as dark as black tea. 'If I told you I had other motives, would you trust me?'

'No,' Sapir said.

'You are a hard man. But then, you are an Israeli.' He drew on the cigarette a small flame appeared at the tip, then died.

'What other motives?'

'I have to kill a man.'

'Here?'

'Across the ravine,' the Chechen said. 'A man called Ruchkin. He tried to outsmart me.'

Blair said: 'Succeeded.'

The Chechen looked at him thoughtfully. 'Obviously I shall have to kill two men.'

Sapir said: 'I still don't understand.'

'It's what the Chinese call face. I have lost face. Viktor Ruchkin was a leader of organised crime in Moscow but he got greedy. We, Chechens, Georgians and Armenians, threw him out. *Gave* him Siberia.'

'Generous of you,' Blair said.

'I was going to rob the armoured train at Novosibirsk. I was on the Trans-Siberian, that's where I met Mr Blair.'

The Chechen's hand strayed to the belt beneath his sheepskin coat. Sapir noticed a blade as bright as a leaping fish.

The Chechen said: 'The Trans-Siberian was delayed. I found a telephone and

358

summoned a helicopter. Mr Blair interrupted me. As a matter of fact, I thought he was dead.'

'So how did Ruchkin make you lose face?'

'He anticipated me. Rushed Novosibirsk station on the armoured train. I managed to get away to the helicopter waiting in Central Park. Now I have to kill him.'

'We have a lot in common,' Sapir said. 'What else have you got to offer?'

'What else is there?'

'Your expertise? You say you're a professional.'

'I know how to blow safes,' the Chechen said. 'In fact I was going to blow this one in Novosibirsk.'

Sapir said: 'I accept your offer.'

The clouds had briefly stopped shedding snow and were picking up the bruised tones of late-afternoon. The countryside was steppe, flat and white, and Rachel Wolf felt hollow with failure—she had even lost the road. Sapir had been right: a couple of sorties into Lebanon was no qualification for a mission in Siberia.

She paused. The men behind her paused too and she could sense their doubt. The wind blew tufts of snow on the fields and mauve shadows were collecting in the hollows.

Should she turn and say: 'Okay, I fucked up. What now? Could any of you have done any better?' To hell with it. One more push in the direction the road had been pointing before they had lost it.

She struck west again. And suddenly there was a church, domes gold on blue against the dying sky. She glanced round, held up one fisted hand. *Did you ever doubt me?*

The west door of the church flapped in the wind. Sacks of rotting grain lay in the nave. Abandon God and look what happens! She waited for the rest of them to join her at the chancel.

'Okay,' she said, 'we approach the strip with extreme caution because the Russians may know we landed here. So fan out.'

She went first along a line of dead, half-buried sunflowers with heads like black berets.

They were nearing the strip when a helicopter materialised, rotor blades scissoring the cloud base.

Rachel flung herself to the ground but she and the others were all easily discernible, black flies against the snow. A couple of bursts from a 12.7mm machine gun and they would be swatted.

The helicopter dropped lower. Rachel turned so that she was lying on her back and drew her pistol.

The helicopter settled, spraying plumes of snow, and the young pilot from Netanya climbed out. 'What kept you?' he shouted.

In the cockpit he told her he had fixed the helicopter and the Ilyushin with the Chinese markings. When the ambulance was overdue he and the other Israeli had bound and gagged the Russians at the airstrip, locked them in the control tower and come looking for it.

'Incidentally, where's Katz?'

She told him what had happened and said: 'So what we do now is fly to Naked Boy Halt, pick up Sapir and his men—'

'Not forgetting the diamonds?'

'—and fly back here. Is there enough fuel in the Ilyushin?'

'Enough to get us to China.'

The helicopter lifted, banked and headed through the shards of the dying day towards Naked Boy Halt.

In the waiting room of the station the Chechen took a packet of three condoms from his bag. 'They have more than one use,' he said to the Israelis sitting on the floor.

'No doubt you'll enlighten us,' Sapir said. Gangsters liked a stage, he thought.

'I won't go on to the bridge until it's dark in case it suddenly stops snowing. I don't want to be stuck up there like a

361

target in a shooting gallery.'

He delved into the canvas bag. 'I'm going to use nitroglycerine. Made by the action of nitric and sulphuric acids on glycerol which, like soap, is made by adding caustic soda to oils and fats.'

Arie, the demolition expert, stood up, sinewy body taut. Sapir had told him the special reason why the Chechen had been chosen to blow the safe but he couldn't resist sniping. 'Nitro's very volatile. You brought it all the way from Moscow?'

'From Novosibirsk,' the Chechen said. 'I don't know about volatile: I do know it can blow your head off.' He turned to the other Israelis. 'But don't worry about it. You mix it with kisselgur, a sort of porous earth, for dynamite; with collodion cotton for blasting gelignite. This is mixed with cotton—I learned my stuff in the coal mines.'

'I learned mine in the Israeli army,' Arie said.

'They taught you to blow safes?'

'No, but—'

Sapir said: 'You're good, Arie, the best. But he knows about safes. Leave this one to him.'

Arie sat down and stared at the floor.

The Chechen took his equipment from the bag and laid it on the small table. Primers, detonators... From a box packed with sawdust he extracted a thin cylinder. 'Pencil time fuse.' He shook his head. 'Not today. Direct detonation, the old-fashioned way. Cordtex and fulminate of mercury.'

He took a condom from the pink packet. 'British—the Russian ones are too thick. Wading boots.' He placed it on the table and took a cartridge from his bag. 'This contains Nobel 808. Smells like bitter almonds and if you play around with it too long you get the mother of all headaches. Known as jelly head in the trade.'

'And the condom?' Sapir asked.

'Insert it into the lock of the safe with a rubber-tipped erasing pencil. Then pour the 808 in. The rubber confines the explosive.'

'And then?'

The Chechen picked up a length of Cordtex which looked like a clothes line. 'Insert this, light it, and run like hell.' He turned to Sapir. 'Then you hit those bastards on the other side of the ravine with everything you've got while I go back for the diamonds.'

'Don't get any ideas,' Sapir told him.

'In the middle of Siberia?'

'You yourself said you had men posted all the way to the Pacific coast.'

'Three billion dollars worth, that's all I want. You have my word on it.'

'Your word? One diamond is worth more than that.'

'Emblem of fearlessness,' the Chechen said.

'But not trust.' I wouldn't want it any other way, Sapir thought.

At nightfall the Chechen made his move.

He replaced his equipment in the bag, walked to the door of the station, peered out. It had stopped snowing and Sapir and his men were spreading out to give him cover; Blair and Noland stood at the entrance.

The Chechen said to Blair: 'So you finally got your big story.'

'They don't come any bigger,' Blair said.

'If you live to send it.'

And then he was gone. Running across the snow sparkling in the moonlight to the cover of the pines lining the ravine that had been too dangerous to put to the axe.

Crouching, he kept to the centre of the track, hoping that Ruchkin wouldn't be able to see him behind the train. Gaps in the sleepers yawned beneath him; one fell away and he watched it tumble to the bed of the ravine. Stars glittered like diamonds.

It took him five minutes to reach the rear coach. The door was unlocked. He frowned: he had expected it to be locked.

He opened it, climbed in and closed his eyes to accustom them to the darkness.

It wasn't so different from being in a tunnel in a coal mine. Waiting for the dynamite—a special mixture so that it didn't ignite fire damp or shatter the coal to dust—to explode. Watching a mouse in a cage to see if it was affected by carbon monoxide.

He opened his eyes. There were signs of recent habitation but no safe. That would be in the coach next to the locomotive.

When he saw the sticks of dynamite protruding from an ammunition box he knew he had seen them too late, that he had already tripped the booby trap.

He thought: I have been betrayed, but he was not surprised. You lived by betrayal and you died by it.

Blair, standing on the fringe of the pines, heard the explosion and said: 'Aren't you supposed to be giving the Chechen covering fire?'

'That won't be necessary,' Sapir said.

'Because that wasn't a safe blowing, was it?'

'I don't think so,' Sapir said.

'You knew the train was booby-trapped?'

'It was an educated guess.'

Sapir's face in the moonlight was bleak. 'So you sent him to his death?'

'Hasn't anyone ever told you, war is hell?'

' "*I am tired and sick of war. Its glory is all moonshine... War is hell*"— General Sherman. But this isn't a war: this is armed robbery.'

'It's war,' Sapir said. 'Israel has been at war since it was born on May 14th, 1948. A long war, Mr Blair. Did you expect me to send one of my own men to his death?'

'You realise I'll put this in my story?'

Sapir looked at him wearily. 'I don't think so, Mr Blair. You see, I've been thinking. I know I promised you a good story. But I didn't say you could send it.'

It was 1750 hours. The snow was still holding off and in the moonlight bridge and train were frozen in a tableau of glacial serenity. But not for long.

Chapter Twenty-Three

After breakfast with the chairman Harry Sampson flew to Amsterdam, with Antwerp one of the two diamond-cutting meccas of Europe.

He made his headquarters in the Krasnapolsky Hotel on Dam Square. He strolled round the square, past the Royal Palace and the World War II memorial complete with 12 urns containing the ashes of some of its victims, and then headed in the general direction of the Rijksmuseum, the national art gallery.

He enjoyed Amsterdam. Its patrician houses, its canals, its bridges, its floating flower market... Antwerp had Rubens, Amsterdam had Rembrandt. Both had diamonds.

Sampson knew all Amsterdam's finest cutters: the van Moppes, Drukkers and, of course, the Asschers. It was Joseph Asscher who in 1907 cleaved the massive Cullinan into two principal gemstones which, part of the Crown Jewels in the Tower of London, were still the biggest in the world, 530 and 317 carats. What would they be worth tomorrow? Sampson wondered.

Amsterdam, he remembered, was also the scene of a heroic diamond heist. On May 13th, 1940, a British raiding party had landed in Holland from the destroyer *HMS Walpole,* filled a kitbag full of industrial diamonds and escaped with it under the noses of the advancing Germans.

In any case you had to admire a city whose main tourist attractions were art, good food, diamonds and sex.

It was a fine morning with rain lurking behind silver-fringed clouds and he walked briskly until he reached the sharp-roofed offices of his agent overlooking a canal reflecting the clouds.

The agent, who looked like a well-nourished burgomaster, offered him coffee and pastries wearing bonnets of cream. Sampson accepted the coffee, waved aside the pastry cook's millinery and asked for a private room and a telephone line.

From the room he called the number in Moscow that Viktor Ruchkin had given him. A man answered breathily as though he had been caught *in flagrante delicto*. Sampson identified himself and gave the code word, Orloff. The man's voice steadied. He said the Syndicate had asked for an extension.

'Playing for time,' Sampson said.

'Exactly. And now we know why.' He hesitated.

'So tell me.'

'This is confidential at the moment.'

'Okay, so it's confidential.'

'The Israelis have mounted an operation to hijack the diamonds.'

'Holy shit!' Harry Sampson gazed at the silvery clouds and the copies floating on the canal. So that was why the chairman had said: 'Supposing I told you that I *know* diamonds are going to survive.'

'Exactly, Mr Sampson. Holy shit. They seem to think we're playing some sort of game. They must be taught a lesson. We want you to sell your third diamond, Mr Sampson.'

'You realise that could scuttle the market?'

'Scuttle?'

'Torpedo it.'

'But it will recover when it becomes apparent that we are not going to saturate the market.'

'If you get the 50 billion bucks.'

'We're getting tougher than that, Mr Sampson. We want you to tell the Syndicate that if we don't receive the first five billion by 2 a.m London time tomorrow morning we go ahead and flood the market anyway. Two a.m, no extensions, this is the end of the line.'

'And you really mean that?'

'Naturally we'd prefer 50 billion.'

'Why 2 a.m?'

'Eight Novosibirsk time, just after dawn. By that time we will have destroyed the Israelis and the diamonds will be on their way to Moscow.'

'There's more to it than that, isn't there?'

'Is there, Mr Sampson?'

'I figure that's your deadline, too. Eight a.m Novosibirsk time... If the Israelis haven't been eliminated by then you've lost because the army will move in. Am I right?'

'Let's just say 2 a.m London is the deadline, leave it at that.'

'There is another possibility—the Israelis could pull it off.'

'We beat three million Germans in the last war; I don't think a handful of Israelis will give us much trouble.'

'We? We're not talking about the Red Army—we're talking about a handful of gangsters. Until the army moves in at dawn.'

A pause. 'You're very shrewd, Mr Sampson. But you'll find that Spetsnaz... ex-Spetsnaz,' he corrected himself, 'are a match for any Israeli elite force.'

'Yeah? Well, I hope you're right. *Dasvidanya*, Comrade Orloff.'

Sampson smiled at the receiver: even if the Israelis did pull it off he would still be calling the shots.

He went back to the agent's office. Two pastries had disappeared and the burgomaster was cat-licking cream off his lips.

Sampson sat opposite him. Small burgomasters peered from frames on the walls; a Lady Burgomaster smiled ominously from another, daring her husband to eat another pastry.

Sampson took the pouch from the inside pocket of his jacket and placed the diamond from the Udachnaya pipe on the desk in front of the agent. It had a greenish tinge and, when cut, might lend weight to the unfounded rumour that the Russians were manufacturing gem-size stones that colour.

He said: 'I want you to sell this.'

The agent cradled the stone in one hand. 'For peanuts? Like the other two?'

'Fifteen thousand bucks,' Sampson said.

'I can't do it,' the agent said. He tried a smile but it didn't reach beyond his plump cheeks. 'We'll all be ruined. You too, Harry.'

'The market will recover.'

'A risk I can't take.'

'I'll pay you commission on what the stone is really worth.'

'No, please.' Sweat started on his forehead; he pressed a finger on a crumb of pastry, won it and nibbled it.

'Okay,' Sampson said, replacing the stone in the pouch. 'I respect your right to make your own decision—you're fired.'

'Please, Harry.'

'And I'll get someone else to sell and you'll lose the commission and, if things work out the way you figure, you'll still be ruined.'

The agent looked at his wife and their

little burgomasters. 'Okay,' he said. 'I'll do it.'

'You won't regret it. Now don't forget, "Harry Sampson's the vendor and he reckons there are plenty more where that came from." Got it?'

'Okay, Harry, I hope you know what you're doing.'

One hour later the carat price of diamonds in London, Paris and Rome had slumped to an all time low. When the bourse opened on New York's 47th Street vendors didn't bother to offer. In South Africa, South America and Australia mines suspended production. Trade in diamond-studded heirlooms ceased. Only jewellers sold stocks because the public hadn't yet heard about the latest threat to compressed carbon—and they offered more than generous discounts.

One dealer did buy. Harry Sampson. He knew that you could never underestimate the Israelis. He should know: he had been doing business with them since they came of age in 1948.

Ruchkin heard the explosion from beyond the pines fringing the ravine. When the snow had faltered he had evacuated the rest house taking the American, Loder, with him. The terrain was studded with pine stumps interspersed with young trees that had grown since the woodmen had left.

Had Sapir blown himself up? He doubted it. Who then? Could the Chechen have reached Naked Boy Halt from Novosibirsk? He had been a safe blower, Ruchkin remembered, and smiled.

So what now? Ruchkin posted two observers in the pines and approached Loder, sitting against a stump, hands and feet bound by rope.

He said: 'So who exactly are you?'

'Name, rank and number, Geneva Convention.'

'Okay, name, rank and number.'

'Loder, Donal. No rank, no number.'

'But you're wearing Russian combat uniform. You must have a rank and number.'

'Loder, Donal.'

'Don't give me shit, Donal Loder. Donal? You look more like an Italian than an Irishman.'

'A question of parentage.'

'You dropped with the Israelis?'

'Loder, Donal.'

'Cut the crap, Mr Loder. You see? I speak passable English. What were you doing with the Israelis?'

'I got on the wrong flight.'

'Let me tell you then. You're the Syndicate's man. Sent in to make sure the

Jews don't escape with the diamonds.'

'To make sure *you* don't escape with the diamonds.'

'I'll tell you what I'll do,' Ruchkin said.

'If I play ball with you, you'll play ball with me?'

'I could kill you now.'

'Except that you want information.'

'The Israelis' strength and weapons. Give me that and we might spare you when we hit them.'

'Supposing they hit you first?'

Ruchkin knelt down and pulled the combat boot off Loder's swollen foot. Then he brought his own boot down on Loder's shin, on to the swollen discoloured flesh.

Loder screamed.

Ruchkin said: 'I think you will tell us, Mr Loder. I really do.'

Most of the equipment, weapons and ammunition was stashed in the ruined helicopter. Ruchkin dispatched Simenov to fetch the emergency radio and white winter combat uniforms.

Loder, sitting in a corner of the rest house, hands and feet still bound, watched Ruchkin's men transform themselves into bulky phantoms, blue helmets covered by white hoods.

Simenov dropped the belt of his discarded combat jacket. As he bent to retrieve it he cut through the rope on one of Loder's wrists with a clasp knife.

'You untie the rest,' he whispered. 'As soon as there's a diversion—as soon as I create one—you get out through the rear exit.'

'I can't, not with this foot.'

'Don't worry,' Simenov said softly, 'I'm coming with you.'

The diversion came five minutes later: hunters turned poachers by new laws of conservation who had journeyed south on reindeer skin sleighs.

They mostly hunted sable and fox but tonight their prey was a pack of wolves which they had stalked for more than 100 miles. They were members of the Evenk tribe but there was nothing primitive about their weapons: they were armed with automatic rifles.

Shortly after nightfall the leader of the poachers who had already been in one gun battle that week, spotted what he assumed to be a militiaman co-operating with game wardens.

As he turned to warn the others the militiaman shouted a challenge. A light blazed and the poacher fired, a coughing burst of bullets that caught the guard posted by Ruchkin in the legs.

Realising how appalling his mistake was, the poacher ran for the pines beside the ravine. But he wasn't quick enough—the blade of a fighting spade caught him in the back of the neck, the classic attack point, partially severing it.

Hearing the shots, Ruchkin ordered his men out of the rest house. Everyone left except Simenov and Loder.

Loder tore the rope, which he had loosened, from his feet and, leaning on Simenov, limped to the rear exit. Then they headed south through the tree stumps, keeping close to the fringe of pines.

Ten minutes later Loder leaned against a pine. 'I can't make it. You go by yourself.'

'We go together,' said Simenov, 'or not at all. Just imagine the police are after you.'

'Why should I do that?'

'You look like someone who's been chased by them.'

'You've got a nerve. Why are you escaping anyway?'

'Because I've just found my identity. Like my brother I didn't know whether I was Russian or Jewish. Ruchkin killed my brother...'

'I don't understand,' Loder said. His foot, covered only by a sock, was still swelling but the cold had numbed the pain.

'I'll explain later. But can you imagine what it's like being Jewish and knowing there are Israelis on the other side of the ravine? Knowing that I might have to kill them...' Simenov took Loder's arm and placed it on his own shoulder and started to walk again. 'Do you know what Ruchkin said to me?'

Loder shook his head.

'He said: "They're Jews, they have to be eliminated. Executed" Then I knew I was one of them and I had to join them.'

'You don't need me,' Loder said.

'Sure I do. When we get across the ravine you've got to tell them who I am. That I'm not a spy. So come on, lean harder on me—I might be clumsy but I'm strong.'

They had taken a few more steps when the ground collapsed beneath them. They fell down the side of the ravine, clutching at roots, bouncing off boulders. Down, down, and it seemed as though the fall would never stop.

When it did Loder felt like a heap of garbage tossed over a cliff from a passing car.

He whispered: 'Simenov?'

'Over here, testing my bones.'

'Test mine, too. Can we fall any further?'

'You can't fall much further than the bottom of a ravine. But I think my bones are okay. Yours?'

'You should have left me.'

'Nonsense, you're my passport. Now all we've got to do is climb up the other side of the ravine.'

'That I can't do, no kidding.'

'That you've got to do, no kidding. Here, lean on me again. But not too hard this time.'

As they began to climb the snow cleared and a bullet thudded into the rock beside them. They ducked and lay still beside a thicket of prickly oak.

'Infra-red gunsights,' Simenov said. 'I forgot to put them on my list. Up here,' tapping his forehead, 'for the Israelis.'

'List?'

'Everything they've got, how many men...'

Another thudding impact. 'When you hear them they've missed you,' Simenov said.

'When you don't?'

'You're dead.'

'Have you got a spotlight on your list?'

'Nothing that will reach this far.'

Rock splintered. A pain like a wasp sting jabbed Loder's cheek. When he took his hand away his fingers were dark with blood.

'We can't stay here,' he said.

'Up or down?'

'Up.'

Simenov put his hand to his chest. 'I *have* broken something. A rib.'

'Christ,' Loder said, 'the walking wounded.'

They began to climb, Loder hauling his leg behind him, Simenov grunting with pain.

Loder said: 'They'll be looking for us on the rock face.'

'For target practice,' Simenov said. 'An old tradition in Spetsnaz.'

'Why did you join them?'

'To prove something. I forget what.'

They reached a ledge and paused.

Another bullet smacked into the rock between the two of them.

'That's a guy called Gusev,' Simenov said. 'A marksman with a Dragunov sniper rifle.'

'Not the greatest.'

'Maybe he's only playing with us.'

'Good sense of humour.' Loder started to climb again.

A burst of gunfire. This time from the Israeli side of the ravine. They heard the bullets rip into the pines on the other side of the ravine.

'A Kalashnikov,' Simenov said. 'Gusev doesn't like rapid fire: he thinks it's beneath him. He believes a man should die from one bullet, not a clutch of them. He gets quite poetic about it.'

Simenov dropped back to the ledge as a single shot came from Ruchkin's side of the ravine. He said: 'I'm going to follow this ledge: Gusev will still be looking for us above it.'

Loder slithered down to the ledge, managing to land on his good leg, and followed Simenov. The ledge led to what looked like a path beneath the snow. They started to climb again.

'I'll bring up the rear,' Simenov said, falling back. 'I'm in white: I'll give you cover.'

'Would Ruchkin have killed me?' Loder asked.

'With a spade.' Simenov tapped Loder on the shoulder. 'Have you got a good memory?'

'I can remember my childhood, not what happened last night.'

'Remember this,' Simenov said. 'In case Gusev picks me off.' He began to recite weapons and probable deployment of the Spetsnaz.

Another burst of fire came from the Israelis and from across the ravine a scream, short and sharp like the screech of a small dying animal.

'That must have been Gusev,' Simenov

380

said. He finished reciting. 'Come on,' giving Loder a push. 'I'm about to become an Israeli. Maybe I'll even get to see Masada. Swear the oath that recruits swear there, "Masada shall not fall again".'

The bullet took him in the back.

Loder knelt beside him and turned him so that he was looking at the stars. 'I'll get help,' he said.

'Too late. Odd, isn't it, that I'm going to die between the Russians and the Israelis?'

'You're not going to die,' Loder said, but he knew that wasn't true.

Simenov grabbed Loder's arm tightly. 'I underestimated Gusev. Even though he's dying or wounded he only needed one bullet.' He raised his head. 'Have you been to Israel?'

'Many times.'

'Jerusalem?'

'Of course.'

'Tell me about it.'

But Loder never got around to it because blood suddenly appeared at Simenov's mouth and his head fell back and he whispered, 'Masada shall not fall again,' and his eyes were staring at the stars but he could no longer see them.

When Loder staggered into the Israelis' position they were still firing. Holding

381

up his hands, shouting, 'Don't shoot,' he pushed open the door of the waiting room and leaned against it.

Then he recited the intelligence Simenov had given him to Sapir. 'His last will and testament.' He held up one hand. 'You don't have to say it—you wish it was mine.'

Sapir said: 'Get Kol to look at your foot—he's our medic.'

'I also know the exact position of the safe in the carriage next to the Skoda.'

'So do I,' Sapir said. 'Your informant in Mirny told the Syndicate—we have good sources inside the Syndicate.' He went outside to direct the Israeli fire, according to the intelligence provided by Simenov. Except that Ruchkin would have changed the deployment as soon as he realised Simenov had gone.

The main Israeli weakness was shortage of ammunition. Enough assault rifles to go round, the light machine gun, hand grenades, mortars and the RPG-75 rocket launcher. But only three magazines per rifle, no shells for the mortars and only one missile left for the rocket launcher.

Ruchkin's strength lay in his reserves in the crashed helicopter. Thoughtfully Sapir approached Allon, a thin-faced marksman, and told him where to direct his fire.

Ruchkin, who had re-deployed his men immediately he realised that Simenov had defected, waited until he had established the positions from which the Israelis were shooting, then gave the order to return fire.

The night was torn apart by gunfire.

What weapons did the Jews possess? Ruchkin wondered. How much ammunition had they got? Perhaps we should take a prisoner? He shook his head. What was the point? On a mission like this the Israelis wouldn't send the sort of soldier who would break under torture.

Probably, he reasoned, we have the advantage with the weapons still under wraps in the Mi-8. Weapons which Simenov might not have counted. But he *would* have given the Israelis the position of the helicopter!

Ruchkin began to run towards the crippled helicopter—as bullets ripped into it detonating explosives and ammunition. Chunks of fusilage and lengths of rotor blade crashed into the forest and tumbled into the ravine.

Shooting stopped on both sides.

Silence except for flames licking what was left of the helicopter.

Ruchkin, lying face down in the snow, raised his head. Now we are equal, he thought.

Then it began to snow again.

Chapter Twenty-Four

There was only one way to shift the armoured train. And it hadn't occurred to anyone else, Chukovsky thought.

From the rest room he took the driver's cap with the small peak and the goggles and put them in his pocket. Then he found an old red scarf under one of the bunks and tied it round his neck, buttoned his reefer jacket, put on his *shapka* and set off down the track in a westerly direction.

Somewhere along the track, not far from the rest house, there had to be a siding used to deposit the old engines in the locomotive cemetery. At the end of that a turntable, the type used in marshalling yards. And, he prayed, an old E class freight switcher, the work horse that was invariably used to shunt has-beens into retirement.

Snow poured from the sky. The cold nipped his face beneath his fur *shapka* and made his eyes water. He put on the goggles but kept the driver's cap in his pocket because there was a time and place for everything.

A gap in the forest to his right. Stooping,

he plunged one hand through the snow to the track and felt points. The siding! Stumbling, he made his way along it. Ahead he saw the fuzzy silhouettes of what looked like wood-burning, eight-wheel freight engines. He tried to run, fell, picked himself up and strode forward.

There was the turntable. And on it an E class.

Chukovsky clapped his mittened hands. Reached for it. Ran his hands along its pistons and knew from its smell, its vibrancy, that anything was possible.

He climbed on to the footplate, in command once again, driver and fireman and lighterman. Behind him stood a glistening mound of snow-capped coal. Water on tap, firebox clean of clinkers and ash.

He jumped from the footplate to look for the fuel that had been used to get the fire going and found a towering pile of logs with kindling wood beside it.

He returned to the engine and built the fire, laying black jewels of coal in the wood, and lit it with a match.

Flames explored the fuel inquisitively, found sustenance, climbed hungrily.

He found an oil can with a long spout and filled the cups on the axles and connecting rods, just as he had in the valiant days before diesel and electricity

385

had replaced wood, coal and oil.

Then he turned his attention to the controls that had been waiting for him for so long, and only then did he put on the peaked cap.

Inside the station, Blair employed an old pro's trick: if you can't think of a good intro write the rest of the story first.

Then a sportswriter's ruse. Alternative intros—the Israelis won, the Russians won, a draw.

When he had finished he taught Noland how to use a laptop 'in case I don't make it'. How to unscrew a telephone, connect the laptop and transmit the story.

'Got that?'

Noland said he had.

'Why so gloomy?'

'I was thinking about my wife. How she would have enjoyed all this.'

'Enjoyed it?' Blair stared at the bird-watcher incredulously.

'We used to make up adventures in the firelight. Change the ending when a coal fell. We should have taken our chances then. Everyone should, while they still have time.'

'We did it the other way round,' Blair said. 'We had our adventures first and we should have relived them later. In front of a fire,' he added.

'Can you tell me what went wrong?'

'I was two people. She didn't know which she was married to.'

'I don't understand,' Noland said.

'I worked for British intelligence. I didn't tell her. She said our whole marriage had been a mockery.'

'And was it?'

'Not as far as I was concerned.'

'But now you're only one person?'

'The one she married,' Blair said.

'The one she loved. She'll forgive you.'

'What gives you that idea?'

'I'm an observer.'

'I'm not a bird,' Blair said.

'People don't notice me but I notice them.'

'You can't see Barbara.'

'I know the man she married: I know the sort of woman she is. Were you ever unfaithful to her?'

'There have always been two sets of rules, haven't there? If a wife commits adultery it's a betrayal of the marriage vows. If a husband is unfaithful it's just a little harmless fooling around.'

'You haven't answered the question,' Noland said.

'No, I haven't been unfaithful.'

'Neither of you?'

'Neither.'

Had she ever been back to the house on

the banks of the St Laurence—St Laurent as, being French Canadian, she insisted on calling it? Peered through the Douglas firs at the water jostling with coins of sunlight?

He said: 'If I die, promise me one thing—you'll go and see her and tell her I always loved her.'

'I promise. Will you do something for me?'

'If you die? Don't be pessimistic: you're a survivor.'

'Go to Hampstead. To the Spaniards Inn. Tell Harry and Syd that I spotted the three birds—if I see the Baikal teal, that is. Collect the cheque and give it to the Royal Society for the Protection of Birds.'

'A big *if*—Baikal teal won't take kindly to all this shooting. What shall I do if you don't see one?'

'Give the Society a cheque on my behalf. You can take my camera as collateral.'

'Don't worry. I can just about raise £100. And then I'm going to set up another organisation, the Royal Society for the Protection of Bird Watchers.'

'It seems to me,' Noland said, 'that *you're* the one who needs protecting.'

The helicopter with the Israelis on board didn't fly direct to Naked Boy Halt. Shortly after lift off with Rachel and her squad on board it developed gear box trouble. The pilot put down at the strip and stared at the gearbox as though it were some ancient and implacable enemy.

'I'm not a mechanic,' he said. 'Come to that I'm not a chopper pilot, either.'

Shapiro said: 'Maybe I can help?'

'What would you know about VR-8A gearboxes?'

'I know about locomotive engines.'

'A great help,' the pilot said.

While they worked Rachel checked out the prisoners in the control tower and the Chinese Ilyushin. It was painted dark green with a grey, shark belly. Its number was 1313; she hoped that was lucky in *T'ung Shu*, the Chinese almanac.

An hour later they still hadn't fixed the gearbox.

She inspected the crippled Antonov. On the floor near the ramp doors she found a diamond ring attached to a gold chain. She remembered that Loder had worn one round his neck. She slipped it into the pocket of her combat jacket.

A telephone shrilled in the control tower. The Israeli they were leaving behind, a bespectacled Latvian, answered it in Russian. 'No, colonel, no aircraft has landed here. Yes, everything is under control.'

The helicopter finally lifted into the black

and white night at 10.30. Below Rachel glimpsed shapes moving ponderously west.

The pilot said: 'T-72 battle tanks. They're on to us.'

When the shooting stopped Ruchkin counted his casualties, two dead, one injured, all victims of the helicopter explosion detonated by Israeli bullets. He wondered vaguely where Chukovsky was, then reviewed his options.

1. Advance along the bridge, blow the safe, bring back the diamonds to the rest house. *Negative.* As soon as they heard the explosion the Jews would saturate the bridge with gunfire. In any case if the snow suddenly lifted they could pick us off with AK-47s fitted with IR.

2. Blow the bridge. *Last resort.*

3. Withdraw south beside the ravine, cross it and take the Israelis from the rear. *Affirmative.*

On the other side of the ravine Sapir counted his casualties. One dead, two wounded—one seriously.

Kol, the medic, who wore wire-framed spectacles and tried hard to look inured to suffering, treated an Israeli with an abdominal wound first.

'If we don't get him to a hospital, soon he's going to die,' he whispered to Sapir.

The other injured Israeli had a flesh

wound in the thigh and Kol applied a field dressing to it.

Sapir gazed at the dead man. Young with freckles. Born to be a farmer. Married with two children. A hole the size of a fist in his chest.

Had he died for the Promised Land? Or for diamonds?

Sapir laid him on the snow just as he had laid others to rest on desert sand.

Then he considered strategy. What would I do now if I were Ruchkin?

Sapir sat at the table in the waiting room, head in his hands.

Go for the train. No one in their right mind would attempt that.

Blow the bridge? Only as a last resort. A safe full of diamonds buried in wreckage at the bottom of the ravine was scarcely the triumphant climax Ruchkin sought.

Mount an attack from the rear? Yes, Sapir thought, that's what I would do.

He told Allon to mount the light machine gun between two tree stumps behind the halt and deployed Arie and two other Israelis.

He then radioed Tel Aviv and at midnight joined Allon beside the machine gun to wait for the attack.

The Israeli chief of staff, the director of Mossad and Reisfeld met in an unoccupied house in south Tel Aviv, near the ancient port of Yafo, where military intelligence housed clandestine visitors.

The living room was barely furnished— bookshelves lined with military manuals, white vacation furniture and a photograph on the wall of the late Defence Minister, Moshe Dayan, black patch over one eye making a brigand of him.

The general told Reisfeld: 'We've heard from Major Sapir: the news is not good.'

'I know,' Reisfeld lowered his bulk into a chair testing its fragile legs.

'You know?'

'Yosef told me,' nodding at the Mossad Director.

'A conspiracy within a conspiracy?' The general stroked the baldness encompassed by his monk's fringe of hair.

The Mossad director said: 'Conspiracy is my business—I don't burden you with the details.' The sunspots at his temples moved fractionally.

'Perhaps you would be good enough to burden me now.'

The director said: 'The train with the diamonds on board is suspended on a bridge over a ravine in Siberia. On one side the hijackers, on the other Israelis. I have also been in touch with the Syndicate in London. They have asked for an extension of the first deadline for the advance of five billion dollars. They've been granted until 0200 hours tomorrow London time. If the money isn't forthcoming then the diamonds will be put on the open market.'

'Except that they haven't got them,' Reisfeld said.

The director said: 'I've also heard from Moscow. From an informant...' He uttered the word softly and reverently. 'The Minister of Defence has ordered the army to attack our position at dawn.'

'Which I presume,' the general said, 'is 0200 hours London time?'

'Precisely. In other words we have eight hours in which to snatch the diamonds from Ruchkin.'

The general turned to Reisfeld. 'Did Sapir say how he intended to complete Operation Joshua?'

'He didn't,' Reisfeld said. 'But he is an inventive officer.'

'He'll have to be,' the general said. 'If the armoured train has been diverted then the Russians must know about it and the airstrip isn't far away.'

The Mossad director loosened his brown shirt by one button as though releasing a secret. 'If all else fails we may have to do a deal with the Russians.'

'What the hell are you talking about?' the general demanded.

'If we can't snatch the diamonds we

don't have another option. We'll offer a division of the spoils. We'll cut, polish and market the stones...'

'But the Russians are going to swamp the market, make them worthless.'

'Surely a better option for them would be to take whatever money the Syndicate can get together then go into business with us. After all, we have the expertise and the markets for cut stones.'

'Thank God I'm a soldier,' the general said.

'I think there's something else we should tell you. Right, Theo?' And when Reisfeld nodded: 'Lieutenant Rachel Wolf is under orders to appropriate the diamonds for Israel, not the Syndicate.'

A Lavi fighter plane flew overhead, splitting the sky.

The general said calmly: 'Why didn't you tell me before?'

Reisfeld shifted in his seat; the chair creaked. 'We didn't think you'd approve. Just the same it would be for the good of Israel. How many times have we been betrayed?'

'Does Major Sapir know?'

The director averted his face from Moshe Dayan's single accusing eye. 'Sapir is an honest soldier like you.'

'And how was Lieutenant Wolf expected to steal the diamonds?'

'Not that difficult,' Reisfeld said, resting one dusty boot on the top of the other, 'if things had gone according to plan. All she had to do was eliminate Loder.'

'Kill him?'

Reisfeld said: 'He is no friend of Israel.'

'And then?'

'The diamonds would have been handed over to a Mossad representative in Kabul. And he would have brought them straight back to Tel Aviv. With that many diamonds in our coffers we wouldn't have given a damn about the Syndicate.'

'Unfortunately,' the Mossad director said, 'everything has changed. But if we can get the diamonds before the deadline expires there's still a chance.'

'If Lieutenant Wolf takes out Loder?'

'He is expendable,' Reisfeld remarked.

'If we try to take on the Syndicate at their own business they will make sure sanctions are imposed against us. They're powerful enough...'

The director said: 'If we are backed by 50 billion dollars worth of diamonds? It's debatable—we would constitute the same threat as the Russians are posing now.'

'So what would happen?'

'We'd strike another deal,' the director said. 'With the Syndicate.'

'Another deal? If they made duplicity

an Olympic event you would win a gold medal!'

'Or survival, general. You have your weapons, I have my wits. We have had our backs against the sea for 40 years and, to avoid drowning, we need both.'

The helicopter with the Israelis on board landed gently at the edge of the plateau, the noise of its two Isotov engines and rotor blades lost in the shooting.

Standing in the snow, one foot on a pine stump, Rachel Wolf said: 'It sounds bad. They should have blown the train hours ago, taken out the Russians.' She drew her pistol. 'Spread out, keep in contact with the man next to you. You,' to Shapiro, 'follow me, that way we should all keep together.'

She advanced across the plateau which had once reverberated with the buzzing roar of chain saws and the chop of axe on resinous wood.

The shooting stopped and quiet closed in on her. A stick snapping triggered a miniature shock wave inside her. She heard a muffled curse. What had gone wrong at the halt? Could Sapir be hurt, dead?

She glanced behind her. There was no sign of Shapiro in the curtain of snow. She waited. No one materialised. She whispered Shapiro's name. No reply. She walked on, hand tight on the butt of her pistol.

The soldier appeared in front as though an illusionist had snapped his fingers. He wore white combat uniform, helmet, paratrooper's flashes on his jacket.

White? Not one of the Israelis had been kitted out with winter uniforms...

Chapter Twenty-Five

At a military airfield to the north of Novosibirsk a unit of the 105th Guards Airborne Division which had led the attack on Kabul airport in 1972 stood by on category one alert.

The colonel in charge had been given to understand that an attack against unidentified insurgents on the east bank of a ravine beside a deserted station called Naked Boy Halt was to be mounted at dawn. But not until the order came from Moscow.

From Moscow! The colonel, refined features marred by a prizefighter's nose, shook his head in disbelief. It was a long time since there had been any cooperation between the Siberian military district and Moscow 3,340 miles to the west. A long time since there had been any collaboration between any of the military districts. Transbaikal, Urals, Volga...

Who were these insurgents? Kazakhs, perhaps, trying to push north from what had been Soviet Central Asia. Maverick Siberians who had always asserted their independence from Moscow. And why not? They lived in heroic circumstances. The colonel hoped he wouldn't have to fight Siberians because he admired them.

Americans? The colonel smiled. Now that would be something. The enemy the Red Army had been trained to fight ever since the Great Patriotic War. The colonel occasionally enjoyed a fantasy in which the United States invaded Russia—after all it was only $4\frac{1}{2}$ kilometres across the Bering Strait from Little Diomede in Alaska to Big Diomede in Siberia. Or the other way round, perhaps, with the Russians reclaiming Alaska which Alexander II had sold to the US for 2 cents an acre.

An obsequious young captain approached. 'May I share the joke, colonel?'

'I was working out my tactics if we engaged Delta or the Rangers or the 82nd Airborne.'

The captain smiled uncertainly. 'I'm sorry—'

'I sometimes think we need a war to unify us once more. Peace is a terrible burden.'

He tapped the knuckle of his nose. 'What have you got to report, captain?'

'The tanks are in position, colonel. Just north of the Trans-Siberian.'

'Tanks? Who needs tanks?'

'We don't know the enemy strength, colonel.'

'Strength? We don't even know who they are. Maybe they're the United States Marine Corps, captain.'

The captain smiled even more uncertainly.

In London it was 7.30 in the evening. The house phone rang. Cronin. 'Message from the Israeli Embassy, sir. I knew they'd only contact us if anything went wrong. Well, I'm afraid it has.'

The chairman sighed. 'Tell me the worst.'

'Their team in Siberia has made contact with the Russians. But it's an impasse—the consignment is stranded halfway between the Israelis and the Russians. On a bridge,' he added.

So it's all over, the chairman thought.

'I know what you're thinking, sir. But anything's possible. Remember the Six Day War, Entebbe...'

The chairman hung up. He glanced behind him at his father. No knowing wink.

He consulted his watch. They had eight

hours until the ultimatum expired.

Chukovsky laboured like one of the convicts who had built the Trans-Siberian under the *plet* and offered thanks to the God of his Russian Orthodox ancestors for releasing the snow that was still falling thickly, hiding the smoke drifting from the chimney of the E class.

He worked first as fireman, or stoker, shovelling coal into the scorching mouth of the firebox, checking the main controls—steam valve, blower, damper, water valve for the exhaust steam injector...

It was up to Fireman Chukovsky to regulate the iron horse in such a way that the fire in its belly heated the water in the boiler to a temperature where it vaporised into steam that strove to take up 1,325 times the space occupied by the water, thus driving the pistons.

Chukovsky remembered the old cry as an engine pounded along the track. 'How is the water?' If the water level in the boiler fell below the top plate of the firebox the engine exploded.

Driver Chukovsky checked his main controls—regulator, reversing screw, cylinder cock, air brake valve, whistle cord... He heard the whistle sounding down the ages, saw the banner of smoke streaming behind the chimney.

What he hoped to do was sharp enough in concept, blurred in ultimate detail. Get up steam, rejoin the feeder line from the turntable and, under cover of falling snow, propel the armoured train stranded on the bridge back on to the Trans-Siberian.

Peering from the sturdy E class Chukovsky could see beautiful silhouettes. An Iosif Stalin type which he had once driven on the Odessa-Moscow run; a semi-streamlined P36—the last steam passenger engine to be built in Russia... But no sign of the loco that had pulled the Blue train with Stalin on board.

Instead there was a statue of Stalin lying on his back. And there, too, was Khruschev, face down, one clenched hand looking as though it was pounding the ground in impotent fury.

Chukovsky stopped stoking the fire. Sweat dripped from his forehead and his heart thudded.

He touched the gauges, levers and handles with love. Then he got back to work.

By 3 a.m the steam was struggling to expand. Time to go. Check that the cylinder cocks are open. Reverse lever into full forward. Suppress the instinctive urge to pull the whistle cord! Hand on the regulator instead. Pistons pumping in the cylinders. Man and machine as one as they had been in the bold days before electricity snuffled along the track.

Except that they weren't moving because the wheels were failing to grip on the icy rails. The sanding control! How could he have overlooked it? He engaged it and knew instinctively that what it lacked was sand. He cut off the steam power and turned to the hummock of coal behind him.

Ruchkin had led six men south. They had kept behind the pines beside the ravine, scrambled down the near side and scaled the opposite bank. On the way up they came across the body of Simenov on a ledge.

Ruchkin kicked the corpse. 'A traitor,' he said. Leaning his back against the wall of the ravine, he pushed with his heel. The body toppled from the ledge. 'Into Devil's Ditch,' he said, 'along with your brother.'

The men spread out among the stumps on the far side of the ravine. Earlier Ruchkin thought he had heard the noise of a helicopter above the gunfire. But he couldn't be sure. In any case the Israelis couldn't have summoned reinforcements.

Moving in an arc, veering north, he picked up the earlier thread of his reasoning. Sapir would first expect him to attack from the south. Then he would think, *No, too obvious—I'll prepare for an attack from the north.* Which is why I'm mounting the assault from the south.

A shot.

Could he be wrong?

It came from his right. A pistol shot. A scream dying as a man died with it.

Ruchkin followed the scream, swiping with one arm at the folds of snow.

As the soldier swung his assault rifle towards her Rachel Wolf pulled the trigger of her P6 pistol. The explosion shocked her: it was supposed to be silenced.

The Russian screamed and dropped his Kalashnikov and reached for the rosette of blood spreading its petals on his combat jacket.

Staring at her, perplexed, he folded, knelt and pitched forward into the snow.

Then she was running, tripping over stumps. Gunfire behind her. Gunfire in front of her.

Sapir was sitting beside Allon who was squinting along the barrel of the light machine-gun when he heard the single shot.

He moved to the right of the LMG and lay down. So his anticipation had been correct: Ruchkin was mounting an attack from the south.

Only one shot?

He peered through the sight of his rifle, moving it gently from side to side.

A movement in the falling snow. A thickening.

He caressed the trigger, held his breath, closed one eye.

The thickening gained human shape.

Sapir's finger tightened on the trigger.

The figure was now so substantial that he could recognise her.

Her!

'No!' He flung himself at Allon, knocking him to one side of the machine-gun.

As Rachel Wolf raced past she tripped and fell face down in the snow.

Sapir ran to her. Behind him Allon let off a burst into the void.

Rachel turned over, sat up.

Sapir said: 'Are you all right?'

Rachel said: 'Sure, I'm all right. What about you?'

Sapir stood up. 'I'm okay.'

'I wondered. You know, we did what we had to do in Novosibirsk but here things seem to be out of control.'

Sapir led her back to the halt.

Hearing the snarl of the machine-gun, listening to the bulets rip the trunks of the pines, Ruchkin thought: He has given away his position.

He took a RGD-5 hand grenade from his belt, lay down and began to slither towards the LMG.

What worried him was the single pistol shot that had triggered the burst of fire from the machine-gun and the return fire from his own men. It had sounded more like an execution than an act of war.

Was there some miscalculation in his reasoning?

And the fleeing figure, presumably an advance look-out... There had been something not right about it. If he hadn't known better he would have said it was a woman.

Of course there were women in the Israeli Army. But there wouldn't be any reason to include a woman in a hit squad in Siberia... Unless she was Russian!

Suddenly Ruchkin saw the silhouette of the Israeli swivelling the barrel of the machine-gun. He looked very professional, Ruchkin thought. And he would die professionally, in combat.

His fingers tightened on the thin, olive-green sheet steel body of the grenade. Twenty metres from the LMG he drew the pin, keeping his hand on the release arm of the 3.5 second fuse.

He waited for a moment until the

gunner angled the barrel away from him. Then he lobbed the grenade and ducked because the fragmentation radius was 25 metres.

The explosion thudded in his ears. He saw orange light flash behind his closed eyelids. Felt a wave of heat. Kept his head down as lethal fragments fizzed above him.

When it was over he raised his head. Flames were feeling their way around the mangled gun. And there was an arc of clarity where the heat was melting the falling snow. Of the gunner's body little was left.

Cautiously Ruchkin stood up and backed away, poised to pick off any rescuers with his rifle.

But no rescuers appeared. Instead he heard shooting from the rear. And realised he *had* made a miscalculation: there were Israelis behind him. They must have landed in the helicopter he thought he had heard. Where from? Novosibirsk. That was how they had switched the points on the Trans-Siberian.

Sapir, you devious bastard!

Ruchkin blew a whistle. Two blasts, the pre-arranged signal to withdraw. Not retreat. They had taken out a machine-gun, probably the Jews' main weapon: they had won the engagement.

He reached the pines. Waited for the others to join him. Automatic fire kicked snow around him. He saw a figure rear, fall.

He counted his men. Four survivors, two presumed dead. One killed by the single pistol shot. Fired by a woman!

He led the survivors down the bank of the ravine.

In the rest house he sat at the table and, cupping his head in hands, planned his next move. No, two moves ahead because Sapir would anticipate the first. Possibly the second. Ruchkin closed his eyes and tried to perceive what Sapir would *not* be anticipating.

Chapter Twenty-Six

Hunger sharpened by cold knifed Sapir's stomach. He remembered his mother's specialities—*gedemptfteh fleisch,* spiced beef stew, and poppy seed cake—and salivated painfully.

Sheltering in the broken shell of the saw mill, he tried to concentrate on casualties. Four dead now—the seriously wounded soldier had died—and one wounded. Fourteen men, one of those at the airstrip, and one woman fit for active service.

Latkes, potato cakes fried until they were golden crisp...emptiness ached inside him.

Tactics. Obviously Ruchkin wasn't acting with the connivance of the Russian Government—just one maverick, the Minister of Defence. And very soon he would have to order the army—airborne troops—to attack. At dawn.

Such an attack would be mounted from Novosibirsk. So, if the snow had stopped, Ruchkin would make a last bid to recapture the diamonds at daybreak while the attack was being mounted. Then, after we had been eliminated, the Defence Minister could call off the assault.

Hummus, a purée of cooked chick peas, garlic, oil and lemon juice served in pita...

So what he must do was pre-empt Ruchkin. Reach the train under cover of snow and stand guard while Arie blew the safe. Chances of escaping? Slightly less than a Jesuit taking his seat in the Knesset.

But he had got a Russian helicopter and the Russians would be scared of shooting that down; he had got a Chinese Ilyushin and they wouldn't attack that without consulting Beijing.

Had the Russians grasped the fact that the An-12 had put down at the airstrip? Possibly not—the blizzard, the impenetrable night, the Latvian taking all calls...

Sapir imagined the first velvet touch of mushroom and barley soup on his tongue and made his way past the rusty teeth of the circular saw to the waiting room.

Where they were eating!

Rachel Wolf said: 'I bought bread in Novosibirsk. Someone has to think of these things.' She tossed him half a loaf. *'Bete-avon.'*

Coal dust instead of sand.

Chukovsky manhandled the lumps of coal aside, shovelled up the coal dust, jumped from the footplate and sprinkled it on to the rails. A dozen times, maybe more.

Despite the cold he could feel sweat trickling down his chest. Face masked black with dust, goggles still in place, cap turned backwards the way they used to wear them peering along the track, Chukovsky ran his hand once more over the controls. Regulator, reversing and brake handles, damper, cylinder cock left open...

He made sure the reverse lever was in full forward gear and eased open the throttle. The wheels moved, spun, but the E class didn't move.

Chukovsky jumped from the footplate

and inspected the track. The coal dust had been ground so finely by the wheels that it was more lubricant than adhesive.

Stepping over the clenched fist of Khruschev in bronze, Chukovsky went in search of sand.

Rachel Wolf stood in the porch outside the waiting room debating when to kill Loder.

She had weighed up everything. Loder claimed that if she took the diamonds back to Israel then the Syndicate would make sure sanctions were imposed.

She now doubted that: the Syndicate, scared of being brought to its knees, would do a deal. 'Mutually beneficial'—she could hear the words of the Syndicate negotiator.

That, of course, was if they got away from Naked Boy Halt. If they reached China. Once across the border the Syndicate would promise to process and market Chinese diamonds if it was allowed to keep the 50 billion dollar haul.

Syndicate's man on the spot: Loder. Without him Mossad might be able to strike an entirely different deal. Lavi fighter planes, Galil assault rifles, electronics... 'And we can help you cut, polish and market diamonds.' Now she could hear the voice of the Mossad director. 'We Jews were in business centuries before the

Syndicate cut its teeth.'

Rachel tried to think of one reason why she should not kill Loder; she failed.

Loder joined her in the porch, dragging his bandaged foot behind him.

He said: 'When you landed at the strip in the chopper did you check out the An-12?'

She handed him the diamond ring attached to the broken chain. 'Is this what you're looking for?'

He took it, kissed it.

'Why did you do that?'

'It belonged to my mother. It was all she had, I guess.'

Rachel wished he wouldn't talk about his mother.

'You said I reminded you of a gangster who loved his mother. Right on the button.'

'I said your mother was the Syndicate.'

'Stepmother,' Loder said. He slipped the ring and chain into the pocket of his jacket. 'Thanks anyway. A last request—it's usually a cigarette.'

'What are you talking about?'

'You aim to kill me, don't you? A stray bullet from the other side of the ravine?'

'I could shoot you now,' she said.

'But Mikhail Sapir would know.'

'I don't care about Mikhail Sapir,' she said.

'But you do love him?'

'No,' she said.

'I left a girl in Africa. You remind me of her a little. She isn't headstrong like you but, you know, she's her own person, always questioning, doubting... Are you doubting now, Lieutenant Wolf?'

'No doubts,' she said.

She wished he hadn't brought his foot along like an offering.

'A pity. We should all doubt.'

'But you don't, do you? The Syndicate... You've ruined lives for it.'

'I doubt all the time,' Loder said. 'In particular what I'm doing here.'

He told her how he had been recruited, how the Syndicate had threatened to make sure his mentor was prosecuted if he didn't collaborate.

She wished he would stop talking.

She said: 'You can change your way of life.'

'I figure you're going to do that for me.'

She felt the butt of her pistol. Remembered that the silencer was defective—the shot would bring everyone out of the waiting room.

'This girl,' she said. 'Is she waiting for you?'

'She doesn't know who she's waiting for.'

Rachel found this unfathomably sad. But not as sad as the ruination of her father. She undid the flap of the pistol holster.

Loder said: 'You know what they say now, don't you?'

'What do they say?'

'Come on, buddy, let's take a little walk.'

She drew the pistol. 'Okay, let's walk.'

'And then either I walk tamely or I go for your gun and it goes off and one of us gets killed. It all depends on the character of the guy at the wrong end of the gun.'

'So which are you going to do?'

'I'm going to talk,' Loder said. He gestured in the direction of the armoured train. 'There is a solution to this which no one has thought of. Not you, not Sapir.'

Rachel loosened her grip on the pistol. 'And you're going to tell me?'

'Not right now,' Loder said. 'But don't forget; kill me and you'll never know.'

Sapir took Arie with him and an Israeli who had been born in Moldavia, sleek-faced with cunning and swagger locked in his features, dance hall Romeo and buccaneer.

Arie, thin frame like a question mark

in the snow, carried his equipment in a shoulder bag, plastic explosive and detonators. Sapir and the Moldavian were armed with rifles and one RGD-5 each. Behind them they dragged the back-up bag for the diamonds.

Leaving two men at the end of the bridge to give covering fire, they struck out across the ravine. A breeze made the snowflakes dance and played music in the bridge's single girder.

Delicately, Sapir explored track and sleepers with his feet. Once a sleeper snapped beneath his foraging left foot. It sounded like a pistol shot to him but there was no response on the far bank.

They progressed with infinite patience.

Sapir, brain numbed with cold, imagined he was advancing on the Spetsnaz who, blue berets like cornflowers, had strutted into the square in Kazan and thrown their fighting spades at the young and the old.

He bit the inside of his bottom lip and tasted blood.

Once he leaned against the handrail. It bent outwards. He released it and it came back slowly.

Nocturnal sounds reached them, the hoot of an owl, the call of a wolf, and lodged in the falling snow.

The rectangle of the rear coach loomed ahead. Sapir knew that the safe was in the farther coach directly behind the locomotive.

Guessed, too, that infra-red field glasses and gunsights were trained on the bridge, but their sights would be blinded by the snow.

It took them five minutes to reach the rear coach. The turret reared above them.

Sapir told the Moldavian to keep watch. He and Arie entered the coach.

It still smelled strongly of explosive. He took half a dozen steps forward and felt frozen meat beneath his foot.

He stopped.

Arie stopped behind him.

'What is it?' he whispered.

'The Chechen,' Sapir said. He skirted the body, one foot kicking a stiff limb.

They passed through the door connecting the two coaches.

Kneeling, Sapir located the safe, sharp-edged and steel-cold and as solid as a tank.

He said to Arie: 'You can't see it. How can you work?'

'I can feel it,' Arie said.

Sapir leaned against the wall of the coach while Arie eased himself past.

'Give me 15 minutes.'

Sapir went ahead and peered through the gap where the windshield had been in the locomotive.

Five minutes passed.

Sapir heard the tick of his watch and the beat of his heart.

He returned to the first coach. 'How's it going?'

'It *feels* all right,' Arie said.

Another five minutes.

Sapir made his way to the exit from the second coach.

The Moldavian said: 'All quiet.' His teeth gleamed as though he was smiling wickedly at a girl.

Another four minutes by the illuminated dial on Sapir's watch.

He went back.

Arie said: 'Almost finished.'

At that moment the breeze strengthened and took the snow with it along the ravine. Moonlight lit the plateau. Shooting broke out from the far side of the ravine.

Arie said: 'I think it's okay,' as bullets hammered into the armour plating. 'I think...If only I could see.'

'Let's get out of here,' Sapir said and blundered towards the second coach and the rectangle of pale light at its extremity.

'How long before it blows?' he asked Arie.

'Two minutes, no more.'

Outside the Moldavian was shooting at the source of the automatic fire. The noise reached for the stars and filled the ravine.

'You get out of here,' the Moldavian shouted. 'I'll follow.'

They were shooting, too, from the Israeli's bank of the ravine and Sapir could hear the crack of the bullets parting the air above him.

He pushed Arie in front of him, then followed using the bending handrail as a crutch.

He glanced behind. The Moldavian was following, pausing to fire his AK-47 but scarcely bothering to take aim.

The two back-ups at the end of the bridge were clearly visible now, firing selectively, saving ammunition.

A scream. Sapir turned. The Moldavian dropped his rifle. Fell to his knees. Slipped sideways beneath the handrail and disappeared into the void.

Sapir stopped and crouched in the snow, Arie beside him.

They waited a long time, three or four minutes, and when they both knew that there would be no explosion Arie said: 'If only I could have seen.'

The Minister of Defence's voice sounded as though it were issuing from the gates of Berlin, static crackling like sporadic gunfire.

'Are you receiving me, Orloff?'

Ruchkin, talking into the mouthpiece of the emergency short-wave radio, said he was receiving him loud and clear.

'One and a half hours to dawn Novosibirsk time, am I right?'

Ruchkin said he was right.

'At dawn I'm sending in the army.'

Ruchkin adjusted the headset. 'You mustn't do that, general.'

'...no alternative,' static shot-gunning his voice.

'That means we've lost. Spetsnaz never lose.'

'...have to remind you that you aren't Spetsnaz any more, you're...'

A gangster? 'I can't hand over to the army, general. You must understand that.'

'It's an order.'

'But I'm not a soldier anymore, you just reminded me.'

'...if you want to avoid being tried and executed for treason.'

'Treason, general? I'm helping to save Mother Russia and you're my accomplice.'

'If you comply I will do my best to ensure that you get a fair trial. That you believed what you did was in Russia's best interests.'

'It is,' Ruchkin said into the mouthpiece.

'But I must stop you.'

Shit, what was the old fool babbling about? Did he really think anyone would believe he hadn't been implicated?

Ruchkin said: 'I respect your judgement, general, but I must do what I believe to be best.'

'And that is?'

'Take out the Israelis and get the diamonds to Moscow.'

'You've got one hour and twenty-five minutes.'

'Dawn, general—that's the time.'

'But...'

'When they're least expecting it, when they see the paratroopers jumping, hear the tanks rolling.'

'Do you really think...'

'Your last victory, general. Your very last.'

The static sounded like a volley from an execution squad. Then the line went dead.

'One hour until the ultimatum runs out,' the chairman said, staring at his secretary through sore eyes. 'You shouldn't be here at this time. One in the morning...'

'I wanted to make sure you were taking your tablets.'

'I fear it's all over,' the chairman said.

'You've never talked like that before.'

'What can the Israelis do? We haven't got the five billion. Even if we had the Defence Minister would have to send in the army: he has no choice. No,' he shook his head which felt heavy, 'there's no way out.'

He put his elbows on the desk. His eyelids were heavy too, like shutters that had just been released. He closed his eyes and he was a boy again in Kimberley gazing into the Big Hole, site of the Colesburg Kopje, where in 1871 the first Kimberley diamond had been found and his father was saying: 'Diamonds come from the heart of the world, son. They are its story and its beauty. It is up to us to make sure they endure.'

Part V

Pre-empt

Chapter Twenty-Seven

December 3rd.

Day pushing aside night. At first a greenish glow rimming the edge of the world to the east.

Mikhail Sapir, red beret inside his jacket, led his men up the steepening slope of the hill behind the fringe of pines to the forest that hadn't been touched by axe or saw.

There he paused and wondered if he had been right in striking north. He knew Ruchkin was going to mount an attack at dawn when all would seem to be lost and he had to pre-empt him.

North or south? That was the dilemma, and he had agonised over it ever since the abortive attempt to blow the safe. If he were Ruchkin, he reasoned, he would first consider moving north because the assault in the night had been from the south.

Too predictable: it had to be south.

So he had left Loder, Blair and Noland at the halt, posted Rachel and Shapiro in the pines opposite Ruchkin's position and moved north. Now he had to make his way through a short stretch of forest, cross the ravine and sweep south in a flanking movement.

Ruchkin would not expect such a maneouvre because he would assume ammunition was running short—their return fire had been thin—and in that assumption he would be correct.

He moved swiftly through the forest towards the strengthening light where the pines made way for the ravine. The light was clear and snowless and he wished this was not so.

As he reached the edge of the ravine a figure materialised on the opposite bank and it seemed for a single beat of time that this sighting had been arranged long ago. That they had always known each other and that one of them had to die.

They gazed at each other for a moment, then withdrew into their own sanctuaries within the forest.

The new day lay still for a while. Shoals of pink cloud hung motionless to the east of the broad pale sky and the snow lay deeply and quietly.

Then the day began to breathe. The sun inched above the skyline and the clouds faded from pink to pigeon grey and the snow found its sparkle. A homeward fox hurried through the forest; an eagle took to the sky. From the direction of the locomotive cemetery a stem of smoke rose.

In the cemetery Ivan Chukovsky had searched many engines for sand and finally found it in an antique Fairlie used on the Trans-Caucasus before he was born. A heap of it spilled like gold dust on the footplate. He shovelled it into a sack and picked his way back through the abandoned iron horses to the E class. Then he scattered the sand on the track, got back on the footplate and eased open the throttle.

The wheels spun. Gripped.

The E class got up a little steam and began to reverse. It left the turntable and followed the siding on to the loopline. There Chukovsky closed the throttle, allowed the engine to roll to a standstill and engaged forward gear. As the E class gathered a modest speed, a banner of steam and smoke settled on the cold air behind it, part of an old black and white photograph from another age.

Unable to control impulses from that age, Chukovsky reached for the whistle cord.

Ruchkin had waited until an explosive charge had been attached to the bridge—the last resort—before moving north in the waking light.

Now, in the fringe of the forest, he gripped his fighting spade and said to Gusev, the wounded marksman cradling the Dragunov sniper rifle: 'They're running short of ammunition. Draw their fire.' He gripped Gusev's shoulder. 'But don't shoot Sapir, he's mine.'

Gusev, who had been shot in the calf, a flesh wound, while Simenov and Blair were escaping, said: 'How am I supposed to know Sapir?'

'The way you were taught in Spetsnaz, the way snipers have always been taught in Russia—spot the badge of rank through the sight. Sapir is a major and he's wearing a major's insignia—I saw it.'

Gusev, pale-eyed and chip-toothed, fired one shot into the pines, then waited, rubber rim of the PSO-1 sight pressed to his eye, skeletel butt of the Dragunov tight into his shoulder.

An answering burst of fire from the far bank. Granite spat from a boulder beside them.

Ruchkin, sighting said: 'Third pine to the left of the prickly oak.'

Gusev said: 'A private soldier,' and squeezed the trigger of the Dragunov.

The Israeli threw up his rifle and fell backwards into the pines.

To the east the sun rose higher, shedding gold on the ermine countryside.

The dead Israeli was Arie.

What did you die for? Sapir asked the corpse. Ten years of your life handling explosive that at any moment could have blown you to pieces and you die from a single bullet in the head.

Diamonds, is that what you were sacrificed for? A 25-carat gemstone sparkling on the finger of a rich man's whore? A necklace cossetted in a bank vault?

He fired his rifle in the direction from which the single shot had come. A long vengeful burst.

Stupid.

The Israelis looked at him curiously.

Gunfire is infectious and bullets thudded into the wall of the waiting room where Blair, sitting on the floor beside Noland and Loder, was writing in his notebook.

He handed the book to Noland. 'Keep it in your bird book in case they try to take it away from me.'

Noland ran one finger along the scrawled lines.

'Don't forget the alternative intros,' Blair said. 'Send whichever turns out to be right.'

'Who do you think is going to win?'

'No one ever wins,' Blair said.

' "A private vendetta within a battle

within a war",' Noland read aloud, finger invisibly underlining the words on the second page ' "Ironically the prize was diamonds, symbol of love".'

'And courage,' Loder said.

'Put that in when you file the story,' Blair told Noland.

'Don't worry, you'll file it,' Noland said.

'Maybe. But neither side wants me alive, do they?'

'Your wife does,' Noland said.

'Don't forget, if I don't make it...'

'Tell her you loved her.'

'Frank Blair loved her. The other guy was an imposter.'

'And if I—'

'I'll tell Harry Cardoza and...' Blair hesitated.

'Sydney Collet,' Noland said.

'That you've spotted all three birds. Although you'd better spot the Baikal teal pretty damn' quick!'

As another fusilade of shots rang out Loder got to his feet and limped to the door.

Blair said: 'Where the hell are you going?'

'I have something to do.' He addressed Noland. 'What month were you born in?'

'April,' Noland said. 'Why?'

'Birthstone diamond—you'll survive.' He

turned and was gone.

'Don't be frightened to decorate the story,' Blair said to Noland. 'Background, colour... Do you know what a desk, foreign or news, always says? "Call in on the way back." Don't forget that.'

'Supposing you're on a plane?'

'It doesn't matter,' Blair said. 'They still want you to do it.' He picked up a Kalashnikov rifle. 'Hey, look what I've found.' He stood up and made for the door.

'Where are you going?'

'I've got to write a first-hand account of the vendetta, the battle, the war...not skulk in a waiting room, taking cover—that's what I've been doing for months.'

'I'm coming with you.'

'You stay here.'

'I've got the camera,' Noland said.

As they went outside an eagle swooped, inspected the positions on both sides of the ravine and soared into the blue sky.

Rachel Wolf, lying behind a pine on the edge of the ravine, rifle butt pressed into her shoulder, looked round and shouted: 'Get down, both of you.'

Bullets ripped into the wall of the derelict mill: one hit the rusty saw and ricocheted.

Blair pushed Noland and he fell. Then, sighting a white figure through a gap in the pines, he swung the Kalashnikov and fired a burst. The figure reared, fell.

'Very unethical,' Blair said. 'A foreign correspondent in combat. I could be shot for that.'

One bullet hit him on the inside of the thigh, the other in the belly.

Blood gouted from his thigh.

Rachel Wolf ran back, grabbed a field dressing and a tourniquet left in the waiting room by Kol. She applied the tourniquet above the thigh wound; the flow of blood eased.

Blair touched the tourniquet but he knew it wouldn't help because he was bleeding inside. He could feel his strength flowing away. Like a river to the sea, he thought.

He stared at the sky. 'What sort of eagle is that?' he asked Noland.

'Imperial,' Noland said. 'The blood's stopped—you're going to be all right.'

'I thought it was a golden.'

'It's got white shoulders, that's how you can tell.'

Rachel Wolf opened Blair's topcoat and his jacket and searched for the second wound.

'Don't worry,' he said. 'Get back to your gun.'

She found the wound, frowned and withdrew her hand.

Blair said to Noland: 'Are you *sure* you can read my writing?'

'It's bad but I can read it.'

'All journalists have bad handwriting, like doctors.'

'You'll be writing the end of the story,' Noland said.

'Not this time,' Blair said. 'You asked me just now who I thought was going to win. Who do you think, the good guys or the bad guys?'

'I'm not sure which is which,' Noland said.

'It's never easy,' Blair said. 'It takes one to create the other.'

He touches the field dressing below the tourniquet but it doesn't feel as if there's anything beneath it, not even bone.

'I took photographs just now,' Noland says.

'Get the story out first...rule number one...no Pulitzers for stories that never get sent...' The sky is fading now. 'Tell Barbara...tell her I'm sorry...'

The eagle is flying high, out of his vision, and through the Douglas firs the water on the St Laurence—St Laurent—dances with light and, holding Barbara's hand, he walks towards it and he is Frank Blair and no one else.

Israelis? The paratroop colonel listened in

disbelief through the headset. What was this, another Patriotic War?

'Bandits,' said the Minister of Defence. Dissidents had always been bandits, the colonel remembered. Or, if they were second division, hooligans. 'Take them out swiftly.'

The colonel spoke into the handset. 'With respect, Comrade Minister, may I ask what Israelis are doing in the middle of Siberia?'

'They are there, colonel. That's all you need to know. Except that they're wearing Russian uniforms, they speak Russian, and they're on the east side of the ravine.'

'Who's on the west side?'

'Patriots. Outnumbered patriots.'

The frequency went off the air.

The colonel tapped his dented nose thoughtfully, then joined the paratroopers waiting in the Antonov at the end of the runway and told the pilot to take off.

Slates of grey cloud lay over Novosibirsk, a legacy of the Soviet determination to pollute Siberia, but beyond the Ob the sky was pale blue and infinite and the Ob was a dark wound bandaged on either side by the white taiga.

Ten minutes later the Antonov was circling the hills to the north of the Trans-Siberian.

The colonel saw T-72 tanks on the

move through a valley. A plateau divided by a ravine which split the hills. Dabs of gunsmoke on either side of the ravine, a small engine on the move, a bridge with a two-coach train stranded half way across it.

He told the pilot to fly over the plateau, then gave the order to jump.

Ruchkin saw the Antonov circling, then the mushrooms in the sky as parachutes opened. He had expected this. What he hadn't anticipated was a banner of smoke trailing over the windbreak of pines behind the rest house.

He frowned. A whistle blew. Then he understood. Should have realised when Chukovsky went missing. What the crazy old fool was trying to do was shunt *Little Eagle* on to the main Trans-Siberian track.

The ultimate humiliation. He imagined the headlines: EX-SPETSNAZ MAFIA BOSS OUTWITTED BY ENGINE DRIVER... Gripping his fighting spade, Ruchkin ran south.

The smoke was long and low-lying like a skein of grey wool. Hearing the pipe of a whistle, Sapir remembered the locomotive cemetery he had noticed when he first arrived at Naked Boy Halt.

Dear God, they were trying to butt the armoured train on to the main track. And if a locomotive struck it with sufficient force, it might succeed.

And we will have lost.

Sapir began to run because the only hope was to reach the rocket launcher and knock out the approaching engine with the one remaining missile.

He saw parachutes hanging prettily in the sky. Hope? Are you crazy, Mikhail Sapir? But at least the gunfire had left his skull, dispatched by reality. Of course there was hope. But not much.

He cannoned into a tree stump, fell grazing his shin, struggled to his feet, ran faster.

On the other side of the ravine, hidden by pines, someone else was running. Ruchkin. It was as though they were running as an entity, sharing each harsh intake of breath.

Below a small black engine came into view blowing gasps of smoke from its lungs. The driver was leaning out of the cab peering along the track. A flame flickered at his neck. A red scarf, Sapir realised.

But why was Ruchkin racing towards the engine? Logic jolted Sapir's shocked thoughts. Because he didn't want the diamonds to be shunted out of his grasp either: the engine driver was acting independently, a wild card.

The engine was approaching the rest house. Ruchkin and he were running neck and neck but Ruchkin had the advantage because it was on his side of the ravine. He could jump on the footplate, kill the driver, apply the brake...

And I can fire the missile, knock the locomotive off the bridge and Ruchkin with it! Sapir hoped it wouldn't end like that.

Gunfire spurted from the other side of the ravine, to the north. Bullets tore into the pines around him and lost themselves over the stumps.

An Israeli gunner aiming at Ruchkin opened up but he was shooting high. Sapir glanced to his right and through gaps in the pines on both sides of the ravine saw the blurred figure of Ruchkin.

And for the first time in a long while it occurred to Sapir that there was a sort of nobility in what he was doing and that Ruchkin, embodiment of every humiliation imposed on his parents and all the other Jews in Russia, had to be killed.

The engine was accelerating now, smoke streaming behind it, and he could hear its voice like the bark of a lazy dog.

Once more he glimpsed Ruchkin, white uniform ghostly against the pines, and it seemed to Sapir that they were timing each other. That they intended to reach the bridge at the same time although, of course, that was ridiculous.

His lungs, sucking in iced air, laboured, his heart thumped. Suddenly Ruchkin veered to the left, stumbled and fell, legs over the brink of the ravine. He caught hold of a birch sapling and hauled himself to safety as bullets thudded into the cliff face. His hood had fallen back and his short fair hair was bright in the sunlight.

Then he was gone behind the pines.

The parachutists were nearing the ground. They would land at the southern end of the plateau six kilometres away. Before attacking they would have to muster and deploy.

Ruchkin calculated that he had half an hour.

To stop the old locomotive. Order Chukovsky on to the footplate of the armoured train. Eliminate the Israelis. *Kill Sapir*.

Take charge once more of *Little Eagle* which would leave the bridge carrying the old loco before it. They could jettison the engine at the locomotive cemetery and, with the connivance of the Minister of Defence, proceed to Moscow. Who would dare to challenge his word?

But if the airborne troops get here first they will take over because that's what they have been ordered to do. Rescue us. And not even the Defence Minister will be able to rescind that order. How could he justify faith in a handful of bloodied and depleted desperados whose helicopter has been blown up, whose armoured train is stranded without a windshield in front of another locomotive?

He tripped again and rolled, still holding his spade. Past the wreckage of the Mi-8 towards the gap between the rest house and the end of the bridge.

Bullets fired from the direction of the halt whipped across the ravine. Head height, he thought. Who was shooting? The girl he had seen during the night? That's what he would have done. Left her guarding the station.

He stopped rolling when he reached the track. Sprawled across it for a moment then, seeing the engine bearing down on him, hurled himself to one side.

He leaped to his feet and shouted at Chukovsky to stop. Tried to jump on to the footplate but there was no hold to grasp.

He fired his pistol into the air but there was no stopping an old rider on the saddle of an iron horse. The engine proceeded inexorably and with venerable majesty on to the bridge.

Chukovsky, goggles in place, peaked cap rakishly back to front, scarf whipping at his throat, leaned further out of the cab.

On either side space. Ahead the armour-sheathed Skoda.

All his working life Chukovsky had striven to avoid every engine driver's nightmare, a collision. Now he was deliberately engineering one. Could there be a more perverse climax to his career?

The E class picked up more steam. The armoured train loomed.

Contact. The familiar metallic shudder of the shunting yard. The two engines hesitated. Then the E class prevailed and the whole train, two engines now and two coaches, began to move in the direction of the Trans-Siberian.

Chapter Twenty-Eight

Loder located the RPG-75 launcher covered with tarpaulin in the ruined saw mill. The missile wrapped in greased paper lay beside the saw.

Hidden from Rachel Wolf and Shapiro

by the mill, Loder manhandled the launcher to a vantage point where, through the pines, he could see the two locomotives and the coaches. Then he returned for the projectile which, according to Sapir, could penetrate the thickest tank armour.

He fitted the pointed, lemon-shaped missile to the muzzle, knelt and got the feel of the launcher. He had never fired one but neither had he flown a 747! Butt like a flared exhaust resting on his right shoulder, left hand below the stock, forefinger of the right hand on the trigger...

Pain from his bandaged foot leaped up his leg.

Sapir, stumbling across the snow, shouted: 'Don't.'

As the locomotive hit the Skoda Loder peered through the optical sight.

Sapir was almost on him. 'Hit the armoured train and we lose the diamonds.'

Loder was about to shout: 'That's what I want to hit,' when his bandaged foot slipped on the snow and he lurched to one side.

The launcher fell in the snow. Sapir hit him on the side of the head with his fist, grabbed the launcher and aimed it at the old locomotive.

'No.' Loder took his weight on his injured foot and karate kicked with the other.

They fell, launcher between them.

The locomotive, Skoda and two coaches inched towards them.

Sapir got to his feet, drew his pistol and aimed it at Loder's head. Fell as Loder, coming in beneath his outstretched arm, charged him.

The launcher was now beside Sapir. Loder flung himself across him, possessed by an intensity of purpose that cancelled the pain in his foot.

They wrestled with the launcher. As Rachel Wolf ran towards them, hugging her assault rifle to her breast.

Sapir yelled at Loder: 'You're crazy...all those diamonds...at the bottom of the ravine.'

Loder head-butted him; blood spotted the snow.

Sapir's grip on the launcher loosened and Loder wrested it from him.

'Drop it!' Rachel Wolf aimed her rifle.

'Remember what I told you? There is a way and this is it.'

She hesitated and, kneeling, he levelled the launcher, got the target in sight and pulled the trigger.

As he did so Sapir clubbed him on the temple with the butt of his pistol.

Loder felt the release of the missile, then pitched forward still holding the launcher.

He heard an explosion. Felt heat gust

past him. But whether or not he had done what he had set out to achieve, the ultimate solution, he couldn't tell.

Sapir ran towards the bridge. The train was crippled but it was still there, wheels off the track, stationary. The rocket had struck the coach containing the diamonds, pierced the armour and exploded inside, buckling the sides. Flames searched the metal but, finding nothing on which to feed, died. Smoke rose sedately from the chimney of the E class.

Rachel called: 'Mikhail...'

He shouted: 'Stay there,' and ran on.

Beyond the E class Ruchkin was making his way along the bridge, wearing his blue beret. Sapir took his own red beret from his combat jacket, put it on and edged round the wrecked coach, feeling its hot breath on his face.

They faced each other on the middle of the bridge.

Ruchkin's men watched from one extremity, Israelis from the other.

Ruchkin held up his short-handled fighting spade. Sunlight splintered on the sharpened edge of the green blade. 'My only weapon.'

Sapir drew a combat knife with a serrated edge. 'My only weapon.'

They moved towards each other.

441

Behind them blue-helmeted paratroopers ran through the pine stumps, bayonets fixed.

Taking his weight on the heel of his right foot, Ruchkin aimed the spade as though it were a javelin. Sapir weighed the knife in the palm of his hand, wrapped his fingers lightly round the handle.

Ruchkin threw the spade suddenly but as he did so a rotted sleeper snapped beneath his foot. The jolt changed the trajectory of the spade and it struck Sapir on the shoulder, slicing the muscle, just as a spade had sliced it long ago in Kazan.

The bridge swayed.

Sapir, left arm hanging limp, threw the knife. Heard the thud as the blade hit Ruchkin's chest.

Leave it there, Ruchkin remembered. That way you don't release the blood and you still have a weapon for the ultimate act. The blade felt like an icicle between his ribs.

He advanced on Sapir who was advancing too, clenching and unclenching the fingers of his left hand. Blood oozed darkly on to his combat jacket but the blood on Ruchkin's white jacket was as bright as poppies in the field.

They were close to each other now and it seemed that if they each took a couple more steps they would merge into a single silhouette high on the bridge.

Ruchkin said: 'So what are you going to fight with now, Jew?'

Sapir raised the fist. 'This.'

'And I am going to fight with this.' Ruchkin pulled the knife from his chest, felt the serrated blade saw against bone, felt the warm flow of blood. Then lunged.

Sapir parried the thrust with his right arm and swung it to the right, forcing Ruchkin against the handrail. The rail broke with a rusty snap and Ruchkin fell backwards into space.

He grabbed the edge of the bridge, stared for a moment, and in his eyes Sapir saw a terrible understanding. Then he lost his grip and as he fell it seemed to Ruchkin that, like the Devil's Ditch, the ravine was armed with spikes.

Sapir, feeling his strength drain, leaned against the side of the old locomotive.

The body of the driver lay on the footplate. There was a wound on his head as though he had been flung there by the blast from the missile.

Sapir climbed on to the footplate and knew as he knelt beside him that he was dead. He untied the red scarf and laid it over his face.

Then he jumped to the side of the track and made his way on rubber legs to the coach where the diamonds were.

He peered inside and, after a few moments of incomprehension, began to laugh.

Chapter Twenty-Nine

He was still laughing on his way back to the Israeli-held bank of the ravine when Gusev, the sniper, blew the bridge.

At first the stretch at that end reared, angling the extremity with the train on it downwards. Engines and coaches held but Sapir sprawled forward.

Then he was on his feet running with clumsy strides. Ahead a figure was running towards him. Uphill. Absurd. His legs buckled and he stared up at Rachel's blurred face.

'Come.' She stretched out her hand.

'I can't.'

The bridge was straightening in majestic see-saw motion and Sapir knew that in a moment the whole structure would plunge to the bottom of the ravine.

'Must.' She grasped his hand.

And she was pulling him and he was loping along with a curious, bent stride and their stretch of bridge was rising, a gap at the end as it lifted above the lip of the ravine.

'Jump.'

'No.'

'Together.'

And they were together in space and he was falling but she had made it. She was above him on the edge pulling his good arm and he was scrabbling against the side of the precipice and there were other faces beside her, other hands, and then he was beside her on the snow and she was holding him. Very tightly.

This time the engines and coaches did shift, moving ponderously towards the opposite bank as the whole bridge plunged to the bottom of the ravine taking them with it.

Sapir, sitting slumped against the wall inside the waiting room said to Loder: 'So no one has won.'

Kol had cleaned the wound on his shoulder and was applying a field dressing. Outside Sapir could hear a Russian officer talking on a radio.

Now it was all over and they were prisoners they had lit the stove and its heat reached him like a salve.

Loder said: 'In the end it was the only way. The Russians don't get the diamonds, the Syndicate doesn't get them, you don't get them,' glancing at Rachel Wolf who was sitting beside Sapir. 'You see, diamonds aren't forever: they burn. Why not? They're not far removed from coal. Drop one in a fire and if it's hot enough it will burn.'

'But these turned to powder,' Sapir said.

Loder leaned against the old ticket window. 'Don't rush me: I don't often destroy 50 billion dollars worth of gem-stones.'

He shifted his bandaged foot and winced. 'In fact diamonds begin to burn in normal conditions at 700 degrees Centigrade. Which is why polishers using heat can damage them. Which is why diamonds in an air crash involving fire are sometimes written off.'

'But these did more than burn,' Rachel said.

'At a temperature of 1,750 degrees the *thermal agitation* of the atoms becomes so frantic that they break away from the diamond lattice—arrangement, if you like—and regroup in a more stable form: graphite powder. Jesus Christ, I hit the safe with a warhead. What chance did those atoms stand?'

'Why didn't you do it before?' Sapir asked. 'If you had destroyed them earlier the Russian threat would have been blown.'

'Because, although I knew where the safe was, I wasn't sure whether the missile would penetrate the coach and the safe.'

'It didn't matter,' Sapir said. 'An RPG-75 missile exploding in a confined space like that would destroy everything inside it.'

'Also I had never fired a missile before. Supposing I had hit the Skoda? I might have punched the whole train *and* the diamonds to the bottom of the ravine.'

'The greatest heist in history and you blew it... What's the value of the powder?'

'One price, take it or leave it.'

'How much?'

'For anyone else 50 cents. For you a dollar.'

And now it was dawn in London and in the headquarters of the Syndicate a single light burned in the office of the chairman who was sitting at his desk opposite Cronin.

Both were drinking coffee, even though it was bad for the chairman's heart, and beginning at last to digest the facts that had been relayed to them from their office in Moscow.

The chairman closed his eyes for a moment like a man sucking down oxygen. When he opened them he said: 'So it's over.'

Cronin, bony face sombre, said: 'We've survived once again. That's all there is to it. One day maybe...' He opened his briefcase and took out a typewritten document. 'Remember that prospector, Vogel, who found the gemstones in Namibia—a possible lead to the source of all the alluvial diamonds there?'

The chairman remembered.

'Well, the bastard's found another. If the source is traced then we could face a crisis as critical as the Russian threat.'

'Send Loder,' the chairman said.

He felt that any other crises were beyond his life expectancy. In a few days he would quit, retire to his vineyards in the Cape and leave all decisions to his son. Luxuriate in the culminating victory of his life.

He turned, seeking approbation from his father, and could have sworn that once again he winked. Well done, boy, the wink said.

Cronin said: 'So what are you going to do about the Russians?'

'Bring them to heel. Threaten to withdraw all marketing facilities if they don't release the Israelis. Make them sweat. Make them understand that no commodity on earth has any value if you can't sell it.'

The pain made itself known in his chest, then vanished without any encouragement from a tablet.

448

He put in a call to his wife in Cape Province. 'Get ready to listen to the Kalahari lions roaring,' he said when she came on the line.

'Do you really mean it?'

'I'm catching the next plane to Cape Town.' With the tips of his fingers he wiped the weariness from his eyelids. 'We have proved once again that no one can take us on and win.'

He was quite wrong.

Harry Sampson arrived at the Syndicate's offices at 5 p.m carrying a late edition of the *Evening Standard*. He was wearing a navy suit, blue shirt and silver tie, and reminded the chairman of a fragile version of the late George Raft.

He sat on the other side of the desk, crossed his legs, tapped the *Standard* with one finger and said: 'Doesn't look so good, huh? All things considered.'

'What do you mean?' asked the chairman who knew exactly what he meant—no one was buying diamonds.

Sampson said: 'The feeling is that the Russians still have the resources to wipe out the market. No one wants to take any risks. Can you blame them?'

'Now is the time to buy.'

'You tell 'em, Mr Chairman. But take it from me, they won't believe you: the rumours are too strong. And no one outside the Syndicate, outside Russia, outside the Israeli military, really knows what happened.'

'You do?'

'That diamonds bit the dust in Siberia? Sure I do—50 billion dollars of them. You see, I had a contact in Moscow who was going to sell me a lot of those diamonds. For dollars. He was a Chechen hood and he's dead. But he had contacts in the know. Boy, did he have contacts...'

'But of course you aren't going to tell anyone what happened...'

'I'm not?'

'That the Russians actually had 50 billion dollars worth of rough diamonds to put on the open market? You're too smart, Harry. The implication is too obvious: they've done it once, they could do it again.'

'What have I got to lose? I sold all my diamonds. But I can do you a nice line in emeralds or rubies or sapphires.'

'But you *have* been buying.'

'So your spooks are as smart as ever. I'm happy for you. Okay, so I've been buying. In a small way, you understand. At bottom prices. To cover any eventuality.'

'So what's your proposition? You never come here without one.'

'You asked me once before to buy, buy, buy to restore confidence. Harry Sampson

450

buys, he must know something—all that shit.'

'And you refused.'

'Circumstances have changed. The Russian threat has been zapped. For the time being anyway. But they'll come again, you can bet on it.'

'So you're willing to buy?'

'Maybe,' Harry Sampson said. 'Just maybe.'

'You want your sights restored?'

'Fifty million bucks each parcel.'

'That's preposterous. The biggest is 25 million.'

'No more preposterous than the story I'll put around if you don't agree. The Syndicate conspired with the Israelis to hijack Russian diamonds... Diamonds turned to dust by missile. And, wait for it...' Sampson leaned forward. 'Russians say plenty more where they came from. Now that really is preposterous, isn't it?'

The chairman sighed. 'All right, you win. The biggest sight ever alloted to one dealer. I have your word you'll buy and you won't leak the story?'

Harry Sampson stretched his hand across the desk. *'Mazel und Brucha,'* he said.

Rachel Wolf, sitting in the corridor of the special coach coupled to the end of the Trans-Siberian taking the Israelis to

451

Moscow with Loder and Noland, pointed out of the window. 'Tyumen, the oldest town in Siberia—the Russians used to lock up convicts here and let them die.'

Sapir, arm in a sling, said: 'Don't point—they might get ideas. As it is we're lucky to be flying back to Tel Aviv.'

'Not lucky,' Loder said. 'The Russians didn't have any choice. The Syndicate threatened to withdraw all facilities if you weren't released. You *owe* the Syndicate,' he said to Rachel.

'Mikhail and I are getting married in April,' she replied. 'You're not invited.'

Noland turned to Loder. 'Where will you be then?'

'In a desert. Same job, same scene, different climate.' With an effort he moved his foot, encased in plaster, and turned to Rachel. 'April—that's diamond. Make it a Sunday, that's diamond too. A double indemnity. God knows, maybe your marriage will be forever.'

They were interrupted by the green-eyed provodnik minding the samovar, who had run down the corridor to shake Noland's shoulder.

'Look!' She pointed out of the window at a lone bird with a green, cream and black head flying steadily beside the train, long neck thrust forward.

'That's it,' Noland said. 'That's a Baikal teal, all right.'

As he spoke the bird wheeled and flew back in the direction from whence they had come.

Post-Mortem

I received the call at my house in Denia on Spain's Costa Blanca one February day when I was packing to fly to London to see my agent, Sonia Land. The caller said his name was Tom Noland; he had heard that I had once been a newspaper correspondent in Moscow. Could he see me on a matter of great urgency?

When I told him I was leaving for London he expressed relief. Could we meet in a pub—the Spaniards Inn—on the edge of Hampstead Heath, where, for him, it all began?

'Where all *what* began?'

'It's a long story. But I'm sure you, as a writer, would be interested.'

I knew the Spaniards well enough: an old tavern, one of Dick Turpin's haunts, frequented by Shelley, Keats and Byron. I could certainly think of no objection to drinking a couple of mellow pints there.

It was a fine, gusty morning; a few kites flew high over the heath where, long ago, washerwomen had hung out the laundry to dry. Noland, paradoxically identifiable from his description of himself—'brown hair, spectacles, easily missed'—was sitting at a table in the bar next to a copper-hooded fireplace and four framed cases containing ancient pistols. Beside him sat a girl with green eyes and a Russian accent, whom he introduced as his fiancée.

He bought me a pint of bitter and told me about a bet he had made in the Spaniards—and its sequel in Siberia.

'Did you know Frank Blair?' he asked.

'After my time. But he was very good—before he went into a decline.'

'I promised I would see his wife. And get his story into his newspaper. Well, I achieved the first. She loved him, you know.'

'And the second?'

'I discovered how wary newspapers are about reports from unknown informants.'

'With good reason,' I said.

'Anyway some of them got reporters to make inquiries in London, Moscow, New York and Tel Aviv, but they got nowhere. The Syndicate closed ranks.'

'So what do you want me to do?'

I ordered two more pints and asked his

fiancée what she would like. Nothing, she said, smiling: it occurred to me that if Noland's story were to be believed she would prefer tea.

'You were once a journalist. Now you write novels. Isn't there something called faction—fiction based on fact?'

'It would take a hell of a lot of research.'

He took off his spectacles and polished them. His face was vulnerable, naked, without them. The girl held on to his arm and looked at me; I still think it may have been those green eyes which persuaded me to take on the project.

Like Noland before me, I encountered many hostile denials and two threats. Hardly surprising in the tense climate of diamond control. As I pursued my enquiries the scenario changed. The White House in Moscow was stormed, hard-line opponents of reform killed, ringleaders captured. Subsequently fascists, the most unlikely of all contenders, won a formidable number of votes in a general election. From its office in Moscow the Syndicate took steps to monitor the output of rough diamonds more closely; the Russians fell out among themselves about who should control diamond production, Moscow or the regional governments. And the Syndicate enjoyed one of its best years of trading.

In the context of the characters in *Diamond Express*...the chairman of the Syndicate did retire and gave his wife a small but perfect gemstone; he called it *Mooi Klip*, a pretty stone, after the first authenticated diamond found in Cape Colony by a 15-year-old Afrikaner farm boy, Erasmus Stephanus Jacobs.

Mikhail Sapir and Rachel Wolf married. When she became pregnant, after the attempted accord between Israelis and Arabs, she quit the army and joined him on his farm where the white, star-shaped flowers of orange trees were just beginning to bloom.

Loder went first to Namibia to seal the possible source of that country's alluvial diamonds, then to Angola where another diamond rush was threatening to get under way, then to Canada to try and gain control of the strike near Yellowknife in the N.W Territories.

Harry Sampson, a pseudonym, prospered until his untimely death.

Finally I sat down and wrote the prologue to this book—the fact that, in April 1993, the G7 countries, the wealthiest industrial nations in the West agreed in Tokyo to inject 43.4 billion dollars into the chaotic economy of Russia. I also hinted that there might have been an ulterior motive to such unprecedented generosity. On September 24, '93 the US Senate voted to give Russia 2.5 billion dollars...

Blackmail? A threat by Russia to saturate the market with diamonds if a substantial payment in dollars wasn't forthcoming? But how can that be? you might ask. The diamonds were destroyed, the teeth of the Russian threat drawn.

The answer to this apparent contradiction lay in the Siberian town of Mirny which I visited. There I met a young man named Yuri Suvorov, son of the former chief executive of the Mirny Diamond Administration whom Ruchkin shot when he rashly asserted that he wasn't a member of GRU, military intelligence.

Yuri Suvorov, sick of rumours, promised to tell me the truth provided I changed some of the identities—the persona of the Russian Defence Minister, for instance—and circumstances in the book. His father, he said, *had* known the combination of the safe containing the diamonds. And as a precaution he had dispatched 25 billion dollars worth of diamonds east to Tokyo. From there they had been flown in the diplomatic bag to Moscow. So the Russians had still possessed ample reserves of prime compressed carbon to exact an unparalleled gesture of benificence from the West.

That left one last question unanswered.

If the Russians, by now enthusiastically but secretly behind what appeared to be the Defence Minister's inspired duplicity, possessed 25 billion dollars worth of diamonds, why did they heed the Syndicate's threat to withdraw facilities if they didn't release the Israelis?

The answer came from what Frank Blair would have termed 'a usually well-informed source'. An Israeli diplomat in fact.

The release of the soldiers had nothing to do with any pressure brought by the Syndicate. But if the Russians had protested to the United Nations and put them on trial they would have been forced to admit that their defences were so chaotic that 20 Israelis had managed to penetrate more than 2,000 kilometres into their country and land unobserved in Siberia.

Not only would they have been held up to ridicule but other countries might have got ideas, notably China. Much better to seek a diplomatic solution with Israel who wouldn't want the affair publicised either. Forget the deaths and the casualties: the episode never occurred.

To detail what is fact and what is embellishment in this book would only spoil the narrative. Suffice it to say that, although Frank Blair is also a pseudonym, I had no difficulty in writing the dedication.

Other MAGNA Mystery Titles In Large Print

WILLIAM HAGGARD
The Vendettists

C. F. ROE
Death By Fire

MARJORIE ECCLES
Cast A Cold Eye

KEITH MILES
Bullet Hole

PAULINE G. WINSLOW
A Cry In The City

DEAN KOONTZ
Watchers

KEN McCLURE
Pestilence